# Lostlings

## Susan Day

Leaping Boy Publications

Published by Leaping Boy Publications
partners@neallscott.co.uk
www.leapingboy.com

Cover illustration and design by Ken Rutter

A CIP catalogue record for this title is available
from the British Library.

ISBN 978-1-9998401-8-1

The first they knew of it was when Jamie texted his father that he needed to talk about something. This was so alarmingly unlike Jamie that Dave phoned Lynn at work and she called Jamie back. He was tiling a kitchen floor at the time and conversation was limited but they agreed that he would call round to see his parents after work. Lynn thought about it while she carried on with her tasks and then, without telling her husband or son, texted her daughters and asked them if they were able to come round too.

'What for?' says Dave. 'You know it will only get more complicated.'

'You didn't need to Mum,' says Jamie. 'I never asked you to.'

'Too late now,' says Lynn. 'They'll be here any minute.'

Jamie is a large person – not fat but broad like his father, with a pink clean face and guileless blue eyes. He is watching out of the window to see his sisters arrive. Sarah parks her car in front of the house, and she and Gemma get out and walk up the path. They do not know what this is all about; you can see by the way they hurry, heads down, not speaking, that they are anxious.

There is hardly space in the front room for five adults; it is hard to believe that they once fitted in, all of them, without somebody sitting on the arm of a chair, but then, in those days the TV was much smaller, and there was no coffee table and no shelves in the alcoves loaded with photo frames and small ornamental articles offered by the grandchildren and souvenirs brought back from holidays. Lynn brings in tea and coffee and a plate of biscuits. Sarah lets her shoulders sag – only a little, but perceptibly – perhaps with relief; nobody is dead, where there are jaffa cakes and gypsy creams the world is still functioning.

'Sit there Jamie,' says Lynn, pointing to what is usually her chair. He comes away from the window and sits.

No one has asked anyone how things are going, or commented on the lovely midsummer day it has been, or asked Dave how his bad knee is. They have not asked after anyone's children or partners. They pick up their cups and their biscuits in silence, waiting for someone to start.

'Now then, our Jamie,' says Dave, and stops.

Jamie looks past him, at the world outside the window.

'Jamie,' says Lynn. 'Tell your Dad and your sisters what you told me.'

Instead he pulls from his back pocket a folded piece of paper. No, two pieces, folded together. He hands them to his mother.

She unfolds them, smoothes them out, silently reads one, then the other. Passes them to her husband.

Dave seems to take a long time to inspect them, as if he suspects a forgery. Then he takes off his spectacles and passes the papers to Sarah. They are soft, creased, much handled. She and Gemma look at them together. Sarah lifts her head and is the first one to speak.

'I don't get it,' she says. 'Whose children are these?'

Gemma has taken longer to read the information. 'They're twins,' she says. 'Two birth certificates, same place, same day, same parents. Boy and girl twins. They're –' she pauses to work it out '– thirteen, nearly fourteen.'

'Same as my Melissa,' says Sarah. 'What does this have to do with us?'

'Jamie?' says Lynn.

He is silent. He has never been one to say a lot in company, but this evening he seems even less inclined. Struck dumb.

'Look at the mother's name,' says Lynn.

'Denise Wilson,' reads Gemma. 'Father – Adrian Wilson.'

'Niecey,' says Lynn. 'Niecey's name is Denise – you know that. These must be her children.'

'Must be?' says Sarah. 'Has anyone asked her?'

'Not yet,' says Jamie all of a sudden. He stands up. 'I'll go and ask her now, shall I?'

'Sit down,' says Sarah. 'Let's not do anything in a hurry. Start from the beginning Jamie. Where did you get these?'

'In her box,' he says.

'Come on,' says Sarah. 'Look we're family here, you can say it, whatever it is. Just spit it out.'

'In her box,' he says again. 'She lost her earring, see, one of her silver ones, and I said I'd look for it so I were looking in her things, in case it slipped down the back of a drawer or something, like, you know, like things do, or it might have done anyway.' He stops.

'Get to the box,' says Sarah.

'She's got this box,' he says. 'Just a box, nothing special, wood. I think she picked it up in a charity shop –'

'Actually,' says Gemma, 'I think you'll find I gave it her one birthday. Not last year, year before. It did *not* come from a charity shop.'

'Never mind that,' says Lynn. 'Let him speak. Go on Jamie love.'

'So I've tipped everything out,' he says, 'and then I thought, well, it might have slipped under the base – it were a loose base you see – so I just shook it and the base came out, and there were all this stuff.'

'Stuff,' says Sarah.

'Papers,' he says. 'These were the first ones I looked at, but then she starts coming up the stairs so I put the others back, and put everything back in the box, so she don't know.'

'She doesn't know you've seen these?' says Lynn.

'I just put them in my pocket, and then later, when she were putting Leo to bed, I took them out and had another look.'

'This was yesterday?' says Sarah.

'Yesterday,' he says, as if he can't believe what he is hearing himself say.

'So what did you say to her?' says Gemma.

'Nowt,' says Dave. 'He's said nothing to her yet. Is that right Jamie?'

'I didn't know what to say,' he says.

'I don't know what to think,' says Dave. 'Here's Niecey, that we've known all this time, and all those years she's never said a word to us about these children. And ever since Jamie's told your mother on the phone about this, I've been thinking, What if they died and she's just carrying it around with her, and us – who's her family, really, all she's got – we haven't been able to help.'

'Oh Dad,' says Sarah. 'You are such an old softie.'

'Or,' says Gemma. 'What if there's some other reason, like – I don't know – like their dad's got them?'

'Why though?' says Dave. 'Why would she let that happen?'

'*I* don't know do I? I'm only saying there are other possibilities. Like if someone's a bad mother.'

'Why would you even say that, Gem?' says Dave. 'Why would you think it?'

Jamie says, 'I don't know why she didn't tell me. I tell her everything.'

'But hold on,' says Sarah. 'She wasn't Denise Wilson was she, when you married her?'

'Nuttall,' says Jamie. 'That were her name.'

'Did you know she'd been married before?'

'She hadn't,' he says.

'Shall I put the kettle on Mum,' says Sarah. 'Mum. Did you hear me?'

Lynn shakes herself. 'Sorry love. I were just thinking. Do you want another cup?'

'I think Dad does,' says Sarah.

'I can do it myself,' says Dave, but he does not move and eventually Sarah takes his mug into the kitchen and calls out, 'Does anyone else?'

No one else does, though Jamie takes a handful of jaffa cakes off the plate and eats them, one at a time, whole, possibly without noticing.

'What were you thinking Mum?' says Gemma, and Lynn shakes her head again, as if it's too difficult to explain.

'We need a plan,' says Sarah. 'Jamie, what are you going to do?'

'I'm going to put them back,' he says, suddenly, decisively. 'I shouldn't have went in her things. I'm going to wait till she tells me herself.'

'Good luck with that,' says Gemma.

'Are you sure love?' says Lynn. 'What were all this about then?'

'I just had to tell someone,' says Jamie, very quietly. 'If it's bothering you – well, I'm sorry I suppose. But I'm done with it now.'

'He don't need any scenes,' says Dave.

Gemma and Sarah and Lynn catch each other's eyes and roll their own, ever so slightly, meaning, What are they like, these men? One's as bad as the other.

'Time I were off,' says Jamie. "Don't tell anyone, will you?'

'Don't be daft,' says Dave. 'They'll tell their husbands, surely they will. You don't want them to start having secrets, now do you?'

'Just them, then' says Jamie. 'I don't want it all round entire estate. Don't tell the kids.'

'Like we'd do that,' says Gemma. As Jamie stands to go she begins to get up herself – to stop him, or accompany him, who knows? Her sister pulls her back down.

4

Lynn sees him to the door. 'Take care love. You know we're here for you.'

'Oh my god,' says Gemma, as the door closes behind him. 'That were a bolt from the blue weren't it.'

'Poor Jamie,' says Sarah.

The daughters get up to go too; they have children to pick up from football training, from friends' houses, they have homework and showers to chivvy them through.

In the car Sarah says, 'I never liked her really, from the off. You didn't either.'

'She's not so bad,' says Gemma. 'And it's Jamie that counts really, isn't it.'

'Hm,' says Sarah.

There is more to say but no time to say it. Their text messages will be full of their thoughts for the next few days at least, as the new information about their sister-in-law – really? truly? – settles into their brains.

Lynn sits back down in her usual chair, the one Jamie has been sitting in, and stares through the window at the houses opposite, as he did.

'What were you thinking then?' says Dave.

'Oh nothing. Just what you said really. How long we've known her, all that sort of thing. I can't believe this, Dave. And yet.'

'I know,' he says.

Lynn has been at work all day; Dave, as usual, has shopped and tidied the house and prepared their evening meal. They eat in the kitchen with the back door open to the summer evening; salad and pork pie. Lynn raises her eyebrows in disapproval.

'Gemma brought it,' says Dave. 'Anyway, salad's nowt without a bit of something tasty.' He is verging on the diabetic, says his doctor, and should avoid all of the things that make eating worthwhile.

'That was nice of her,' says Lynn. She has some herself to stop Dave eating all of it. 'How's your day been?' This is the conversation they usually have straightaway when she comes in; it has been postponed by the meeting, which as yet they are not quite ready to talk about.

'Good,' says Dave. 'I've walked right up to the Common.'

'Busy?'

'Not really. A few dog walkers. Then I've done a bit of shopping on the way back. Had a chat with a couple of folk at the bus stop –'

'You've not been getting the bus, just from the shops?'

'If I did I wouldn't let on, would I? No, *they* were at the bus stop, waiting.'

'Who?'

'Fella from the bowls club and his wife. No one you know.' He finishes his last mouthful of pie, along with his last quarter of tomato. He always saves the best bit until last; Lynn read in a magazine, once, that it was a sign of an optimistic and secure personality, someone who knows that they are not going to be robbed. For herself, though she tries not to do it, she is much more inclined to eat the best bits first, and then let the less attractive items go to waste. It may be why she is thin and Dave is not.

Between them, they clear the dishes away. Lynn puts the leftovers in the fridge; Dave runs hot water into the washing-up bowl. Lynn puts the kettle on.

'I'll make the tea,' says Dave. 'Have a walk round the garden, clear your head a bit. Them yellow roses are starting to come out.'

Obediently she goes out. The air is soft and scented, the grass is cut and tidy, the plants are staked and sturdy. This is Dave's project. His wife, his children and grandchildren, his garden, in that order. His life. Lynn looks at his yellow roses and pulls one down to her face to smell it. She watches a bee bumbling in and out of the cones of a tall white foxglove, and turns back to the house.

They sit together outside the back door in the last of the sunshine with their cups of tea. It used to be a council house, but they bought it back in the early eighties, among the first to do so. 'I'd never have voted for that woman,' Dave has been known to say, 'but I didn't mind taking a house off her.'

Lynn slips off her shoes and puts her feet on the cool grass.

'What did you think of how the girls took it?' says Dave. 'Will they be all right, do you think?'

Lynn understands him. Sarah has never been wholeheartedly accepting of Niecey, but it is Gemma they need to worry about more. She has always set herself up as Jamie's protector and has been known to act without thinking first. 'I hope she won't do anything,' she says. 'Should I call her?'

'Better not,' says Dave. 'Let's not stir anything up.'

'Too late,' says Lynn.

They sit, hearing without listening their neighbours' television on one side and on the other, two little girls toddling about with cups of water, splashing water on the grass and laughing. It's nice, having children nearby, especially, says Lynn sometimes, when you don't have to do all the worrying and the getting up in the night, and the boring bits like reading the same story over and over again, or building up those interminable towers of bricks just so that Jamie could knock them down.

'Do you remember Jamie and his towers?' she says. 'And then he learned to build them himself, and he used to get really upset when they fell down before he was ready. Remember?'

'He loved his bricks didn't he?' says Dave. 'Should have been a brickie, not a tiler.'

He was not a bad looking boy, Jamie, he is not a bad looking man – not too tall, not too short, with square shoulders and the long arms of a plasterer. He has brown hair which he keeps very short, a heavy chin and very pale blue eyes which rarely blink so that he seems to be looking right into you, Lynn says, though the evidence is that he has very little curiosity about other people. His default expression is anxious, but when he is with his little boy – Leo, his and Niecey's little boy – then he can laugh and have fun.

There is a faint feeling that they are talking about someone who has disappeared – not died, they wouldn't allow themselves to even come close to thinking that – no, just someone who is no longer quite what he was.

'He was a good lad,' says Lynn.

'He's a good man,' says Dave. 'Isn't he? He don't deserve this. Whatever it is.'

'What should we do?' she asks.

'Leave it alone,' he says. 'See if it sorts itself out. Let's not go looking for trouble.'

'That's all right for you to say,' says Lynn. 'You forget, I've to go to work tomorrow, and see her all day long. I've to keep my mouth shut all that time.'

'Yes,' he says, after considering, 'that's what you've got to do.'

'What do you think though? Do you think Denise Wilson is Niecey?'

'I don't, no. I don't. I can't believe it. Can you?'

'I can,' says Lynn, 'and I'll tell you why. The names of those twins – Did you notice?'

Well,' he says, 'I saw them – I'm not sure now if –'

'Lila and Oliver,' she says.

'Quite posh names aren't they?' He says this doubtfully, as if searching for an answer that will suit her.

'You're being a bit slow on the uptake,' she says. 'Think about Leo. L for Lila, O for Oliver. You can't tell me that's a coincidence.'

'Oh,' he says slowly. 'Yes. I see what you mean.'

'I wonder if our Jamie has picked up on it.'

'I wonder.'

Jamie drives the van home. Niecey is sitting on the settee with Leo snugged in beside her, watching a cartoon about dragons. Dinosaurs and dragons are Leo's favourite things.

'Time you were in bed,' says Jamie.

'Mummy said I could wait for you,' says Leo, though without taking his eyes off the screen.

'I'm here now,' says Jamie. 'Bedtime for you, my man.'

After tucking Leo into his bed Jamie goes into the other bedroom and carefully, quietly, tips out Niecey's jumble of chains and earrings from her box, and slides the two birth certificates back in, without looking at them again. When he goes downstairs she is in the kitchen, warming up his tea in the microwave.

'All right?'

'Fine.'

When the sun has gone down Lynn and Dave go inside.

'I wouldn't mind a beer,' says Dave.

'You shouldn't,' says Lynn. 'Oh go on then, just this once. I'll have one too.'

'You know it's true,' says Dave, though Lynn hasn't mentioned Niecey for half an hour, 'we still don't know anything about her.'

'Like what?'

'Where she grew up, what happened to her parents, where she lived before she came to Sheffield. What jobs she did. What friends did she have? Why did she even come here?'

'Oh Dave,' says Lynn, 'don't you wish things were simple? Why are families so much trouble?'

He reaches his foot across the room and prods her foot with it, gently. 'Now then, they're not so bad are they. You love em anyway, don't you.'

'If I didn't,' says Lynn, 'it might not be so bad.' She finishes her beer. 'I'm never going to get to sleep tonight,' she says. 'Time for bed anyway.'

Dave is almost asleep when Lynn says into the dark, 'I did wonder you know, at the time, whether Jamie was Leo's father. You know, whether she was marrying him just because she was pregnant and someone had gone off and left her.'

'Or,' says Dave, rolling over towards her, 'whether she didn't even know who the father might be.'

'I never thought of that,' says Lynn. 'But anyway, the more I see of Leo, the more I see Jamie in him. Don't you?'

Dave is quiet for so long he could be properly asleep. Then he says. 'Yes, I do see Jamie. Not much – he certainly favours Niecey more. But yes, he has Jamie's build I would say. The shape of his face, now that he's not a baby any more. And he has that determination that Jamie had as a little one. Would you say that?'

'I would,' says Lynn. 'I'm glad you think that. I don't like to think of Jamie being deceived.'

'You mean, even more deceived,' says Dave. 'She's not been straight with us, whichever way you look at it. She's deceived us all, one way or another. I don't know if we'll ever get to the bottom of it.'

'I don't know if we should even want to,' says Lynn. 'What worries me most, at the moment, is what Gemma might do. Or what Sarah might say.'

Dave makes a sound that means he is going to go to sleep and rolls back onto his right side. He does not hear Lynn a few minutes later when she says, 'We don't even know how they met, do we?'

New Year's Eve. The big pub on the corner was heaving with folk, young, old and loud. Jamie Wilde stood wedged between two people he had been at school with, and failed to follow what was being said, what with the noise of the music and the sheer number of conversations surging around him. Across the room his two sisters and their husbands were sitting at a table – having made an early start – with some friends. They would not be staying much longer; they would go back home to watch the fireworks on the TV and have a last drink before going to bed, leaving their children asleep at grandparents' to be collected in the morning. Jamie's friends would be going down town any time now and he was supposed to go with them; one of them was already phoning for a cab.

At the bar there was a crush, naturally. Behind it the staff weaved through and past each other, taking orders, pulling pints, pouring bottles, taking money, giving change, never, apparently, making a mistake. Jamie wondered how they could be so quick; he would never be able to do that job, under pressure, people shouting, people changing their minds, handling the things he had never been comfortable with, liquids and money, and noisy demanding people.

He saw a woman in the crush at the bar; a woman he had never seen before round here. Although she was quite tall she was not managing to get noticed and served; Jamie could see her looking along the bar to find a better place but there was none, it was all one mass of people pushing forward, calling out their orders, passing full glasses back to people behind them. She manoeuvred herself forward but was now sideways on to the bar between two men; Jamie couldn't see her face any more but he was still watching her.

She straightened her back, as if she was taking a deep breath. She shouldered the smaller of the two men out of her way. She banged one hand down on the bar and then with both hands she lifted up her top to reveal her breasts. Jamie couldn't see them properly, only the edge of the left one, and the ridges of her ribs. He deduced though that the breasts were quite nice – not big but firm and round; she was not wearing a bra – there would not have been a lot of point in her gesture if she were. What she said to the barman was lost in the noise.

The barman – Jamie knew him from school too – laughed and started to serve her but the manager bustled across and stopped him.

'We'll not have that,' Jamie heard her above the music and above the noise. 'You can get yourself out of here young lady. I'm not having that in my pub.'

The young woman seemed not to even think of arguing. She had pulled her top back down and she stood still at the bar, looking towards the barman as if he might serve her when his boss's back was turned. Jamie saw him shake his head, and the manager was back.

'I told you to get lost didn't I. Go on, get yourself off home. You've had enough already.'

The barman caught Jamie's eye and beckoned him over. 'Do us a favour,' he said. 'See this young lady home for us. She'll only get herself in trouble.'

'Where does she live?'

'No idea mate. Ask her.'

Jamie turned to her but she had already turned her back on him, and was walking back towards a group of women – girls really, noticeably younger than her – who were standing together and had not noticed what had happened. Jamie followed.

'Shall I see you home?' he offered but she appeared not to hear.

One of the girls turned towards them; someone else Jamie vaguely remembered from school, from a couple of years below him.

'Is she with you?' he said.

The girl shrugged her plump shoulders. 'Just met her tonight.'

'What do they call her?'

'Niecey.'

'Niecey?'

'That's what she told us.'

'Niecey Nuttall,' said another of the girls. 'What do you want to know for?'

'Barman wants me to see her home.'

'Good idea,' said the plump one. 'She's not got much money, she can't buy a round. We don't want her down town with us anyway.'

'Know where she lives?'

They shrugged again.

Jamie turned to the woman. She was nearly as tall as him and he guessed four or five years older. Her eyes – the brown side of hazel – were looking vaguely round the big room but she was standing steadily, without swaying. Her lipstick had rubbed off except at the very corners of her mouth.

'Have you got a coat?'

She pulled something from a heap on the floor and put it round her shoulders.

'Come on,' said Jamie. 'I'm supposed to take you home.' The barman waved and shouted something but Jamie didn't see or hear.

Outside it was mild for the last night of December, and a small rain was falling steadily. The woman's hair – dark blond, thick and cut short – was soon spattered by drops which caught the light as they passed under streetlamps.

'Where do you live?'

'You don't have to do this,' she said. 'I can find my own way home. I'm not drunk.' Her accent showed that she was not local. She was not someone he had gone to school with.

'I'll see you to your door,' he said, and she shrugged as if she couldn't be bothered to argue.

As they walked she lifted her face to the sky and let the rain fall on it.

'You'll bash into something,' he said. She seemed not to hear him and he took hold of her arm so that she didn't walk into lamp posts.

'Your mascara will run,' he said. He had sisters and knew about things like mascara.

'Worth it,' she said. 'Isn't it nice, being out in the dark.'

'Nicer than the pub.' It was not quite a question, not quite a statement.

They walked through streets where Christmas trees twinkled and flashed in front windows and sad garish packaging was heaped beside the wheelie bins waiting for the next collection. She stopped at a low anonymous block.

'This where you live?'

'Anything wrong with that?'

'No,' he said, although there was. 'I'll see you to your front door.'

'No don't,' she said.

'Someone there? Boyfriend?'

'Fat chance,' she said, and then, 'Oh, come in if you must.'

She opened the window wide before she closed the door.

'Cold?' she said.

'It's a bit cold,' he said, 'but I don't mind it. I work in cold places.'

She didn't ask where he worked and he didn't tell her. He didn't ask why she would have the window open in December and she didn't explain.

'Shall I make you a coffee?' he said.

'I'm not drunk,' she said. 'But go ahead, if you like.'

He put coffee in one mug and did not look for another one.

'There's another mug in the cupboard,' she said. 'I didn't intend for me to have some and not you.'

'Thank you,' he said.

'There's no milk,' she said.

'That's all right,' he said.

There was only one chair which she had sat on – probably she did not want him getting more ideas than he might already have – so he was forced to sit on the bed.

'Where do you live?'

'Wisewood.'

'I don't know where that is. I'm not from Sheffield.'

'Just up the hill from Hillsborough.'

'So is that your local?'

He smiled, nicely. 'There's not really any locals in Wisewood. It's just a big estate. I come down to Hillsborough when I want a night out.'

'What about going into town?'

He shuffled his feet a bit on the floor. 'I don't really like night clubs. Too loud. I'd rather have a quiet drink with a mate.'

She was quiet. He said, 'I'm a bit boring.'

She looked at him properly for the first time. 'You do what's best for you. What's your name?'

'Jamie. Jamie Wilde. What do they call you?'

'Niecey,' she said.

'I've never heard that before.'

'Short for Denise,' she said. 'I don't like Denise.'

'Niecey,' he said.

He drank his coffee slowly, as if it was too hot. Then he stood up. 'I should be off then.'

Niecey stood too and as she did so, fireworks shot into the sky. Spasmodically, here and there, from all around, people were letting off fireworks. They crackled and fizzed and shed coloured stars which fell slowly to earth. Jamie watched Niecey watching them, as if she was entranced. As if, maybe, she had never seen fireworks before.

'Happy New Year,' he said.

'Happy New Year,' she said, and gave him a small kiss on the cheek. 'Thank you for bringing me home.'

'Would you like to come out with me?' he said, in a rush. 'Tomorrow?'

'All right,' she said.

When he was gone she wondered why she had said that. He was too young for her, she could see that even if he couldn't. He was too respectable, he was too boring. He was a gentle soul. He wouldn't like her when he got to know her. But she said yes. What else could she say, in her position?

She got into bed and lay with the window still wide open, lay awake a long time listening to people going past in the street, singing, vomiting, shouting, arguing, racketing. Heard a girl crying, some friends trying to cajole her along.

Wondered about Jamie. Mr Wilde of Wisewood.

She hadn't been drunk at all, in fact. A little giddy, from some cannabis earlier in the evening, but that had mostly worn off, and afterwards, when she thought about what she had done, she knew it was simply (simply!) that she wanted to be *seen*. She was tired of being insignificant. She was fed up of being passed in the street and not noticed. She had had enough of being invisible.

She didn't go to the pub with the idea of exposing herself. She didn't want to be exposed, either to ridicule or to lewdness or to censure. She didn't plan it. There was this big pub and she thought to herself, I'll just go in and have one drink and talk to some people and feel a little bit as if I'm still alive. *When night comes,* she thought, *I'll go to places fit for woe.* Because, she said aloud, I just had Christmas without you babes and even though I was free to do what I wanted, I wasn't free at all, if you know what I mean.

She went in this place and it was noisy as you'd expect, crammed with people, they all knew each other it seemed, they'd been drinking all afternoon, at least most of them had, you could hear their voices getting louder and louder. There was a party of people about her age sitting round a

14

table, about eight of them and one of the men smiled at her but they were all couples and she knew, too respectable for her, and there was no spare chair to be seen of course, so she attached herself loosely to this party of girls – young women – early twenties maybe; they didn't look to her as if they would be too fussy about who they spoke to and she hovered on the edges of them until one of them turned to her and asked her name.

She tried talking to that group of young women, she introduced herself, she asked their names, she enquired what they were doing later in the evening. One of them offered to include her in their round but she said no, I don't have enough to reciprocate. Maybe it was that word that made them turn, very slightly, away from her.

She thought she would go and get herself a drink. A double vodka and maybe borrow a little bit of tonic or something from somebody to make it go a bit further, but when she got to the bar – it was like you had to have lived on that road for a century, going back three generations, before they would take any notice of you. And it felt like no one had taken any notice of her for weeks. She was invisible and insignificant and she did not matter. She tried to remember if anyone – apart from Orla, once a week, – had taken any interest in her and she couldn't remember a single one. Proper interest, not just, Cold out isn't it, that's eighty-nine p dear, and eleven pence change.

So when she went to the bar, by herself, she wanted to shout so loud that everyone in the place would hear her. 'See me,' she would shout. 'I'm here. I live here. I want to be a part of this.' Shouting, though, wouldn't have worked, that was clear. What else, then, was possible? She hated doing it. Even as she banged her hands on the bar, even as she grasped the edge of her decent black top, she knew what she was going to do and she hated it. She knew she would be embarrassed by it, she knew she would cringe – if not today, then tomorrow and for weeks and months. She could already see people pointing at her in the street – that's that mad woman, you know –

It was quite funny though. A small corner of her imagined how anybody who knew her would be surprised. Disbelieving. So on the one hand it was humiliating, being ejected from the place, and she felt sorry for that poor young man who was detailed to take her home, on the other hand, it gave her a bit of a buzz. When she walked with him back home – she couldn't think what else to call it but home – she kept smiling to herself, though she tried not to let him see.

*I said my prayers for you babes, like I always do. You couldn't see the stars tonight, what with the rain and the mist, and the smoke from the fireworks hanging in the air, and I always feel more hopeful when I can see the stars. But this year, babes, this year.*

Mr Wilde of Wisewood. It sounded lucky. Maybe it could be lucky.

Lynn and Dave spent that New Year's Eve quietly at home. Sarah dropped her children off with them before going on to the pub to meet some friends. Gemma and Mark would be there too, their children having been dropped in a similar manner with Mark's parents.

'We can have all of them,' Lynn had said, but Gemma said, No, they would get no sleep at all if all four children were sharing a room, she would only worry, better to let Mark's parents do something for a change. So it was just Melissa and Dom who came with their little backpacks crammed with pyjamas and toys and books and cough medicine. They spread their belongings round the house and climbed all over Dave and delayed going to bed by all the stratagems they could think of, and finally, – after more stories than they would ever have had at home, after cleaning their teeth, drinking more Ribena, cleaning teeth again, getting up to pee again, arguing over the landing light being on or off, arguing about who would have which bed, losing the favourite soft dog and finding it again – they went to sleep in the same bed, and Lynn came downstairs ready for the one small drink that she would allow herself when she had responsibilities.

'Not bad,' said Dave. 'I've known them be worse than that.'

Lynn was on her knees picking up a disassembled Lego helicopter which had been upsettingly difficult for Dom's little fingers, a set of unpleasant-looking toy dogs who appeared to be running a sweet shop ('What sort of example is that?' she'd said to Sarah) a few books and two sets of discarded clothes.

'It's a good thing we're not expecting company,' she said to Dave, though in fact they rarely socialised outside the family.

'Pass them toys over here,' said Dave. 'I'll put them back in the boxes.'

Lynn folded the clothes and piled them neatly on the arm of the settee. 'I'll do it,' she said. 'You go and get me a drink. I'll have a gin – small gin, mind – and a bit of tonic. There's half a lemon in the fridge.'

They sat quietly with their drinks. The children were quiet and must therefore be asleep.

'Where was Jamie going tonight? Did he say?'

'Just that they were meeting at the Park.'

'Then where?'

'He didn't say.'

'Didn't you ask him?'

'He most likely wouldn't know would he? They make it up as they go along.'

'I suppose he'll come back in the early hours. I hope he doesn't wake the little ones.'

'Maybe he won't come back. Some years – New Year – he's stayed out all night hasn't he.'

'Did he say who he was going with?'

'No.'

'I wonder if he's got a girl at the moment. He's not mentioned anyone lately.'

'If he has I doubt we'll ever get to see her.'

'Funny isn't it. Our girls weren't like that at all. I could have done with less information a lot of the time. But him – well, he's never been one to bring girls home.'

This was true. Sometimes Lynn and Dave would notice that he had gone out of an evening looking a bit more dressed up than usual; he might buy some new clothes, or have his hair cut, or go a bit heavy on the aftershave, but they knew better than to ask him if he had a girlfriend. He might have told them but it would have been unwillingly. It was better to wait and see, and usually – always – it turned out to come to nothing.

He was always, from a child, a private person. It was always hard to know what Jamie was thinking, or if he was thinking at all. When he was growing up there were people who thought he was a bit slow, but really it was just that he was a natural bystander. An onlooker. He had spent his boyhood on the fringes of football games, spectating at playground fights, staying out of his sisters' arguments, not getting involved. His schoolteachers said that he was hard to engage – willing enough, but without enthusiasm or initiative.

'He's just one of those people,' said Lynn, 'who don't like to push themselves forward. He's all there, he just keeps to himself.'

Dave, who was – he said so himself – not someone who normally cared about success in a worldly sense, used to worry. 'How's he going to make his way in the world? Can you see him going for a job interview?'

'He's good with his hands,' said Lynn. This was when Jamie was fourteen and had to choose his options at school. When asked if he wanted to study history or geography, IT

18

or food technology, he said he didn't mind. Whatever. In the end, when he finished school he went to work with his uncle, Dave's brother, who ran a plumbing business. Jamie became a tiler, which suited his methodical ways. He went round in the van as Uncle Steve fixed people's clapped out boilers and cracked shower trays and put in new bathrooms. Steve did all the complicated stuff with pipework and electrics, and Jamie assisted. As soon as he learned to drive he could go to the store and get parts and materials; he would do the heavy work of stripping out an old bathroom, he went on courses so that he could learn plastering and tiling so that then, when all the new shiny parts were in place, Steve could go away and leave Jamie on his own, with his boxes of tiles and his cutting implements and his measuring tapes, where he worked steadily through a day or two, only interrupted sometimes by the customer offering coffee. Usually he said no.

He still seemed content to live with his parents. He kept his little bedroom, even though he could have had the bigger one that Gemma and Sarah used to share until they left home.

'I don't need a big room,' he said. 'I only use it for sleeping.' This was not true though. He spent a lot of time up there, on his own, with his TV and his X-box and listening to music through headphones, so as not to disturb his parents.

He was a good boy. The girls as teenagers had been a lot more trouble. Sarah with her obsession with her weight, which looked at one point like turning into a proper eating disorder; Gemma with her temper and her habit of getting into long involved arguments with her friends. How many evenings Dave and Lynn had had to spend with one or the other of them – or both – cajoling and counselling and comforting while one or the other – or both – sobbed and accused and beat herself up (Sarah) or blamed everyone else (Gemma), while Jamie kept to his room protected by screens and headphones.

'Are we neglecting him?' wondered Lynn, but whenever she asked him how he was he said everything was fine.

'What have we done wrong?' she said. 'Why are we the ones with a dysfunctional family?'

'Don't use that word,' said Dave. 'I hate that word. We're not that. We're functional, we're working. Every family has a problem at some time or other, and we're working on it.'

'On all of them,' said Lynn.

'The point I'm making,' said Dave, 'is that *we* are doing the work. We've not gone snivelling to some psychologist to sort it out, have we? *We're* working on it, as a family. *Working,* that's what functioning means.'

Dave didn't often go off like that, and as it turned out he'd been right. In the end Sarah has got over her apparent hatred of her body after she turned her energies to her schoolwork, and later, her career. Gemma has learned to control her temper and become a person who has friends, although she still has a snippy side to her. They each have a husband, and a daughter and a son, all very right and proper, as Lynn and Dave see it. They are happy, as far as anyone can tell. Things are fine.

As a very minor homage to the fact that it was New Year's Eve, Lynn and Dave stayed up until twelve, with the TV on mute.

'At last,' said Lynn, as the first fireworks showed on the screen. 'We can go to bed now. I'll just glance in at the children.'

'They're fast asleep,' she reported. 'That Jamie just better not wake them up at four in the morning.'

In fact, Lynn and Dave had not been long in bed before she heard Jamie come in, very quietly, and go to his room.

Her room. A bed, a chair, a table. A washbasin, a chest of drawers. A shelf, a hook. A window, open to the cold air.

Morning came and Niecey stayed in her bed, there being nothing yet to get up for. Single bed, wood frame, plain, like the one she had as a child. Thin mattress, one pillow, no duvet, but sheets and two blankets, like something from long ago, her parents' childhoods maybe, or prison. Small table next to the bed, one small book upon it, slim volume, hardback, dusty red cover, and a copy of the Metro, several days old. Chair – some sort of compromise between hard and comfortable, placed by the window, facing outwards, yesterday's clothes hung over the back of it.

Washbasin, her toothbrush, two coffee mugs waiting to be washed up, two.

Storage options – the chest of drawers, a hook on the back of the door for her coat, a shelf holding a jar of coffee, a small packet of rolling tobacco and a packet of rizlas.

The floor was woodblock like an old school hall, the walls were cream and bare, the window had a pair of curtains, green, with white flowers. Someone once went to the trouble of designing that material, and someone else chose it and went to the trouble of making curtains with it, and hanging them in some other room – a girl's maybe – and probably stood back and looked at them with pride. And then, years later, became tired of them, repainted the walls perhaps in a colour that didn't go, so took the curtains down and passed them on to a good cause. Here.

Niecey herself, as a girl, had a bedroom with curtains run up by her mother on her sewing machine. She remembered being eight years old and choosing stuff with rainbows on. She remembered – this may not have been true but she remembered it this way – that her mother approved of the rainbows; that she sewed them without complaining and hung them and took advantage of an educational opportunity to teach her daughter the mnemonic for remembering the colour sequence. It is a happy memory and all the more hurtful. Not many years later the rainbows were seriously despised and Niecey – Denise as she was at home – was agitating for new ones, and by then things were different. It was unthinkable that her mother would go shopping with her for something as frivolous as new curtains when the old ones were perfectly serviceable; it was not to be expected that she would have the time to get the sewing machine out and make new ones.

Niecey rolled slowly out of bed. No appointments. Orla was on her Christmas break, the Job Centre was closed. Jamie had said that he would see her at four o'clock outside the hostel door but the more she thought about it the less she believed it. She could not take seriously the idea that Jamie Wilde would actually turn up. She did not particularly want to see him – *him* specifically – but the prospect of seeing *someone* in the course of what had to be a long flat New Year's Day was appealing.

She especially did not want him to see her room, again, in daylight, or walk along the cold bare corridor with laminated rules stapled to the notice boards, telling you everything you were not allowed to bring in – dogs, cats, any other pets, untested electrical devices, takeaway meals, alcohol, and illegal substances. Also people. You were not allowed visitors, though there was a little bare cell near the front door where you were allowed to see your probation officer or – with permission – your parents. Niecey could not imagine that many of the residents had parents who might make a visit.

But then, what did she know? She could hear the woman in the next room sometimes - hear her push her chair across the floor, hear her door open and shut as she went down the corridor to the bathroom, hear her turn on a tap or open a window – but she had never seen or spoken to her. Sometimes – very seldom – she heard what must be a phone ringing; it was the same burst of music each time – some heavy drum beats and someone singing Why don't you call me? And then the low flat voice of the woman in the next room saying words Niecey couldn't quite make out. The calls did not last long, but still Niecey was hoping that Orla could get her a phone, just so that her appointments didn't have to be made by letter, just so that once a week the phone would ring and a voice would be there.

Niecey went down the corridor for a pee, came back, made a cup of coffee and got back into bed. She picked up the book from the table and opened it at random. She said the words softly to herself. *So I turn'd into a sty and laid me down among the swine.* A little twist of her lips and she closed Blake and put him back on the table.

Jamie was waiting outside for her at four o'clock, just as he said he would. In her memory he looked quite different from what he turned out to look like; if she had passed him in the street she would not have recognised him.

'Why do you live here?' he said.

She did not look him in the eye. 'Just till I find somewhere. Where are we going?'

'Everything's shut,' he said, 'except the pubs.' He seemed to take it for granted that she would not want to go in one.

'We could go for a walk.' She said it hesitantly but he agreed straight away.

'You a stranger to Sheffield?'

'Been here a few weeks,' she said.

'Seven hills,' he said.

'What?'

'There are seven hills in Sheffield. Seven hills, same as Rome.'

'Have you ever been to Rome?'

'No. Have you?'

'When I was a kid,' she said.

'Been to Spain,' he said. 'Mallorca too. Long time ago though, with me Mum and Dad. Want to see a river?'

'All right.'

They walked without touching each other, hands in pockets. Her coat was a thin affair, never meant for winter.

'Are you cold?'

'No,' she said.

'Want some gloves?' He pulled a pair out of his pocket, thin black fleecy ones, and she accepted them.

They crossed a dual carriageway, quiet today.

'See that?'

'Football ground?'

'Know which one?'

She shook her head.

'Where do you come from? Don't they have football where you come from?'

'Is it Sheffield Wednesday? I used to know someone who supported Sheffield Wednesday.'

'There's a lot of people do.'

'Do you know him? Adrian –?'

'Don't know any Adrians,' he said. 'Here,' he said. 'Down there, that's the River Don. It all flooded two-three years ago. Ruined the pitch.'

'Where does it go?'

'The river? Doncaster. After that, I don't know. Sea I suppose.'

'Where are we going now?'

'I don't know,' he said. 'I've got to be at my sisters at six o'clock. New Year Day meal, all the family.'

'Oh.'

They walked through the park, came out on the dual carriageway again. She was watchful, looking everywhere, looking hard at the few people to be seen walking about. She did not say anything about what she saw. The outing could not be said to be a success.

'I think I'll go home now,' she said. 'I'm getting cold.'

'Why did you do it?' he said.

She hunched her shoulders, kept them up by her ears. 'I just did,' she said at last. 'It just happened.'

'So,' he said, 'ever done it before?'

She made a noise that was almost a laugh. 'No,' she said. 'Never before. Never again either.'

'Right,' he said. After a few minutes he spoke again. 'Sunday tomorrow,' he said. 'I could show you another river. Or we could go to Meadowhall. Meadowhall will be open for the sales.'

'I haven't got any money,' she said.

'Tell me your phone number.'

'I haven't got a phone,' she said. 'I'm saving up to get one. Not there yet.'

'Tomorrow,' he said. 'Eleven o'clock. We'll get a tram and go to Meadowhall. You don't need money. We'll just be looking.'

He saw her back to her door.

'I can't ask you in,' she said. 'Not in daylight. Someone might tell and I'd be out on my ear.'

'Not really daylight is it?'

'Daytime I mean. People are about. In the corridors.'

'All right. But see you tomorrow, all right.'

\*

The New Year's Day gathering was a family expectation – of course in the past it would have been at Lynn and Dave's, but the growing family were too many now for the small house and the gathering had moved to the biggest one available. Sarah, her husband Jon and two children lived fairly near to her parents, not in an ex-council house but in a modern detached house with four bedrooms. They were the first in the family – if you didn't count their Aunt Janet – to live in a detached house.

Lynn contributed food, and Gemma always provided dessert. Jamie was supposed to bring wine, which he found problematic – beer he could cope with, wine sent him into an embarrassed confusion. He had to take the advice of the woman in the off-licence and arrived with a plastic bag, clinking.

His sisters amused themselves with trying to find out who he has been seeing.

'That were a short date though, weren't it? Going back later are you?'

Jamie blushed a little and said nothing. 'And where did you get to last night?' said Sarah. 'One minute you were there and then when we looked to say goodbye – no Jamie. Disappeared.'

He couldn't think of an answer, and Gemma joined in. 'So who were you with? Those two you always knock about with – they were still there, but where were you?'

'Went out.'

'Who with though? Where'd you go?'

Jamie turned to his nephew to rescue himself. 'Hey Dom. Show me your cars. Let's see that garage of yours. Come on Jake, you too, let's play cars shall we.'

'He's not going to tell us. Who is she? Come on, tell us.'

When his parents arrived the sisters stopped their teasing and became part of the grown up world again. Jamie sat with his brothers-in-law and drank gently – it was a particularly long holiday weekend and care had to be taken.

'No work till Tuesday for you then Jame,' said Mark. 'Me, I've to go in Monday to get it all set up for the night shift. People will be all out of bread by Tuesday morning.'

'Sales start tomorrow,' said Jon. 'No rest for the wicked.' He was a manager at a big department store; Christmas and New Year were far from restful for him and he wouldn't see daylight now until February.

'Now then,' said Sarah, coming in from the kitchen, 'I thought we'd put the children on a separate table – we can use Melissa's little table, I've given it a clean – otherwise we'll not have enough chairs.'

This was the first year that Dominic and Jake were allowed to stay up and eat with everyone else and it made fitting seven adults and four children round the table less easy.

'One of us can sit at the table,' said Tasha, counting chairs.

'Which one though?' said her uncle Jon.

'Jake and Dom are too little,' she said. 'Melissa can sit here every day anyway, so I think it should be me.'

'Dream on,' said Gemma to her daughter. 'Even if that was fair, which it isn't, you'd be wanting to sit with the others within two minutes.'

'Look,' said Lynn, laying out cutlery, 'Here's your serviettes, all folded like ours, and here's your party poppers – *not yet* –' as Dom reached for one – 'they're for later, when you've eaten your dinner.'

'Come over here boys,' said Dave. 'Come and show me what this does.' He held up a box.

'Actually Grandad,' said Melissa, 'that's mine. Shall I show you?'

He pulled her to his side and whispered, 'I'm just trying to distract the boys while your mum and them get that food out. Can you find something for them to show me?' But before she had finished ferreting through the pile of toys and games in the corner, her mother was rounding everybody up and telling them to sit at the table.

'No matter what you do,' Sarah said to her mother, 'they never sit in the right places.'

The four men were clustered at one end, leaving the women to sit together, closest to where the children were now, for the time being amicably, at their own small table.

'Brung up rotten,' joked Dave. 'Too late to change us now.'

Later, as they walked up the hill to their home, Lynn said, 'I know we've always done it – New Year's Day – but it's not as enjoyable going to someone else's house. Don't you think?'

'Swings and roundabouts,' said Dave, after a pause for thought. 'We don't have the pots to wash, that's a big plus, and we can get away whenever we want and come home early if we feel like it. On t'other hand, you never feel quite as at home, do you. Best behaviour job, isn't it.'

'I know I shouldn't feel this way,' said Lynn, 'but I don't like not being in control. I do all I can to help, but I'm not allowed to do things my way. What did you think of the gravy?'

'Not a patch on yours,' he said.

'And Mark always carves the meat. Just because he's a baker doesn't make him a chef does it. Even with that big kitchen it was like Paddington station – all that coming and going and nobody knowing what was what.'

'You're tired,' he said. 'It all went off perfect.'

'And why hasn't Jamie come home with us? Where can he be going at this time of night?'

'He said he was going for a bit of a walk. Probably meeting up with a mate.'

'Hm,' said Lynn.

Niecey liked this about him, that although he asked her questions, to make conversation, he didn't push her for answers. She asked him questions too; it was a good way of deflecting him from discovering her.

'Just one sister?'

'Two,' he said. 'Sarah and Gemma. Older than me, I'm the baby. You got a sister?'

'No.'

'Brother?'

'No.'

'Mum? Dad?'

'No.'

'Neither?'

She shook her head and he stopped asking.

They were walking to look at another of Sheffield's rivers, everything else being shut – except Meadowhall, for which Niecey showed no enthusiasm.

'My sisters are always there,' he said. 'Specially Sarah. She loves shopping, Sarah. Me mum don't like it there though. She says she feels shut in – no windows, see – and she gets into a panic to get out.'

'Yes.' Niecey said it as if she understood.

They looked at the River Loxley as it flowed grey over its stony bed and under the road on its way to join the Don. Rain was beginning to fall.

'Shall we go back to yours?'

'I can't let you in,' she said. 'Rules.'

'You let me in the other night.'

'I shouldn't have. Honestly, if I break the rules I won't have anywhere to live.'

'So why do you live there? It's a bit –'

'Horrible,' she said. 'I know. I'm looking for somewhere better.'

'What sort of place?'

'I don't know,' she said, sadly.

As she keyed the number into the entrance panel he said again, 'Let me come in. I've hardly seen you today. I'll be really quiet. Anyway, I know the number now. I could let myself in. And if they throw you out I'll find somewhere else for you. Better than this.'

'You don't understand,' she said, but she did not explain.

In the room he kissed her firmly. 'Sorry about the stubble,' he said. Though his hair was a dull mid-brown the stubble had a ginger tinge and caught the light from the one overhead bulb. They lay down on the bed.

'All right,' said Niecey. 'But no noise.'

He was very polite, prepared with a condom; he seemed to do his best to make no noise and Niecey was prepared to enjoy the experience but the creaking of the bed made her nervous, the fear that he would make incriminating, sexual noise – not just any old noise – over-rode any pleasure.

'I'm sorry,' she said.

'Thing is,' he said, 'I still live with my Mum and Dad. I've only got a single bed too – bit more comfortable than this one though.' He seemed inclined to do it all again but she pushed him away.

'Look, you make me scared. Someone will hear us talking, let alone –'

'I really like you,' he said. 'I want to see you again. We'll have to find you another place to live.'

'Yeah right,' she said.

'What's this?' Picking up Blake from the table. 'Is it poems?'

'You can see it is.'

'We had poems at school,' he said. 'Never made no sense.'

'It's the only book I've got now,' she said. 'I know it by heart.'

He shook his head slightly, conveying bewilderment, and said no more.

When he was gone she opened Blake again, standing by the open window. *Secrecy the Human Dress*. She sighed.

*

'How is the job going?' said Orla.

'It's all right,' said Niecey.

'It's not for ever. It's so that you have something to put on a CV. Some skills.'

So far, thought Niecey, So far I have learnt the skill of emptying a black bin bag on to the floor, and picking up the contents very carefully. You would not believe what some people think is all right to palm off on to a charity. You would not believe how much soiled clothing and bedding and curtains and I don't know what else we have to throw out –

'Nice people?' said Orla.

'All right.' Mostly retired ladies, and the occasional young offender, and another person like me – a man –His skill is lifting heavy stuff.

'Denise,' said Orla. 'I need you to talk to me. We have fifteen minutes together and I need to know how you're getting on.' She was from Northern Ireland and the way she said 'how' was a continual diversion; Niecey was always waiting for her to say it again. Or 'now.' 'How was your Christmas?'

What do you think? But Niecey did not tell her how bad it had been. The loneliness. The boredom. They were the easy bits.

'Have you made any friends? At the shop? Anywhere? Come on Denise, tell me something.'

She is only young, Orla. She's doing her best. 'Well, I do have one friend.'

'That's great.'

Too much enthusiasm. But it gave Niecey a warmish feeling, to be able to say that she had a friend. Though maybe that wasn't quite what Jamie was.

'Have you heard from your parents?' Orla asked her now. She always said this before closing the session, a sort of final, desperate attempt to find something had been achieved.

'No,' said Niecey.

'Well then,' said Orla, still cheerful, still hopeful. 'Shall we say two weeks? Unless there's a problem – you know you can call me if there's a problem.'

Niecey pulled her phone from her pocket, to show that she had one. It wasn't new, it was an old one that used to be Jamie's, but it enabled them to arrange meeting times and places. Niecey enjoyed knowing that when it rang the woman in the next room – still never seen – would know that she too had someone who would call her.

If there's a problem, Niecey thought, walking out of the building. Because, babes, there is a problem, isn't there. *Where are you?*

Now that the evenings were getting lighter and sometimes the weather was drier, she and Jamie went out in the evenings for longer walks. Niecey always kept her eyes open, looking all around. They talked about what they saw, in the present, just things like, Oh look at that funny coloured car, look at that house, would you like to live in a house like that, look at that kid on roller blades he needs someone to hold his hand till he gets his balance. Things like that. It has become clear that he thinks he is her boyfriend. He talks of things that will happen in the future. We could go to Scarborough, he says, stay for a weekend. Have you ever been to Cornwall? Nice there. We could go in the summer. But there was a gap, she realised, between the immediate scene in front of them and some nebulous future. When she asked him, one time, what his parents thought about him spending so much time with her, he said he hadn't told them about her. Not yet.

They held hands. They made love – as quietly as they could, in her room. When they said goodbye they kissed. They rarely looked each other straight in the eyes. *The look of soft deceit*, she thought.

Lynn worked at an old people's home – properly a Residential Home for the Elderly and Infirm – called The Hedges. She had not grown up with the idea of what would be called a career. When she left school, and up until Sarah was born she worked at the sweet factory and then stayed at home with the children until Jamie started going to nursery school. It was just chance that found her working at the old people's home, a chance remark from someone at a bus stop, that they were short-staffed and looking for sensible people to work there.

'You can more or less choose your shifts,' said this person. 'It suits me fine. And they're nice people you know.'

It suited Lynn fine too. When she started there she was untrained. Nothing more was expected of her than common sense and a kind heart. They were understanding of the demands of family life. In school holidays she used sometimes to bring Jamie in to work with her, sometimes one of her girls as well, and they would sit with the old people and pick up the pieces of the jigsaw puzzles when they fell on the floor, or hold a skein of wool between their two hands for someone to roll it into a ball. Nowadays there are fewer of the residents who are capable of doing a jigsaw, or knitting so much as a square piece for a blanket.

Later her daughter Sarah worked with her there for a few months before she started her nursing training. Lynn too acquired certificates. She was the oldest, and longest-serving, member of staff, a support for everyone and a trusted second in command.

Dave, though, had been thinking for some time now about retiring from work. Every morning he thought about it, when Lynn shook him and he turned over to try for a few more minutes of sleep.

'You're like a big teenager,' she said. 'What's the matter with you?'

'I'll have to go to bed earlier,' he said, most mornings, drinking strong coffee to wake himself up. 'Either that, or retire.'

Several times he had thought he might be in line for being made redundant, but each time he was considered too valuable a worker to let go. This time he was determined – pay-off or no pay-off, he was going to pack it in.

'What do we need a redundancy package for anyway,' he said. 'I've been working since I were fifteen. The house is paid off, I've got a pension, we're not big spenders, we'll be fine.'

'What will you do all day?' said Lynn.

'Do? I'll just do exactly what I feel like doing.'

'For example though?'

'I can pick up the children from school, if I'm needed. There's the garden. I can join the bowls team at the club. I can do the shopping.'

'That would be nice,' said Lynn. 'It would be nice to come home from work and not have to start thinking about shopping and cooking.'

'Well,' he said, 'you'll be retired too. You don't have to go to work.'

'I will retire soon,' said Lynn. 'But maybe not quite yet. Who would I talk to all day if I didn't have work to go to?'

'Me?' said Dave.

'I'm not ready yet,' she said. 'You retire if you want to, and I know you do, but I'm not ready. See how we go. Maybe when I see you having a good time I'll think differently, but at the moment –'

'I heard you,' he said. 'You're not ready.'

'You won't want me under your feet all day,' she said.

'I would,' he said. 'Anyway, I thought we might go on a cruise.'

'You didn't,' she cried. 'David Wilde, that's the worst idea that's ever come out of your mouth. You'd hate it.'

'I thought you might like it,' he said. 'Your sister's always on about cruises.'

She shook her head. 'You think you know someone,' she said, half laughing. 'I thought you knew me, and then you come out with that. Don't you remember I'm scared of boats.'

'Not a boat,' said Dave. 'It's a ship, and a great big one. You wouldn't even know you weren't on dry land.'

'Then what's the point?' she said. 'And I've heard all about them, these cruises. It's nothing but eating and drinking.'

'There's dancing and things, in the evenings.'

'And when did we last dance? About 1964 if I remember rightly. And you were rubbish at it then.'

'Ah well,' he said, equably. 'We'll see how we go. You might come round to the idea, when you see me enjoying myself.'

'I might,' she said, but her tone of voice suggested that it was unlikely.

'My Dad's retiring from Stanley,' said Jamie. 'Stanley tools, you must have heard of them?'

'I don't think so,' said Niecey. She was looking out of her window at an old railway bridge, with old graffiti painted on it in big white letters. Someone loved someone – she wondered if they still did.

'You must have heard of a Stanley knife.'

'Oh yes. I knew –'

'What?'

'Nothing really. Someone I heard of got arrested for having one. I mean in the street.'

'Well yes. You can do damage with a Stanley knife. What did *your* dad do?'

'What?'

'I mean as a job? What was his job?'

'Teacher,' she said at last.

Jamie made a face. 'Teaching what?'

'Geography.'

'Oh. Tell you what, do you want to come round my house? My Mum and Dad have gone to Gemma's to look after the kids. No one at home.'

It was a Saturday afternoon. They walked up there, hearing the shouts and cheers and groans from the football ground.

'I thought you would be at the match,' she said.

He said, 'I've got a season ticket, but I let my mate have it for today.'

'Why did you do that?' she said, and he did not answer.

His parents' house was quite small, and very neat and well-cared-for. There were three Mother's Day cards on the windowsill. Niecey glanced their way once and didn't look again. They went as if by arrangement straight up to his bedroom – small, and also neat and tidy – and took off their clothes.

After they made love Niecey asked him, 'Why do you still live with your parents?'

He looked surprised, as if he'd never thought he had a choice. Then he said, 'I give me mum money for my keep, but I always save some as well. I've got quite a bit put away.'

'What will you do with it?'

'It's for when I get married,' he said. 'To buy a house.'

'Are you planning to?' she said, and he just said, 'One day.'

Later they went on a bus to Meadowhall, and there they happened to meet his sister Sarah, and her daughter Melissa. Niecey took deep breaths and held herself together. Sarah was a year or two older than her, and brisk. She had eyes of the same colour blue as Jamie's and a sharp-featured face. Melissa was a pretty child, not shy at all.

'Are you our Jamie's girlfriend?'

'I suppose so,' said Niecey. 'How old are you?'

'Nearly seven.'

'Nearly seven,' said Niecey and it seemed, the way she said it, to be an important age.

Sarah looked at her carefully, covertly, while saying to Jamie something not very important about somebody's birthday.

'There,' he said as they parted from them. 'It'll be all round family by now.'

'What will?' Though she knew what he meant.

'That I've got a girlfriend. And she's a stunner.'

Dave and Lynn had the sort of family where everyday plans were communicated, so it was to be expected that they would know what Gemma's plans were for the weekend.

'I'm going in to work Sunday,' she said to Lynn. 'There's a bunch of equipment wants giving a proper clean. Not that it's bad, of course, but you never know when Public Health are going to come through the door. Just letting you know so you don't come round. Mark will take the kids to the park if it's not raining.'

'I'm at work too,' said Lynn. 'Manager's weekend off so I'm in charge. I'll see you next week.'

It wasn't raining. The sun shone quite warmly for March, though the wind was a cold one, and Dave was in the garden raking up winter debris when the phone rang.

It was hard to tell what was going on. There was a great deal of noise which he took at first to be the children playing, with Mark's voice raised above them.

'Dave, mate,' said Mark. There was an urgency in his voice. 'Can you come. Can you come now. I'm in the playground at Rivelin. Jake's had an accident. Gem's took the car.'

'What's happened? Is he all right?' Though he could tell now from the noise that he wasn't very all right.

'I've called an ambulance,' said Mark.

'Oh Christ,' said Dave. 'I'm on my way.'

He drove there in his gardening boots and arrived at the same time as the ambulance did. It was easy to see where they were – a small crowd of passers-by had formed and were trying to help. Mark was sitting on the cold ground holding Jake – Jake with his face already swelling and blood dripping down the front of his coat from his mouth. He had stopped screaming though and was softly groaning, as if anything else would take too much out of him. An elderly lady had hold of Tasha who was struggling and making a lot more noise than her injured brother. 'I didn't mean it,' she was wailing. 'He's my brother. I didn't mean it.' When she saw Dave she broke free from the woman – who tried hard to keep a hold on her but failed – and ran to him.

'Grandad, I didn't mean it. Grandad, is he going to die?' Though genuinely upset, she was using the occasion to full dramatic advantage.

Dave picked her up. She was skinny like her dad, but eight years old now and heavy enough to make his knees buckle slightly before he stiffened them.

'Hey, hey,' said Dave. 'Let's quieten down shall we. You'll scare the ducks with all that noise.' He turned to thank the woman.

'I tried to calm her down,' she was saying, as if affronted that Tasha hadn't been compliant. 'Hysterics never helps anyone.'

'Shock,' said someone else.

Mark was on his feet now, as a young ambulance woman – looking too young to drive, never mind do the job she was doing, and pretty enough to be on the telly – lay Jake down and felt all over his body.

'What happened?' said Dave.

'He jumped,' said Mark. 'I only took my eyes off him for a second. He jumped off the roundabout while it was going.'

'Can happen to anyone,' said Dave. 'You couldn't have stopped him even if you'd been looking, probably.'

'His foot got caught,' said Tasha. 'I was on the monkey bars, I shouted him to look at me. It was my fault.' She said this soberly now, as if she had just realised the truth of it.

Her dad was not listening. 'What's Gem going to say?'

The ambulance crew called him over. They were loading Jake on to a stretcher. 'That ankle looks broken,' said the man. 'How bad, we can't tell. His face – looks bad I know, but no bones broken, I don't think. They'll X-ray him when we get him to t'Children's.'

Dave and Tasha had joined the little group.

'I want to come with you,' cried Tasha. 'Dad, let me come too.'

'You'll need to come home with me,' said Dave. He put her down on the ground and straightened his back with some difficulty. 'Your mum will want to know all about it. We'll go home and call her. I bet she'll take you to see Jake when he's been cleaned up.'

The woman who had previously been holding on to Tasha put in her opinion. 'Listen to your grandad,' she advised. 'Hospitals are no places to be hanging about in.'

'I'm going to be a nurse,' Tasha informed her. 'It will be educational.'

The woman gave Dave a look which informed him he needed to get a grip on this child.

'All right then Jake,' said the ambulance man cheerily. 'Let's take you for a ride in the ambulance. Your dad's coming too.'

As Mark turned to go he paused and held out his hand to give something to Dave. 'It's his teeth,' he said. 'Look after them for us.' He appeared to be on the edge of crying. 'He's lost his top teeth even before his bottom ones have started wobbling.'

Dave took the little bloody stumps and patted Mark's shoulder with his other hand. 'Off you go,' he said. 'It'll never be as bad as it looks. I'll call Gemma and tell her.'

*

Niecey was waiting for Jamie. Twice already she had gone down to the outer door to see if he was there – as if he didn't know the key code. She looked down the road; she went back inside. She was more than usually anxious.

She opened Blake. *The night was dark, no father was there.*

Did he know? Had he figured it out somehow, that she was pregnant? Had he dumped her because of it?

She lay on her bed and looked at the ceiling. It was her own fault. Had she not learned, over the past years, that it did not do, it never did, to trust a man? Had she not learned that a man would always let you down? And that therefore it was down to her to be responsible?

And she had not been responsible. The conversation had been had, though, about condoms and alternatives, and she had said she would go and get contraceptive pills – and had she? No, she had put it off, and not told him, and why was that? Because – she knew this and was ashamed of herself – because she wanted a baby.

Her phone announced a text message.

'At hopital with jake. CU later. X'

He explained it all when he arrived, driving his uncle's van with 'Steve Wilde Bathrooms' on both sides.

'Dad called me to pick up Mum from work, cos he'd got Tasha off to sleep – she were that upset – and he didn't want her waking up. Then Mum wanted to go to the hospital so I took her and I waited for her.'

'So you didn't see Jake?'

'He were sleeping as well. He's had his ankle set and plastered. Mum says his face is a proper state, but it's what they call soft tissue injuries – it will all heal she says.'

He saw that Niecey was almost crying.

'What's up love? He'll be all right.'

'I know. It's just the thought – children – you know – hurt – and happening suddenly, when you don't expect it. Poor little boy. Poor Gemma too, what a shock.'

'I never thought you'd care that much,' said Jamie. 'You don't hardly know him – fact, you've never met him have you, or our Gemma.'

Niecey sniffed and blew her nose. 'I don't know what happened to me there. Sorry. I just came over all emotional. I've stopped now.'

'I don't mind,' he said. 'Come out for a walk.'

The wind had dropped, it was a spring evening, cool and light, the sort that makes people believe that summer is really and truly coming. He drove them down to the Rivelin valley – another river of Sheffield – and they walked past the playground where the drama had taken place and on along the river where the bushes were coming into leaf and the birds were cheeping in the twilight.

'The thing is,' said Niecey, 'I have to tell you this – what it is – I'm pregnant.'

He did not stop walking, he did not let go her hand, he did not speak.

'I'm sorry,' she said.

'Are you?'

She said nothing because she was both sorry and not sorry.

'What are you thinking of doing then?'

'What do you mean?'

'You know what I mean. If you're sorry about having a baby – what are you going to do?'

She grasped his meaning then. 'What I'm not going to do is – I'm not having an abortion. Whatever you say, I'm not doing that.'

'Did I say that?'

'You meant that.'

'I never meant that. Nee, I would never say that, I just thought that's what you were thinking – I'd be – I'd be over the moon if we had a baby. Yeah I would –'

'Do you mean that? I thought –'

'I mean it,' he said. 'Look, my Mum and Dad would kill me – they'd disown me – if I let you go on and do this without me. It's not how I've been brought up. We'll get married, I've had my eye on a house as it is – I were going to ask you anyway – when's baby due?'

'December.'
'Brilliant,' he said.
'I've given up smoking,' she said.
'Brilliant,' he said again.

Lynn and Dave had for a long time now been settled in the idea that Jamie shared their house, and though they sometimes talked as if he would one day get married and move out, there wasn't any sense in them that it was a real possibility. So it was a shock when he came home late one evening and told his parents that his girlfriend was pregnant and that he would soon be moving out of his boyhood bedroom and setting up home with her. More than this – it was both a relief and a further worry – he was going to marry her, as soon as it could be arranged.

'He seems quite sure of himself,' said Dave.

'I'm glad,' said Lynn, 'that they're getting married – in one way I'm glad at least. I've known that many people lose touch with their grandchildren when everything breaks down, and I know, before you tell me, that a marriage can break up just as much as living together can, but it at least shows they're serious don't you think. But I wish we'd known her before this happened. He can't have known her long enough to be sure. What did he say?'

'He said, Since Christmas.'

'Not even six months,' she said.

'We didn't even know he had a girlfriend,' said Lynn to her daughters. 'Did you?'

They looked at each other – they were all sitting in Sarah's conservatory at the time, watching Jake practise using his crutches up and down the garden path – and Sarah said Yes at the same time as Gemma said No, so that Lynn did not know what to think.

'What's the matter with her?' she said suspiciously. 'What are you not telling me?'

'It's all right Mum,' said Sarah. 'He was going to tell you about her – it's just events have overtaken them, if you see what I mean.'

'She's not some daft teenager is she?' Jamie was twenty-four at the time and Lynn didn't want him being charged with having sex with a minor or anything like that.

'Not at all,' said Sarah.

'You've met her then?'

'Briefly,' said Sarah. 'Just bumped into them in Meadowhall the other day.'

'And?'

'Nice enough. She's all right Mum, honestly. The only thing I wonder is –'

42

'Well, what?'
'Well, what she sees in our Jamie.'
'Oh,' said Lynn.

Lynn spent all morning in the kitchen. It was a warm June day and a big roast seemed too hot and heavy a meal to be cooking and offering. But an effort had to be made, and in the end she decided on chicken and new potatoes and asparagus (though the price of both was ruinous) followed by a cold dessert of fresh fruit salad – not tinned – and ice cream.

'Should we have a starter?' she asked Dave.

'I always like a starter,' he said. 'That one you do at Christmas?'

'Not suitable,' she said. 'No, I mean, is it appropriate, or will it look as if we're trying to be posh?'

'How should I know?' he said. 'What does Jamie say?'

'Forget it,' said Lynn. 'I'll make up my own mind.'

She had asked Jamie questions about this girl – this woman – this daughter-in-law to-be – but he was unable to give her answers that made her feel that she knew anything. She was hoping that when she came for Sunday lunch that they would be able to get on with her, and be able to feel comfortable about letting Jamie go.

Jamie took his Dad's car to pick Niecey up.

'Niecey,' said Lynn, when he was gone. 'What sort of name is that? For a grown woman.'

'Lynnie,' said Dave. His voice had a pleading sound to it. 'Like it or not, she's our Jamie's choice. Whatever she's like we'll make the best of it won't we. We'll have to. Don't let's start by finding fault before we've even met her.'

Lynn continued cutting peaches into slices as carefully as ever and did not answer.

In spite of the heat of the day Niecey was wearing a loose dark blue top with long sleeves, and black leggings that looked quite thick and hot. She wore a lot of make-up too. Dave hugged her and Lynn came out of the kitchen and did her best to smile in a welcoming manner. She saw that Niecey was older than she had expected, clearly older than Jamie.

They sat inside, it being cooler there. Niecey, not being offered a specific chair, sat in Dave's chair, which left him looking around the room as if he didn't know what other furniture was available.

'That's Dad's chair,' said Jamie, coming through from the kitchen. 'You can sit with me on t'settee.'

'Take no notice of him lass,' said Dave. 'You sit where you like.' Which made matters worse until Lynn, hearing it all, called Dave into the kitchen and allowed Niecey to move as if it was her own idea.

Soon Lynn called them from the kitchen to come and eat. 'I'll leave the back door open,' she said, 'as it's so hot. Is that all right?'

'Niecey always has her windows open,' said Jamie, as if it was some endearing characteristic.

'Always?'

'I like fresh air,' said Niecey. Her voice was low and quiet and empty of expression. Then she seemed to make an effort, and smiled at Jamie, briefly.

'You're not from round here,' said Dave. 'I can hear that in your voice. Have you been in Sheffield long?'

'Not long,' she said.

'Where are you from then?' he said. 'I mean where are your folks from?'

'Plymouth.'

'Well,' said Dave. 'That's a long way to come. We've never been there have we Lynn?'

Niecey smiled again, without showing her teeth.

'So what brought you to Sheffield?'

Niecey chewed carefully and finally said, 'I thought it sounded like a good place.'

'Were you in Plymouth before then?'

'Oh I haven't lived in Plymouth for a long time,' she said. 'Not since I left home.'

'What do you do?' said Lynn.

'I work in a shop. A charity shop.'

'Manager, are you?'

'No.'

'Well,' said Dave, 'you'll have to have some time off when the baby comes. When are we talking?' Though he already knew of course.

'December,' said Jamie. 'In time for Christmas.'

'What do your parents think about it?' said Lynn. There was some emphasis on the 'your.'

Niecey did not answer.

'They'll be coming up for the wedding of course,' said Lynn.

'No,' said Niecey.

'Niecey hasn't got any parents,' said Jamie.

'I'm sorry,' said Lynn. 'I didn't want to upset you.'

'It's fine,' she said. 'It's a long time ago.'

'What about your friend?' said Jamie. 'Nicola. Have you asked her?'

'I did,' said Niecey, 'but she can't get way from work on a Friday.' She put her knife and fork carefully side by side on her empty plate. 'Thank you,' she said. 'That was delicious.'

'Do you like cooking?' said Lynn.

'I'm not very good at it,' she said. 'But I suppose I can learn.'

After the meal she offered to help with the dishes but Lynn waved her away. 'Dave will help if I need it,' she said. 'What are you and Jamie going to do this afternoon?'

'I'm taking her round to see Gemma,' said Jamie. 'She's met Sarah – there's only Gem left.'

'And then come back here,' said Dave. 'We need to discuss this wedding.'

'What did you think?' he asked Lynn when they were sitting at last in the shade in the garden and Jamie and Niecey had gone.

'Fishy,' she said.

'What do you mean?'

'You know what I mean. Keeps herself to herself, doesn't give anything away. Shifty if you ask me.'

'Lovely table manners,' he said. 'You can tell she's been well brought up.'

'Anyone can learn to hold a knife and fork,' said Lynn, 'and say please and thank you at the right times. What about eye contact though? Did you see any?'

'Shy,' said Dave.

'Well she shouldn't be, not at her age. She's got things to hide, David Wilde, and you can't tell me any different.'

'Well,' said Dave, 'I thought she seemed a nice enough lass. She'll soon get used to us, she'll turn into one of the family. I think Jamie's done all right for himself there.'

'We'll see,' said Lynn.

'What did you think?' said Gemma to her mother next day.

'Well –'

'You don't know what to say do you? You want to say something nice but you can't think of anything.'

'Not exactly,' said Lynn.

'Yes exactly,' said Gemma. 'Well I thought she was all right. I mean, she brought some books for the children –

46

second-hand, but she was up-front about that, and she talked to the children as if she was interested in them, and she didn't just talk to Jake, she spoke nicely to Tasha, Tasha really likes her and I think if children like someone that's a good sign.'

'You're not sure though?'

'She's not like us, is she?'

'That's it,' said Lynn. 'She's not like us.'

'And he's moving out straightaway, our Jamie?'

'So it seems,' said Lynn. 'Says he's renting a house off someone he knows – might talk him round into selling it to him. Needs a lot of work doing though he says. He hopes he'll get it done by the time the baby's born.'

Gemma laughed. 'Who'd have thought it?' she said. 'I thought he'd never grow up and leave and now he's doing it – well – in spades. I hope it works out for him.' Which was as gracious as Gemma was ever likely to be.

'I hope so too,' said Lynn, a trifle grimly.

Niecey told Jamie she was going to see a friend – it was a lie, but there was a little bit of truth in it. She told him about Nicola who had been her friend since nursery school, Nicola with her round red face and her lovely hair that her mother did in big loose curls that were envied by everyone.

'It was Nicola who gave me the name Niecey,' she said. 'We wanted to have the same initial. I guess little girls get funny ideas like that. We just used to talk and talk, and share everything and we sat together all through until secondary school.'

She let him believe that they have been in touch all their lives, by text and letter and phone calls, and that she wanted to go and spend a day with her for the last time before she was married. She did not tell him that she had had no contact with Nicola ever since their primary school days, because at the end of the summer holiday one of them went to the comprehensive and one of them had to go, against her wishes, to the grammar school where her father was headteacher. Jamie half-listened to her story, and did not even ask enough questions for Niecey to use all the fictitious biography she had invented for Nicola.

Niecey told the charity shop she couldn't work because of a meeting and set off, travelling by train and then a series of buses, to the village where she used to live. The journey was tedious and complicated – Manchester, Macclesfield, the village – and though she started as early as she could, it was well into the afternoon before she arrived. She hadn't seen it for – she calculated – eight or nine years. There were new houses, some built on land that used to be the gardens of the larger houses, and a whole new development, a couple of streets, tucked away behind the main road, of modern family houses, each one detached from its neighbours, each with its double garage and front lawn and driveway. The pub had a new sign with a more cartoonish portrait of the head of some indeterminate queen.

The school looked, to her relief, the same. She had been concerned that it might have closed down, but it seemed that the influx of new families would be keeping it going. She avoided the shop, for fear of being recognised and went to stand near, but not too near, the women – a few men too – who were waiting at the school gate. Skulking, she thought. Skulking is what I'm doing. She turned her coat collar up, not only because of the cold wind.

When the caretaker came out to open the gate the waiting parents moved in a little closer. Niecey stood up a little straighter. The children were let out a sedate class at a time, it seemed, not in a frantic mass as she remembered. She watched them closely, not knowing what she wanted to see. Soon the Infants were all out of school and the Juniors began to appear from a different doorway. There were no more parents waiting except those who had moved along to the other gate to collect older children.

It was a negative result. Niecey was disappointed, but above and beyond that, greatly relieved. She walked along the road to the edge of the village, turned down a footpath and into a field. Over the hedge she could see into the back gardens of the houses. Largish, solid houses, built of stone, with attics and cellars, and inside, she knew, Agas and drinks cabinets and well-stocked fridges and freezers. Dining rooms and matching crockery, mirrors and pictures on the walls. A hall stand with several coats for different weathers and occasions; a place for briefcases to stand, containing work brought home for the evening. Her parents were like all the rest, busy, driven, prosperous. They had aspirations and expectations; they had standards. She wondered how they had explained to people what had become of her, but she was as sure as she could be that they would not have left this house, not on her account or any other.

Another negative result. There were no objects in the garden that were even remotely child-related. There was washing on the rotary line – though cold, it had been until now a good drying day and probably the cleaner had hung it outside instead of in the utility room. The washing was mostly shirts, voluminous and white; some socks and pants, a bra, a jumper. While she watched a woman – no one she recognised – came out and began taking the washing down and putting into a plastic laundry basket. She took it into the house and a light came on in the utility room – it had always been a dark little room with only a small frosted window. After a short time – long enough to fold the clothes roughly ready for ironing – the light went off.

Niecey retraced her steps and, turning her collar up again, walked along the road in front of the houses. There were no cars on the driveway, which did not surprise her. It was way too early for them to be home from work. The cleaner came out of the front door, turned and locked it. She came through the gate and passed Niecey without looking at her, making for her own cosy home, perhaps, and waiting for a couple of teenage children to come home from the comprehensive.

Niecey – though the day could be said to have been a success – came over sad. She was used to it. There were angry times and hopeful times; there was sometimes excitement, when she thought of some new plan. There were defeated and hopeless times, but mostly there were sad times.

She made her way to the bus stop, hoping that she would not have to find a taxi to get to town. She stood under the shelter, shivering, and searched her memory for some words of comfort. *Under every grief and pine Runs a joy with silken twine.* It didn't make sense, it didn't seem true, but was better than some words of comfort she could recall.

*

It seemed to take hardly any time at all before they were busy with a house. It belonged to one of Jamie's friends who was a builder hoping to branch out into renting out properties. He had bought this house as a first go but hadn't yet had time to do anything to it in the way of improvement, or even clearing or cleaning. The evidence of the old man who had lived in it and been taken away from it to die was still there – the fabric of the chairs shiny with wear and sweat, the ancient gas stove splashed with soup and beans, the empty tins of which were stored in a black bag hanging on the door, the bed where he had slept in a sleeping bag because he had no clean sheets, the tobacco stained ceiling and the ashtray beside the bed overflowing with dog ends. The first plan was that they would be renting this house until they – Jamie – could buy one of their own.

'You know what though,' he said. 'I reckon he'd sell it to us instead of renting. He's bored with it already, he needs the cash for some other project he's got.'

'It needs a lot of work just to make it liveable,' said Niecey. 'It needs cleaning top to bottom for a start. It'll take me a week at least.'

'You don't have to do it,' said Jamie. 'I can get one of them cleaning companies in.'

'No,' said Niecey. 'I've got nothing to bring to you, nothing at all, no money, no family, nothing. *I'll* do it.'

She told Orla she had a new job, helping to do up a property and Orla told her in turn that she also had a new job, with the Youth Offending Team and that Niecey would be seen from now on, if necessary, by a colleague. 'OK,' said Niecey. Orla had been the only friendly face she had known here until Jamie turned up but she parted with her without, as it were, a backward look.

She stopped going to the charity shop, stopped going to the Job Centre, and spent her last benefit money on cloths and sprays and scourers and a new roll of black bin bags, a broom and a dustpan and a new washing-up bowl. She would keep on living in her room at the hostel while she got rid of the worst of the dirt. She started with the bathroom.

'You don't need to bother too much,' said Jamie. 'It'll only be taken out.'

'If we're going to live here,' said Niecey, 'it has to be clean, even if we're going to have a new one.' She was feeling strong and purposeful, and her morning sickness disappeared, which she put down to the caustic smell of toilet cleaner. It took her a whole day, and a chemical onslaught. She threw out everything – towels and flannel, toothpaste and denture fixative, toilet paper and brush. She stood on a stool and washed down the walls – green tiles – while the sink and the bath and the toilet – pink – soaked in cleansers. She washed the little window and the windowsill that was rotting under its flaking paint. The bath was not too badly stained, only covered in dust; it was clear the old man had not used it for at least a year. The sink was blocked and crusty, the toilet required a scraper and a strong stomach. She boiled kettles for hot water and scrubbed at the taps with wire wool, and when it was all done, she knelt down and scrubbed the black and white tile-effect vinyl that covered the floor until the white was whitish again.

She stood at the door looking in and felt powerful. When Jamie came, though he looked and approved, he did not seem to appreciate how much work had gone into it and seemed surprised that she had done only one room.

'I've not stopped all day,' she said, realising. 'I've not had anything to eat.'

'Do you want to go for fish and chips?' he said. 'We can eat them in the park.'

'I didn't notice,' she said – they were sitting side by side on a bench – 'what a lovely day it must have been.'

'I wouldn't know,' he said. 'I've been stuck in a bathroom all day.'

'You and me both,' she said and laughed delightedly.

'You know what,' he said, 'I think that's the first time I've seen you laugh.'

Next day she worked on the kitchen. Jamie's plumber mate came first thing and disconnected the gas and dragged the old cooker out into the back yard.

'Needs two of us to get it down the passage,' he said. 'I'll come back with Jamie after work and we'll put it in the van.'

Niecey opened the fridge and shut it quickly again to keep the smell in. She would ask Jamie to take it away too and dump it with its contents. She emptied all the cupboards – old packets of things like suet and gravy powder, gone solid, a tin of treacle, empty but stuck to the shelf, dried up coffee powder, mouldy jam. At the back of the cupboard there was a copy of Delia Smith's Cooking For One; she imagined the old man's wife dying and one of his children – a daughter – giving him the book to help him manage. She blinked hard to stop a tear coming. *I must be getting soft. This pregnancy is making me daft.*

She spent the day again scouring and brushing. She threw away the bedraggled curtains and took up the worn out vinyl. There were flagstones underneath, and woodlice and black beetles, and the slime trails of slugs. Jamie called by on his lunch break and she showed him. 'They come in through the air bricks,' he said. 'They'll go away when it's all dry and warm in here.' He passed her a cheese sandwich. 'What do you think of it then? When it's all done up and decorated?'

It was a terraced house, two bedrooms, in a street of houses inhabited by other old people, or else students. They were sitting on the wall in the tiny back yard.

'Could you live here? I mean permanent? If Colin would sell?'

She thought of the bathroom, she thought of the black corners of the kitchen which she had still to clean up, she thought of the bedroom that she hadn't looked into yet.

She thought, briefly like a light going on and then off, of the house she had grown up in.

'We'd make it nice?'

'Sure we would. Before the baby comes it'll be perfect. New bathroom, new kitchen, central heating. Lot.'

'Can we afford it?'

'I know what he paid for it,' said Jamie. 'Looked it up online. He'll owe me for the work we're doing – even the cleaning you're doing would cost him if he had to pay. So if I offer to pay what he paid and take it off his hands – you know I've got my mortgage arranged already. Steve will put in a bathroom for us, I've got a mate will do electric, we can be in before the wedding.'

'Jamie,' said Niecey. 'The wedding is in three weeks. It'll never be ready.'

'Evenings,' he said, 'weekends. You helping, me Dad helping. It may not be all done – fact, the decorating won't be done but we can do that once we're in. What do you think?'

'Let's go for it,' said Niecey. It felt to her, suddenly, even more than the baby, to be something they were engaged in together. A joint enterprise.

At the weekend they spent all day there in the house. Lynn was working but Dave came and set about stripping the bedroom of its furniture and carpet, its spiders and dust, and then its wallpaper.

'Easy job,' he said. 'This wallpaper can't wait to fall off. Then it'll just want washing down and we can paint and paper again.'

'I've never done decorating,' said Niecey.

'Never? Where have you been living?'

'Different places,' she said, turning away, and went downstairs where she was doing a similar job in the sitting room, taking the lightest pieces of furniture out to the skip and ripping up the carpet. Jamie and his uncle Steve worked on the kitchen with the radio on loud.

'I can't believe,' said Niecey to Jamie on Sunday evening, 'I just can't believe we got so much done in one weekend. I thought it would take weeks.'

'Only little rooms,' he said. 'My Dad's a quick worker, he's done all this a hundred times, knows what he's doing.'

'That bedroom's lovely,' she said.

'Tell you what,' he said, 'if you go tomorrow and order a bed – make sure they can deliver straightaway – we can move in.'

'With only a bed?'

'What more do we need?' he said.

*

'I miss Jamie,' said Lynn.

'Of course you do,' said Dave. There was a pause and then he put down his paper and said, in a less distant tone, 'So do I.'

'It's not,' said Lynn, 'as if he ever made much noise here, did he. It's not as if he often sat down here with us of an evening. I don't know why the house feels so empty.'

'We'll have to get used to it,' said Dave. 'It's just us now.'

'Maybe after the wedding I'll get used to it. Maybe that will bring it home to me.' Lynn picked up her magazine again and sighed.

'You're not disappointed are you love?' said Dave. 'You didn't expect them to have a big do?'

'It's not that,' said Lynn. 'I just feel sad about her, you know, having no one to invite. I don't see how that's possible, do you?'

'She's not been in Sheffield long.'

'But before that? She must have been somewhere. She must have had friends. She must have a family.'

'She clammed up didn't she, when you asked if her parents were coming to the wedding.'

'Like slamming a door,' said Lynn. 'But even if her parents are dead, or she's not speaking to them, whatever reason it is – even if she's no parents, she must have a sister or a brother, or an aunt, or *something*. Surely.'

'Nothing we can do about it,' said Dave. 'We'll just have to make the best of it. And make her feel welcome.'

'We've never had someone in the family that didn't come from Sheffield,' said Lynn. 'Do you think that's unusual? We've always known, like, someone who knew of the family. Even Sarah's Jon – we didn't know him but then we found out our Janet knew his mum from church or something.'

'Janet,' said Dave, with the particular huff of breath he always used when Lynn's sister was mentioned. 'Church.' Another sceptical huff.

54

'I'm only saying,' she said.

'I suppose you'll be asking Janet to this wedding?'

'We have to make up the numbers somehow,' she said. 'Even though it shouldn't be you and me making these decisions. I think if it wasn't for us they would just go off and be married on their own. *She* would anyway. I hope our Jamie would know better.'

*

The night before the wedding Jamie slept at his parents' house on instructions from Lynn. 'You're not to see her before the ceremony,' she said.

'I've seen dress already,' he said. 'I were with her when she bought it.'

'Yes I know,' said Lynn. 'But we don't have to go on doing things wrong. We'll do the wedding day properly or –'

'Or what Mum?'

'Or else,' she said.

*

Niecey woke early, alone for the first time in ten days, and lay in bed worrying. Not about her dress – that would be fine. It was blue, a nice soft blue with the long sleeves that she insisted on, and was loose enough to hide the baby bump, which however was not so evident yet as to cause comment from people like Lynn's father, who was known to be coarse. When she and Jamie went shopping for the dress together, it had felt to her once again as if they really were some kind of partnership, and that as long as they were doing practical things together they would be able to make a go of it. She clung on to this hope.

Today she was worrying about the wedding. His family, all of them, everyone that they could round up was going to be there, all with names to learn and remember, all looking at her and judging, trying to work her out, who she was, where she had come from, why was she so alone. She thought of Jane Eyre – she had read it for A level – and wondered if someone would burst into the registry office and announce that the wedding could not take place. The thought should have made her smile but did not.

She forced herself to eat a biscuit. A proper breakfast felt not possible. She washed herself standing in the bath, maybe for the last time because the bathroom was due to be ripped out and a new one put in on Monday. She put on the dress. She took great care over her hair and makeup. Whatever else they found to criticise it should not be too much blusher, or too harsh eye liner. Then she sat on the only chair they so far possessed and waited, looking out at the street.

Sarah, because she had a car of her own, was coming to pick Niecey up and take her to the Town Hall. *The marriage hearse* – the words came into her mind and she pushed them away, kept them away by finding other things to worry about. She might not recognise Sarah, having seen her only once that time at Meadowhall. Would she find the house, would she be able to turn her car round in the narrow street? Would she be late? What would she want to talk about while on the way there? Was she annoyed that they weren't having bridesmaids? Lynn had certainly strongly put forward the idea of Melissa and Tasha playing a bigger part than just guests, but Dave must have seen Niecey's face and said, kindly, that it wasn't really that sort of do.

Apart from going with Jamie to fill in the forms Niecey had had nothing to do with the organisation of the day. It was a Friday, at eleven o'clock – they had been lucky enough to get a cancellation, though Niecey could not help wondering about the couple who had cancelled and wondering how lucky it could be to get married through someone else's misfortune. After the ceremony they were going for a meal; there had been a deal of discussion between Dave and Lynn as to where it should be. Places in town had been rejected on account of a lack of parking space, or else the idea that they would be full of rowdy Friday-lunch-time drinkers. Places outside town were put forward by either Lynn or Dave and dismissed by either Dave or Lynn on the grounds of being too dear or too cheap, too quiet or too noisy, too far, too posey, too old-fashioned, too modern. In the end Lynn got on the phone to Janet, her sister, and her advice was taken, not without some grumbling from Dave. It was going to be out in Derbyshire, in a village Niecey had never been to, or even heard of. She didn't care.

Sarah turned up absolutely at the time she said she would and came in by the back door and into the room where Niecey was still sitting, looking out but apparently noticing nothing.

'Are you ready? You look nice.'

'Thank you,' said Niecey. 'You do too.'

Sarah looked round the bare room. 'I must say, you've been getting on with it. Mum tells me our Jamie's buying this to live in.'

'That's right.'

'Small,' said Sarah.

'It's fine,' said Niecey.

'When the baby comes –'

'Babies don't take up much room.'

'Well,' said Sarah, 'it's easy to think that but you wait and see, you'll find you've got their clobber all over the place. Take it from me.'

Niecey did not reply.

'Anyway,' said Sarah. 'Are you ready? Got everything? Where's your flowers?'

'In the kitchen.'

Sarah went and fetched them, seemed to approve of the small bouquet – more a posy really – of cornflowers and gypsophila. Niecey put on her shoes – new shoes – and picked up her handbag.

'What am I supposed to do with this? You know, while the –'

'I'll keep it for you. You don't need it really do you?'

'Just my lipstick. Tissues.'

'You don't need tissues. You're not going to cry are you?'

'Of course not.'

Sarah suddenly became solemn. 'You *are* happy really aren't you? Only Mum says you don't smile much. She's a bit worried about you.'

Niecey smiled as best she could. 'I'm fine. Really.'

'Excited?' Niecey knew the correct answer was a yes, but if she was it was the sort of excitement you'd have before a bungee jump – a really dodgy bungee jump where the ropes were frayed and people had died already.

She could never remember much about the actual ceremony, only Jamie grinning as if he'd only just learned how to, and the sound of his grandfather coughing into his handkerchief behind them. They stood on the steps afterwards and people took photographs with their phones – except Dave who had a serious camera and wanted to arrange everyone into proper groups. Then there was some confusion as another wedding group encroached on their space and Uncle Steve and his wife somehow managed to be in the wrong photo call.

'You have to throw your bouquet,' said Gemma but Niecey held on to it firmly, loving the cornflowers too much to give them away, and besides seeing no one who could be qualified to be the next one married.

'You've missed your chance there our Janet,' said Grandad. Niecey thought he was a malicious old man and hoped not to be sitting near him at the meal.

They drove out into the country, Jamie and Niecey holding hands in the back of his parents' car. The sun shone on hills and rocks and fields and Niecey was entranced.

'I never knew it was like this,' she said. 'I've never seen this before.' The broad sky and the racing clouds were so beautiful that she wanted to cry.

'Never seen the Peak District before?' said Lynn from the front seat. 'Wait for this bit – look to your left as we go round this corner.'

And there was a wide valley stretching down and away, green fields in the bottom of it and the heather not yet in bloom on the high slopes. Jamie's hand tightened on hers. 'I'll bring you out here one day.' She squeezed his hand back in gratitude.

She and Jamie sat side by side at the top of the table, Lynn and Dave to their right and left. Lynn's father sat next to her so that she could attempt to keep him in order, and next to Dave his mother, a fidgety little lady who liked to ask people how old they thought she might be. Then Gemma and Sarah, facing each other, with their daughters beside them, then their sons and then their husbands. So far so symmetrical. At the bottom end of the table was Uncle Steve and his wife with, putting the arrangement out of balance, Lynn's sister Janet. Younger than Lynn, and weightier, and the only person in headgear – a rather arresting fascinator, which made her appear to be a more important part of the family than Dave at least thought she should be. Niecey found her, even on this brief acquaintance, rather overpowering and was glad she was as far away as she could be.

The grandparents were chiefly concerned with where Niecey was from, as if being from somewhere that wasn't Sheffield put her outside what could normally be expected.

'Plymouth,' Dave explained to his mother.

'By the sea, Plymouth,' said Grandad. 'Sheffield ant got no sea. Long way from the sea, Sheffield.'

'At least she's not from south side,' said Nan. 'Not from Darnall or Manor. Rough places.'

'Now Mother,' said Dave. 'There's rough bits in North Sheffield too, as you know.'

'We've always lived north side of Sheffield,' she said, leaning past her son to explain.

'Scarborough,' said Grandad. 'You'll find sea at Scarborough. You want to get our Jamie to take you there. Bracing Scarborough is.'

'Skegness,' said Nan. 'It's Skegness that's bracing, not Scarborough.'

'Here's your starters,' said Lynn. 'For goodness sake Dad, don't start arguing. It's smoked salmon and no, there isn't anything else, we've all got the same.'

He poked at it disdainfully. 'Price of this,' he said, 'we could have had fish and chips and come out with enough change for a beer.'

'You'll get a drink,' said Lynn. 'Just eat your starter, you'll like it.'

'Could do with some chips,' he said, and Niecey could see that he was winding Lynn up for the fun of it.

'I prefer Whitby to Scarborough,' said Nan, provocatively. 'They do lovely fish and chips in Whitby. Have you ever been there – er – what's her name again?'

'Niecey,' said Dave. 'It's short for Denise.'

'Well, it's no shorter,' said Nan.

'It's like a pet name, Nan,' said Jamie. 'She doesn't like Denise.'

'Nothing wrong with Denise,' said Nan. 'Her who does my hair, they call her Denise.'

Niecey looked down at her plate and kept her eyes there. She felt she might laugh, she might choke, she might be forced to stand up and hurl her plate down the table if they didn't shut up. Was this really what it was like, being part of a family? She had a picture in her head of more and more weddings down the years – Melissa and Tasha, Jake and Dom. These two old people would be dead by then but their place would be taken by Dave and Lynn, each with a daughter beside them encouraging them to behave nicely, rolling their eyes at each other. She had never known her own grandparents – at the moment it did not seem such a big loss.

In the pause between the starter – which Grandad polished off with enjoyment – and the main course, they started on about honeymoons. Niecey and Jamie were not having one, being for the moment busy – obsessed even – with getting their house fit to live in.

'We didn't have one either,' said Dave. 'It were February and we thought we'd save it till the weather were better.'

'I couldn't afford one,' said Nan. 'Didn't have them in my day. Didn't know what a holiday were. Sunday school day out were as near as we got to a holiday.'

'Give over Mother,' said Dave with affection. 'You went to Blackpool, I've seen a photo of you.'

'That were later,' she said.

'Scarborough,' said Grandad again. 'Nowt to beat Scarborough.'

'Is the food all right?' said Lynn to Niecey.

It occurred to Niecey that she was not the only one who was anxious about the day. 'Lovely,' she said, though in fact she had hardly noticed what she was eating. 'Thank you,' she added, and remembering what Sarah had said, tried her best to smile at her new mother-in-law.

Further down the table Tasha was being threatened with going outside to sit in the car if she didn't stop moaning about having chicken nuggets instead of what the adults were having and saying that Jake was annoying her and shoving him with her sharp little elbow. Across the table Melissa and Dom sat together more peacefully and talked politely.

'See,' said Gemma. 'Nothing's ever right for her. Argues with everything.'

'Ow,' said Jake, needlessly, and Tasha kicked him under the table for trying to get her into more trouble.

'She'll grow out of it,' said Sarah.

'She'd better do,' said Gemma. 'She's nearly eight.'

Tasha held up six fingers. 'Six weeks,' she said. 'I'm not eight for six weeks, not nearly.'

'Nearly eight,' repeated Gemma.

'Anyway,' said Tasha, 'I don't want to be eight.'

'I wish I was eight Mummy,' said Melissa.

'Not much I can do about that darling,' said Sarah.

'Can I get down?' said Tasha. 'I don't want any more.'

'I've finished,' said Melissa. 'Can I get down too?'

'Can I get down?' said Dom.

The little boys went off together to the end of the room and the two girls came shyly round the table to Niecey and looked at her closely and touched her dress with sticky hands.

'I thought you would have a long white dress,' said Tasha. 'Why is yours blue?'

'You can wear whatever colour you like,' said Niecey. 'What's your favourite colour?'

'Purple,' said Tasha. 'I used to like pink but I've gone off it now. She –' waving a hand at Melissa '– she still likes pink. Her bedroom is all pink.'

'I don't,' said Melissa. 'I like blue now. Blue and pink.'

'Blue and pink is purple,' said Tasha. 'So you like purple too.'

'No I don't.'

'You do just because you're copying me. Because I'm older.'

'See what I mean,' said Gemma to Sarah. 'She can make an argument out of nothing. She goes through life looking for things to argue about. It drives me crazy.'

'I can remember,' said Dave, leaning past his mother, 'having a few arguments with you when you were younger. Like mother like daughter, maybe.'

Niecey, sitting between Dave and Jamie, suddenly aware of how alike they are, how Jamie will grow to be just like his father and how she will be there, along with him, to see it, was overcome with a brief dizziness and leaned her head on her hand.

'Are you all right?' said Lynn. 'Sarah, come here, I think our Niecey's feeling faint.'

'I'm fine,' said Niecey, lifting her head and trying once again to smile. 'Honestly, I'm fine.' And thought to herself, *Our Niecey. So I belong to them now.* Which was a pleasant thought, in a way, but is followed by, *If they only knew.*

Dave drove the new couple back to their new home. Sharing the back seat with them was a wedding cake – single tier but still large, even after it had been ceremonially cut and pieces given out. Mark had made it, and decorated it.

'You'll have plenty there to send to your friends,' he said. *Friends?* wondered Niecey and said hurriedly, 'Jamie can take some to work. They'll love it.'

Dave halted his car outside the house. Even from the outside it looked different, with the windows cleaned and the front path swept.

'Come in and have a look,' said Jamie, but Dave said, 'No thanks, son, I've seen it already and Niecey looks as if she needs a lie down. Me and your mother will come after the weekend, if that's all right, and see how you're going on. You look after her now.'

'I will,' said Jamie.

Lynn got out of the front seat and gave Jamie a big hug and Niecey what was possibly a smaller hug, and Dave hugged her too, tight, and shook Jamie's hand and punched him on the arm and then they drove away, back home for a nice cup of tea and a paracetamol for Lynn's headache. Jamie and Niecey went inside and stood for a moment in the kitchen, as if wondering what to do next.

'You all right?' he said.

'I ache,' she said. 'I ache all over. You know, like when you've been out in the cold and all hunched up.'

He put his arm round her shoulders. 'Not ill are you?'

'No,' she said. 'It must be the tension. I'm glad it's over, aren't you.'

'Go and sit down,' he said. 'I'll make us a cup of tea.'

*

The house was beginning to be furnished by now. Lynn and Sarah and Gemma had all been through their cupboards and found that they had sheets and towels and saucepans and dishes that they could spare – that indeed, they had no use for whatever and had only been keeping them until such time as Jamie would need them. Carpets and curtains were more of a problem, but as Jamie said, their rooms were only little and end-of-rolls were cheap. Gemma found some curtains in a charity shop – she loved a charity shop, did Gemma – and Lynn altered them on her sewing machine. Even Jake and Dom sorted through their toys and, under pressure from their mothers, donated some of the most babyish ones to their new cousin. Melissa drew a picture for the baby's bedroom. Dave came round with geraniums in pots and arranged them on the wall of the back yard.

Jamie and Niecey spent the first weekend of their married life painting and papering the baby's bedroom.

'It's starting to feel real,' he said, setting up his ladder so that he could paint the ceiling.

Niecey was standing in the doorway. 'Real,' she said. 'None of it feels real to me, not yet. I keep thinking it will all vanish in the night.'

'No chance,' he said. 'You're stuck with me now.'

*What do you know?* thought Niecey. *You know nothing.*

Aloud she said, 'I'll get out of your way while you're up a ladder. Call me when you've finished and I'll make us some tea.'

*

'And I worry about the baby,' said Lynn. 'I don't know why, I just do.'

Nothing wrong is there?' said Dave.

'No, nothing. As far as I know. But if there was she wouldn't tell us would she.'

'She would tell Jamie. Jamie would tell us.'

'You think. We hardly see Jamie any more.'

'I wouldn't expect to see him. Think about it Lynnie – he works all day, he's just got married, he's in the middle of buying a house, he's looking forward to the baby – we're going to come well down his list of people to see. When we got married – did we spend our evenings round at your dad's? Didn't we have better things to do?'

'I knew you'd say that,' said Lynn. 'I'm not saying he ought to come round, I'm just telling you how I feel.'

'Look,' said Dave 'We're on holiday soon. This time next week we'll be packed up and on our way. With everything that's been going on we haven't had chance to think about ourselves. You'll feel better when you see the sea. Put a bit of space between us and the family. What do you think?'

'You're right,' said Lynn. 'I'm looking forward to that, but as you say, it's been pushed out.'

'Now get off to work woman, and earn some money for us.' And he kissed her on the cheek and ushered her out of the door.

While Jamie was working, at times when Niecey was not doing anything to the house, or shopping or cooking, she walked. She took the street map out of Jamie's van, now that he'd acquired a satnav, and she walked, starting from the house, in each direction in turn. She walked into town, particularly if it was a weekend, scanning the families as they walked past her, watching the children on the roundabouts in Fargate; on her way back, calling in at the museum and paying attention to the people in the parks. She crossed the dual carriageway and walked up the hill but it was clear to her that what she was looking for was unlikely to be in that sort of area. She walked uphill in the other direction and found areas which were more possible. She walked round the western edge of the city, finding houses not unlike the one she had lived in as a child. She noted where the schools were and sometimes found herself walking past one at playtime, or home time. She made pencil marks in the A to Z, little ticks and crosses and question marks. When he asked her what she had been doing with her day she told him, Walking. Getting to know Sheffield, getting so that I can find my way around. If the weather was too bad to go out in she cleaned the house, although it was already clean. Lynn, and Gemma, and Sarah – all with a professional interest in hygiene – noticed how clean Niecey's house was.

She registered with a GP and attended her appointments. She went for her scan and gave the photo to Jamie to show to his family. As her pregnancy progressed she walked less far but not less often. She had a warm coat now, gloves and boots, an umbrella. Foreseeing that a winter with a baby would limit her excursions, she joined the library, and if there was nothing Jamie wanted to watch on TV, she read books in the evenings, while he passed the time on his games console.

*

Christmas was fast approaching. Lynn and Dave had been stockpiling presents for weeks, wandering – and wondering – round Toys R Us for the little boys and hiding the boxes on the top shelf of the wardrobe where even nosy Melissa wouldn't be able to see them hidden behind the spare pillows.

'What about Jamie's baby though?' said Lynn. 'Should we get a present? I mean as well as paying for the crib and the car seat?'

'Something small,' said Dave. 'It's not going to know, is it?'

'I wish we knew if it was a boy or a girl,' said Lynn. 'I want to be able to picture her. Or him. I wish they would tell us, it's perverse I think, not telling us, it's just being difficult.'

'Jamie says they haven't asked,' said Dave. 'They want to wait and see.'

'Do you believe him?'

'Jamie doesn't tell lies,' said Dave firmly.

'He never used to,' said Lynn.

The Hedges, where Lynn worked, had four Christmas trees, two on each floor, with fake presents underneath them, since if there were real ones some of the residents might have been tempted to open them, or steal them. The seasonal songs CD played on a repeat setting. In the lounge the television seemed to carry mainly advertisements for things that the residents were unlikely to want, even if they grasped what they were for. Cards, and the occasional present arrived through the post for the residents and staff. Lynn and her manager wrestled with the holiday rota and checked the stocks of food and medications. Other staff were busy planning the Christmas party.

Through the front door came Jamie, though he should have been at work, and stood as if he didn't know where to go next.

'Hello,' said a friendly staff member – they were all friendly. 'Are you lost? Who have you come to see?'

'Lynn,' he said. 'Mrs Wilde.' His eyes looked tired but glittery at the same time. 'Can you tell her Jamie's here.'

Lynn knew of course as soon as the message reached her, and ran down the stairs to where he stood in the hall. He grinned. 'It's a boy,' he said 'Everything's good.'

*

The baby – little Leo David, David after his grandad and Leo because Niecey liked it – was a joy. Lynn visited as much as she could, reasoning that Niecey did not appear to have anyone else to help and advise her. She had done the same for Gemma and Sarah when they had their first babies and she knew it had been appreciated.

Niecey seemed to take to motherhood as if it was easy. Whatever time of day Lynn called – Sarah and Gemma said the same – the house was tidy, the baby was either asleep or smiling, Niecey was apparently cheerful and busy and in control.

'I don't know how she manages it,' said Sarah. 'When I think of what I was like – I couldn't even get round to combing my hair most days, and there she is with full make up, cooking home made meals, from a *recipe book*, for god's sake.'

'I think you had a touch of that post-natal depression,' said Lynn.

'I did *not*,' said Sarah. 'It's just that it's bloody difficult, adjusting to a first baby and getting insufficient sleep. You should know that.'

'I know,' said Lynn. 'I didn't mean to –'

'I'm with you Sis,' said Gemma. 'It's like being on another planet all of a sudden, with this alien screaming at you in another language.'

'What a thing to say about your Tash,' said Lynn, laughing. 'Alien! As if a baby is an alien.'

'I think you've forgotten mum,' said Gemma. 'Or else you had nice easy babies.'

'Not at all,' said Lynn. 'And remember I didn't have a mother to give me any advice. Apart from the health visitor and the baby clinic I was on my own. Except for your dad of course.'

'Well as to that,' said Gemma, 'I'm pretty sure our Jamie does his fair share. He's besotted with that baby. I don't think my Mark was ever quite so daft about his.'

Gemma and Sarah always – it seemed – moved on quickly whenever their mother mentioned her own history. They knew the story well enough – how Lynn's mother left her and her little sister Janet at school one day and ran off with some man, leaving her husband to bring up two small girls on his own. They knew that Lynn had no proper childhood after that, being always the one who had to do housework and look after Janet. They knew that Lynn never saw their mother again – even though she was living in Sheffield and eager to see her children, their father would not allow it.

'You have to understand,' their own father explained to them, 'times were different then. He felt he'd been wronged. He *had* been wronged. Whether there were any fault in him I don't know, and neither does your mother, but the fact remains that *she* walked out on *him*.'

Gemma and Sarah, as young teenagers in their beds at night, discussed whether running off was the same as walking out, and if not, which was worse.

They knew as well that years later, when Lynn was already working at the liquorice allsorts factory, Janet, still at school, tracked down their mother and went to live with her. It was only after many more years that she managed to make it up with her father and sister, and by that time she had grown into a woman with a more refined accent, a job as a qualified book-keeper, a driving licence and a house on the west side of the city. She had been married but was divorced from her husband, which Lynn seemed to feel was some sort of deserved retribution.

'Your mother had a hard time as a child,' Dave used to remind them, on occasions when Lynn was snappy or harsh with them. 'She doesn't always see that times have changed.'

'You ask her for us Dad,' they would say, and sure enough, usually Lynn would come round, and permission would be given for the outing, or the new jeans, or whatever it was.

Time has passed, years have passed. Lynn's father and Dave's mother have both died, which was only to be expected. Life goes on. Lynn has clung on to her job and has not retired, and Dave has stopped mentioning the possibility. By now, he has got used to his routine; he likes it, and they still have separate things to talk about when she comes home. They still worry about their children and grandchildren, but as a routine, not because there has been anything particular to worry about. Yes, Melissa is a trifle overweight and Dom is rather full of himself; Tasha is still inclined to excessive drama and Jake is physically quite fearful, ever since his nasty accident. He has needed a brace on his teeth too as a consequence and is self-conscious about it. These have been no more than the ups and downs that any family could expect. Leo – Dave and Lynn agree – is just lovely. Jamie has turned out to be a good, friendly, attentive father, Leo has been the making of him, Lynn has often said.

'And Niecey,' Dave would add. 'She's been good to him. Good for him.'

Dave has always been more fond of Niecey than Lynn was. He could get her to soften and relax, like bread dough. He is the same with animals – cats, dogs, cage birds – they all seem to trust him and will rub themselves round his legs or perch on his fingers.

'I don't know how you do it,' Lynn has said, often.

'You could do it too,' he said. 'It's nowt special. All you have to do unbend. You're a bit prickly, you. You don't need to hold yourself so stiff. They won't hurt you.' But Lynn has never got the knack, and to be truthful, she has never really wanted it, it seems somehow dishonest. Except she would have liked to be better friends with Niecey.

Things have happened in the family as things do. Dave has had an operation on his dodgy knee. His brother Steve has retired and Jamie has taken over running the business. Gemma's Mark has won a prize for his Eccles cakes. Niecey has learned to drive. Both Sarah and Jon have been promoted at work and between them now do so many hours that they have had to employ a cleaner. 'Or else nothing would ever get done,' explained Sarah to her sister.

Niecey has become part of the family. Not an indispensible part, not a first-to-go-to, first-to-be-informed sort of part, but a frequent part, weekly if not daily. Lynn has continued to call in to see her every week at least, sometimes on her way home from work, sometimes on her day off – the awkwardness might sometimes wear off and they might laugh together, and then another day it would be back again and they would wonder what to say to one another.

She is useful, Niecey, in that she doesn't have a job to go to and has therefore been available, if Dave isn't, to collect the other children from school sometimes and keep them at home until their mothers are able to come and get them. Gemma can normally finish work by mid-afternoon but she has her shopping to do and a million other things to fit in. Sarah's hours and shifts change from week to week, and Jon is never home till after six. Tasha and Jake and Melissa and Dom lead patchwork lives of after-school clubs and grandparents and friends and other arrangements. Niecey is reliable and willing; she never says she can't do it, or complains to any of the family about any of the others.

One time though, Dom's father asked him, 'What did you do after school today? Did Niecey come and meet you?'

'Yeah,' said Dom. 'But what I don't get, she stands at the gate, you know, and she never sees me till I'm right next to her. Like, she's looking at me but she doesn't see me.'

'I've noticed that too,' said Melissa. 'She kind of looks right through you and then when you speak to her she kind of wakes up and it's all right.'

Sarah was listening but said nothing except, 'Have you brought any letters home? Mel, did you remember your PE kit? It needs to go in the wash.'

If they knew – which they don't – there are things about Niecey which they would find unusual. Odd. There is the walking, the exploring of odd corners of Sheffield, pushing Leo in his buggy, the A-Z in her pocket. There is the fresh air fixation, so that when Jamie comes home he has to put more clothes on; it is so cold with the back door always standing open. There is the book of Blake's poems, which never leaves her bedside. There is the fact – if it is a fact – that she has no family. Not a parent or grandparent, not a brother or a sister, not even a cousin or an aunt, not even a friend. And there are the outbursts, as if something builds up inside her and sometimes – maybe once a year or so – she might do something stupid.

It can only be stupid, can't it, to throw paint at the wall, or cut a sweater – a perfectly new one – into shreds. It can only be stupid to throw a saucepan at the kitchen window, or to get up in the night and be found next morning asleep on the back doorstep. No one ever sees her do these things – there may have been others too – she does them secretly but she never tries to hide the results, or lies about how the paint made a mess of the wall, or how the window came to be broken. And she never said sorry, although for a few days afterwards she is quiet, thoughtful, subdued. Jamie does not tell anyone about these incidents either. He shrugs them off as he does other inexplicable or unpleasant events. As long as she is all right, and Leo is all right – and he knows she would never harm Leo – why waste time worrying?

They moved to a bigger house once they started feeling the need of a proper garden for Leo to play in.

'I'm sad to move out of here,' said Niecey. 'I love this house.'

But they were not going far, only two streets away, to a house of a similar age – late Victorian – but bigger. An extra room downstairs, three bedrooms and an attic. A parking space for the van and the car, and a garden for children to play in.

Tasha and Melissa, though they have been in different primary schools, have moved up to the same secondary school – the academy – though Gemma says scornfully that it is no more an academy than it was when she went there, for all its new building and fancy uniform. By a trick of fate, Tasha is the oldest in the year group, having a birthday in September, while Melissa is almost the youngest. Tasha is bright and quick, but chatty and mischievous, Melissa is well-behaved and hardworking – there has been debate in the family about whether or not they should be in the same class – would it be good for one and not the other? And if so, which one? In the end, the school decides to separate them and they are only together for PE.

Dave and Lynn have been watching with satisfaction as their children did well. Everything is good.

\*

The weather stayed fine for the celebration of Dave's seventieth birthday, in late July. It was held in Sarah's garden, because hers was the biggest. The barbecue was set up by the kitchen door and Jon and Mark put on aprons – Mark's a businesslike one from work, white, and Jon's a jokey one which made the little boys giggle and the big girls pretend to vomit.

'Take it off Dad,' said Melissa. 'You're embarrassing me.'

'Your dad's got boobies,' said Leo confidently, and Jamie laughed and spluttered into his drink.

But Jon ignored them and kept it on, as if it was a task he'd set himself.

Inside the kitchen a cake – made and decorated by Mark of course – sat underneath a muslin cover, waiting for its moment.

'Let's go up to my bedroom,' said Melissa to Tasha. 'I've got things to show you.'

The boys, Dom, Jake and little Leo, went to the bottom of the garden where there was a football net and set about kicking a ball. In this formless time before the food Dave prowled round the garden looking at the plants and pulling out weeds. 'You're letting this go,' he called to Sarah. 'I've told you, keep on top of the weeds. You'll have nothing but dandelions if you don't watch out.'

The mothers – Gemma, Sarah and Niecey – sat together sipping white wine while Lynn came and went from the kitchen with bowls and implements. When she passed one or other of the younger ones would look up and offer to help, to which she replied each time that Jamie was helping and between them they could manage fine. Through the open window of Melissa's bedroom came the sound of the girls laughing – sometimes shrieking – at what was coming through on their phones.

'I should go and see what that's all about,' said Sarah, but she remained where she was. It was too good, just sitting, sipping, in the sun, other people doing all the work – it was too good to spoil.

'What were you doing up at Meadowhead then?' said Gemma suddenly, to Niecey.

'Meadowhead?' said Sarah, and Niecey did too – 'Meadowhead?'

'I saw you,' said Gemma. 'Dinnertime, it were, all the kids coming out of school. You were standing by the gate. I saw Leo too.'

71

Niecey shook her head and drew her brows together as if she couldn't understand but was thinking hard how to help Gemma.

Sarah said,' What were you doing up there, Gem?'

'Delivery,' said Gemma. 'Driver were off so I had to take this stuff up. Buffet lunch for ten – interviewing I think.'

'You'd think they'd choose somewhere more local,' said Sarah.

'Not if we're the best,' said Gemma. 'Which we are.'

'Of course you are,' said Sarah. 'I didn't mean you're not really good, just that –'

'Leo,' called Niecey, 'come here, I want to tie your shoelaces.'

And then Lynn came over with a big bowl of salad and Niecey got up and went to stand with Dave on the grass, looking up at the house and then away to a view of the hills just glimpsed in the gap between two houses opposite.

'I did see her,' Gemma said to Sarah. 'It was her, I'd swear on my life. It *was* her. What was she doing up there, she don't know anyone up there.'

'You could have made a mistake,' said Sarah. 'Why would she be standing outside a secondary school? It doesn't make sense Gem.'

Lynn came and sat down in Niecey's chair. 'Nearly ready,' she said.

'I'm not stupid,' said Gemma. 'I know my own sister-in-law when I see her.'

'But you didn't speak to her.'

'I'd to get the delivery in,' said Gemma. 'I were late as it was. Traffic were a nightmare. And when I came out she were gone.'

'What are you talking about?' said Lynn, but Gemma said it was nothing, and no more was said.

After the food Dave's cake was unveiled. There they all were – Dave and Lynn, in icing, their three children with their partners, and five grandchildren. Six of those present took out their phones and took a photograph of it, and then of Dave standing close to tears in front of the sugar – moulded, coloured sugar – version of what was most important to him in his life.

'How have you done that Mark?' he was saying. 'Look at this, kids, see how you can recognise everyone. Look

Lynnie, he's got us exactly, sitting in us armchairs, and all t'grandkids on the floor, right down to little Leo.'

'I'm not really little, Grandad,' said Leo.

'Are we going to eat ourselves?' said Jake, but Dave said no, they would all have a piece of cake, later when some other people had arrived but these little figures were going to be kept untouched, to remind him of this day.

'Won't they go mouldy?' said Tasha, and Mark told her, not for years and Lynn told her they would be kept in the fridge.

Then other guests arrived – Lynn's sister Janet and Dave's brother Steve with his wife and one of their daughters with a husband who no one seemed to like.

Then Dave made a speech. 'It's all about family,' he said. 'You all know that my belief is we are put on this earth to be a support to our families. And look at us all, growing older, and growing up. Here's Dom and Jake, going into top class at school in September, and little Leo, starting proper school. And these two young ladies, Melissa and Tash, getting lovelier by the day and with everything in front of them.'

Dave's brother's daughter's husband gave a shaven-headed smirk and said, 'You're not wrong there,' looking at Melissa from top to bottom in a way that made her blush and made his wife turn away from him. Dave ignored him.

'And I want to say that no one could have a better family than I've got,' he said. 'There's not one of them wouldn't go out of their way to help another one and there's not one I wouldn't want beside me in a crisis. And last and most important of all I have to raise my glass' – and he did – 'to the most wonderful woman – to Lynn, the best wife and mother and grandmother you'll ever meet.'

After Leo started proper full time school, something shifted in Niecey's life. It started when Lynn called in on her way home from work one day, looking more tired than usual.

'We had a death,' she said, and eased off her shoes, one by one, under the table.

Niecey poured tea from the pot into a mug and put it down in front of her.

'Oh?' she said.

'One of the men. Stroke.'

'Shame,' said Niecey.

'Nothing to cry for,' said Lynn. 'Sometimes it's the best thing that can happen. And anyway, he weren't one of them I could really take to. I shouldn't speak ill I know, but he weren't a very nice man, from all accounts. His daughter used to go away in tears from the way he spoke to her, and his sons wouldn't even come and see him, only about once a year.'

'Still,' said Niecey.

They sat together, quietly, looking into their mugs. Having a conversation with Niecey was never the easiest thing in the world. It was a chilly October day and the back door stood wide open, as did every other door in the house. From the front room came the relentless sound of children's TV.

'And one of our cleaners has given her notice,' said Lynn. 'It's been that sort of day. And you know the other cleaner – you've heard me talk about her – well, she's been on the list for knee surgery, and she's had a letter to go in next week. That manager – well, she's only a stand-in one, she usually stays calm but she were getting a bit flustered, phoning agencies, and what not. This is her last week, we've got a new one coming next week, permanent.'

'I could do it,' said Niecey.

'What, clean? You?'

'I can clean,' she said. 'It's what I do every day isn't it? I can't do an early start but once I've got Leo dropped off at school, I can do what I like till three o'clock.'

'You can get a better job than cleaning,' said Lynn. 'You've had an education, anyone can tell. And you don't need to go out to work, our Jamie earns enough doesn't he.'

'It's not to do with money,' said Niecey. 'It would do me good to get out of the house. Jamie won't mind, he's not –'

'Old-fashioned? I think you might find he is.'

'Honestly,' said Niecey, 'I know you all think I'm cleverer than some people, but I'm not, not at all. I haven't got any qualifications, I'm not trained to do anything.'

'You've got A levels,' said Lynn. 'No one in our family ever stayed on at school. Even Sarah, as you know.'

'Everyone in your family has got skills,' said Niecey, 'because of how you and their dad brought them up. I can write an essay about Shakespeare – or I could once upon a time – but I haven't got any skill that someone would pay me for. Still, I'm sure I can come and clean an old people's home.'

'What about school holidays?'

'Other people manage. I'll sort something out.'

'I could have him some of the time,' said Lynn, 'if we could sort out our shifts. I'd like that. It's nice to have a young grandchild, the others are all so big now, they're off doing their own thing, they barely come near their Nannan. And if I'm working Dave would certainly have him.'

'He'd like that?'

'How can you even ask? He'd love it, you know he would. Him and Leo could have a great time out in the shed, fixing things.'

'Will you ask her then?'

'Are you really serious?'

'Really.'

'I'll ask her first thing tomorrow. But think about it, talk it over with Jamie when he gets home. If I don't hear from you – if you don't change your mind – I'll ask her. She'll bite your hand off I can tell you.'

Leo came running into the room.

'Slow down,' said Lynn. 'You run in like that you'll bump into something. You're like your mum, can't wait, everything's got to be right now, this minute. Come and give your Nannan a kiss.'

He sidled up to her so that she could kiss his cheek, while he launched into a story from school – 'and this boy says – and Miss told him to get down – and his trainers were flashing –'

Lynn watched his face as his words came rushing out, she looked from him to his mother, how alike they were, such large hazel eyes, such heavy eyebrows, such a widely smiling mouth. When it smiled.

Different music came from the TV and he ran back to watch.

Lynn finished her coffee. 'I'll be off then.'

'Don't forget to ask, will you.'

'I won't forget. I'll probably be knocking on your door by half nine, with your overall and your mop and bucket.'

Lynn never thought she would take to it; Niecey seemed more the sort of young woman who would work in an office, or maybe some kind of studio, doing something artistic. Or maybe selling, not the sort of way that Gemma does, working in the baker's shop, but in a more high-powered sort of way. But she did take to it. She always turned up on time, cheerful, never grumbling about her shifts, or the mess some of the residents made of their rooms; and she got on well with the residents, chatting with them easily as she moved around the Home with her hoover and her bucket of cloths and sprays.

Sarah of course was sceptical.

'I never thought she'd do that,' said Sarah. She was sitting opposite Lynn in Marks and Spencers' cafe. 'I thought she would just sit at home putting on her make up and cleaning it off again. I thought she was quite happy letting our Jamie do all the work.'

'You're not being really fair,' said Lynn. 'She looks after the house, she's very clean, and she's always took good care of Leo. She doesn't just sit around.'

'I clean my house too,' said Sarah. 'Or I used to, *and* I look after my kids, and my husband, *and* I work full time. If I can do it, so can she.'

'Sarah love,' said Lynn, 'it's not a competition. Anyway, I was telling you, she's started working with us and I have to say, she's really good. Lovely with the residents, doesn't get flustered or irritated, good worker, everybody likes her.'

'Perfect in every way then,' said Sarah.

'Have you finished?' said Lynn.

'I've finished my coffee,' said Sarah, and they gathered their coats and handbags and left the Marks and Spencers café.

On the escalator Lynn took her daughter's arm. 'Don't be grumpy now. It's not that often I get to have a day out with you.'

'I get sick of hearing about her,' said Sarah. 'How many times have we had conversations about her? *Is she right for Jamie? Where did she come from? Why don't we see her family?'*

Lynn paused on the ground floor and checked the price of a purple sweater. Sarah looked around her as if searching for someone else to argue with.

'What do you think?' said Lynn.

'Not your colour,' said Sarah. *'Isn't Niecey pretty? Isn't Niecey nice? Isn't Jamie lucky?* Like we're trying to convince ourselves. All right, I'll shut up. Let's go and look at the market, and then we can call in Debenhams. All right?'

It was not possible to have a conversation as they walked down Fargate in the teeth of a cold wind, weaving among shoppers and pushchairs and chuggers and rag magazine sellers. Lynn stopped and gave fifty p to a young man singing, and smiled encouragingly at him while Sarah stood by, disapproving.

'I like that song,' said Lynn in her own defence. 'And he was quite good.'

Sarah had had enough of arguing, perhaps, and said nothing.

'I miss the old market,' said Lynn, as they enter the new one. 'This one doesn't smell the same.'

'Your point being?'

'It's not the same.'

'No. It's got more space, more light, no stairs, less smell. What's your problem Mum?'

'It's further from the bus stop.'

'Can't argue with that,' said Sarah. 'Are we getting vegetables?'

They missed out on Debenhams because their bags of vegetables were too cumbersome, and so hauled themselves and their shopping back to the bus stop.

'Going out tonight?' said Lynn as they took their seats.

'Not a chance. Football on telly, wall to wall. *She's* out, Melissa, at some sleepover –'

'Have you checked?'

'Of course. It's a birthday, the mum says she's going to be there all evening. All night. You just have to grit your teeth and trust them.'

Sarah got off the bus first and Lynn continued on home. She told Dave all about it while she was putting the shopping away and he was making a pot of tea.

'You can see where she's coming from,' said Dave. He put the tea cosy on to the pot and leaned back against the worktop. 'There was never two women less alike than Niecey and our Sarah.'

'Let me get to that cupboard.' Lynn had her hands full of packets and boxes. 'But Sarah – she's so *hard* sometimes. What's Niecey ever done to her?'

'You know what she's like – heart of gold but she can't help looking out for faults.'

'I think she's getting more picky lately. Seems to have lost her sense of humour. Maybe something's wrong at home?'

'There is something Gem told me – she said she doesn't know if she should tell or not – Mel's been getting into trouble at school, according to what our Tasha's been saying.'

'What sort of trouble?'

'Not sure. Tash saw her outside the Head of Year's room, with some others, bad girls she said.'

'Remember when Tash was the naughty one and Mel was the good girl? She's getting to be a little madam, much as I love her.'

'But it might be nothing.'

'Let's hope so,' said Lynn.

Later, when they were sitting quietly in front of the TV, Lynn came back again to her afternoon.

'Thing is,' she said, 'our Sarah had a right moan about Niecey. I've never heard her before being so down on her. Anyone would think she was jealous.'

'You said,' said Dave. 'Are you watching this? Because if not I'll turn it off.'

'I just want to see who gets voted off,' said Lynn. 'You can turn the sound off if you like.'

'Don't worry so much,' he said. 'Sarah's working too hard, and she asks a lot of herself, you know she does. She can't be jealous, can she, what's Niecey got that she hasn't.'

'You're right,' said Lynn. 'I'm fretting for nothing. It just feels like Sarah – or even Gem – might go searching for something to hold against Niecey.'

'Give over,' said Dave. 'Put it out of your mind before it gives you a headache. You've been watching too many of those soaps. We'll not have nothing like that in our family.'

But as it has turned out it isn't Sarah – or Gemma – who has found the something; it is Jamie, with those two birth certificates in his pocket and the worried and baffled frown on his face, who has set it all off.

The family meeting breaks up. Jamie is the first to leave, out of the door with barely a goodbye while Lynn stares after him wondering what she should have said, or done, to help. Then the sisters go, as they came, together, back to their busy lives where Jamie's troubles will be something they only have time to think about after everything else has been sorted out.

Sarah, at first anyway, does not tell her husband Jon what the family has been discussing, and actually, he doesn't ask, assuming that it was something ordinary like asking for a recipe or a loan of a pair of knitting needles. Although he has been part of this family for several years he pays little attention to what goes on between them.

After she has loaded the dishwasher and put on a load of washing, chased Melissa to do her homework, gone through Dom's school bag looking for a lost letter and incidentally removing crisp packets and black banana skins, taken yesterday's washing out of the dryer and sorted and folded it, kicked the pile of shoes by the front door into a smaller pile and then shouted for the kids to come and take some of them into the utility room, put the kettle on twice without ever getting round to actually making or drinking a cup of coffee, called Dom in from the street and sent him to have a shower, taken Melissa's phone away from her – after all that and before she begins to chase the kids to turn off their lights and get to sleep – Sarah calls Gemma.

'Hi Gem. Kids in bed?'

'Just going myself.' Gemma's family, being bakers, have to keep early hours.

'What are you thinking?'

'What's the matter?' says Gemma. 'Do you think I'm on my way round there to beat the truth out of her. Credit me with a bit of sense, please.'

'Did I say that?'

'You thought it.'

'Gem, I didn't. I just wondered if you'd had any thoughts that make sense of it.'

'I haven't had time to have a thought,' says Gemma. 'You know what it's like.'

'What I think,' says Sarah, 'is that those twins died. Twins are often early aren't they. They could have been very small. Too small to be viable.'

'That's a horrible word.'

'I know. Sorry. But you know what I mean.'

'Look,' says Gemma, 'I'm actually in the bathroom now. I was just starting to brush my teeth. I'll talk to you tomorrow.'

I tell her everything, Jamie said, and it is true, that's what he does. Every day when he comes home he starts talking, after being mostly silent all day while he is working on his own. Before he's changed out of his work clothes, between playing with Leo, while Niecey is cooking their tea, while eating, while they are doing the pots together, he tells her about his day, where he was working, what the weather has been like, who he saw, what they said, what the job was, sometimes tile by tile he tells her. She listens. She knows more about what plumbers do and the unreasonableness of customers and the relative merits of the Sheffield sandwich shops than she ever thought she would need to know.

After Leo has gone to bed and the TV is on he slows down. Sometimes he remembers something and tells her. Sometimes he asks her what she has been doing and she replies, 'Oh nothing much. Just the usual.' The she will tell him about something Leo has said or done.

Since she started to work at The Hedges there is more variety in what she has to tell him. He learns about Hilda and her books that she can't read any more but won't part with; about Peggy and her bad temper when Niecey has to go in and make her bed and clean her room. She can tell him about the other staff and their everyday human gossip about their children and grandchildren, their boyfriends, their girlfriends, their plans and outings. Their broken washing machines and new hairstyles. Their diets and their lapsed gym memberships. Jamie listens amiably, though not attentively; he can never remember afterwards who is who and who said what.

He has put the two birth certificates in Niecey's box, and to the back of his mind – the silver earring will never be found – and though he has not forgotten about them, he tells himself not to think too much about it. He understands that Niecey had a life before she met him, he gets that she is unwilling to talk about it, that she pretends it never happened, whatever it was, he has no wish to force her to tell him anything, but at the same time he believes, mildly, that one day she will. He has not even looked at the other papers she has kept. He can wait.

Lynn and Dave, next morning, have not put the subject aside.

'I don't know,' says Lynn, tipping a small mound of muesli into a bowl, 'how I'm going to look at her today. How am I going to pretend I don't know anything?'

'Easy,' says Dave. 'Because you *don't* know anything. Do we?'

'Very clever,' says Lynn. 'You know what I mean. She'll come in all bright and breezy and there'll be this *thing* between her and me. And I can't tell anyone about it, because they all know her –'

'You wouldn't anyway,' says Dave. 'You're not telling me that you would go discussing private family business outside this house? To all and sundry.'

'Of course not to all and sundry,' says Lynn. 'Whatever that means. But –'

'Not at all but,' says Dave. 'I know love, I know it's weighing on you. Just hold on to it till you get home, then you and me'll talk about it some more.'

*

The Hedges is divided into two parts, known as Upstairs and the Corridor. Upstairs the residents are more confused – or, to put it more bluntly, demented. The Corridor, downstairs, is named from the way the bedroom extension has been designed, and there most of the residents are physically limited by illnesses that are not acute enough for them to be in hospital, but too chronic for them to be looking after themselves. Their memories are often sound, which makes their infirmities all the more difficult for them to accept, and their moods are often hard to manage, whereas the baffled occupants of Upstairs can usually be distracted or jollied out of any bad temper by a cup of tea and a biscuit.

Niecey wrings out her cloth and wipes the windowsill of Peggy's room. She takes the duster from her overall pocket and gives all the little photographs a quick going over. If Peggy was there she would be squawking at this point because she is very possessive about her photographs, but she has been taken to the lounge so that her room can have a proper clean.

It is an easy job. She likes doing it, and – or but – it allows her time to think. Peggy's framed relatives – monochrome parents in the thirties to technicoloured grandchildren in the eighties – always set off a memory or two. Today it's the granddaughter's graduation that Niecey notices. There she is, with her long brown hair under her mortar board, holding her scroll, a parent on either side. How many homes up and down the land must have a photo identical except for the facial features.

Not that my parents have one, says Niecey quietly to herself.

She carefully puts the photo frames back in the order she found them – though Peggy will not remember how they were. She looks around. She has changed the bed, dusted the furniture, hoovered the floor, cleaned the wash basin, put some dirty clothes in the bag to go to the laundry, checked the commode (empty; Peggy doesn't bother with it), closed the drawers and the wardrobe doors, and is ready to move on to the next room, Hilda's.

Hilda is there, sitting, leaning heavily to one side so that her head is dropping off the back of the chair.

'Shall I straighten you up a bit?' Touching the residents was difficult at first but Katie the manager explained to her when it was all right to do it, and when it was necessary to call one of the trained staff. Now her squeamishness has gone, she has watched Lynn and the others to see how they do it, she has got to know the residents enough to know how they like to be arranged and what is acceptable to them. 'Here, let me put this cushion behind you.'

'Hello dear,' says Hilda, with every sign of recognition. 'It's nice of you to come and see me. Is it Christmas?' Outside the sun is high in the sky and the trees, in full leaf, are motionless.

'Not yet,' says Niecey brightly. 'A little longer.' She has already taken on the lying cheeriness which seems to be the accepted way of speaking in this place. Upstairs, there is no point trying to explain.

'What are you doing for Christmas?' says Hilda. She has a strong deep voice with more than a trace of Irishness; her eyes as she looks at Niecey are bright and knowing – if you only spoke to her for one sentence you would think that she knew what was what.

'Just family,' says Niecey.

'Oh well,' says Hilda, 'never mind, it will soon be over.'

There are no photographs in Hilda's room, but there are books, a whole shelf of them, Jane Austen and Charles Dickens in hard covers, the Brontes and works that Niecey, in spite of her 'education' hasn't read – George Gissing and Wilkie Collins.

'Shall I dust these Hilda? Shall I take them down and dust them properly?'

'In the right order,' says Hilda. 'Don't go getting them out of order now. I know what you girls are like.'

Niecey flicks her duster over the spines and blows along the row of books. That will do.

On the floor by the wardrobe is an old brown purse, bare and colourless at the corners. Niecey picks it up. 'Where shall I put this for you Hilda?'

'Throw it away,' she says, without looking. 'Put it in the bin, it's only rubbish.'

'There's something in it though,' says Niecey. 'Is it all right if I look?'

Inside the purse there is a pair of small stud earrings, gold probably, a broken gold chain, very delicate, and a heavy wedding ring.

'Throw it away, I said. I told you, throw it away.'

'All right Hilda,' says Niecey.

'In the bin, now,' she cries. 'Let me see you put it in the bin.'

Niecey drops it into the plastic bin under the washbasin. 'There, it's gone.'

Hilda's eyes go back to her books, then on to look out of the window. 'Look at those leaves now, they'll soon be all over the ground. Who'll be sweeping them up I wonder.'

Niecey gathers her hoover and her cleaning materials, and picks up the bin to take it outside. 'See you later Hilda.'

The staff of the Hedges have taken to their new manager, though at first they were doubtful. She is a heavy woman, in her forties, who pulls her dark shiny hair away from her face as if she wants to disown it. She has a lazy eye which makes her look as if she is about to wink. She is a Londoner, but it is known that she moved up from Bristol for this job, with her younger son. Her older son, she has told someone, has finished university and is working in the Middle East. She has proved to be a fair person to work for, not above clearing up mess herself if necessary, reasonable about swapping shifts or having to take children for dentist appointments and the like; and at the same time, making sure everyone pulls their weight and there is not overmuch gossiping in the kitchen. Not a cheery person though – she earns every penny they pay her and takes her work very seriously.

As it happens Lynn is with her in her office when Niecey knocks on the door. She shows them the purse and the pathetic bits of jewellery. 'She made me put it in the bin. She got quite upset about it. But I don't want her to think I've robbed her.'

Lynn and Katie seem quite unbothered by the event. Lynn fetches out a large envelope and they write on it Hilda's name and the date and the words 'brown leather purse, broken gold chain, pair stud earrings, gold wedding ring.' And put the whole thing in a small safe that sits under the manager's desk.

'I wonder about the ring,' says Lynn. 'She's never been married, as far as we know. She's our only Miss.'

'Except for me,' says Katie, and then, 'Could have been her mother's I expect. Something like that.'

Lynn looks at Niecey's retreating back. So far today she hasn't spoken directly to her, but it doesn't appear that Niecey has noticed anything unusual.

'What do you think of her?' she asks Katie.

'She's great,' says Katie. 'Sometimes a little late for work, but I understand she has a little boy to get off to school. Always makes up the time anyway. No, I've no complaints at all. I've even wondered whether she'd like to start training as a carer. She could do her NVQs here, no trouble. Do you want to ask her?'

'You ask her,' says Lynn. 'It will be better coming from you. I think she might say no, though.'

'Why would she? She'd be paid more – not much more, but a little bit.'

'She'd have to do different shifts wouldn't she? I think at the moment she can only manage this nine while three. With Leo you know.'

Katie nods. 'I understand. We've all been there haven't we. She seems like a devoted mum.'

'Yes,' says Lynn. 'Yes, she is.'

The Corridor is not where Niecey usually cleans but the other cleaner is off and she has been asked to do Ron's room.

He is ninety, Ron, ninety last month, and his birthday was celebrated only by the staff and residents because he has nobody else.

'Never had children,' he says. 'Had a wife once, been without her nearly thirty years. Without her more years than I was with her.'

Ron is crooked with arthritis; his knees and hips don't bend, and hardly bear his weight – though his weight is only that of a child. He watches what the staff call 'clever' things on television and reads. Today he has a book open on his knee, but he is looking at the wall opposite, or maybe through it.

'What are you reading?'

He shows her – Lyrical Ballads it is.

'You like poetry?' says Niecey.

'Ah yes,' he says. 'Poetry is what keeps me going. If I can be said to be going.' He chuckles.

'Not novels?' says Niecey.

'Too long,' he says. 'I don't want to be popping off in the middle of Bleak House do I? No, I used to read novels but now poems do the job. I can read one and then sit here and let it roll round in my head. A good poem needs a whole day, but I've got a whole day I hope. A good novel needs a couple of weeks, and who knows if I'll have time to finish it.'

Niecey knows that some of the staff – Lynn for example – try to jolly him out of these dreary statements, but she doesn't herself feel able to do it.

'Which poets do you like best?'

'Ah now,' he says, 'it's not so much the poet as the poem. Any of them can write something that doesn't hit the mark, and at the same time any of them, even someone you've never heard of, can come up with something that can make you think, That's right, that's spot on that is, I'll never forget that.'

'So,' says Niecey, emptying his wastepaper bin into her sack, 'what's one of the poems you read again and again?'

He thinks, watching her as she moves about his room, straightening and dusting. 'Ulysses,' he says at last. 'Or no, Gray's Elegy. Or some of Keats – Ode to Melancholy. Some days I would say Hardy, other days he's too clumsy for me. Today – today I would say the Lucy poems – "rolled round in Earth's diurnal course, with rocks and stones and trees." There's comfort in that.'

'I like William Blake,' says Niecey.

'Do you indeed? Tell me then, what it is you like about his mystical nonsense?'

Niecey closes the wardrobe door and puts a fresh towel by the washbasin before she replies. 'He loves children,' she says.

'That's so,' says Ron.

'And his words seem not to make sense at first, but they stay with you,' says Niecey. 'They can be a comfort.'

'Tell me some Blake then,' he says, daring her, perhaps, to prove that she can.

She stops moving about the room, she considers. Then: '*A weeping babe upon the wild, And weeping Woman, pale, reclined; And in the open air again I fill'd with woes the passing Wind.*'

'Each to his own,' says Ron. 'Or her own.'

'You know it's true,' says Dave, though Lynn hasn't mentioned Niecey for half an hour, 'we still don't know anything about her.'

'Like what?'

'Where she grew up, what happened to her parents, where she lived before she came to Sheffield. What jobs she did. What friends did she have? Why did she even come here?'

'Haven't we said all this before?'

'I know,' says Dave. 'I know we used to sit and wonder about her, but it might be worth going over it again, in case something has come out in recent times. You know, Jamie might have said something to us that we haven't properly taken notice of.'

'Do you think Jamie knows more than we do? I don't.'

'All right, *you* might know more. You've worked with her for six months or more.'

'Seems unlikely,' she says. 'But go on. Where shall we start?'

'At the beginning. Where was she born? I seem to remember somewhere on the south coast.'

'I think so. Portsmouth was it? Or Plymouth?'

'And her parents. Has she ever said anything about them?'

'I have the impression that they died.'

'How do you get that impression though? What did she say?'

'Remember when we were sorting out the wedding? I'm sure I said her parents would want to be there and she said something – maybe something like, They won't be able to, or, They can't come.'

'Not, They're both dead?'

'No, nothing as clear as that. But I didn't want to ask her. I didn't want to upset her. Because if they were alive surely she would want them there?'

'Lynnie,' he says fondly, 'you know better than most that families are awful things. Not everyone's as lucky as us. OK. What else do we know? What was she like when we first met her? Can you remember?'

'She was nervous,' says Lynn. 'I remember that. Mainly I remember thinking that she wasn't like us. Do you know what I mean?'

'Not really.'

'Some minutes I thought she was posher than us, and then I'd find myself thinking she was a bit rough. Does that make sense? She were wearing a lot of make up but her clothes looked as if they'd come out of a junk shop. Nothing fitted her properly. And her face were made up lovely but her hands were rougher than mine and her nails were all bitten right down. But she had manners didn't she. Do you remember, we had a Sunday dinner and she was all please and thank you and very appreciative.'

'As who wouldn't be,' says Dave. 'But did she say anything about herself?'

'I think we talked more about the future,' says Lynn. 'You know, when the baby was expected and how Jamie wanted to get married straight away –'

'Did she not want to then?'

'She said it was all right with her. But I got the impression she didn't want to force him. Or else she didn't really love him – I don't know which it was. And we talked about where they could live and she was very evasive about where she was living, I remember that, and to this day I don't know where she was living when she got together with our Jamie. But she did say she couldn't stay there once the baby was born.'

'Then they moved into that little house. What a state that was in, do you remember? But they worked on it.'

'It was just the job for a starter home wasn't it. And Jamie had saved the money for a deposit – remember what a shock that was?'

'He was a dark horse too,' says Dave. 'Maybe they suit each other.'

'I know she said – maybe not on that occasion, but around that time – she said she wouldn't be able to put anything towards buying the house.'

'Women are amazing,' says Dave. 'How can you recall things that someone has said – how many years ago? So she'd no money saved, she didn't have a job? Did she even have a trade? A profession?'

'She went to university,' says Lynn. 'I distinctly remember her saying that quite recently, when our Tash was talking about what she wanted to do when she leaves school. Niecey said something like, One step at a time. Get your GCSEs she said, then work hard for your A levels, that's the hard part, then you can start thinking about what you want to study at uni.'

'That doesn't mean she went does it? Anyone could say that.'

'No, she did. Tash asked her and she said she went but she dropped out because she was ill and she failed her exams.'

'Did she say what university it was? Sheffield?'

'No. I think what she said was Liverpool, I wasn't listening that much, Gemma was talking to me at the same time. But she never got her degree.'

'So she must have gone to work then, after that.'

'She must have. But I've never heard her talk about it.'

'So maybe it was something she's ashamed of?'

'Like what?'

'I don't know,' says Dave, exasperated. 'It's like we're making up a story for a fictional character here. It's as if she's just dropped from the sky without any childhood, or any history, just landed like she's from Mars.'

'Men are from Mars,' says Lynn, and he looks at her crossly for a second before he allows himself to laugh.

'I mean, that wedding,' says Dave. 'It were a good thing we only booked the small room at the Town Hall weren't it. She didn't even have any friends to ask. Why was that? What was wrong with her, that she'd no friends?'

'We had to spread out didn't we,' says Lynn. 'Do you remember, we asked everyone we could think of – your mum and my dad, your Steve, Janet and her bloke –'

'Who never turned up and we still had to pay for his meal –'

'– all the kids – and we still didn't make an impression on that room.'

'It was a good do though weren't it,' says Dave. 'I could see everyone thinking he'd done well for himself, our Jamie. I know it were a rush job, but folk don't mind that these days, even my mum never said a word about it.'

'It was a good day, I know. But I thought, even then, I thought, We don't know anything about her. I believed it wouldn't matter. I thought she'd open up as time went on, to Jamie if not to us. But it seems as if she hasn't.'

'At least,' says Dave, 'she hasn't told him about those twins, if they really are hers. And if they are, where are they now?'

Oliver and Lila are not far away, as the crow flies. They live in a nice house, enclosed by a garden; they have bedrooms with windows that look out on water meadows and rocky edges. They go to school – they are approaching the end of Year Nine; they have chosen their options. They have friends, and nice clothes, they have a smartphone and an iPad each – though they are not allowed any screen time after nine o'clock in the evening. They have each other. They have books and hobbies and aspirations. They are loved. They are lucky.

'Tell me about Adrian,' says Dave.

It is Saturday, three days after Jamie shared his discovery with his family. Dave and Niecey are sitting in her garden, watching Leo and Jake jump from the slide into the paddling pool. Niecey does not look at him, or appear even to have heard him; she sits still, looking down the garden at the children splashing.

'Jake's getting a bit old to play with Leo,' she says.

'He'll grow up soon enough,' says Dave. He waits, then he says again, 'Tell me about Adrian.'

She says nothing.

'I suppose you're still in touch with him?'

Nothing.

'You'll have told Jamie all about him?'

Unexpectedly, she smiles, as if to herself. 'He's old history,' she says. 'An old boyfriend. It was years ago.'

'How old were you?'

'Eighteen. My first boyfriend, really. I never had a boyfriend till I left home. I wasn't allowed.'

'Not allowed? Why was that?'

'Oh, my parents. They were strict, that's all. Anyway, I didn't know any boys. So when I went to university I went a little bit wild.'

'You went to University?'

'You know I did. I'm sure I've told you that before.'

'In Liverpool? Was that it?'

She pauses, as if thinking. 'Actually no. No, I don't know what gave you that idea. University of East Anglia. It's in Norwich. UEA, they say, for short.'

'So Adrian, was he a student too?'

'He was a graduate student. He was very clever, doing a Ph.D in psychology.'

'Psychologists,' says Dave. 'I'm not a fan of them. Thinking they can tell what you're thinking all the time. Don't like people who try to see through you. Dreams and so on.'

Niecey laughs. 'They're not like that. It's all data and statistics. I don't think I ever knew Adrian deal with a real person.'

'So, serious boyfriend was he?'

'We went out for a couple of years, on and off.'

'Not that serious then?'

'There were some breaks. He used to go to the States in the vacations sometimes, because his dad lived there. He was some big professor. Adrian was hoping to get a job out there when he finished his Ph.D.'

'And did he?'

'I wouldn't know,' she said. 'We lost touch.'

'Plenty more fish in the sea,' says Dave. 'Plenty more boyfriends I'm sure.'

'Not really,' she says. 'Shall I go and put the kettle on?'

When Dave has gone, taking Jake with him, Niecey sets about changing the beds. It is a job – like most that she does – that allows her to think. Adrian. When she said his name, out loud, it was nothing, like it could just float away. No harm done. She kept a lid on it. She held him at arm's length. She kept it casual. She didn't give anything away, nothing that Jamie can't know. If he tells him, that won't matter. But it did – *oh it did* – feel good to say some words. How does that happen, she wonders.

Adrian. Of course when she first fell for him she said his name to herself all the time. Adrian. Adrian. She behaved as if she was fourteen, not eighteen. She only just stopped short of writing his name on her books and carving it onto her desk. What an unbelievable catch he was. Everyone thought so, not just her, all the other girls too. Graduate students were definitely superior to boys who had only just left school, but Adrian – not only older, but good-looking, tall and brown and so so cool. When the other girls saw her talking to him in the bar, in a corridor, outside a lecture hall – they were so envious, so interested. What's his name, what does he do, god, Denny (she was Denny then) he's fit, if you don't know what to do with him, just pass him on to me.

She had not the first idea how to get on with boys. Every boy she'd ever been in the same room with had been a pupil at her school, and knew her as the headmaster's daughter. They might smirk, or even laugh at her as she passed them in the corridor but they wouldn't say anything, because they knew she could have – though she never would have – gone straight to her dad and told on them. So to be singled out by Adrian – the dreadlocks, the smile, the casual way he could say he was going to the States for Christmas – it was like being chatted up by royalty. Better.

What he saw in her she didn't know, then. Now she does, she knows now. She was not bad looking, certainly better than she'd ever been before, convincingly bright enough on the surface, and she was giddy enough with her newly acquired freedom to go along with whatever he wanted. He didn't need to be Freud to know that she was needy, uncritical, inexperienced, totally available. She was perfect for him, just as much as she thought he was perfect for her.

Leo comes to find her, bored with the garden now that Jake has gone. 'Can I ride my bike?'

'Let me finish this,' she says. 'You can help me – look, take that washing basket downstairs and put it by the washing machine. Can you manage it? I think you're strong enough.'

'I'm strong,' he says. 'Can I ride my bike then?' He has only just got the hang of riding without stabilisers.

'Five minutes,' she says. 'Then I'll take you out.'

Sitting on the park bench she tries to summon up images of the twins.

*

'She weren't bad,' says Dave to Lynn. 'She were quite happy to tell me Adrian were an old boyfriend. From her student days. Says she's not in touch with him any more.'

'Did you believe her?'

'Why not? It's normal isn't it, to lose touch with your old flames. Or is there something you're not telling me?'

Lynn gives him a push on the shoulder. 'Go on, you. You know as well as I do you were my first boyfriend.'

'So you say.'

'Well I'm going to change my story now am I, after all these years.' They laugh together, as they do often.

'So, you didn't get the impression that she still cares for this Adrian?'

'Not at all. Seemed as if he were well in the past. And you wouldn't expect her *not* to have boyfriends before our Jamie.'

'He didn't have girlfriends.'

'As far as we know. He went out with girls sometimes I'm sure. It's just none of them ever got to a settled stage. All this is beside the point anyway. What we know now is that Adrian Wilson is someone Niecey knew at one time.'

'So what about the children? What about his name and hers on them certificates? That's the important thing, not how many boyfriends she had when she were a teenager.'

'I didn't get to that bit,' he admits.

'Why not? That was the whole point weren't it.' She slams a cupboard door so hard that she makes herself jump with shock.

'Calm down dear.' He stops and waits for her to laugh and relax.

'I've waited days,' she says. 'I thought you would get it all cleared up. I can't go on thinking about it every minute of the day. And night.'

'Softly softly catchee monkey,' he says. 'I couldn't, love. She were spooked enough talking about Adrian. We have to take this thing slowly. I'm picking Leo up from school on Wednesday. I'll try again then.'

'You make sure you do,' says Lynn. 'Else I might have to do it myself.'

'Come into the garden,' says Dave. 'Come and get a breath of air before bedtime – it's hardly dark yet.'

They take a turn round the garden, breathing in the scents of roses and pinks. The bees are silent now and only a stray moth flutters among the flowers. The last of the light, the very last glimmer, goes as they stand by the sweet peas, but they stay outside in the warm darkness, hearing distant traffic, occasional voices, tiny rustlings in the hedge.

'Longest day's past now,' says Dave. 'Dark will start coming earlier from now on.'

'Don't be an old misery,' says Lynn. 'There's plenty more summer still to come. Isn't it still, tonight? Isn't it peaceful?'

'Lovely,' agrees Dave. 'Time for bed now I think. Is that our phone?'

It is Sarah on the phone. 'You haven't seen Melissa have you?'

'Not today,' says Dave. 'Is she late home then?'

'She wasn't even supposed to go out,' says Sarah. 'She's grounded. I thought she was in her bedroom all evening, sulking, and now, when I've gone to tell her to go to bed, I find she's not there at all. Little minx has skipped out when my back was turned.'

'Have you asked Dom?'

'He's asleep. But he wouldn't know, she doesn't tell him things. No, she'll be hanging around on some street corner with her mates. Jon's just gone out to see if he can find her.

I thought I'd ask you, just in case. I'll get off the phone, she might be trying to ring.'

'Do you want me to go and look for her?' says Dave.

'I don't know Dad. We've not had to deal with this before. I don't know what time I should call the police – what do you think? It's just gone eleven.'

'Maybe give it half an hour?' says Dave. 'She's probably in someone's house and they've forgot what time it is.'

'She's got a phone that tells her what time it is,' says Sarah crossly. 'She's only grounded because she was late home last night. She'll get worse than grounding this time, I can tell you.'

'You were young once,' says Dave. 'Tell you what, we'll stay up till midnight – let us know when she's home, so that we don't worry all night.'

'I'll text you,' promises Sarah.

'So Leo tells me he's going to be a footballer,' says Dave. He ruffles the hair of his grandson, and his grandson smoothes it down again, crossly.

'Jamie's taking him on Saturday,' says Niecey. 'You're a bit excited, aren't you sweetheart. You'd think he'd been picked for England, not going for a kickabout with twenty other five year olds.'

Dave has just brought Leo home after looking after him while Niecey did a longer shift at The Hedges. He hovers at the back door until Niecey smiles at him and fills the kettle. Then he sits down at the table, looking out through the open door at a fine warm drizzle.

'Do you know, I'd rather have a proper rainstorm, clear the air and let the sun come out,' he says.

'Here's your tea. Was Leo good?'

'He always is. You've done a good job with him, you and Jamie, he's a lovely little boy.'

'I know.'

Leo has gone up to his bedroom, eager to construct his latest dragon cave.

Dave's hand is hovering towards the biscuit tin, 'We're blessed, me and Lynn,' he says, not looking at Niecey. 'Five lovely grandchildren, we couldn't ask for more. All good kids.'

Niecey has left her mug on the table and is rummaging through the freezer compartment.

'What happened to Oliver and Lila?' says Dave. He takes a broken biscuit out of the tin – broken ones don't count – and waits.

Niecey keeps the freezer door open until it begins to bleep. Dave waits, biscuit in hand.

'Come and drink your tea love,' he says as she closes the door at last, and she comes slowly to the table and sits down. She holds her hands round her mug as if she needs warmth and says nothing.

'You've never even told Jamie,' says Dave. He does not sound as if he's accusing her, more that he's commiserating.

Still she says nothing, and he watches. At last he says, 'Drink your tea.'

'Eat your biscuit,' she says, and he looks and realises he is still holding it.

'Niecey love,' he says. 'We don't want to give you a hard time. We can see it's not easy.'

'"We?"' she says.

'All the family.'

'I can't say anything,' she says.

'You've told us lies,' he says, 'but that's not the point. We know there's a story to you and we know you want to keep it quiet, but it's not fair is it. It's not fair on Jamie.'

'What does Jamie say about that?'

'He says – he says he's going to wait for you to tell him.'

'Why? Why did he say that? What have you told him?' She stands up. 'I'm going to call Leo down for his tea.'

'His tea's not ready is it,' says Dave. 'And you know you won't sleep tonight if you leave it like this. Let me just say this. Niecey, you're family, you know you are. But secrets don't belong in families. I've never kept the littlest thing from Lynn, ever since we've been together. Not the littlest thing. It'll come between you if you do.'

'We're fine,' she says. 'Jamie and me, we're fine.'

'You might be,' he says 'Actually, I take that back, *you're* not, and neither, whether you notice it or not, neither is he. He's worrying, to himself, and you know it. Tell Jamie, even if you don't tell the rest of us, that's my advice to you.'

'When I want it,' she says, suddenly loud, 'when I want your advice I'll ask for it. All right?'

'No,' says Dave slowly. 'It's not going to be like that. I'll finish for today. But this is my job, holding the family together, and I'm not giving up on you, Niecey Wilde. Time to tell him. You hear? Time to come clean.'

She has her back to him now, twisting away in her chair.

He goes to the foot of the stairs and calls goodbye to Leo, then leaves her, patting her shoulder as he goes past.

To hear their names come out of his mouth – she never thought that would happen. All the times she'd imagined how she would find them again, all the scenarios she has made up, all the dreams and ideas – they never included her father-in-law, old Dave, sitting across the table from her and asking her that.

What does he know? How does he know? Who else knows – Lynn obviously since he tells her every little thing. Gemma and Sarah – do they know? Are they at this moment planning how they're going to tell Jamie?

She should have a plan. Maybe she should write a letter – who to? To Jamie? He'll find that very weird – writing anything down is just not his style, and it would come hard to her too, after all this time. She's got out of the habit of putting pen to paper. A text wouldn't really do the job.

She even smiles to herself at this thought, then the worry comes back into her face.

Dave would read a letter – but then it would be a real thing, that he could show to the others. She can't bear the thought of all of them clucking over it, and plotting how to get rid of her. She can't bear the idea of Gemma turning up on her doorstep and shouting at her before she's even let her in the house, and calling her a stuck up bitch and a liar and a con artist, and whatever else. And Sarah meeting her somewhere and turning away, sneering. Whatever else they find out.

How have they done it? What do they know?

Or, have they found them? How would that be possible? Did he come here with the idea that he was giving her a present – knowledge of her babies, a contact with them, and she didn't react as he wanted and he went away disappointed? Is that possible?

She puts fish fingers under the grill for Leo and starts to peel potatoes for Jamie, working in a sort of fog. Thoughts and questions are misting up her brain. She can't see anything clearly, she's going round and round, like someone lost on the moors, round and round and back to the same place, tired and despairing. *Folly is an endless maze, Tangled roots perplex her ways.*

Jamie comes home, they eat, he talks to Leo, about school, and football, and the best sort of car to have. Niecey stays quiet but he doesn't seem to notice anything about her that is new or strange. He puts Leo to bed, as usual, and sits with her in front of the TV. He doesn't seem any different from how he usually is.

She is very fond of Jamie. She appreciates what he has done for her; she appreciates what a good person he is. If she says she loves him, it is true; but it is the sort of love where his goodness has to keep reminding her that she loves him. She wonders if it is now that she's going to lose him. Is that what his family want? Well, she could cope without him, as long as she has Leo. No way is she going to give up Leo.

'Nothing,' says Dave to Lynn. 'Couldn't get anything out of her.'

'What do you mean? She didn't speak?'

'Oh words were said all right. On both sides. But she weren't going to tell me anything. I think I went in a bit too sudden. It upset her though, I could see that. She's lost them children one way or another.'

'What kind of a mother does that?' says Lynn. 'If their father's got them, why doesn't she see them, and what's the big secret anyway. If they were mine I wouldn't just let them go without making damn well sure I saw them. She doesn't write them letters, she doesn't have anything to do with them. How does she live with herself?' She is biting her bottom lip to keep herself from crying.

'Whoa,' says Dave. 'Give the woman a chance Lynnie. We don't know the story do we. She might not be the same as your mother, there might be a better reason. Our Sarah says they might have died as babies, maybe being very small or premature as they say. You can't go jumping to conclusions.'

'If she'd lost them that way,' says Lynn, more calmly, 'then I can't see what would stop her being open about it. Wouldn't she have told Jamie? What about when she were expecting Leo? Wouldn't she have said, if something had gone wrong before? Wouldn't it have been on her mind?'

'All good questions Lynnie,' he says. 'But she's not ready to tell us. This could be a long job. What I'm going to do, I'm going to go back to Adrian. She were all right with that. I'll talk about Adrian until she's at ease and then gradually introduce children into the conversation, that's what I'll do. My mistake were, I tried to shock it out of her, but she were so shocked – this is what I think – that she just about froze. I'll pop in and see her Saturday morning.'

Adrian lives in the USA. His visits to England are irregular and brief. He has divorced Niecey and has an American ex-wife, and an American ex-girlfriend and an American daughter with whom he is tenuously in touch. He has American citizenship and a well-paid job to do with marketing. He is a disappointment to his mother, and to his English children he is someone whose promised visits provoke excitement and then, quite quickly, dissolve into a bitter dissatisfaction that they cannot communicate, not even to each other.

Saturday again. Niecey puts Leo's football boots and a bottle of water and a cereal bar into his backpack and waves him off with his dad. And very soon after Dave is stepping through her back door, smiling as though he has no purpose on his mind beyond a cup of tea.

'Now then lass,' he says. 'Jamie's out for the morning, Lynn's at work as you know, till three o'clock. There's just you and me, having a good talk.'

'Fine,' says Niecey. 'There are things I want to ask you too.'

Dave's eyebrows go up in mild surprise. 'Fair enough,' he says.

She boils the water for the tea, deliberately leaves the biscuit tin on the shelf. She carries on with her tidying of the kitchen, wiping down the surfaces and taking the rubbish out to the bin. She picks up some Lego and some small cars from the floor and puts them in a plastic box, and the box at the bottom of the stairs, ready to be taken up to Leo's room. She pours the tea and sits down across from Dave, looking directly at him.

'What do you know?' she says. 'Or what do you think you know?'

'I don't know any more than I've told you,' he says. 'I just know those names. I feel like you should be telling me what I need to know.'

'Where did you hear those names?'

'I can't tell you that,' he says. 'I have to protect my sources.' He laughs, gently.

'It was Gemma wasn't it?' says Niecey. 'What has she been saying about me? What does she thinks gives her the right to go nosing through the internet for me? What is it to her anyway? Or Sarah?'

Dave looks a little shocked. 'Our Gemma's never said a word to me,' he says. 'Honestly love, I didn't get this from Gemma, but I don't have – what's the word? clearance – to tell you where I did get it from. Understand? And I won't tell people what you and I say either, unless you agree.'

'Not even Lynn?'

'Ah well,' he says. 'I don't see how I can keep anything from Lynn.'

'And what about Jamie? Are you telling him?'

'I think that's up to you to do,' says Dave. 'To be honest Niecey, it seems to me that you and our Jamie have a funny relationship, if you don't talk to each other. But that's not my business is it.'

'No,' says Niecey, 'it's not.'

'So,' says Dave, 'Why don't we go back to Adrian. Adrian Wilson, weren't it.'

'Do you know him, that's what I want to know? Is he here, in Sheffield? Do you know his mother? I don't mind telling – I'll tell Jamie everything if –'

'So he's a Sheffield lad, is he? But you said his dad's in America?'

'OK,' says Niecey, 'What I know, what I think I know – Adrian was born somewhere in America. His mum went there – I don't know why – and she took up with this man and they had Adrian, and then later they split up and she came back to England and he went to school in Sheffield.'

'So she came from Sheffield?'

'I suppose so.'

'So what were her name? Is she a Wilson? And do you know what school he went to?'

Niecey shakes her head. 'I've tried and tried,' she says. 'Sometimes I think I remember it was this school or that school – I've got a list – but then I think, no it was this other one. The honest answer is I've forgotten, or else I never knew. And his mum was a Wilson when he was born and her name is Jacqui, but she married again, or maybe for the first time, I don't know, and I never knew her surname.'

'Jackie Wilson –' says Dave. '– he were a singer. Reet Petite.'

'Different Jacqui Wilson,' says Niecey, and they both smile a little. 'With a Q, you know?'

'But to get back to Adrian,' says Dave. 'Do you know where he is now?'

'No,' she says. 'Completely lost touch.'

'When was the last time you saw him?'

'What does it matter?' she says. 'It's got nothing to do with anything that's going on now. I haven't seen him for years.'

'But you've been looking for him.'

'No I haven't.'

'What's this then about a list of schools? What's this about trying to remember what school he went to? What's this about trying to find his mother?'

'No,' she says. 'You've got it all wrong. I don't care for Adrian at all. If he's abroad, or dead, or married to someone else, it's all the same to me.'

'Married to someone else?'

'Married to anyone, it's still all the same to me.'

'You were married to him weren't you.'

'Dave,' she says. 'I like you, I really do. You and Lynn have been lovely to me. But all this – interrogation. It's not on. You're imposing it on me without me agreeing to it. I know you've found out some names – Sarah or Gemma have looked something up and you think you know something about me – so if you know something, tell me what it is. Don't expect me to tell you things so you can say, That's wrong, that's not enough, that's not what it says on the internet or wherever. I'm not going to play this game Dave, I don't have to tell you anything, I don't have to tell Jamie anything if I don't want to, and I certainly don't have to answer to Sarah. Or Gemma.'

He waits and she waits. She looks through the open door at the garden and he looks at her. Then he says, 'Niecey love, you've mentioned our Gemma.'

'I knew it.'

'Now then, I never said that did I? I just think it's fair to warn you that she has got her hooks into finding stuff out about you. She's a dab hand at that internet, Gemma is. So far I suppose she's not come up with owt but she will, I'm certain, if it's there she'll find it. Wouldn't it be better for you to come clean before she does. She's not a bad girl, she don't dislike you, not at all, but she won't have her little brother made a fool of, know what I mean? Wouldn't you be better telling me now, so I can tell her it's all out in the open and there's nothing to get excited about?'

Niecey sits very still, looking at the garden, showing no sign that she has heard him. At last she says, 'Tell you what Dave, this is my position. You're right, there are things that Jamie has a right to know. You back off, you get Gemma to back off, and I'll talk to Jamie. It wouldn't be right for him to think I've told you things before I've told him, would it.'

'But will you come clean? How will I know you've done it?'

'If I say I'll do it,' says Niecey, 'then I'll do it. Give me a week.'

'A week?'

'It might take some time,' says Niecey. 'But I'll do it. I've said.'

'That's a promise?'

'That's a promise.'

When people talk about getting things off your chest, when they talk about a great weight being lifted off them – when she hears those things it's like someone saying they believe in Santa Claus. Wishful thinking.

She knows now that she has to tell him. She has to say something at least. What is the least she can get away with? Put another way, what does he deserve to know?

Poor Jamie, he deserves, if there is such a thing as deserving, he deserves to know nothing. Will he feel better for knowing? She doesn't think so. Will she feel better for him knowing? No, she doesn't believe that she will.

*

Dave and Lynn are clearing away their evening meal, a bit later than usual, when there is a knock at the front door and a simultaneous ring on the bell.

'Who can that be?' says Lynn.

On the doorstep Melissa is standing, accompanied by a policewoman.

'Mrs Wilde? Melissa's Nannan?'

'Yes.'

'Can I come in for a moment?'

'You can tell me here,' says Lynn, indicating the doorstep. 'What's gone off?'

'Nothing much,' says the policewoman. 'Bit of a to-do down by the chip shop. We've just been to sort it out and I'm just bringing Melissa home to get her out of the way.'

Melissa has said nothing but her eyes have been fixed on Lynn, imploring, unblinking.

'She lives with you?' says the policewoman.

Lynn lets only half a second go by before saying, 'At the moment.'

'Fine. You'll let her parents know, then, when they come back? And you, Melissa, keep away from people drinking in the street – next time you might find it works out worse for you.'

Dave has been listening from the front room. 'What did you say that for?' he demands of Lynn. 'You can't go lying to the police – in front of Melissa too.'

'Give over,' says Lynn calmly. 'You know Melissa won't have done anything. Have you love?'

Melissa subsides, now that she can, into tears, and through her sobs, tells her version of the story. 'Dani and me, we weren't doing anything, and this girl Bethany, she starts shouting at us – not at me, she's all right with me – at Dani, and she's got these other kids with her, and boys, and they come over to us and she wants Dani a fight, and Dani goes, What have I done to you? and she says, Don't give me that, you know what you've done and she was swearing Nannan, so I'm missing those bits out. And Dani says to her, Look at how many you've got with you and there's only two of us so it's not fair is it, and then this Bethany, she went for Dani and they started fighting and I couldn't leave her could I, and the chip shop woman she called the police and they came –'

'Is Dani all right?'

'I don't know – she didn't fall down or nothing – they took her in the car and I said I lived up here – you don't mind do you. Mum'll kill me if she finds out, I'm supposed to be at home with Dom, Mum and Dad have gone to this do, but I'll be home before they get there. You'll take me won't you Grandad.'

'You can walk,' says Lynn. 'This is all a big fuss about nothing.'

Melissa's tears start again, as if a tap has been turned. 'I'm scared Nannan. Those kids, they might be still around. I'd be on my own.'

'I'll take her,' says Dave. 'You put the kettle on lass, I'll be back in five minutes.'

In the car he looks sideways at her, his younger and possibly dearer granddaughter. (Of course he loves Tash dearly as well, but she's self-contained, doesn't have the open need of Melissa to be loved.) She looks as she usually looks when out of school – long loose brown hair, chubby knees bursting through ripped jeans, pointed nose like her mother's and a brace on her teeth – but he detects something different.

'Have you been smoking?' he says.

'No Grandad.'

'What can I smell then?'

'It's the others,' she says. 'It must be Bethany – she smokes.'

'You must have got pretty close to her then.'

'You know I don't smoke Grandad.'

'You make sure it stays that way,' he says.

It is well over half an hour before he returns home. 'Dom were in his room, on t'Playstation,' he says. 'I don't think he even knew our Melissa had gone out and left him, so no worries there. But what Sarah's going to say I don't know.'

'We don't need to tell her,' says Lynn. 'It will only cause trouble.'

'So what then, just pretend it never happened?'

'Why not?' she says. 'Melissa's done nothing. It's only what kids do all the time, you did it when you were a kid, went around with a bunch of kids, saw a fight now and again. Did it do you any harm? Did your mum and dad ever find out? It will only stress our Sarah out.'

'So who are we protecting here?' says Dave. 'And what if Melissa tells her?'

'She probably won't,' says Lynn, 'and if she does, well, we just explain don't we.'

'Have it your way,' says Dave, and goes unhappily to the kitchen to make the long-awaited cup of tea.

Until they are settled in bed that night, neither of them speaks again. It is as near as they get to a disagreement. Dave gets into bed beside Lynn and cannot stop himself.

'What's going to happen Lynnie? Why are we keeping a secret from Sarah all of a sudden? You know I don't like it.'

'I don't see,' says Lynn, 'that one more secret is going to make any difference.'

She reaches out and turns off the bedside light, leaving Dave staring into the darkness.

The Hedges is hot. It's hot and muggy outside and hot with heating inside. They feel the cold, the residents, they keep their cardigans on winter and summer, they shiver, most of them, if you open a window.

Niecey closes Hilda's door and opens her window. 'Tell me if you feel a draught,' she says. 'Just want to get a bit of air in.'

Hilda is incontinent. She has been washed and changed and installed in her chair, but her bed has now to be dealt with.

'Raining outside,' she observes. Niecey does not argue, but strips the bed and sprays and wipes down the plastic cover.

'Not talking to me this morning?' says Hilda. She is not completely daft.

'Sorry,' says Niecey. 'I was just thinking. Things on my mind.'

'Who opened that window?' says Hilda. 'All the warmth will go out, you know that don't you. You young girls, you don't think.'

'I'll close it in a minute,' says Niecey. 'The thing is though, there's all this stuff that I haven't told anyone, and now I've got to.'

'The rain will be coming in,' says Hilda. 'All my books will get wet.'

'See,' says Niecey, 'when I was young I did some silly things. Worse than silly. Bad.'

'You'll get told off,' says Hilda. 'I always tell people off when they do something like that. That soon stops them.'

'It's a long time ago,' says Niecey. 'I've paid for it, don't think I got away with anything, I've paid for it more than you can imagine. Just, now, people are asking questions.'

'Well, tell them,' says Hilda. 'Who opened that window, tell me that. When are you going to shut it?'

Niecey finishes the bed and moves to the washbasin. 'You never had children, did you Hilda? I did, and I was a bad mother. They took my children away.'

'Nothing but trouble, children,' says Hilda. 'I know, I worked in a school. I cooked the dinners.'

'Did you? I thought you were a teacher. Weren't you a teacher? You've got all these books.'

'You leave my books alone,' says Hilda. 'I did everything in that school. Nothing would have got done if

107

it wasn't for me. I told them all off *and* I cooked the dinners.'

Niecey switches on the vacuum cleaner. When she's done she closes the window, fills Hilda's water cup and puts it within reach, pats her hand and says goodbye.

'Goodbye,' says Hilda. 'Will you be coming next week?'

'I'll see you tomorrow,' says Niecey, and moves on to Beryl's room.

Beryl is bedbound. She lifts her hand feebly as Niecey comes in. This is an easy room to do as the bed is made later, when they come to turn Beryl, and as she can't get up she can't throw all her belongings about the way some people like to do. She is not taking much notice today, of anything.

'Hello Beryl,' says Niecey loudly. 'How are you today?'

Beryl whimpers a little, as if to say she is too ill to bother to speak, which is probably the case, but Niecey knows she likes to be talked to.

'I was a terrible mother,' she says. 'Not at first, when they were babies I was good at it, it was hard work but it was the best time, except me and Adrian were fighting all the time. Not fighting as in punching each other, but arguing. I was a disappointment to him, but he was a disappointment to me too. Well, Beryl, I can tell you this because I know you won't be telling anyone, I went right off sex, you know, I couldn't see the point, can you? I'll just open your window a tiny bit, for some fresh air. There, you'll be able to hear the birds singing.' Though this is untrue because, as Niecey well knows, Beryl is very deaf indeed.

'He was playing around with other girls,' she says. 'It wasn't even that I cared that much but it was costing money and we didn't have a lot. So we had rows about money. That was the beginning of the bad times. All right Beryl, they'll be in in a little while to see to you. And I'll see you soon, all right.'

She hoovers the corridor outside the two rooms she has done and takes the laundry bag down to the basement, using the stairs because she can hear Lynn's voice down by the lift. She and Lynn have been forced to avoid one another, neither of them admitting why this is.

She cleans the rooms of Peggy and Joyce, Derek and Norman – they are all in the day room so there is no conversation needed.

'Come for your coffee,' calls a colleague, and she goes, but takes hers into the residents' lounge, to avoid sitting with Lynn. On the TV screen a middle-aged housewife is confessing to a shopping habit. There are photographs of her wardrobe stuffed with shoes and handbags, and dresses still with their labels on. The woman says it's all because her mother died and left a gap in her life and the glossy presenter – who probably has just as many clothes in her own wardrobe – nods sympathetically. Of the residents only Margot appears to be taking an interest.

'Poor lady,' she says to Niecey. 'What's the matter with her?'

'Too many clothes,' says Niecey.

'Ah well,' says Margot as if philosophically. 'Could be worse.'

'You're right there,' says Niecey.

As she leaves the lounge Katie the manager pops her head out of her office. 'Can I have a word Niecey?'

The filing cabinet is open and she is flicking through the staff files. 'I can't find your DBS check,' she says. 'Did you ever get one done?'

'DBS?'

'What they used to call a CRB check. Criminal records. Same thing, different name. Did you ever fill in a form? Like this? The previous manager – what's her name? – she would have given you one.'

'I don't think she did,' says Niecey. 'I was only here three days before she left, and then you came.'

'My fault then,' says Katie cheerfully. 'Here you are, just fill in all your details and then you'll need to bring in some documents to prove who you are. It's just routine, we all have to do it.'

Niecey goes and locks herself in a bathroom and studies the form. 'Things can't get any worse,' she says aloud.

On Friday, the day a little cooler now, Niecey is in time to pick Leo up from school and stroll back home via the swings. He dashes up the steps of the slide, and down, then up again to show her how he can come down face first. He swarms up the climbing frame and down the fireman's pole. 'Watch me. Watch me.' She watches, intensely.

She buys him an ice cream as a Friday treat. The deadline is tomorrow. Jamie will come home, as usual. They will eat, he will play with Leo a while, then put him to bed, come back down, fetch himself a beer maybe, look to see what's on TV. Then she will have to tell him.

'I have to talk to you,' says Niecey.

'Don't sound so serious,' he says. 'You'll make me worried.'

'It's me who should be worried,' she says. She is standing in the doorway as if she might decide to leave.

'Come and sit down,' he says. 'Beside me, not over there. There's nowt on telly. Do you want a beer?'

'No,' she says. 'Thank you.' This is what she always says.

'Go on then.'

'Has your dad said anything to you? Or your mum?'

'What about?'

'About me.'

'Like what?'

'I've never told you this before – I didn't know how you'd take it – I had two children before.'

He lifts the can to his mouth but doesn't drink. After a bit he says, 'I thought maybe that was it.'

'Did you know?'

'Not as such. Was it them twins?'

'You knew.'

Now he takes a drink, not looking at her. 'I thought something of the sort.'

'And you never said.'

'I said to them you'd tell me, in the end.'

'Jamie.' She reaches her hand to his shoulder and he puts his hand over hers.

'Is that it then? Is that all you're going to tell me? Sarah thinks they died.'

'No,' she says. 'Not as bad as that. Or maybe worse, depending how you look at it.'

'You can tell me you know,' he says. 'Anything at all, it don't matter to me.'

She has been rehearsing this to herself for a week but still shakes her head as if she doesn't know what to say.

'They didn't die?' he says, trying to help. 'Where are they then?'

'Their dad's got them.'

'Adrian.'

'How did you know that? Dave *has* said something hasn't he.'

Jamie drains his can. 'I should have asked you straight out. When I found them certificates I mean. I should have asked you, not gone round to me mum and dad.'

'You found them?'

'In your box. When I were looking for that earring, remember.'

'When?'

'About three weeks since.'

'You could have asked me.'

'I were scared to. I shouldn't have gone to me mum though. I weren't thinking straight. Anyway, what would you have said?'

She looks him in the eye and almost smiles. 'I would most probably have lied.'

'Why would you though? If you didn't do anything wrong.'

'I made mistakes,' she says. 'I made a mess of my life. I'll tell you about it if you want to hear.'

'I don't know,' he says. 'After all this time – six years we've been together, more even – I don't know if it matters.'

'You can ask me anything you want,' she says. 'Any time you want. I'll tell you anything you want to know. And if your dad, or Gemma – any of them – if they ask you, you can say I've told you and it's all – all right?'

'It's all right,' he says. 'Of course it's all right. When I think of something to ask you, I'll ask you.'

They sit in silence for a little while. Then Niecey says, 'I think I might go to bed.'

'What now?' he says. 'It's not even dark yet.'

'I'm tired.'

'Want me to come with you?'

She hesitates. 'If you want to.'

'Course I do,' he says.

And she is relieved, she wants so much to be held, to be stroked, to be comforted. She wants to be where he can't see her face and to tell him how her heart is hollow because her children are gone. How Leo makes up for it – even Jamie makes up for it a little, but it is not enough. They are gone and she does not know where they are, or how they are, or who they are with; and how she has spent years of her life walking the streets of Sheffield, looking for someone, some two, who might be them. How she has had to cry in secret because there has been no one she can tell about what had happened. How her whole life has been a lie, because when she is being cheerful with Leo she is thinking of them, the other two; and when she is being polite and friendly with his family it is all an act, put on to cover up her grief and unhappiness.

How, even, she wants to love Jamie better, as he deserves. She always has wished that she could, but it feels as if she can only love children, even the ones who are not here in her life to be loved. She and Jamie lie together in bed as the light fades outside and she says none of these things out loud. *And I wept both day and night, And hid from him my heart's delight.*

Next morning though, early, she feels better, for telling him something at least. Dave will be off her case now. He was lovely, Jamie but – somehow – not interested enough. And why had he gone running off to his mother, instead of being brave enough to ask her? Six years they've been married, and not many cross words have passed between them – because he's so placid and she's so grateful – but why did he not trust her? What did he think she would do? And what now – will they have more conversations? Anything he asks she'll tell him, but why should she load him with all the crap that she carries around? Maybe he'll ask, maybe she'll tell, but there's a sense of disappointment that she hadn't been able to tell him everything. He hadn't wanted to know. Their lives started, for him, when they got together, but for Niecey, the most important things happened before she met him. Except for Leo. Nothing, now, is more important than Leo.

She sleeps a little and wakes again to find herself curled on her side, and Jamie curled around her, holding her. He's right behind me, she thinks, he's got my back, isn't that what they say. She must have moved and woken him. He moves his hand to hold her breast and she feels his penis twitch against her.

'Leo's awake,' she says. They can hear him muttering to himself and then a crackling crash as some Lego construction fails and falls. 'Not now,' she says.

She did want to love him. She does want to love him. He deserves all the love she can manage to spare. *Love seeketh not itself to please.*

'All right?' says Dave. He has been waiting at the sports field for Jamie to turn up with Leo.

'All right Dad,' says Jamie. He looks exactly as he usually does, solid and calm, and his pale blue eyes are steady and innocent.

Dave waits until Leo has run off to join the others. Then, 'Has Niecey said owt to you?'

'She told me you'd ask,' says Jamie. 'Yes, she's told me things. It's all OK.'

'You're all right?' Dave tries to look at him intently but Jamie seems not to notice; his eyes are following Leo as he struggles into his tabard and lines up with the others.

'No problem,' says Jamie.

As soon as the weather forecast finishes, Dave turns off the TV and gets to his feet, pushing himself up on the arms of the chair. 'That's that,' he says.

Lynn puts aside her magazine and takes off her glasses.

Dave checks that the front and back doors are locked and starts up the stairs. Lynn is already in the bathroom. The phone rings.

'Dad.'

'Gem? What's wrong?' Something has to be wrong for Gemma to be calling at this time of night, when she will be up before six tomorrow morning.

'Dad. I've found her. I know all about it. I've googled her, she's there, I've sent you a link.'

'Hold up a minute,' says Dave. Three minutes ago he was all but asleep and now Gemma's voice – urgent, almost panicky – threatens to wake him up again. 'Can this wait till tomorrow?'

Gemma pauses. Dave can imagine her looking at her phone to see the time. 'Shit,' she says. 'I need to get to sleep. I've sent you a link Dad. Check your email.'

'All right,' he says, and puts the phone down.

Lynn comes out of the bathroom. 'Who was that?'

'Gemma.'

'At this time of night? What's wrong?'

'I don't know. She says she's found something on the internet.'

'What, about Niecey?'

'I think so. She was a bit garbled. I said we'd leave it while tomorrow.'

But while Lynn is getting undressed he fetches his tablet and goes to his email. There is the one from Gemma. He can't not open it.

'Look, Lynn.'

She is already lying down. She says without opening her eyes, 'I thought you were leaving it till the morning.'

He says, 'You'll want to see this.'

'My glasses are downstairs. If you want me to read something you'll have to go and get them.' The fact that Dave does this without argument makes her sit up and look at the screen. She can see, even without her glasses, that it is an article from a Norwich local paper. The headline can be read by anyone not totally blind.

# DRUG DEALING MUM

and then, in smaller type:

### Children were filthy and starving

Lynn and Dave sit side by side, she under the duvet, he, still fully dressed, on top of it, and read the article.

Neglectful mother denies dealing drugs.

Denise Wilson, 24, pleaded not guilty yesterday to possession of Class A substances, with intent to supply.

The court heard that when police, alerted by her estranged husband, broke into a flat in Sprowston, they found what Detective Sergeant Bacon called 'a treasure trove of drugs and stolen goods' under the defendant's bed and in the wardrobe. He said the defendant claimed that she was not involved in the drug-dealing enterprise, but was unable to give the police details of who was responsible.

In another bedroom, continued DS Bacon, the police found the defendant's two children, three year old twins, 'filthy and cold.' It appeared that they had been given only biscuits to eat for some days, according to the doctor who examined them.

Wilson was found guilty on three counts of drug dealing and a number of counts of theft and handling stolen goods and sentenced to four years in prison.

Her children are being cared for by their father's family and a prosecution for neglect is likely to be brought in due course.

'I've read it four times,' says Lynn. 'I still can't take it in. Is it her? Is it Niecey?'

Dave is still on his fourth reading.

'I won't sleep,' says Lynn. 'How can we get to sleep now? What was Gemma thinking of?'

'I won't sleep either lass,' says Dave.

But they do.

*

'I can't go to work,' says Lynn. 'There's no way I can face her is there. I'm going to have to call in sick.' She is dressed for work, except for her shoes, and is standing with her hand on the kitchen door, holding it closed as if burglars are trying to get in.

'I don't get it,' says Dave. He is sitting at the table in pyjama bottoms and vest, looking into his coffee cup as if it will tell him something. 'I told you didn't I, that Jamie spoke to me on Saturday, when I saw him. He's told me, clear as anything, that it's all right, she's explained it to him, he knows all about it, nothing to worry about, water under the bridge, done and dusted, all that. I've said to him haven't I, have a word with our Gemma, put her mind at ease. And now –'

'I can't go,' says Lynn. 'I just can't. If I could stay out of her way I would, but you know what it's like, you can't tell where anyone's going to be at any one time, I could pass her in the corridor or on the stairs, I could be in the same room. She won't know I know, I'd have to say something, I can't trust myself –'

'I don't know where to go from here,' says Dave. 'Do we just leave it to Jamie to sort it out? Do we tell Gemma to stay out of it, she won't forget it will she. She'll tell Sarah, she'll tell Mark, Sarah will tell Jon, one of them will say something to Jamie, then where will we be? There's no keeping control of this –'

'I should be doing the medications this morning,' says Lynn. 'Katie's in a meeting with the managing group, then she's on leave for the rest of the week, and there's a funeral I said I'd show me face at. I don't like to let them down, but I can't trust meself –'

'They'll all be at work by now,' says Dave. 'Maybe I can catch Gemma when she's on her break. Maybe I should go and see Jamie, he's only working on Halifax Road –'

'Don't you say anything to Jamie without me there,' says Lynn. 'Don't you dare. You know what's happened don't you. She's told him enough of a story to explain those birth certificates, she's told him it was her sister, or her cousin, or something, some lie, and he's believed it and now she thinks it's all over and he thinks there's no problem, and I don't want to upset him all over again, and I don't want him to fall out with his sisters – I just want it all to be all right.'

'Go to work,' says Dave. 'What will you do all day if you don't? Tough it out Lynnie, that's all you can do. You're going to see her sooner or later, just keep out of her way as much as you can, try to have someone else by you all the time so you don't get tempted to say – well, whatever you feel like saying. Once you're there it will feel better.'

'What will you do? Remember, don't say anything to Jamie – I want to be there.'

'You're right, it wouldn't do, not while he's at work. To be honest love, I don't know what I'll do. I had the day all planned and now I can hardly remember what I meant to do. It looks like rain as well.'

'You're right,' says Lynn. 'I'd better go to work. Putting it off won't make it any easier.' She goes to the front door now and slips her shoes on.

'Go on then,' he says. 'Get off before you're too late. What time are you on till?'

'Till four. See you about half past.'

'I'll have the kettle on.'

*

Sarah has been at work all day and has just come home. Jon, for a change, has been home for a while and he and the children have already eaten. Now Dom, unusually, is quietly doing his homework in front of the TV; Melissa is loading the dishwasher; Jon is taking washing out of the drier and folding it. He stops when he sees Sarah and goes to put her meal in the microwave.

'That is really nice,' she says, to him and to Melissa. 'It's so great to come home and find everything under control. Thanks for doing that Mel. Don't switch it on – I'll put my plate in when I'm done. Have you got homework?'

'Finished it,' she says. 'Can I go round and see Dani?'

'Back here by nine then.'

'OK.'

Sarah takes her plate from the microwave. 'Isn't it brilliant,' she says to Jon. 'Sometimes?'

'Gemma's been on the phone,' he says. 'Sounding a bit agitated. I said you'd call her back.'

'I will, after I've eaten.' But the phone rings again just as Sarah is finishing her meal – by the time she has ended the call her plate will be dried and encrusted and the dishwasher will still be waiting to be switched on.

'What was that all about?' says Jon. He has been lightly dozing in front of the news.

Sarah flops onto the settee. 'I don't know where to start,' she says. 'It's serious, I can tell you that much, Mum and Dad already know, Gemma told them last night but she hasn't had time to speak to them today –'

'What though?'

'I don't know how to begin,' she says again. 'It's about Niecey.'

'Something about those birth certificates?' Jon does not sound very interested; he had not seemed to feel that Jamie's discovery was anything to make a fuss over in the first place.

'Well yes, sort of. Except it's got much more serious. Gemma's found this report on the internet –'

'She doesn't want to believe everything she reads on there.'

'No, I know, but this sounds real enough. She's found a woman called Denise Wilson who was done for drug offences, and thieving, in Norwich, and got sent to prison.'

'Denise Wilson – must be plenty of those around.'

'I know, but wait. This one had twins – it doesn't say their names – but they were only little. We're going back ten years or more. But the dates fit. And how many of all these Denise Wilsons have a pair of twins.'

'Doesn't prove that it's Niecey though does it? Or was there a photo of her?'

'No. But why would she have those certificates if they're not her children?'

'So what happens now?' Jon is apparently not interested any further in the ins and outs and ifs and buts that Sarah has gone through at length with Gemma. He is the sort of man who calls a committee back to the main issue, gets a decision, knows who will do it and by when. Next item.

'We don't know. We're going round to Mum and Dad's now.'

'Again.'

'It's important. We need to think about Jamie.'

'Sarah, he's a grown up. Which is something his family don't seem to recognise.'

'If something like this happened to Dom, wouldn't you be concerned. I bet you would.'

'Sure I would. But the difference is – at least I hope so – Dom isn't going to be the sort of person to get himself mixed up with a person like that.'

'What do you mean, a person like that? I thought you liked Niecey.'

'I do, as far as it goes. Or I did. But you know she's a wreck, mentally, always has been. And if all this stuff is true, well, that changes how we think of her, doesn't it?'

'I think so too. I tried to like her, but now I think it was only because she was part of the family. And you know – well I thought Gemma felt the same about her, but now she's saying we've been mean to her and there might be two sides to it.'

'No doubt,' says Jon, turning up the volume on the TV, 'no doubt you'll be hearing all the sides there are in due course. It'll all come out in the end. It always does.'

\*

The sun has gone down when, though no one has asked them to, Gemma and Sarah appear, together. Lynn is lying back in her chair with her feet on a footstool and her eyes closed. She opens them as her daughters come into the room, but says nothing. Dave comes through, drying his hands.

'What now then,' says Sarah. Not so much a question, more like an accusation.

'Jamie told me he knows everything,' says Dave. 'He told me Saturday morning, at Leo's football.'

'How did he seem about it then?'

'He were fine. I would say very happy. He said – if I can remember exactly – he said, "Niecey says to tell you she told me all about it, and that's an end to it."'

'And you didn't ask him any more?'

'Didn't seem necessary. He were happy enough and that's what it were all about weren't it.'

'She's not told him,' says Sarah. 'There's no way he'd be feeling all right if she's told him all we know. She's told him part of it, maybe, what she thinks she can get away with, that's all.'

'So who is going to tell him?' says Gemma. 'I think it should be you two.' She waves a hand to take in Dave and Lynn.

'I think just Mum,' says Sarah. 'Dad's too much on her side. Niecey's side I mean. He always sticks up for her.'

'But he's better at breaking something gently,' says Gemma.

'You think there's a gentle way to break this, do you? How would you do that then?'

'Girls,' says Dave. 'Can we take this a bit more slowly? Your mother and I haven't seen each other all day. She's been at work and I –'

'Did you see her?' says Sarah. 'What was she like? How did you look her in the face?'

Lynn closes her eyes again, and shrugs.

'She's had a hard day,' says Dave. 'Manager's day off, you know, and a funeral to go to. Bit of a headache.'

'Sorry Mum,' says Gemma. 'We didn't know what to do so we thought we ought to come round. Probably I shouldn't have sent that to you late at night, I should have waited for a better time.'

'Like what?' says Sarah. 'What sort of better time could there conceivably be?' She is the most wound up of all of them, ready to snap. 'Look, I'll go round there right now and tell him, if no one else will. I'm not scared of her, whatever she's like.'

'Hey Sis,' says Gemma. 'Don't get yourself in a state. I'll come with you, just as soon as we've talked it through with Mum and Dad. But let's not go off half-cock.'

Dave smiles at her. 'That's what I always say,' he says. 'Tell you what, I'll put the kettle on, we'll think it through. We don't want to make things worse than they are –'

'How could they be?' says Sarah, but she gets up before Dave does and goes to the kitchen herself.

'I couldn't find any more online,' says Gemma. 'It doesn't seem to have been in any of the national papers, just that local one.'

'So no report of the court case for neglecting them children?' says Dave.

Gemma shrugs. 'Couldn't find it.'

Sarah returns with mugs on a tray. Lynn levers herself up straight and speaks for the first time. 'I looked for her DBS check,' she says.

'What?' says Dave.

'You know,' she says. 'What used to be called a CRB check – for criminal records. Obviously we have them at work, so I looked in the file for Niecey's.'

'And?'

'Not there,' she says, and sips her tea.

'Not there,' says Sarah. 'How can she not have one? Everyone has one.'

'No idea,' says Lynn. 'But I looked, had a proper look, all through, and it's not there.'

'Could she have taken it out?' says Dave. 'Knowing that we're on to her, as you might say?'

'I suppose she could,' says Lynn. 'Obviously the office is open, even if Katie's not in it, but the filing cabinet is kept locked, and Niecey wouldn't have a key. Even I don't have a key except on a day like today when Katie's not there. So it wouldn't be easy.'

'It's beside the point,' says Sarah. 'We know she wouldn't have a job there if the manager knew about her conviction, so somehow she's got away with it so far, but Mum, you'll have to tell Katie tomorrow.'

Lynn does not respond but leans back again and closes her eyes once more, balancing her mug on the arm of her chair.

'So,' says Sarah. 'What are we doing? Or rather, when are we doing it?'

'I think you're right,' says Dave. 'It will be better coming from his mum and me. Maybe even tonight, if your mum's up to it. Nothing to be gained by putting it off. What do you think Lynnie?'

Lynn does not move, or open her eyes but she says, slowly and loudly, this: '*No one* is going to tell Jamie. No one is going to ruin that boy's life. No one is going to take that away from him.'

'Take what away?' says Sarah, crossly.

'You know perfectly well,' says Lynn. 'He loves Niecey. He's never been so happy in his life. What would he do if he knew all this? Would he leave her?'

'No, he'd chuck her out,' says Gemma softly.

'And what about Leo?'

'He could keep Leo,' says Dave. 'We'd rally round.'

'And how would Leo be without his mum?' says Lynn. 'Do you think it's easy to pull a family apart? Do you think they just shuffle themselves like a pack of cards and carry on as usual?' She's sitting up now and her eyes are open, her forehead creased with headache. 'Anyone – anyone at all – who goes and upsets our Jamie with all of this – I'll never see them, I'll never speak to them again. And that,' she says, 'that goes for you too David Wilde.'

'She means it,' Dave told his daughters, though they did not doubt it. He stands up. 'You'll be wanting to get off home. Your mum's tired. We'll see you soon.' He steps across the small room and gives them each a kiss on the cheek. 'Keep it under your hats for now, eh.'

As they walk together down the path Gemma says, 'She's got a point. I don't want to destroy Jamie and I know you don't. But she never said we couldn't talk to Niecey. Did she?'

'Are you,' says Dave to Lynn, 'serious? What you said, do you really mean it? Would you break up the family, would you break off any sort of relations? What are we supposed to do then?'

Lynn opens her eyes and looks at him for a full half minute before she speaks. 'I do mean it. But I don't know if I could do it, if it came to it.'

'So just an empty threat then?' says Dave.

'Do you want to find out?' She closes her eyes again.

'Are you sure?' says Mark. 'Are you sure Gem, do you know what you're doing?'

'What do you mean?' says Gemma. 'We can't just forget about it can we?'

'If Jamie can, surely you can.'

'We don't think Jamie knows about all this,' she says. 'We think she's told him some lie, or some bit of it that doesn't sound too bad and he's just accepted it. Because that's the sort of person he is – he doesn't want to make a fuss, he won't want to upset anyone, you know what he's like. He doesn't stick up for himself. A bit weak.'

'He's a decent bloke,' says Mark. 'He's not weak, I wouldn't call him weak. Quiet, not pushy, but not weak. You only think that because you've spent your life looking out for him – you and Sarah, and your mum and dad – he's never had to put himself forward.'

'It's Mum,' says Gemma, 'who's running this thing now. We couldn't believe it, me and Sarah, when she said that. Do you think she means it? Sarah says we should go ahead and she'll come round in the end.'

'Do you want to risk it?' says Mark. 'What do you gain?'

'We get to the truth. Jamie gets to know the truth.'

'And what does he lose?'

'But look at what she *did*. How can we ignore that and go, oh, it's fine, we have a criminal in the family but never mind, she's all right really. Mark – *she's looked after our kids.*'

'The kids were fine, weren't they?'

'They like her, but they don't know do they? Suppose –'

'What? Do you think she's doing stuff now that would get her arrested?'

'She might be.'

'Where's your evidence? Gem, you're getting carried away about something that happened a long time ago. Didn't you ever do anything bad?'

'Not *that* bad.'

'No,' he says, 'neither did I. But you've known people who got into bad stuff. It's not always as simple as it seems, is it? Look at our Chris.'

'He didn't mean it.'

'In the paper though it sounded bad didn't it – drinking, driving, going through a garden wall, could have killed somebody.'

'But it weren't like that.'

'Not to us, no, because we know him, don't we. We know he was having a bad time, we know he was getting divorced, he was missing his kids, but if you just see it in the paper, or if you're that woman that's had his car nearly come into her front room, you'd have a different take on it wouldn't you.'

'It's not the same,' says Gemma. 'Anyway, he's only your cousin – not even your first cousin. Niecey is close family. We can't just go on as if we don't know about it.'

'All I'm saying,' says Mark, 'is listen before you accuse her so much that you destroy her. Because all the time I've known her I don't know anything bad about her.'

'You,' says Gemma, 'are too nice for your own good. It's a good thing one of us is tough.'

He puts his arm around her wide shoulders. 'You're not as tough as you think you are. Just think about it,' he says.

She leans her head against him, briefly. 'All right,' she says. 'I'll think about it.'

*

'If it was you though,' says Sarah. 'If someone knew something about me, something like that, wouldn't you want them to tell you?'

'If you knew it for sure – is this the sort of evidence that would stand up in a court of law? Are you absolutely certain that she is this person? Because if you're not sure –'

'We are all sure,' says Sarah. 'She's admitted to Dad and to Jamie that they are her children, she's admitted – as good as – that she was married before, she's told Dad she lived in Norwich. It all adds up.'

'I'll leave it to you,' says Jon. 'You and Gemma won't listen to me will you.' He picks up a pile of papers – some sort of job applications – and starts to leave the room.

'Thanks for your support,' says Sarah bitterly.

'What do you want me to do? You've got it all covered, you're going to see her – two of you. You're going to accuse her, probably threaten her and then what?'

'That's what I want to talk to you about. You know, talk it through, like people do. But you just back out don't you, just like when I want to talk about Melissa, you don't want to discuss it, you don't seem to care.'

'*I* don't seem to care? Seems to me you care more about whatever Niecey did or didn't do than about your own family.'

'Jamie *is* my own family.'

'More important than *our* children?'

'As if you care –'

'I care about Melissa,' he says, on his way out of the room. 'In fact I've got enough to care about here, without bothering about some distant bit of family.'

'You call my own brother distant,' shouts Sarah after him, but the door is closed behind him.

*

'What will you do?' says Dave. 'About the DBR check – whatever you call it – about telling Katie?'

'You know Katie's on leave,' says Lynn. Her eyes are dull with tiredness. 'I can't do anything until she comes back.'

'Shouldn't you tell somebody? To cover yourself?'

'Don't start,' she says. 'I've been worrying about it all night. I've decided – I'm doing nothing. Sooner or later Katie will check; I don't want to be involved.'

'But then won't they think you knew all along? Wouldn't it look bad?'

'I'm past caring,' she says. 'All I want is for things to go back to normal. I want to know that my children are all right and I want to see my grandchildren without getting mixed up in something I know nothing about, and don't want to know anything about. I want it to be like it used to be.'

'Lynnie,' he says, 'you know it can't be. You can't not know something once you know it.'

'I can try,' she says. 'Watch me. I'm stubborn that way.'

Jacqui Thwaite, formerly Wilson, takes a walk round her garden, mug of coffee in her hand, noting that the roses will soon be over, that the delphiniums, having been doctored with slug pellets, are doing better this year, that there are rogue opium poppies where they shouldn't be and if she doesn't act quickly self-sown seedlings will be coming up everywhere. Her favourite clematis – the dark purple one – is just beginning to flower.

One more week until school breaks up for the summer. Six weeks of school holiday. No prospect of Adrian coming over. No prospect of *those other grandparents* helping out in any way at all, even if she would allow them to. No hope of getting the twins into any sort of summer camp, even on a day-basis – Lila might go if she had a friend to go with but Ollie wouldn't even bring himself to discuss the idea. It would only upset him to try. No hope, then, of even a night or two away with Bruce. Every year she has thought with longing of a weekend in a good hotel, one with spa treatments and an award-winning chef, somewhere in the Lake District or the Cotswolds, and every year she has come to the conclusion that it can't be done, and every year she has thought, Next year, maybe by next year they'll be old enough to stay with a friend, or maybe she will have found some way of getting someone to move in for a few days to look after things. Maybe Bruce's sister – but she knows that Ollie wouldn't handle it. There are times when she thinks he will never leave home, not even to go to university, clever though he is.

She is deeply attached to her grandchildren. She loves them. She will miss them when – if – they leave home. *And* she wishes the day could come soon when her life would again be under her own control.

The plan is to invite Niecey round to Sarah's house – having got the family out of the way – and to confront her with the evidence.

'Jon will probably go out,' says Sarah to Gemma. 'He'll go to badminton and then to the pub. Melissa will be out with her friends, so if your Mark will have Dom round at yours we can get on with no interruptions.'

'Are you sure you want to do this?' says Gemma.

'Don't back out on me now,' says Sarah. 'We can't do nothing, you know we can't. It will haunt us for ever.'

'But if she admits it, what then?'

'Of course she'll admit it. There's no way she can talk her way out of it, not with the evidence we've got.'

'But what then?'

'That's all I want,' says Sarah. 'I want to know, from her, from the horse's mouth, what she is and what she's done and want her to know that we know.'

'Why though?'

'Gemma,' says Sarah. 'I never thought I'd hear you talking like this. What's the matter with you? You're the one who spent all that time searching for evidence and now you're not backing me up on this. If I have to do it on my own I will, don't worry, but I thought we were in this together.'

'Fine,' says Gemma. 'I'm just trying to think, what next?'

'Well don't. I'll bring Dom down to you Friday after tea, then we'll pick her up and come back here. We'll have all evening to get through it.'

Sarah drives the short distance from Loxley to Hillsborough, then, with Gemma next to her in the front, up the hill to Walkley.

'Are you sure?' says Gemma.

'Quite sure,' says Sarah, bringing the car to a halt and sounding the horn. She does not look at her sister, and adds, 'So are you. What else can we do? We have to do something.'

'Do we?' says Gemma. 'We could just go for a drink.'

Niecey comes out, freshly showered and made up, dressed as always in leggings and a long-sleeved top. Unsuspecting, presumably.

When they get to Sarah's house she offers tea and coffee and wine, she brings out a bowl of nuts – it's as if it really is a social occasion, a girls' night in, or as if, now, she is putting off the moment when they have to get down to the hard business. Niecey is quiet, still standing looking out at the front garden, a little thrown maybe by the unaccustomed quietness of the other two, by the absence of the children.

'Come and sit down,' says Sarah. 'We want to talk to you.' Her voice comes out harshly, as maybe she meant it to, but she seems to be shocked by it herself and softens it to say, 'There, that's your glass.' She and Niecey are drinking white wine, Gemma is on a diet again and takes only water.

Niecey takes a large, panicky swig of her drink. She does not look at either of them, she puts her glass down, she ruffles through her handbag for something that she never produces, she adjusts the strap of her sandal.

'Niecey,' says Gemma, pleadingly, and stops.

'Here,' says Sarah. She passes Niecey a sheet of paper, printed. Niecey takes it, turns it, reads it. Gemma and Sarah wait – surely she has read it by now, when will she say something, when will she lift her head – until at last Sarah, who seems to be in charge of proceedings says, 'Well?'

Niecey appears to be reading it yet again.

'Is it you?' says Sarah, sharply. 'Do you admit it?'

'Sis,' says Gemma quietly. 'Go easy.'

At last Niecey looks up. 'I suppose it must be,' she says.

'What do you mean, *it must be*? You must know.'

'I've never seen it before,' says Niecey, 'but, yes, it's me.'

'That's all I wanted to know,' says Sarah, and leans back in her chair, and takes a long swallow of her wine.

Gemma looks at her sister in a stunned sort of way; Niecey has looked back down as if she is learning the newspaper report off by heart.

'It's not all I want to know,' says Gemma, and her voice comes out so loud that she seems to startle herself.

'I suppose,' says Niecey, 'that this is why your dad was coming round every Saturday, asking me questions.'

'You didn't tell him though, did you? About this?'

'He never mentioned this.' Niecey waits.

Sarah, usually the more polite of the sisters, is tonight the more wound up, more ungracious. Gemma, who can be outspokenly blunt, is tonight more cautious, holding back, letting Sarah do the talking. But now that Sarah has declared herself satisfied and finished there is a long silence, until Niecey and Gemma speak at once.

'Does Jamie know?'

They listen to the echo of their two voices – they almost laugh at the synchronicity; they realise at the same moment that neither of them can answer the question.

Then Sarah speaks again. 'Yes,' she says forcefully. 'Does Jamie know? What did you tell him? What did he say? He can't be all right with this can he? You can't tell me he knows all this and he's all right about it.'

'Jamie knows some of it,' says Niecey. 'Unless one of you has shown him –' she waves the piece of paper.

'No we haven't,' says Gemma. 'We didn't think it were right to. But you've got to see – it's a bit of a shock to us all – Mum and Dad. I mean, you're part of the family –'

Sarah makes a sort of sceptical honk into her wine glass – her wine is almost gone; Niecey, after her first taste has not looked at hers.

'I can explain,' says Niecey, though there is doubt in her voice.

'*I* don't want any explanations,' says Sarah. 'You'll only be lying. What's the point? In fact,' she says, reaching for the bottle and refilling her glass, 'I don't think there's any more to be said. I think this evening is over. We've got to the truth, that's all we need. Tomorrow I shall be calling your employer and telling her why she needs to check your records again and I dare say that by Monday you'll be suspended and our Mum won't have to see you every day of her life. And I'm *not* going to say anything to Jamie, but that's not out of any sort of feeling for you, it's only because our Mum has forbidden it, and we respect her wishes. And –' She stops to take a drink.

'Sar –' says Gemma.

'I'll go then shall I?' says Niecey.

Sarah does not answer and Gemma looks from one to the other, frowning with confusion. Niecey stands, slowly, still with the piece of paper in her hand. She glances at it once more and then folds it and tucks it into her bag. Still slowly, as if not quite sure that there is no more going to be said to her, she leaves the room, opens the front door, closes it softly behind her and they see her walking slowly past the picture window, not looking in at them.

'How many have you had?' says Gemma. 'You're not driving me home anyway. I'll walk.'

Niecey is not far down the road before she hears Gemma's voice behind her. 'Niecey. Wait.' She pretends she hasn't heard and continues to stroll thoughtfully through the evening, past front gardens full of roses and men mowing their lawns and teenage girls walking about together and boys riding bikes. The sky is still light but the sun has gone, the colours have turned soft and the shadows are dim.

Niecey hears Gemma's footsteps running to catch her and then Gemma is there by her side, gasping a little with the unaccustomed effort.

'Thought I'd come with you – Sarah – can't drive – drunk too many.'

They walk in silence past the family houses with their family cars in the drives and their sense of settling down for the evening after a long warm day, and turn on to the Loxley Road, towards the town.

'Go on then,' says Gemma. 'Explain.'

'It's hard,' says Niecey. 'Even to myself – I don't know why I did some of the things I did.'

They walk for fifty yards or so, down hill. Then Niecey says, 'I wouldn't mind telling someone about it, it's not – well, I am ashamed, but –'

'Did you trick Jamie into marrying you?' says Gemma. 'That's one thing I'd like to know.'

'No,' says Niecey. She sounds shocked. 'No, I didn't even think of it. It was Jamie wanted to get married. He *asked* me.'

'But did you get pregnant on purpose though? I mean, you'd not been together very long had you.'

Niecey, hiding her face from Gemma, looks over towards the Retirement Village, with its banners and reassuring walls. 'It's hard to say isn't it? It wasn't a good time to have a baby – I only had a room in a hostel to live in, and no money and no job – it wasn't very clever to get pregnant, I knew that. But Gem, did you ever *want* a baby so much that – well, that you would just go ahead and do it.'

'Not really,' says Gemma. 'Is that because of the other two?'

'They're nearly fourteen,' says Niecey. 'I haven't seen them since – well, for eleven years. Almost exactly eleven years. Eleven years on July the twentieth. In the afternoon.'

Gemma says nothing. It is here that they would probably go in different directions to their separate houses but they carry on walking together. Then she says, 'Don't you know where they are?'

'Their father has custody of them, but from what I know of him, he won't be looking after them all by himself. I think he might have left them with his mother.'

'Doesn't anybody tell you? Don't you have any rights?'

'Apparently not. They might be somewhere in America, but I thought – well, I hoped, that they might be in Sheffield. His mother lived here you see – I know she had them at first – she had a residence order. That's why I came here. I thought – well, I wasn't thinking very much, I was just on what do they call it? – autopilot. I had the idea that I would see them, I would find them, they would just *be* here, in full view. I thought it would be easy.'

'But they could be anywhere,' says Gemma. 'Sheffield's a big place. She could have taken them somewhere else anyway. You can't find people by just wandering around –' She stops walking for a step, then is beside Niecey again. 'That's what you were doing up at Meadowhead. When I saw you outside the school. Why didn't you *tell* us?'

Niecey waves a hand which communicates, Look what happens when people find out.

'But we could have helped you. What if Tash or Melissa knows them? They might be on Facebook. They might be looking for *you*. But what if they're in another city – you can't search them all. Anyway, what if they've forgotten you, what if they think you're dead? What if their dad has married again?'

'I know,' says Niecey. 'I've thought of all these things. It's exhausting.'

They have reached the junction where they will have to separate. Gemma will go straight on and Niecey right and up the hill. They pause, on the noisy corner among the high-heeled girls and T-shirted youths.

'Are you all right?' says Gemma.

'As all right as I'll ever be,' says Niecey, and smiles, a little.

'I'm sorry about Sarah,' says Gemma. 'I don't know what's got into her. Unless she's had a row with Jon.'

'Maybe she's worried about something. Melissa maybe?'

'Possible,' agrees Gemma.

'You know,' says Niecey, 'I wouldn't mind talking to you again. I feel – I don't know – a bit lighter. As if I've – I don't know – do you know what I mean?'

'I'll text you,' says Gemma. 'When I've got a spare hour. One evening.'

'Soon,' says Niecey. 'Before I change my mind.'

She should have known that telling Jamie half of it would not be the end. But she had relaxed after that, she thought that would be enough. And now there it is, the truth, out. *A truth that's told with bad intent beats all the lies you can invent.*

Telling. Opening the box of horrors again. Admitting to what happened. Saying it out loud.

Oh, she's had counselling. Six sessions with a nice woman at the GP's. She had hopes that she would help find the children but she said there was no way she could get involved in that, and that made Niecey feel there was no point in the whole exercise. Part of her wanted to tell everything but she knew she could only see her six times and she knew that wouldn't be enough. How long would have been enough? She really didn't know, and she doesn't know now, how long it might have taken. Sometimes it feels like it would take the length of her lifetime all over again to explain it to anyone, and other times it feels like she could say it in two sentences. *I fucked up. They sent me to prison and took my kids away. There, two sentences.*

So why does she think that Gemma would listen? Jamie's had the two sentence version, Dave wants the complete and unabridged version, Sarah, she believes, would just like her not to be here any more, she thinks she would want her dead. Gemma is such a complicated person, sometimes friendly, sometimes dismissive and critical; you never know where you are with her, which Gemma will you get today, what will she be like next time? Could she trust her not to tell the worst bits to Sarah? No she couldn't.

The counselling woman had seemed keen to know about her parents and her childhood, so that's what she told her about and it lasted all six sessions and didn't change a thing. Niecey got the impression that she was wasting her time, moaning about her middle class upbringing with parents who only wanted her to do well and get a good education. 'It sounds like,' she said, 'your mum was a really good role model.' As if she ever wanted to be like her in any way at all.

'I don't know where to start,' says Niecey.

Jamie has taken Leo and Jake to the park for a kickabout, Gemma and Niecey are sitting – a little stiffly – in the front room.

'Start at the beginning?' suggests Gemma.

'No, tell you what, you ask me a question.'

'I don't know what to ask.'

'Whatever you like. Something you want to know.'

Pause.

'What was it like in prison?'

It takes a while for Niecey to come up with an answer. 'Vile,' she says at last. 'Hell. Cold, hard, echoey, like an indoor swimming baths, you know?'

'Were you scared?'

'You better believe I was scared. You would be scared, Sarah would.'

'Of the other women? Or the wardens?'

'Warders they're called. Some of them are a bit scary, but you know that they have rules. Most of the prisoners are OK but some – a few – are bad people. They can scare you. Mostly what scares you I think is just the amount of – the amount of misery. It's just miserable. Everyone is miserable. Everyone is missing their mum or their boyfriend –'

'Or their kids,' says Gemma.

'Yeah,' says Niecey, 'their kids. People cry, at night especially, you can hear them, people cut themselves, I shared with one girl who pulled her hair out. Not a little bit – handfuls, just tugged out, screaming all the time.'

'Couldn't you stop her?'

'People don't like being stopped Gem. You want to hurt yourself – cut yourself, say – well, you want to be on your own, but if you can't be, then you don't want anyone watching. You turn away on your bed, you pretend you're asleep or something, but really you're scratching at your arm or something –'

'What with?'

'Whatever you've got. Fingernails, a bit of plastic from somewhere, whatever. You can't stop yourself, you know it's hurting, you want it to hurt more. Even you know they'll put you on watch if they find out but you don't care –'

'What's on watch?'

'Where they check you all the time, in case you do yourself in.'

'Did you do it? Cut yourself?'

'A bit,' says Niecey.

'That's why you always wear long sleeves, isn't it? But Jamie has seen?'

'Of course. Jamie takes me as I am, that's the nice thing about him. One of the nice things.'

'I haven't told Sarah I'm talking to you,' says Gemma. 'In fact I've not spoke to her since that night.'

'That's not like you two.'

'I've thought about it. I don't want to be – I don't know – against her. But she's not called me, or texted, or anything. Mark says I should have called her this weekend – yesterday – and pretend nothing happened, but how can I?'

'It wasn't so bad,' says Niecey. 'She won't hold it against you, surely.'

'Have you got a sister?'

'No.'

'Brother?'

'No.'

'Are your parents really dead then?'

'I don't know,' says Niecey. 'I stopped seeing them.'

'Why?'

'I don't know. Yes, I do know – partly I was scared to go home, partly I wanted to punish them, partly I was happy to be free of them. I dropped out of university and that made it hard for them to find me. I don't even know if they tried to find me – they might have been as pleased to see the back of me as I was to get away.'

Gemma's face shows how stunned – disgusted even – she is by this admission. 'What does Jamie say about that? That you come from that sort of family? None of us could ever say a thing like that.'

'I know,' says Niecey. 'But not all families are like yours.'

'So when they took your children,' says Gemma, 'I suppose it felt quite normal to you?'

'No,' says Niecey loudly, shocked. ''Well I suppose – not normal – I wouldn't say that. I suppose I knew I deserved it. In a way. Not as much as they said though.'

'Who took them? Were it Social Services?'

'Their dad had them. Adrian. I told you.'

135

'But Social Services must know where they are.'

'No. He has Parental Responsibility, just like Mark has for your kids, so he can do as he likes.'

'Mark can't do as he likes.'

'He could if you were – away, or something. Say there's a letter from school that has to be signed, and you're not there to do it – well, he can do it.'

'Of course he can. But he can't just walk off with them.'

'If you were in prison he could.'

'But you said his mother had them.'

'She did at first – they told me that before the trial. Adrian was trying to get a job, he was still backwards and forwards to America – his dad was there, he was ill I think. It was all quite jumbled in my mind at the time – I just wanted to see my babies, they told me she had them in Sheffield, I wasn't allowed to travel away from Norwich – I had to stay in a bail hostel – I couldn't do anything very much. I thought they'd let me off – I couldn't believe that someone like me could go to prison.'

'But you did.'

'Oh I did.'

They sit for several minutes. They sip at their water. They do not look each other in the eye.

'What I really –' begins Gemma, but the sound of Jake and Leo coming through the back door forces her to stop.

When Adrian called his mother, eleven years ago, to say he was back home – she hadn't even known he had been out of the country – and there was a bit of an emergency, it was, for Jacqui, the start of a whole new life. Just like that. No warning, no planning, no training and even – quite honestly – no desire to be a hands-on grandmother. Not even for a weekend, never mind for more than a decade.

She drove down to the address he gave, driving across the fens and down through rural Norfolk, under the impression that his wife was ill, in hospital, and that he needed her for a day or two to look after a pair of children, not quite three years old. They would be a little upset, she anticipated, but they would be charming and talkative. She would take them for walks and read them stories. She had no worries about her competence to deal with them. They would be toilet-trained of course, and Adrian, in between visiting times, would be able to help with them. If it turned out that he and Denny needed help for more than a weekend, then no doubt *her* parents would come down from Cheshire.

She was not prepared for the fact that Adrian was in a hotel with them, as the flat they had been living in was now a crime scene. The children had no clothes other than what they stood up in – which was pyjamas – and no toys. They were crying when she arrived and stopped crying only rarely, when bribed with sweets. Their toilet training was by no means complete; Adrian had acquired nappies from somewhere but they were too small, and so tight round their waists that they had started to pull them off and run about the room half naked. Their hair, which was, naturally, black and curly like Adrian's, was matted and tangled. At least that was something she could deal with – she was a hairdresser, wasn't she, though it was years since she had actually handled hair, rather than accounts spreadsheets.

Jacqui, learning about what had been going on, realised there was nothing to be gained by staying in Norwich. Denny was in a bail hostel, forbidden to see the children; Adrian clearly had no idea how to look after them and was happy to hand them over. It was difficult enough persuading him to come back with her to Sheffield.

'There are things I have to do,' he said. His voice had a distinct American intonation now.

'There is no way,' said Jacqui, 'that I can drive all the way to Sheffield on my own with them crying in the back of the car. You are their father. They need you to be with them and stay until they're settled.'

'I am busy,' he said.

'Yes you are,' she said. 'You are busy looking after your children. You should never have gone off and left them in the first place. How long were you away?'

'A week or two,' he said, but he did not look at her.

'Tell me the truth,' she said. It felt as if he was a little boy again, in trouble for sneaking biscuits from the cupboard, or wandering too far from home.

He went away in February. It was now July. He had had difficulty finding his wife and children because she was no longer in the flat he had left her in.

'Why not?' asked Jacqui. Apparently Denny said she had no money to pay the rent. 'Didn't you send her money?' Apparently he thought she would be able to claim benefits. 'So where was she living?' Apparently in a flat belonging to a drug dealer. He found her after a few days of asking around. When he got to the flat she was not there, she had gone to the shop to buy cigarettes; the children were on their own. He had called the police to break in.

Jacqui called Bruce to warn him that they would have to look after the children for a few days. Adrian accompanied his mother and his children back to Sheffield, but he was not a great deal of use. The journey was one that was memorable for the distress of the children as they were fastened into their newly bought child seats and for the repeated outbursts of crying – one setting the other off – interspersed with peaceful periods where they were hypnotised by the passing scenery. Neither of them was sick, though, which Jacqui counted as an unlooked-for blessing.

She could barely tolerate Adrian, she was so angry with him. For getting involved with that stupid girl in the first place, for getting her pregnant, for allowing himself to get actually married to her, and then for going off and leaving her. She knew that she herself, with all her advantages of experience and confidence would not have been able to manage these children on her own, certainly not without money coming in, so how could a single young woman with no knowledge, and no friends or support make a decent job of it. Denny had been wrong, very wrong to do what – apparently – she had done, but Adrian, for all his excuses, had to take blame as well.

She got them home, she cut off their hair. Strangely, they sat quietly while she did it, and then laughed at each other, at the way they looked quite different, clean and naked, their slender brown necks looking vulnerable and delicate. She sent Adrian to buy them clothes, knowing that he would not do a good job of it. She put them together in a single bed, which they seemed to be happy with.

'Do you sleep in the same bed at home?' she asked and they smiled and said yes they did.

They were never out of each other's sight. The crying diminished gradually, from ninety per cent of the time to eighty, to seventy, and downwards, until, in a matter of weeks, a whole hour could go by without an outbreak of heart-rending sobs. Because they didn't cry in an angry or demanding way; it wasn't out of temper or frustration. It was the weeping of children abandoned and lost; it was grief and mourning and they clung together as they cried and Jacqui, though she tried to comfort them, or at least distract them, found herself filling up with tears of pity, as well as anger. Getting them to sleep at night was a trial. They needed the bedroom door open and the landing light on and Jacqui sitting within sight in the stairs. Bruce offered to help, but the sight of him made them cry harder. She was assured – by the Health Visitor who came once, and the social worker who came three times – that it was all normal and would pass. As it eventually did.

She was shocked to find they had not had their immunisations up to date, and seemed not even to have been registered with a GP. Taking them to her own doctor, filling in the forms (on an impulse she gave them her surname, Thwaite, she could not have explained why), sitting in the room while they were examined and pronounced healthy though a little underweight, made her realise, all of a sudden, that Adrian was not going to step up to the plate, not at all. Oliver and Lila were her responsibility, hers and Bruce's, and apart from abandoning them yet again, there was nothing she could do about it.

They did, naturally, at the beginning, think about Denny's parents. Partly because Jacqui was hoping they could come to some arrangement about the children, partly because she felt sorry for them. They must be worried about their daughter; they must be frantic about their grandchildren. Adrian said he had never met them. They lived somewhere in Cheshire, he believed, in a village. Denny had no contact with them, ever since the end of her second year as a student. She had failed her exams – she hadn't attended for most of the year – and she had lost her place. Her parents, understandably, had cancelled their standing order for her allowance.

'What about the babies?' said Jacqui, and Adrian said he believed they didn't know of their existence.

It was that easy, thought Jacqui. That easy to lose completely the person you had given birth to.

She asked the social worker, who said that she believed contact had been made, but that she couldn't give Jacqui their contact details without their permission.

'Will you get a message to them?' said Jacqui. 'Give them my contact details. They have my permission to contact me, the sooner the better.'

The social worker said she would try, but the next visit was made by a different woman, and she could tell Jacqui nothing.

It was a couple of years later that Adrian, home on a visit, remembered that Denny's father was a headteacher. 'He might have retired though, by now.'

'Where though,' said Jacqui. 'What town?'

Adrian didn't know, but the internet did, when Bruce did some searching.

'Should we though?' said Jacqui. 'After all this time, is it right to get in touch?'

Bruce thought it was probably best to let it lie.

'But in the holidays,' said Jacqui. The children were five now and at school. 'It would be a treat for us to have a week off. And they're old enough, surely. They'd have each other. It wouldn't do any harm to make contact.'

'I wouldn't be so sure,' said Bruce.

She wrote letters nevertheless, and when nothing came in reply she tried the telephone, first to the house, which they never answered, nor replied to her messages, then to the school. The school secretary assured her the house number was correct and she tried again, at different times of the day and evening. Shortly after that the number was no longer recognised.

She suggested to Bruce that they should drive there, with the children, and confront them. Surely they had some responsibility, surely they would want some contact. Bruce dissuaded her.

'Face it Jac,' he said. 'We're on our own.'

She was grateful that he used the word 'we.'

She took on the responsibility herself. Bruce too. What else could they do? She had sold her business; some of the money went to Bruce, to build his business, some into the new house they bought in Derbyshire – for some reason staying in Sheffield made her anxious. Who knew what friends Denny might have; who knew who might be looking for the children?

At the end of her shift, Niecey, holding the DBS form that has been tormenting her for what seems like centuries, knocks on the door of Katie the manager.

'Thank you,' says Katie. 'Just leave it on the desk there.'

'Can I have a word?'

Katie pushes back her chair and waves Niecey to sit down. 'What is it?'

'There's something I have to tell you. About my criminal record.'

'Go on then.'

Niecey begins almost before Katie has finished speaking; the words come out like a waterfall. 'I was in prison. It was years ago. It was drugs, and stolen goods. I got out seven years ago – six and a half. They took my children away. I haven't been in trouble again. It was my fault but I wasn't really bad, it just happened to me, someone used me, I didn't know. Didn't hurt anyone, I don't want to lose my job, I –'

'Slow down,' says Katie. She picks up the form and reads it. 'Have you put everything down on here, previous names and everything?

'Yes.'

'Then we'll send it off and see what comes back.'

Niecey's words have dried up. It seems to cost her an effort to say, 'Can I stay then?'

'For now,' says Katie, 'there's no problem. I need to wait and see what comes back from the DBS, then I can make a decision. There are rules you know, I don't have any discretion in this, I have to do what the management committee want, and what the law says. Does Lynn know about this?'

'She didn't,' says Niecey. 'Until a few weeks ago, nobody knew. But it's all come out and my sister-in-law said she was going to tell you – we had words about it you know – so I thought I'd better tell you myself.'

'You should have told me months ago,' says Katie. 'But then, I should have checked that you'd been given the form months ago so we're both in the wrong.'

'I don't want to lose my job,' says Niecey again.

'I don't want to lose you, if I'm honest,' says Katie. 'But it's out of my hands. I'm sorry.'

'Do you love him though,' says Gemma. 'Jamie, I mean.'

'Who wouldn't love Jamie? Everybody loves him.'

'That's not what I was asking though.'

'I love him, of course I do. But I don't –'

'Fancy him?'

'No it's not that, it's just, we don't seem to have much in common. Leo and the house, and I help with his paperwork but we don't have – I don't know what you'd call it – common ground.'

Gemma is quiet for what seems a long time. They are sitting on a park bench while Jake and Leo ride their bikes round the track in the late afternoon sunshine.

'What do you want to ask me?' says Niecey.

'I think of questions,' says Gemma, 'but then when I see you they don't seem – appropriate, somehow.'

'Go on,' says Niecey. 'It'll be all right.'

'Well, OK. The drugs – what about the drugs?'

Niecey sighs. 'I'll have to start at the beginning. Are you ready?'

'Go on. Stop putting it off.'

'OK then. I started going out with Adrian in my first year. At university I mean. He was my first boyfriend ever, I never had a boyfriend while I was at school, I wasn't really used to it, and what's more, he was a real catch. I mean, he was a graduate student, so he was twenty two – that seemed so mature to me, and he was really really good-looking and the girls I knew all said I was really lucky to be going out with him. But we went out for a few months and then he went off to the States to see his father and I stayed in Norwich for the summer because I didn't want to go home – well, I did go home but I came back after two or three nights because it was just like I was still a little girl, and there were all these rules and I just felt I couldn't stand it, so I came back to Norwich and stayed with another girl and got a summer job in a shop and waited for Adrian to come back. And I met this other guy – even older than Adrian – he'd been a student but he'd dropped out, I never knew why –'

'What do they call him?'

'Hedley, he was called. He knew Adrian. It wasn't anything serious, I mean we slept together a couple of times but he wasn't wanting to get serious or anything, and neither was I, and I knew he was into smoking weed, but everybody did a bit of that, it didn't seem dangerous in any way. I did it myself, Adrian did, it was normal, in fact Hedley was who he bought it from, that's how we knew him. And when Adrian came back at the beginning of term we got back together and I moved into his bedsit with him. And everything was great.'

'Did you make it up with your parents?'

'I went back at Christmas – I don't know why I did it, I knew it would be awful but it seemed to be the thing everyone was doing. Adrian said I could go with him up here, to Sheffield, to meet his mother but – this is silly – I was scared to face her and have her ask why I wasn't at home with my parents. I felt socially unacceptable I suppose. So I went home –'

'Which is where?'

'Over near Macclesfield. Not far away really –'

'Not Plymouth?'

'No. And my dad picked me up from the train and we had nothing to say to each other. And I was stuck there till the trains started up again the day after Boxing Day and I hated it –'

'Just you and them? No one else?'

'We don't have family – well, if we do I don't know them.'

'Funny,' says Gemma, 'how every family does things different. Mark's lot now, at Christmas they have all the neighbours in – they go down the pub and anyone there they know, they ask em back to the house. My mum and dad don't have much to do with people outside the family but they'd think the world was ending if we didn't all go there for Christmas. All of us. As you know.'

'Wonder what it will be like this Christmas then?' says Niecey, and Gemma's face seems to melt.

'I wish I'd never found that bloody report,' she says.

'It's awkward at work,' says Niecey. 'Your mum and I – we're avoiding each other as much as we can. I've not said anything and neither has she. I know she knows, but I don't know if she knows I know –'

'Depends what Sarah has said.'

'– and your dad hasn't been round to see us all week – that must be ten days – Leo's been asking for him.'

'They'll be in Cornwall next week,' says Gemma. 'Maybe they'll forget all about it.'

'Would you put money on that?'

Gemma laughs. 'No. Would you?'

'Look,' says Niecey, 'I've got to go soon. Jamie will be waiting at home.'

'Just finish the bit you were on.'

'Oh right. Christmas. Well, that's the last time I saw my parents. I left and went back to Norwich and at New Year Adrian came back and we got very drunk – and stoned – and sick – and I got pregnant. Accident. Mistake.'

'And you got married?'

'How did you know that?'

'The birth certificates. Denise Wilson. Adrian Wilson.'

'Oh yes. I suppose I put some pressure on him to get married. I felt like he was all I had, after I'd burnt my boats with my parents. I felt like I couldn't risk being left on my own with a baby. As if being married is any guarantee.'

'But he wanted to?'

'He agreed to.'

'He didn't want you to get rid of it?'

'Strangely, no, he didn't. He was quite – I don't know, romantic about it all. Until they were born that is. No, we discussed it, termination – of course we did – but no, that was never on the cards. Another thing was, he wanted to go and live in America – he was close to his dad – and he thought I might not get a visa unless we were married. So that's what we did – got married, then he told his mum afterwards.'

'My mum would have had a blue fit if any of us had done that to her.'

'Mm,' says Niecey. 'I kind of got that.'

'Then what?'

'Then I went and had twins.'

'Not your fault.'

'No. The thing I think though – what was my fault, probably, I was obsessed with them. I took no notice of Adrian. He felt pushed out.'

'Oh, all men say that. How can you help it?'

'I didn't know. I'd never had anything to do with babies.'

'We wondered,' says Gemma, 'why you were so easy with Leo. I mean, you made it look easy. When I had Tash I was all over the place, nothing ever got done, know what I mean? But second ones are easier aren't they.'

'I suppose it was exhausting,' says Niecey. 'But they were good babies, quite sleepy to begin with because they were small – but not too small, they didn't have to be incubated or anything – and then I think having two together means that they have some company all the time so they didn't seem to want attention every waking minute. But you know – I used to spend a lot of time just looking at them. I couldn't believe my luck, I couldn't believe they were mine, I was just entranced by them. I didn't even notice Adrian if he was in the room.'

'Wasn't he – entranced?'

'Not for long. It wore off for him quite quickly. Well, you know don't you, it's one thing having a cute baby – even better having two cute babies – but it's a different thing waking up three times a night, and walking up and down with them, and when they're teething or a bit ill, or just grumpy and fractious.'

'But you didn't mind?'

'I'd rather they were happy and contented. But I didn't mind too much if they had a bad day. But Adrian seemed to take it personally – as if they were doing it especially to annoy him. He went out a lot. And he had his PhD to do. It was a lot of stress, and I didn't really pull my weight – I do see that.'

'And he got no sex I suppose.'

'I was never that good at sex,' says Niecey. 'I don't know why, I just sort of put up with it.'

'We've all been there,' says Gemma. 'Now and again.'

'It's better now though,' says Niecey, 'without obviously wanting to embarrass you, I'd say it's better now than it's ever been. When I think of how I never saw the point – what I used to think was – it was like being the passenger in a car when someone is putting petrol into the tank. You know, you just sit there in the front seat waiting while they jiggle about with this pipe and the car just moves a tiny little bit. And that's it.'

Gemma giggles, tries to stop, fails. 'Don't,' she says eventually. 'Don't because I'll be thinking about it on Saturday night and Mark will think I've gone weird. Don't tell me any more, right.'

'I wasn't going to,' says Niecey but she is laughing too.

Leo brakes his bike in front of them. 'What's funny?'

'Nothing.'

'No, but what though? Tell me.'

Jake pulls up beside him. 'Take no notice,' he advises with the wisdom of being twelve. 'Women do that sort of thing.'

146

'We have to go in a minute,' says Niecey. 'Once more round the track and then home.'

'So hurry up,' says Gemma. 'Get to the drugs bit.'

'Well, says Niecey, 'the long and the short of it is, that Adrian went off back to the States – the children were about two – yes he went soon after Christmas and I thought he'd come back after a week or two but he didn't and there was no money in the account, and I couldn't pay the rent and the landlord threw me out – it was all in Adrian's name and he wasn't there, and I was homeless, nearly, and I ran into Hedley – oh there's lots more to this, this is the short version – and he had this flat – council flat, I don't know how he came to have it, probably rented it off someone who was entitled to it, I don't know. And he let me live in it.'

'Bloody lucky for you,' says Gemma.

'I know. But I knew there was something not right about it. And it was a horrible flat, but it was somewhere to stay. The thing was though –'

'Hedley stayed too?'

'Sort of. He kept stuff there.'

'Drugs?'

'And I can't say that I didn't know. I knew, but it seemed like I couldn't stop him. He was paying the rent. And he'd helped me a lot – to get some benefits and stuff – he knew how it was done. Because Adrian had stopped transferring money to me – I never found out if that was deliberate – and I was clueless – the idea of going to Social Services and asking for help was completely outside anything I'd ever heard of. I'm ashamed of how useless I was. I let Hedley take over my life really –'

'Were you sleeping with him?'

'No – that's a funny thing isn't it. I was useful to him but not in that way. It was more like he was a brother, or an uncle – not that I'd know, never having either – but it didn't feel like he was a bad person. He was truly helpful to me. He didn't like the children, it was always better to have them playing in their bedroom when he came round – but to me he was always helpful and – well, I would say caring. Except for the stash of skunk and cocaine under my bed, and then he was also keeping stolen goods. There was a cupboard full of bags and boxes, all taped up. He used to bring them at night and I never looked in them - it turned out they were all things like computers and phones and stuff that had been nicked – either by him or his friends, I never found out.'

'So did they catch him?'

'No. Never saw him again.'

'Didn't you tell them?'

'The police. I told them everything I knew. They said there was no one with that name. They didn't believe me. But I truly didn't know where he lived, or anything about him. So I think he never got caught – he probably went off to London or somewhere and started again. There are plenty of idiot girls like me.'

Gemma touches her arm. 'Come on,' she says. 'Call Leo. We'll get off home.'

As they walk along, keeping an eye on the children riding their bikes along pavements, Gemma says, 'I never knew you could be funny.'

Niecey says, 'I don't think I ever have been, before.'

Jacqui had met Adrian's wife only four times.

First, when he called her and told her that he had got married. She stormed down to Norwich on that occasion, full of ideas about divorce and annulments. She knew it would not last, even before she saw the girl, and when she saw her there was nothing to help change her mind.

They were living in Adrian's bedsit. Jacqui was invited to sit on the bed or on the chair – she chose the chair, though it was a hard one. The girl – Denny, what sort of name was that? – could have been good-looking enough, under the white powder and black eyeliner, if her hair were not dyed and teased and dried so that it looked like one of those dead crows that lie beside the motorway. It was April, and a warm day but she wore layers of black t-shirts, covered by a black garment that covered her hands. When she stood up and her shawl fell behind her and she twisted to pick it up, Jacqui suspected that she was pregnant. Adrian had not mentioned that.

She was well-spoken, Denny, except that she didn't speak. For every question or comment addressed to her she turned her eyes to Adrian. Adrian fidgeted nervously, rolling skinny cigarettes one after another and smoking each one; sometimes the girl reached and took one from his mouth and took a puff, then put it back in his mouth.

'If you're pregnant,' said Jacqui, 'you shouldn't be smoking. Neither should you,' she added to Adrian.

The girl looked at him accusingly. '*I* didn't tell her,' he said.

'Would you ever have told me?' said Jacqui. 'When is it due?'

'September,' said Denny. 'Fifth.'

'So,' said Jacqui, 'You'll be needing to find somewhere to live. You've no room for a baby in here.'

'I'm on it,' said Adrian. 'Don't worry Mum. I've got somewhere lined up – tenants moving out end of June, then we'll be in. Rent's higher though, obviously.'

'Obviously,' said Jacqui, and thought, That's the only reason he even told me anything about all this.

She saw them again when the babies were born. By that time they had been made aware that it was a twin pregnancy but Adrian hadn't seen fit to tell her, his mother. He did though phone her one morning in early August.

'Premature?' she said, anxious.

'All fine,' he said.

'Boy or girl?'

'One of each,' he said. Did he think she knew already or was he enjoying the shock in her voice?

She went this time with Bruce. They had been together for some years and had just got round to getting married. Adrian had been invited to the wedding but had not turned up, to Jacqui's complete lack of surprise. Bruce drove and they talked about plans to sell Jacqui's small empire of beauty salons and take a year off to go travelling. It was enjoyable, talking about it, but Jacqui – she said later – had a feeling even then that it would never happen.

The girl looked both better and worse this time. She still wore the black clothes – maybe they were all she had – but she had cut off most of her hair – probably done it herself, considered Jacqui – and allowed most of the black dye to grow out. She wore no make-up and looked pasty and tired. Jacqui was not surprised at that. She remembered quite clearly looking after a baby Adrian and looking, maybe once a week, in a mirror, seeing the dry thin hair, the puffy eyes, the dull skin. Not that Adrian hadn't been worth it at the time, and so, no doubt, were the twins, now. They were three weeks old, still unbearably tiny, still squally and squeaky, still scrawny in their arms and legs but beginning to fill out in their faces. Denny was still quiet but she had now an air of purpose about her; twice Jacqui heard her telling Adrian firmly what he should be doing and each time he obeyed. She did, after all, have something about her.

They were still chaotic. There seemed to be no food in the flat. They neither knew how nor had the equipment to make a cup of tea – Adrian borrowed money from Bruce and went out to a cafe to bring some drinks back. Later he went out and brought back fish and chips.

'Is this what you do all the time?' said Jacqui.

'We mostly eat sandwiches,' said Denny. 'Adrian's going to go into town and try to get us some saucepans and things. The last tenants took everything away with them.'

Jacqui had brought some clothes and toys for the babies, of course, and she found herself the next day, with Adrian and Bruce, purchasing the basic requirements to equip a small kitchen. Denny looked at them doubtfully, as if unsure what to do with them, but concealed her feelings after a second and thanked Jacqui and Bruce politely. She had been properly brought up, decided Jacqui.

'And your parents have been to see their new grandchildren?' she said.

Denny pretended she hadn't heard and when Jacqui looked at Adrian he was putting his finger to his lips and mouthing at her not to go there.

It was not, she found, too traumatic to tear herself away from the twins, or from Adrian. She looked at Bruce's profile as they drove out of town and knew that he too was relieved to be going home.

They went again for the twins' first birthday. Adrian was not there when they arrived at the flat and Denny told them he was in the library, just finishing the last checking of his Ph.D. This time she had teabags and milk and a cake, though not a homemade one. The children were clean and happy. Lila was just walking and Oliver was standing and frowning and sitting down again. Denny was quiet and only spoke when spoken to but she was, Jacqui thought, loving and firm enough with the children and the flat seemed orderly. It had, after all, been unfair to judge a pair of very new first-time parents on their housekeeping.

When Adrian came home he seemed distracted. It was the PhD that was worrying him, he said. It was nearly done, but his funding had now finished and he would need to get a job. He could get a job, someone had offered him some hours doing bar work, and he might get something at the university, but then how would he finish writing up.

'I thought it was finished,' said Jacqui. 'Denny said you were just doing a last check.'

'She doesn't understand,' he said. 'You wouldn't understand. There's more to it.'

On their way home Jacqui worried out loud that Adrian was in more trouble with his work than he was letting on. 'I know what he's like,' she said. 'He kids himself that everything's all right, and even more, he tries to kid everyone else.'

Bruce said that he was a grown up. He did not say that it was time to start behaving like one but Jacqui took his meaning.

On the twins second birthday they drove down again. Jacqui had still not sold her business, hadn't even tried to.

She was fifty and could see their idea of travelling drifting away from them. Bruce had not mentioned it for ages and she did not like to, knowing that it was up to her to make the move of selling up. On this long journey, in the heat of August, the dream hung in the air, a forbidden subject, but – was this a premonition? – Jacqui had already taken the first steps towards approaching her lawyer and accountant about the sale.

There was open hostility between Adrian and Denny. She had clearly been crying; he had to make an effort to invite his mother into the flat. The children were watching cartoons on a laptop, sucking their thumbs.

Soon Adrian said he had to go to work, and left. He did not say goodbye to the children and they did not appear to notice. Jacqui and Bruce took Denny and the twins to a cafe and bought them cake. Denny said nothing bad about Adrian – but then she said nothing at all, except to and about the children. They sat in highchairs and looked round them wide-eyed; it was clear that this was the sort of event they were unaccustomed to.

As Jacqui and Bruce got ready for bed in their hotel they discussed how bad things might be.

'You know,' said Jacqui, 'if they break up we may never see the children again.'

But by the time their next birthday came round she had had them living with her for more than a fortnight, and there was no end in sight.

Sarah is in her uniform, tidying the kitchen before setting off for the six o'clock start of her night shift. The meal for Jon and the kids is there, ready to be heated and eaten, whenever they manage to get round to eating it. Jon is up in what he calls his den with a pile of CVs and his laptop. He is always grumpy when she is on night shift, because he has to come home early, and also, she believes, because he is unable to get to badminton, or to the pub for a last half before closing.

School is out, finished yesterday. Dom is out somewhere on his bike, Melissa has gone, that afternoon, to Meadowhall with her friends. Her behaviour, recently, has been better – no late nights, no arguments with her parents, no fights – or not many – with Dom. The school holidays stretch ahead, everyone chilled, friendly, back to normal.

The telephone, ringing in the hall, is an annoyance, when she's so close to going out the door.

'Jon, can you pick it up?' she yells up the stairs.

'On my mobile,' he yells back.

She picks it up. It is her father.

'Sarah? I thought you'd have left by now.'

'What is it?'

'Are you on nights?'

'You know I am.'

'Then you get off, don't let me hold you up, just tell Jon I need to speak to him.'

'He says he's on his phone.'

'Then tell him to ring me as soon as he can. Important.'

'Tell me then. If it's important.'

'No,' says Dave. 'Nothing for you to worry about.'

'Is it mum?'

'No, nothing like that. She's still at work – on till ten tonight.'

'Is it something to do with Niecey?'

'No, not at all. Honestly, Sal, I know you're on your way out the door. Go, I'll tell you tomorrow.'

'Promise.'

'Of course.'

She pounds up the stairs and finds Jon finishing his call, which has not, in truth, been a strictly work call.

'I'm on my way out,' she says. 'Ring my dad. He says it's important.'

'To him,' says Jon, as if to himself.

'Just do it,' she says, and they look at each other with a hostile impatience.

'OK.'

'Now,' she says. 'Before you forget.'

He does that exaggerated sigh that is made to annoy her and waits for the sound of her footsteps on the stairs, before he does anything.

'Have you done it?' she shouts up.

He goes back to his contacts and reluctantly calls his father in law. Looking out of the window he can see Sarah backing out of the drive.

'Jon.'

'Dave. What can I do for you?'

'Has Sarah gone?'

'She's gone. What is this? Why not talk to her, whatever it is?'

'I didn't want her to miss her shift, and I didn't want her to be upset and worrying all night at the hospital. She'll find out soon enough.'

'What then?'

'Melissa,' says Dave. 'She's been arrested. At Meadowhall. She's at the police station. You need to go down there.'

'What for?' says Jon. 'No, I know – shoplifting.'

'Seems so,' says Dave.

'So how have you got to know before we have?'

'She gave them our address,' says Dave. 'Though she must have known you would get to know sooner or later. Anyway, I've told them, she doesn't live here, and I've told them that you would go and get her. You'll need to be there while she's charged.'

'I can't really,' says Jon. 'Dom's out somewhere.'

'I'll come over,' says Dave. 'I'll wait in your house for him. Does that work?'

Dave is home before Lynn comes back from her late shift.

'Good day?' he asks, as he always does.

'Not bad,' she says.

He switches off the TV and brings her tea. He puts her feet up on a stool, even though she protests.

'Anything happened today?' she says.

'Drink your tea.'

'That means yes,' she says. 'Something has happened. Is it Jamie?'

154

'Now, why on earth should it be Jamie?'

'If Gemma's said something to him –'

'Not Jamie.'

He tells her about Melissa, how she was caught coming out of Accessorize in the shopping mall with four Jojo bows and a handful of friendship bracelets in her bag, unpaid for, and that there were also cosmetic items from Boots, with no proof that she had paid for them. There were other girls with her, and one of them, Bethany, was also arrested and charged.

'She had money on her,' says Dave. 'She could have paid.'

'So, Sarah? How did she take it?'

'She doesn't know yet. She were just leaving for work when I called –'

'Why did you call?'

'Police called me. Our Melissa gave them our name and number – made out like she lives with us. Why, I couldn't tell you. I haven't seen her, only for a second when Jon brought her home. She was in the front door and straight up to her room.'

'So Sarah's going to come off shift in the morning and get home to find all this has gone off. And we're off on holiday tomorrow.' She stops to think. 'Do you think we should cancel?'

'I do not,' says Dave. 'They can sort it out by themselves.'

'That,' says Lynn, 'is something I have never heard you say, ever before in all the time I've known you.'

'I must be getting old,' says Dave. 'Keeping track of this family is starting to get me down. I'm feeling I need to get away, just me and you.'

'Sarah will call tomorrow,' says Lynn. 'I hope she gets her sleep in before she finds out about all this. We'll talk to her tomorrow and she'll know we're here for her. Even if we're not at home.'

'What on earth, though?' says Dave. 'That girl has every damn thing money can buy, and she has to go thieving out of some nasty tat shop, I can't imagine what got into her.'

'A dare maybe,' says Lynn. 'Trying to look big in front of that other girl. Or maybe the other girls made her do it.'

'She knows better,' says Dave. 'She should have stood up for herself. She's not been brought up to nicking and dishonesty. She should have walked away. I'm disappointed in her.'

'It's done,' says Lynn. 'They have to just get on with it.' She gets to her feet and puts her hand on the back of Dave's head, stroking his hair. 'Come on. Worse things happen.'

'Not to us,' says Dave. 'When have we ever had the police to our door?'

There is a silence full of thinking and then Lynn says, 'You can't blame Niecey for this.'

'That's not what I was thinking.'

'Yes you were,' she says. 'Because I thought it too. But be logical. Niecey was probably a stupid young woman, once. Maybe bad. Melissa's been a silly girl. Niecey's pulled it together and Melissa will do it too. We'll go on holiday and when we come back it will all be over, and this time next year we won't even remember it.'

\*

Dave and Lynn have been going to Cornwall for their holiday ever since Sarah was a baby. Yes, for sure it was a long way. Scarborough or Bridlington would have been an easier journey with small children, the three of them elbowing and bickering in the back of the car and demanding frequent refreshment and toilet stops. Sometimes Dave, dawdling through traffic queues on the M5 regretted their decision. But once they were arrived it all became worth the journey. Cornwall was like a foreign country. 'You really feel like you're somewhere different,' said Lynn, every year. 'You really know you're on holiday.'

They have stayed in tents and caravans, everywhere from Looe to Mevagissey, Bude to Falmouth, Newquay to St Ives. They have photographs taken on beaches, on ferries, on donkeys, on jetties; of their children in swimwear, in silly hats, in the rain, in the sea, up to their necks in sand. They have memories of Gemma dropping her ice cream at Fowey and being inconsolable, of Jamie getting stuck halfway up a cliff, of all three of them having races across the sand, of the year when Jamie was able to beat Gemma and she didn't speak to anyone for a day and a half, of Sarah being sick in the car, of Dave cutting his foot on rocks. Some of their memories can no longer be placed precisely – was it at Bude where they took a rowing boat up the river? Was it somewhere near Newlyn where they got lost on a walk and ended up dragging the kids for something like ten miles? Happy times.

Once the children, one at a time becoming teenagers, no longer wanted to come with them, they gave up staying on caravan sites and began to rent a cottage or an apartment. This year they have not looked forward to it with the same pleasure; somehow it has felt risky to be too far from home for too long.

'I'm laying down the law here,' says Dave, right at the start of their journey. 'We are not going to spend our week talking about the family. All right?'

'I don't know what we will talk about then' says Lynn, watching fields slide past on her side of the M5. 'It'll be a quiet week.'

'We'll manage,' he says.

'But your kids?' says Gemma. 'Were they really filthy and starving?'

Niecey shrugs. 'I wasn't doing a good job, I can tell you that. I'm not ashamed really, about getting done for the drug offences and the stolen goods – I mean, I am, because I should have had more intelligence, I should have known how to organise my life, I shouldn't have let men control me – so yes. But neglecting the children – I didn't have to do that – I am ashamed of that, that's the worst thing I did.'

'It's the worst thing anyone can do,' says Gemma severely. 'So when you said you could explain – what's your explanation?'

They are sitting, this time, in Gemma's kitchen, at the table. Mark has taken Jake and Leo to the swimming baths, Tash is out somewhere with her friends.

'I was out of it,' says Niecey. 'That's the long and short of it.'

'On drugs?' says Gemma. 'Proper drugs?'

'Drink mainly,' says Niecey. 'Pills too. Hedley gave them to me, to calm me down.'

'What – Valium, something like that?'

'There was Valium. But other stuff too. I think he wanted to keep me from thinking clearly. He didn't want me to work out that I could tell someone about him, or kick him out – not that he was living there with me – he just used to come to pick up stuff, or bring stuff, but if I'd been in my right mind I would have realised what he was doing. I would have pulled myself together somehow.'

'He was using you,' says Gemma. 'I can see that. But Niecey, you're not stupid – you've got exams and that – why did you let him do it?'

'What can I say?' says Niecey. 'I'd like to blame my mum and dad, I'd like to blame Adrian and Hedley, but really – it was my fault. I hadn't grown up. I was passive. I was feeble. And I knew I was doing it, I knew and I kept on thinking I could stop, I would get to bed every night – I used to stay up really late just watching telly and drinking – I thought I was only drinking a little bit – vodka – I used to kid myself about the empties, like, that's a month's worth when it was really only a week. Anyway, then I couldn't wake up in the morning and the kids would wake early of course, as they do, and if Hedley was there – not really often, but sometimes he stayed over, if he was there he used to shout at them and make them go back to their beds and I remember –' she is crying as she speaks, big silent tears are falling down her face – 'they were scared of him because he shouted and I used to hear them outside my bedroom talking to each other, scared to come in, saying, Is he there? I feel bad about that.'

'So were they really hungry?'

Niecey wipes her eyes with the back of her hand. 'I didn't feed them properly. I didn't know how to really – no, that's wrong, I did know, I just didn't get myself together enough to do it. We ate chips and biscuits. No they weren't really hungry, but they weren't properly nourished, I know that.'

'In the newspaper it said they were filthy.'

'I know. I saw it. They weren't – it wasn't like they were sitting in dirty nappies – but they were pretty grimy I suppose. Everything I knew I should do, like give them a bath, and clean clothes, and empty their potties, and go and buy some proper food – I always put it off till the next day, and then the next day came and I would be too tired to do it, and I would take a couple of pills to get me going –'

'What – like amphetamines or something?'

'Whatever. Hedley used to bring me a sort of pick and mix. Mostly I couldn't remember which was which – whatever I took would either perk me up so nothing mattered or else slow me down so that I didn't care. I tried not to drink during the day – my mum was an alcoholic you know, probably still is, but she never – except at Sunday lunchtime – she never drank before six o'clock in the evening. So I didn't either – mostly – I cheated sometimes, but if I held out till six o'clock I felt so virtuous I sometimes poured a bigger one as a reward.'

'Oh yes,' says Gemma. 'Like getting to your target weight and then bingeing on fish and chips. Not' she added, 'that I ever do get to my target weight.'

'I never thought,' says Niecey, 'that I could talk to anyone about all this. I can't believe I'm doing it.'

'Talk to Jamie though,' says Gemma. 'You know you'll have to one day.'

'Yes,' says Niecey.

They sit quietly for a little, while a small drizzle falls on the garden. Then Niecey says, 'Have you heard anything from Sarah?'

'Not a word,' says Gemma. 'It's been a whole week.'

159

'I can't believe,' says Niecey, 'that it was only a week ago.'

'No,' says Gemma. 'We've got through a lot.'

'It's been all right,' says Niecey. 'I wouldn't have thought I could do it, but once you start, you know, it's almost hard to stop. You've been ever so good to me.'

Gemma blushes. 'I haven't done anything. But tell Jamie. He'll cope.'

'Sarah though,' says Niecey. 'Do you think she'll do what she said – I mean at work, telling Katie?'

'I don't know,' says Gemma. 'But you'd probably know by now if she had. The thing is – I don't know if I should tell you this – but Tash says that Melissa has got into trouble with the police.'

'What for?'

'Shoplifting at Meadowhall apparently. It's all over Facebook, so I'm told, and Instagram.'

'Do you think it's true?'

'Going by what Tash says. She doesn't hang around with that crowd – thank goodness – but she knows them well enough. Sarah probably won't want people to know, but these days, what can you do?'

'I won't tell her you've told me.'

'I don't see why I shouldn't,' says Gemma. 'You're family after all.'

*In the morning glad I see my foe outstretch'd beneath a tree.* Niecey knows she shouldn't think like that but it just came to her. Take that, Sarah, not so righteous now are you.

When Jamie and Niecey get to bed it is a hot stuffy night, rare for Sheffield, and twenty minutes in they are both still awake, the covers thrown off them.

'Are you awake?' says Niecey.

'Mm.'

'Awake enough to talk?'

'What about?'

'There are things I want to tell you.'

'Go on then,' he says. 'Make it boring though, so that it sends me to sleep.'

But by four in the morning, when the sky is just beginning to lighten, he is still awake, though Niecey is sleeping, snuffling a little into her damp pillow.

He knows – he suspected all along – that she has been in prison. He knows now what for, he knows both the short version – drugs, Class A, possession and intent to supply, stolen goods, handling of, neglect of children, case dropped – and he has heard some of the long version, the detail, the random, tiny details. The children's first words and their different characters – Oliver so sensitive and timid and clever, Lila so confident and talkative. And how they changed when she stopped being herself – that was how she put it – not herself. The first night in prison – how she cried, how it smelled, how she wanted to die – and all the days afterwards, the ache, the weight, the guilt. The work she did – the cleaning, the scrubbing of floors and scouring of sinks and saucepans, the hot smell of the laundry and the feel of the folded sheets.

'I chose it,' she says. 'It felt like the worst job and I wanted to punish myself. Like I wasn't being punished enough, I knew that. But when I did it, it was all right, I could think to myself, and you know, even now I like making things clean and tidy.'

She has even told him about William Blake, how she did him at school, as part of her A level, and how she found the little book in the prison library and kept it for the whole time she was there, because no one else ever wanted it.

'I would still have it,' she says, 'but they wouldn't let me. Prison property.'

'But you have got it,' he says.

'I got one when I came out,' she says. 'It was the first thing I did, almost, and it was only fifty p – old books, nobody wants them really. Though I knew the poems by heart – but still, I like seeing them written down.'

'Poems,' says Jamie and shakes his head in the darkness.

'I'm sorry.' She says this many times through that night, sometimes snivelling a little, sometimes sobbing, sometimes calm, and Jamie replies to it only once. He says, 'You don't have to be sorry to me. It's not me you did anything to.'

'I kept it all a secret,' she says. It is one of the calm times.

'Look,' he says, 'it's all in the past. Before me. You didn't even need to tell me.'

'Do you mind?'

'What?'

'Do you mind that I *did* tell you? In the end?'

'You're still you,' he says. 'Nothing has to change.'

And she cries some more and this time, falls asleep.

When she wakes in the morning she can hear Leo singing to himself in his room and the sound of it fills her with a rush of love. It must be about seven o'clock; she has had probably less than three hours sleep and her eyes are feeling gritty and dry from all the tears – and she feels simultaneously the anguish of loss as if it is new, and gratitude for her good fortune in having Leo. And Jamie. He is still asleep, turned away from her, his pale back, his reddened neck, his left ear, lobeless and strangely dainty. *Then cherish pity lest you drive an angel from your door.* Her lips form the words, silently. Dull, stolid Jamie, an earthly angel.

Cornwall has been full. Many French people, squeezing their French cars into steep and narrow roads, Japanese in flocks, Australians working in bars and cafes and water sports.

'Never seen it so busy,' says Dave. 'I suppose they're taking a last look before we pull up the drawbridge.'

'That's not funny,' says Lynn.

They are sitting in a teashop in Tintagel while a slow drizzle falls outside. It is Thursday already; almost halfway through. This time next week they'll be thinking about packing to go home, looking forward to seeing the family and getting back to their proper lives.

'When I retire,' says Lynn, 'we can make a longer journey of it. I mean we could stop somewhere along the way for a night or two. There are some nice places between here and Sheffield and yet we've never stopped for so much as a cup of tea.'

'When you retire,' says Dave sceptically. 'Do you mean that Lynnie? Has the sun got to your brain?'

'What sun?' she says, because in truth it hasn't been the best week for weather.

'Are you really thinking about it though? What's brought this on?'

'I'm tired,' she says. 'I've been on holiday all this week and I'm still tired. Maybe I'm getting too old for all this. I'm feeling like I don't want to go back. I don't feel like I've had a holiday.'

'You've been worrying,' says Dave. 'So have I. We haven't made the best of this week. And the weather's not been on our side.'

'But I think it's more than that,' says Lynn. 'In fact, I've decided – when I get back, I'm giving my notice. You'll have me under your feet all day.'

'That's all right by me,' he says gallantly.

They turn their attention to the teapot and the scones and clotted cream. 'Tell me again,' says Dave. 'Do I put the cream on first or the jam?' And she tells him again that he can do it whichever way he likes.

'Do you know,' she says, squinting up at the sky, 'there's a bit of blue up there. Maybe it's clearing up.'

Niecey has just finished cleaning Ron's room – he has recited Gray's Elegy to her, not all of it, just the highlights, he said – when Katie calls her into the office.

'Can I have five minutes?'

Niecey sits on the edge of her chair, holding her hands tightly together to keep from fidgeting.

'How are you managing?' says Katie. 'I mean with the school holidays. Is your little boy at home with his dad?'

'He's with his auntie today,' says Niecey. 'When his grandad comes back – well, I'm not sure really. He can go to Kids Club – he likes it there but it's expensive.'

'As long as you've got options. Now then Niecey, I've been thinking – no, your DBS check hasn't come back yet, I wouldn't expect it to, but I feel that after what you've told me I need to know a little bit more, just to cover myself, and the Home you know. I need to know a little bit more about what happened to get you in prison – because that's quite unusual isn't it – just to do my job and make a judgement about keeping everyone safe. Does that make sense to you?'

'Yes,' says Niecey.

'So, do you want to tell me in your own words, or would it be easier if I ask you questions?'

'I'll tell you,' says Niecey.

Just as she told Gemma and Jamie, although in a more coherent order, she relates her story once again. The relationship with Adrian, the twins, being left alone, Hedley, the drink, the pills, the neglect, the arrest, the loss of the children. The trial, the sentence, the loss of the children. The years in prison, the loss of the children. The loss. Katie listens. Her phone rings but she turns it off without answering it.

'No one knows what it's like,' says Niecey. She has not shed a tear through all this.

'True,' says Katie. 'You were a silly girl. I was a silly girl once too. I had a baby when I was sixteen. It's not the same as what happened to you, but I still feel ashamed of how I handled it. I split up with my son's father and so he grew up without a father. It was irresponsible. I didn't think.'

'I was old enough to know better,' says Niecey. 'I've been telling people, now that it's all come out; I've told my husband all about it, and I've talked to my sister-in-law about it and it makes you see it differently somehow. I always blamed Adrian and Hedley, and I thought it wasn't my fault, but it was. I should have been more grown up, I should have been more – tough.'

There is a knock on the door and one of the care workers puts her head in. 'Sorry Katie. I've got Peggy's son here wanting to speak to you. He's been waiting a while.'

'All I can say to you now,' says Katie, when the woman has gone, 'is that there is no reason I can see why you shouldn't carry on working here for the time being. When your check comes back I will have to make a decision, but for now we'll just carry on as normal.'

'Thank you,' says Niecey and when Katie has left the room she uses her overall to wipe away the tears that have now begun to run down her face.

Jacqui did not attend the trial. How could she when the children would not let go of her legs even to let her go to the toilet. Bruce said he would go.

'I shouldn't let you,' said Jacqui. 'I know you don't want to.'

'We need to know,' he said. 'If she gets off, well, there'll be decisions. She'll want the children back. You'll need to be prepared.'

'We don't know how long it will last,' said Jacqui. 'Will they manage without you at work?'

'It's my business,' he said, 'I can do what I like. There's the phone, and email. It'll be fine.'

'You're a hero,' said Jacqui. 'You don't know how grateful I am.'

As it turned out it was not a long trial. Denise Wilson pleaded guilty to the charges of possession of class A substances, though she denied intent to supply, and guilty to possession of stolen goods. Adrian was called as a witness and spoke on the first day to tell how he had gone to the flat on the advice of an acquaintance and found the children there unattended. The court was told that the neglect of the children was a further offence which might come before them at a later date. A policeman told of breaking into the flat, of Mrs Wilson returning within a very short time, of finding the children shut in a room.'

'Can you describe the state of the children,' he was asked.

'They were distressed,' he said, 'but it might have been the noise of us gaining access that frightened them. They were not too clean, I would say. They had toys in the room.'

A neighbour of the accused was asked if she had noticed other instances of the children being left alone, but objection was made that the question was not relevant to the case being tried. She was then asked about visitors to the flat. 'Yes, there was one man who came often. Yes he came and went most days, sometimes more than once.'

Had she seen him carrying objects in and out of the flat, boxes for example?

'Not boxes but he had these big hold-all bags, like people have at airports.'

Did he appear to be living at the flat?

'He had a key. He usually came and went away again. He didn't stop long, usually.'

Through it all, Bruce reported, Denny sat as if sedated. 'Blank is the only word for it,' he told Jacqui. 'As if she wasn't there at all. Hardly moved, no expression.'

'How did Adrian seem?'

'Seemed to take it in his stride. I would say any feeling he had for her has gone. In fact I think that's quite a mild way of putting it. She looked awful though. Destroyed. Judge had to ask her to speak up when she was being questioned.'

'What did she say?'

'Said she had no money, nowhere to live, this man let her stay in his flat while he was somewhere else. It was hard to believe, Jac, that she didn't know what was going on, surely she would have suspected, especially with stuff arriving in bags and being taken away again. They said there were cupboards full of stolen stuff – mostly from stores, still in boxes. And the drugs were under her bed – she must have known.'

'Four and a half years,' said Jacqui. 'I'll be fifty-six.'

'Where's Dad,' says Dom.

'He's gone to the shop. Some sort of emergency.'

'Like what though?'

'I didn't ask,' says Sarah. She is making a list of jobs that have to be done and things that have to be bought before they go on holiday. 'Do you still have that snorkel?'

'Yeah of course,' he says. 'But Mum, Dad said he would take me to the pictures today if it was raining, and look, it is raining.'

'He'll be back in time.'

'Suppose he isn't.'

'You'll just have to do something else won't you.'

'Like what though?'

'Like tidy your bedroom and bring out all your dirty clothes for washing, so that I can get them ironed and ready before we go on holiday.'

'That will take me two minutes,' he says scornfully. 'Then what am I supposed to do?'

'Go for a walk.'

'Who with?'

'One of your friends?'

'They're all on holiday.'

Sarah has stopped listening.

'If I had a dog,' he says, revisiting an old argument, '*then* I would go for a walk.'

'We're not having a dog,' says Sarah, a conditioned response.

'Why though,' says Dom. 'Why can't we have a dog?'

'How many times do I have to explain this to you,' says Sarah. 'A dog is not like a games console. You can't switch it off when you don't feel like taking it for a walk. It's like a baby – you have to think of it all the time. Does it need food, or water, does it need to go out? It needs exercise. Every day, whether it's raining or not. Every day, whether you feel like it or not.'

'I would do it,' says Dom. 'I would take it for walks.'

'While it was a novelty you would,' she says. 'Then it would end up being me that did it. On top of everything else.'

'Please.'

'No. You heard me. I mean it, it's a red line, no dogs. No pets of any sort, you hear. No more.'

'But we haven't got *any*. We've never had any.'

'I mean,' she says, 'no more arguing and whining. I don't want to discuss this any more. End of.'

'But Mum –'

Now she shouts. 'That's it. Didn't I just tell you no more. That's enough. Give over moaning. I've got enough on my plate without all this.' Somehow the shouting has made her hair stick up and her face go red.

'Just because you're mad with Mel,' says Dom. 'You don't have to take it out on me. Just because Melissa's been a dickhead.'

'Language,' says Sarah automatically, and then, 'What do you know about what Melissa's been doing?'

'Everyone knows,' he says. 'All my friends know, everyone. Bethany's put it on her Facebook.'

'Gem?'

'Sarah?'

'Look I'm sorry,' says Sarah. 'It wasn't your fault.'

'What wasn't?'

'Gem. I'm trying to apologise. It's not you I've got any quarrel with is it?'

'So?'

'Gemma don't be like that. I don't know what I did to upset you.'

'You haven't texted me for a fortnight, you haven't phoned.'

'Neither have you.'

'I've been busy.'

'You've had time enough to see her.'

'So who's told you that?'

'Your Jake.'

'And?'

'No Gem, this isn't what I called you for. I don't want to get into an argument with you. It's done, it's all fine, it's just – I need –'

'So you just call me because you want something?'

'Gem, stop it – you won't know this but we're having some bother with Melissa –'

'I know. I've heard all about it.'

'Who's told you?'

'Tasha. Everyone knows.'

'She's your niece Gem. She's your family.'

'You sound like Dad. That's just what he'd say. Anyway, come on, say what you want.'

169

'I was going to ask – Mum and Dad aren't back yet and I don't trust her to be left on her own – Melissa I mean – I was wondering if she could come round to yours while I'm at work. It would have to be Dom too of course. Tasha's that sensible, she's a good influence. I want to get Melissa away from that Bethany and all that crowd, but they keep on messaging her and she keeps on whingeing about having to stay in. I think if I go to work and leave her she'll go and leave Dom on his own and she'll be out with them – I'm sorry Gem, there's no one else I can ask –'

'OK,' says Gemma.

'But you've looked for them?' says Gemma.

'I look for them all the time,' says Niecey. They are talking in Gemma's kitchen again. 'Let me do that,' adds Niecey, as Gemma opens out her ironing board. 'You've got the kids' tea to get.'

The children, all five of them, are upstairs; outside, rain falls steadily on the garden.

'But you've looked on Facebook and all that kind of thing?'

'Sort of,' says Niecey. 'Obviously I'm on Facebook, you know I am, but I can't find them. I've found a few Oliver Wilsons – loads actually – but none of them are him. I'm pretty sure now that she's changed their names. Maybe just their surnames.'

'Why would she do that?'

'To stop me finding them?'

'Well yes, I suppose so, but won't they know? Won't they be asking? Won't they be trying to find you?'

'I've thought of that,' says Niecey. 'But they won't know I've got married to Jamie will they? So I'm Niecey Wilde, aren't I, and they'll be thinking – that's if they know anything about me – that I'm Niecey Wilson.'

'Or Nuttall? That's your maiden name isn't it. Why don't you put yourself on Facebook as Denise Nuttall – they might be looking for that?'

'So might my parents,' says Niecey.

'Why would that be a bad thing? Don't you miss them?'

'I try not to think about them,' says Niecey. 'I behaved badly towards them – it's only when you have your own children that you realise, isn't it – but they behaved badly too –'

'Maybe they meant well –'

'Meaning well isn't enough though, is it.'

'So what were they like?'

'They didn't like me. And I didn't like them. That's all there is to it.'

'Why though? Why would your mum not like you?'

'I was fat,' says Niecey.

'That's funny,' says Gemma. 'I was proper skinny, like Tash, and look at me now.'

'Well, I was proper fat,' says Niecey.

'Hard to believe,' says Gemma. 'But even if you were – I don't get it. I would still love Tash if she was fat. However fat she was.'

'Now,' says Niecey, 'when I look back, things make more sense. My dad was fat too, or at least overweight, paunchy, not soft and flobbery. And he used to indulge me. *She* – well, I think she had some sort of eating disorder and anyway she got most of her calories from alcohol so it was like they had their arguments through me. He bought me sweets and buns – I had ever such a sweet tooth – and she told me off, and nagged and made me feel miserable and said she couldn't love a fat child.'

'She didn't say that!'

'I don't know if she said it, but I knew it. She was ashamed of me. Also, I wasn't very clever. My dad cheated – he must have done – to get me into the grammar school, and I didn't do very well there. He shouldn't really have let me into the sixth form, but of course he could do what he liked –'

'But you got into university.'

'I pulled it round a bit in the sixth form. I lost a bit of weight too – or at least I grew taller all of a sudden so I didn't look so fat – and that set me off doing diets and exercise. I wanted to get away you see, I wanted to be a different person.'

'So, did your mum – did she like you better?'

'Not that you'd notice.'

'You wouldn't believe,' says Gemma, 'how skinny I was. It was having babies that did it for me. Never lost the pounds. But go on – how could your mum just not even like you?'

'I don't want to talk about them,' says Niecey. 'I never told them I had the twins; I never told them I dropped out of university; I never told them when I got married.'

'Why didn't you ask them for help? I mean when Adrian went off and left you without any money. Surely you could have gone to your mum and dad?'

'I don't think I even thought of it,' says Niecey. 'That's how things were. I dropped out of university and after a bit they must have found that out because they stopped putting money into my account.'

'Probably they did that to make you get in touch,' suggests Gemma.

'I never thought of that. Actually I thought it was quite reasonable of them. They were paying for me to study, if I wasn't studying then why should they pay me. We got by on Adrian's money anyway – his mum was quite generous.'

'Did you meet her?'

'A few times. She came down after we got married. That was pretty awful – she was all glossy and made-up, and she'd got this boyfriend with her, and I was this scruffy pregnant goth, and I had no idea how to cook them a proper meal, and I had nothing to say to her and she had nothing to say to me – nothing she *could* say anyway – I bet there was plenty she'd have liked to say, like, I was ruining her son's life and landing him with a baby – we didn't know then it was twins – oh it was just ghastly, and I could see Adrian wishing I would disappear.'

'Perhaps he was wishing his mum would disappear, not you.'

'No,' says Niecey. 'It was me he wanted to get rid of. He knew he'd made a mistake.'

She shakes out Mark's white work trousers and folds them neatly, and picks up a top of Tasha's, spreading it carefully over the ironing board. Her hair falls over her face and she does not push it back. Gemma tips pasta into a colander to drain.

'What's going on?' says Tasha to Melissa. 'Are people acting kind of weird, or is it me?'

'You mean –?'

'Parents. My mum is forever talking to Niecey – she's never done that before, it's usually your mum she talks to. And then she's talking to my dad every night about Niecey, and I've been trying to listen but I can't work it out. It's all about, does Jamie know, and something about some children.'

'My parents are just arguing,' says Melissa, 'but they always do when Mum's on nights.'

'I think she's had an argument with my Mum too – they haven't talked for ages, until yesterday.'

'I know, I heard her on the phone, it was like she was begging your Mum to have us over here. It's all to get me away from Beth. As if she doesn't trust me.'

'I don't know what you saw in Beth anyway,' says Tasha.

'It was a laugh,' says Melissa. 'That's all.'

'What do they argue about then, your parents?'

'Me,' says Melissa. 'Some of the time anyway. And then, Dad thinks Mum is too close to her mum and dad, and to you lot, and she shouldn't worry so much about Jamie. I didn't know she worried about Jamie but he seems to think she does. And he wants to go and play badminton but when she's on nights he has to stay with us, especially now they don't trust me to stay home with Dom. Like, this is how stupid it is, I can't even go to the shop down the road on my own. As if they've got anything there I'd want to have.'

'Fags?' suggests Tasha.

'You can't shoplift fags, stupid,' says Melissa. 'You are such a Goody-Two-Shoes, you know that don't you.'

'If you don't like it here,' says Tash, waving her arm round her bedroom, 'you might as well go downstairs and sit with my Mum.'

'I know when I'm not wanted,' says Melissa, without moving.

'Obviously you don't.'

'If you're going to be like that –'

'Go on then.'

Once outside the room Melissa listens at the door of Jake's room. No one is speaking; there is just the sound of X-box, and then Leo saying, 'Is it my turn yet?'

She goes quietly down the stairs and stops by the front door. She can hear her two aunts in the kitchen, their voices accompanied by the sounds of stirring and the occasional thunk of the iron going back on its stand. She opens the front door carefully but the rain is falling too heavily to make going out attractive; she closes it again, just as carefully. And sits on the bottom stair.

'There must be ways,' says Gemma's voice. 'Social Services, the Salvation Army, the Education Department. Lila, that's not a common name, even if they've changed the Wilson to something else. Just search on Facebook for Lila.'

'I've tried all those things,' says Niecey's voice. 'I used to think it would be easy, it would just happen, but after all these years, I don't know, it feels like I'd be happier if I could forget them.'

'Could you though? Forget.'

'I've never tried.'

'Niecey, they're your kids. You're not going to pretend they don't exist. You're not going to stop believing, I know you're not.'

Melissa hears the plug of the iron being pulled out of its socket, she hears the sound of plates being put out on the table.

'I'll just call the kids,' says Gemma.

Something mumbled from Niecey.

'You look fine. They won't notice a thing.'

Melissa races upstairs in time not to be seen. All through the meal, as each of the children picks out of their pasta the ingredient they dislike most (mushrooms for Leo, courgette for Jake, tomato for Tasha and Dom) she is repeating in her mind what she has heard, twitchy with impatience to tell it all to Tash.

It has not been too difficult for Tash to get hold of her mother's phone. Gemma is not a person who has it in her hands the whole time – she is a person who leaves it on the table, or on the sideboard or the sofa while she does something that can't wait and goes on to another task without thinking of who might be texting her. She doesn't always recall exactly where she has left it either, so Tash has been able to take it to her room and scroll back through the texts – mostly tedious things about picking up Jake from swimming, or buying milk on the way home from work. But she finds a bunch of texts between her mother and Sarah from a few weeks ago which have a note of surprise in them, of puzzlement and shock. 'OMG!' one of them says, 'do you think it's true?'

And the reply comes back, 'Secret twins – like something on TV.'

'I know. What will J do?'

'Nothing. U know him.'

Tash is able to follow her mother's and her aunt's unpicking of the information, while still not understanding clearly what they are on about.

The laptop – the family laptop to which she has free access for homework purposes – is more expansive. She finds the newspaper article that has brought things to this place, and some emails between her grandad and her mother. She sends an excited text to Melissa, without giving anything away.

Melissa has not been able to get hold of her mother's phone. It is on her person the whole time, except while she is at work when it is locked in a drawer at the nurses' station. There are a number of devices around the house, and a computer in her father's office that she and Dom have been occasionally allowed to use but it is mostly understood that it is part of his work and will not offer anything interesting to anyone else. Her dad also has more than one phone, one for work and one for home. Dom once asked for his old one but he said he had given it back to the shop in part exchange for the new one. This – Melissa finds when she sneaks into his office while he is downstairs having another argument with her mother – was not true. It is there in the drawer. She takes it to her own room to investigate, without expecting much.

Later, using her own phone she texts Tash. 'My dad is having an affair. What shall I do?'

Next day they are back in Tash's bedroom.

'So what did they say? These texts? Were they gross? Did you bring it with you?'

'I couldn't. He uses it all the time. Evenings when he goes upstairs to work.'

'So your mum doesn't know? Or – is that what they've been arguing about?'

'She can't know can she? She would throw him out. It's just everything else they argue about.'

'So what did they say? And who is she?'

'Just things like, Not tonight. Try again next week. Stuff like that. Not smutty stuff.'

'What's her name?'

'He doesn't use her name. I looked in his contacts and there's none. I mean no others, just her. H, that's all. So he doesn't use the phone for anyone else.'

'And were there any from her?'

'He must delete them straight away.'

'Will you tell your mum?'

'I don't dare.'

'She might be mad at you.'

'What I'm going to do – Tash I was awake *all night* thinking what to do – when we're on holiday next week I'm going to watch him and I'm going to see if he's got this phone with him and if he has I'm going to ask him and I'm

176

going to say I'll tell mum if he doesn't give her up. This woman. H. What do you think?'

'Yes,' says Tash slowly. 'That's good Mel, I really think so. Very mature.'

Melissa leans back on the bed. 'You won't tell anyone.'

'Of course not.'

'Not Grandad. Especially not them.'

'I can keep a secret.'

'I don't want my parents to split up.'

'Of course not.'

'I can see why he'd want someone who's not my mum though. She is *so* bad-tempered. I'd rather live with him.'

'It might not happen. You don't know yet.'

'I'm being prepared. Dom could stay with Mum and I could stay with Dad. And they'd have to sell the house and get two small ones. Or flats. Maybe Dad would get a flat in town, somewhere cool.'

'But hey, listen,' says Tash. 'Do you want to know what I found out? All this stuff about Niecey. It will blow your mind, honestly.'

But Melissa has suddenly folded into a tearful heap, curled and sobbing.

'Be quiet,' says Tash. 'You don't want my mum to hear. Look I'm going to show you this on the laptop.'

'I can't look,' moans Melissa. 'It's like everything is falling apart. I want it all to be like it used to be.'

'What,' says Tash, 'like before you starting shoplifting with Bethany and them. Look at this – I've spent all day yesterday finding this, you might take an interest.'

'Not now,' mutters Melissa, and at that point Gemma enters the room (without knocking) to send them to the shop as she has insufficient pasta to feed them all.

'What's the matter?' she says to Melissa.

'She got her court date,' says Tash quickly.

'Well, she knew it was coming,' says Gemma. 'It will be fine Mel. Your mum and dad will go with you, you'll be all right.'

'It's not like you'll go to prison,' says Tash, which might have been meant to be helpful but comes out scornful.

'And that's where the laptop is,' cries Gemma. 'What are you doing with it?'

'Homework,' says Tash.

'I haven't really got a court date,' says Melissa. They are walking down to Morrisons now. 'I've got to wait months probably. There's a backlog.'

'What will you get do you think?'

'Dad says I won't go to prison for a first offence. Actually I think I'd rather *be* in prison, the way things are.'

'Who was more angry, your mum or your dad?'

'Dad, mostly. Cos he works for a shop. He moans all the time about shoplifters. But Mum's really hacked off about having to deal with it. She says it's *one more thing* and she's got enough on her plate.'

'Like what?'

'Don't know.'

'They say that all the time though, don't they. They think they work hard morning to night. They think we have nothing to do. They don't realise do they?'

'They think Year Ten's going to be easy,' says Melissa. 'They don't realise things have changed since their day. And I'm the youngest in the year you know –'

'I know.'

'– and it's hard for me. It's all right for you.'

'You're not the only one born in August you know.'

'Who else then?'

'Anyway, what are you doing for your birthday? You'll be on holiday won't you.'

'Ibiza.'

'They let you go, do they? The police I mean – you're allowed to leave the country?'

'My dad sorted it. Cos it's pending you know.'

'Lucky thing. I wish we could go to Ibiza.'

'Filey again is it?'

'You know it is so don't pretend to be sorry for me.'

'So listen.' They are walking back, carrying a kilo of pasta each. 'Mel, let me tell you what I found out about Niecey.'

'I'm bored with Niecey. I don't care. I've got my own troubles.'

'If that's how you're going to be –'

'Don't start Tash. I told you, I've got enough on my mind.'

'This will take your mind off your troubles. Look, don't start crying again. I bet you've got it all wrong. Isn't he going on holiday with you?'

'Of course he is.'

'Then there can't be another woman can there? Your mum wouldn't want him –'

'What if she knows and she's keeping together for our sake?' Mel was stopped in the street by the idea.

'Mel, whatever you do, don't say anything to her.'

'Why not? Hasn't she got a right to know.'

'Not from you. You could make things worse.'

'Should I tell Dom?'

'That could be an even worse idea. You can't tell Dom. It's only suspicion, you don't know anything for sure.'

'You think you know it all,' says Melissa. 'How come you're the big advice place all of a sudden, who trained you up to be a family counsellor?'

'I'm just looking at it from outside,' says Tash.

'You think you know better than I do, and I've been living with it, I should know what it's like. I'm going to say something.'

'To your mum or your dad?'

'Just my Dad. I'm going to tell him I know everything and I'll tell him I'll tell mum if he doesn't promise to give her up.'

'What if he says you're wrong?'

'I'll know if he's lying.'

'What if you *are* wrong?'

'I'll write it all down, dates of all those texts and what they say, then I'll have it even if he takes his phone and deletes everything. I'll tell him I know everything. I'll do it while Mum's at work.'

'Tell you what,' says Tash, 'why don't you talk to my mum and ask her what you should do? She'll listen to you, honestly she will. She won't shout at you.'

'She'll tell my mum though, before you can turn round. She'll be straight round at my house telling her everything, wouldn't that be the same as me telling her?'

'Or you could wait and tell Grandad when he gets home. He always knows what to do. Just don't do anything stupid.'

'You think I'm stupid, is that what you're saying?'

'You are if you go telling your mum and dad without thinking it through.'

'Here's Goody-Two-Shoes again,' says Mel. 'Mind your own business, Miss Know-All and let me make my own decisions.'

179

'Suit yourself' says Tash. 'And I'll decide what I'm going to do about Niecey and I obviously won't consult you because you've just told me you don't want to be bothered.'

She marches into her mother's kitchen and bangs the pasta on to the worktop. Melissa follows and puts her packet gently on the table.

'You two fell out?' says Gemma pleasantly.

'Not really,' says Melissa. 'Is it all right if I watch TV?'

'Sure,' says Gemma.

'You know what,' says Lynn. 'We should have called Sarah yesterday, just to see how things are going. They're off today, they'll be gone by the time we get home.'

They are driving back from Cornwall, in glorious sunshine, as they have not failed to point out to each other.

'It's been on my mind too,' admits Dave. 'But you can text her tomorrow. Let's not get out of holiday mode before we have to. We'll have a nice quiet evening in front of telly. We don't even need to unpack.'

'Oh,' says Lynn. 'I'll just get a load of washing on and then we'll put our feet up.'

'No washing,' he says firmly. 'I know you. You'll start with a load of washing and then it will be, Oh I'll just do this, I'll change the bed, I'll vacuum the stairs and before I know it you'll be up a ladder cleaning the landing window.'

Lynn is laughing. 'I'm not as bad as that. You do exaggerate, you.'

'No worrying about owt till tomorrow. All right?'

'All right.'

The phone rings before they have finished their first cup of tea.

'It was Sarah,' says Dave. 'Ringing from airport. Telling us about Melissa. She's been charged and she'll have to go to court – don't know yet when that will be. Sounded proper stressed out, Sarah did. I can tell she's getting herself in a state before she even needs to. There's this appointment – some time, she don't know when, not yet, asking can we have Dom when this person comes to do some sort of report.'

'I'll be at work,' says Lynn. 'But you'll have him won't you. It will be nice won't it.'

'I don't mind having Dom,' he says, 'of course I don't. It's just Melissa – we've never had anything like this before have we. I just wish all I had to think about was getting the grass cut and dead-heading them rudbeckias. Honestly Lynnie, we've just had a holiday and all the benefit of it has gone, just like that.'

'Well,' says Dave. 'How have things been?'

'What things?' says Gemma.

'You know. Things in general. Everyone OK?'

'Mm,' says Gemma. 'What about you? Did you have a good time?'

'Of course' says Dave. 'We always do. I told your mother, Forget all them at home, we're here to enjoy ourselves.' He pauses. 'You know about Melissa's little escapade I suppose?'

'Dad, there's not a person in the English-speaking world who doesn't know all about it. Though by now it's old news and they will have found something else to talk about. Yes, I know – not that Sarah told me – and Tash knows and Jake knows, and all their friends, all the neighbours. You know.'

'What about Sarah? How's she taking it? She rang us yesterday from airport – sounded stressed out, but that's airports in't it. So I didn't get anything out of her. Only she's got to go to court some time. But they don't know when – is that right?'

'As far as I can gather,' says Gemma, 'Mel was arrested and charged and now she has to wait for a court date. Tash says she's got one but I'm not sure I believe that. Someone is going to come round and see her before she goes to court, to write some sort of report – it's not Sarah telling me this, it's what I've gathered, you know, online, and from someone at work who knows about these things cos she went through it with her son.'

'So nothing's happened? Is Sarah all right though?'

'Dad, I've not seen her. I've spoke to her on the phone but that's all. I've had her kids here most of this week while she was working.'

'You've not been working yourself?'

'Been home with the kids. Mark's mum has been doing a turn in the shop for us. It's worked out OK.'

'Seen Niecey?'

She looks at him sharply. 'Why are you asking?'

'Just wondering.' His voice is trying to sound casual.

'Yes, as it happens, I've seen her a few times. We've been getting on well. Talking, you know.'

'What does Sarah think about it?'

'What do you mean Dad?'

182

He stops to think. 'I was thinking Sarah might be getting a bit – left out. You know, feeling like you and her aren't as close as you used to be.'

'For goodness sake Dad, where do you get these ideas? We're not eleven years old are we. All right, me and Sar had a bit of an argument, but it's all over, I've been looking after the kids, when she comes back off holiday things will be fine.'

'I hope so,' says Dave. 'Now then, do you want to go into work this week? Shall I take Jake home with me? Tash too if she wants to come.'

When Lynn gets to work on Monday she sees Niecey's back receding down the corridor pulling the vacuum cleaner behind her. Katie comes out of her office smiling, pleased to see her.

'How are you? Did you have a good time?'

'So so,' says Lynn. 'How are things here?'

'Pretty quiet. Come into the office, I'll get you up to speed.'

'Actually,' says Lynn, 'you might not want to bother. I've decided to hand in my notice.'

'Come in,' says Katie. 'We won't do this standing in the hall.'

She fetches two coffees from the kitchen and sits herself down, not behind the desk as she did with Niecey, but beside Lynn, the two mugs on the low table in front of them, steaming gently.

'I'm going to retire,' says Lynn. 'I'm well past sixty you know.'

'You don't have to explain,' says Katie. 'I just want to be sure that you really want to do this – because you always said, didn't you, that you couldn't face the thought of leaving us – and if there's anything that I've done, or anything that's made you unhappy here – you know what I'm saying. If there's something we can put right, then we'll do our best. If retiring is what you really want to do – well, you're entitled and we'll all wish you –'

'I didn't want to stop work,' says Lynn. Her face is tight as if she is struggling against having any sort of expression. 'But I feel needed at home. Everything seems to be going wrong. I can't concentrate on my job, my mind isn't on it –'

'Are you sleeping all right?'

'Not really. I drop off but then I wake up and it all goes round and round in my head and there seems to be no way out –'

'Is your husband –?'

'He's fine. Obviously he's worried too, about our children, two of them anyway, but he says we have to let them get on with it, they're grown up he says. I think he worries though, as much as I do, he only says he's OK.'

'Is Niecey part of your problem?' Katie says this gently, warily.

Lynn does not reply immediately. 'There's something, yes. But I don't know the details and I don't want to talk about it.'

'It makes it hard for you to see her here at work though?'

'It's a bit awkward, yes.'

'You know something, or you think you do, and she knows you know, or she thinks you know, but you haven't said anything to her and she hasn't said anything to you?'

'Yes,' says Lynn.

'I've had a conversation with Niecey,' says Katie. 'Obviously I can't say any more than that, but she is still working here, and I hope she can continue to work here. If you wanted me to sit down with the pair of you to have a conversation, if it would help –'

'I don't think so,' says Lynn quickly. 'Thank you, but not at the moment anyway.'

Katie waits, says nothing.

'I'm going to hand in my notice,' says Lynn. 'I've thought about it while we were on holiday, I've told Dave, I've made up my mind. I'm tired.'

'Lynn,' says Katie. 'I've said already, you're entitled. If it's the right thing for you, then do it. I'm not saying we'll manage without you because we won't manage as well as we do now, but do it. Just remember there are other options we can look at. Part-time? Or do you need some sick leave? If you're not sleeping you could get signed off for a week or two.'

'I've brought the letter with me,' says Lynn, and holds out the envelope.

'If you're sure.'

'I'm sure.' And Lynn does not wait for Katie to leave the room before the tears come.

It is, as promised, a hot clear morning in Ibiza.

Jon and Dominic are in the pool before breakfast. Sarah is in the shower and Melissa is looking at her phone, wondering if Tash is really so hacked off with her that she hasn't texted. She puts it down and brushes her hair while she considers whether she needs to care. Her father and brother come into the room with towels round their shoulders.

'Breakfast,' says Jon loudly. 'Where's your mother?'

Melissa inclines her head towards the shower. She is, when she remembers, not speaking to her Dad.

Sarah comes out of the shower. 'You go on without me,' she says. 'I'll see you when I'm dressed and ready.'

'Just put something on,' says Jon. 'You don't need make-up or whatever to go into breakfast.'

'Don't start,' says Sarah. 'I'll take my time. I'm on holiday, it's not a race, I'll come when I'm ready.'

'And we'll be finished by then,' he says. 'I want to go in as a family.'

'Fine,' says Sarah. 'You go with the kids. You can pretend to be a single-parent family.'

'Funny,' he says, without smiling. He goes into the bedroom and comes out wearing his new holiday shorts.

'Coming kids?'

Dom and Melissa look towards their mother but she has gone back into the bathroom. 'See you later,' she calls, and they get up and follow their father, without speaking.

*

Tash wakes up with an idea. That's not really true – the idea has been there all along, ever since she learned about Niecey's lost children – but she has pushed it away, knowing that she is taking a chance, going out on a limb, as her Grandad would say. Whatever *that* means. At the same time though, in bed at night, or when she has had to do some boring job for her mother, she has been rehearsing the words in her head, she has envisaged the response, and then the acclaim, the gratitude of Niecey, the tears and smiles, and maybe presents, the approval of all her family, even an appearance on Look North. Teenager Reunites Long-Lost Family.

She wakes up, then, determined to do it. Her Mum comes into her room, dressed and ready for work. 'I off now love. Make sure Jake has a proper breakfast won't you. And put the pots in the dishwasher, *please*.'

'Yeah yeah, all right Mum.'

'And you could sort your clothes out ready for Filey. Anything that needs washing – has to be done today or you can't take it.'

'OK.'

'Grandad will come soon after eleven, he says, so you can go there with Jake if you want.'

'I know.'

'If you don't, you'll find plenty in the fridge.'

'Mm.'

'Right then, I off.'

Tash, foregoing breakfast, brings the laptop into her room as soon as she hears the front door click shut. She hears Jake go downstairs but she does not bother to go and monitor his breakfast. She ignores the pictures Melissa has sent of a blue sea, a white hotel, and her own sunburnt feet. She sets her plan in motion.

*

Melissa, sitting by the pool where Dom is jumping and splashing with another boy, hears a message arrive to her phone. Her mother has been nagging her to turn it off and find something better to do, but, she thinks, what is there to do? She is not going to join small boys in their splashy games. She is not going to swim up and down as her father has been doing. She is not going to go for a walk. She has read her magazines, and her mother's magazines. So she looks at her phone; it is a Facebook update, from Tash.

It says: Hi everyone who knows me. This is a very special update. I am searching for two members of my family, my cousins. One is called Oliver and the other is called Lila. They are twins. I don't know how old they are but probably about Year Nine or Ten. I don't know where they live, maybe in the UK, maybe in America. Please pass this message on so that they can get in touch and be reunited with their family.

No surnames, notes Melissa. Tash is supposed to be so clever, why didn't she do the job properly?

'Are you on your phone again?'

Melissa looks up at her mother and turns the phone off. She hopes Tash has filtered out all the people in the family who might have something to say about this. The trouble with Tash is that when she has an idea she can never imagine being wrong.

*

Lynn and Dave are sitting at the table looking at the empty plates that need clearing.

'You've had a hard day,' says Dave. 'I do the pots, you go and sit down.'

The phone rings. 'I'll get it,' says Dave, getting to his feet. 'If it's for you I'll tell them to wait while tomorrow.'

He comes back into the room and passes the phone to her. 'It's your sister. Can't even bother herself to say hello to me.'

'Hello Janet.' Lynn too is guarded.

Dave wanders out into the garden to check on the weeds and the tomatoes. He's still there, pulling up the odd bit of groundsel, when Lynn comes out to join him.

'What did she want?'

Lynn has a stunned look about her. 'You won't believe this.'

'Go on then.'

She sits on the bench. 'Come and sit down,' she says. 'I'm still trying to get my head round this.'

'What's wrong? Not Melissa again is it?'

Lynn closes her eyes briefly and then, without looking at him, begins. 'Now tell me, what were the names of Niecey's twins?' Though she knows perfectly well.

'Oliver and Lila.'

'Well –'

'What then? Don't tell me your Janet is mixed up in this.'

'Just listen. She says to me, I've had this strange thing from your Tash on Facebook.'

'Oh, don't tell me that's all over Facebook as well. How has Tash got hold of it?'

'Now that I don't know, but seemingly our Tash has put something on Facebook to all her mates, asking if anyone knows these two kids. This Lila and Oliver.'

'And Janet's seen it because Janet hasn't got anything better to do than to spy on my family,' says Dave bitterly.

'So Janet's seen it,' says Lynn, 'along with the rest of the world, I know what you're thinking David Wilde, but just listen – so Janet's seen it, and she says to me, well, I can tell you something about them. And I've said, why do you

188

know where they are, and she's said, Not exactly, but I bet I can find them for you.'

'She's not told Tash though, has she?'

'Do credit my sister,' says Lynn, 'with some sense. Why do you think she's told us? So she says, I know a woman who took on a pair of twins that were her son's children, and guess what their names were? So I've waited and she's come out with it – their names, and she says to me, do you know anything about this, because Tash is saying they are long-lost cousins, and – well, Janet's put two and two together –'

'She would,' says Dave.

'– and she says, Is this something to do with Niecey? I always wondered, she says, what was going on there.'

'So what is she telling us, after all this. Are we getting information, or just your Janet's wondering?'

'There were a woman down her road, Janet used to tell me about her, she had hairdressing salons I believe, I think our Janet thought she were bee's knees and all that, with her nice car and her hairdos, you know, and this woman, her name were –'

'Jacqui Wilson I suppose,' says Dave.

'Well yes, a long time ago, but she's got married, she's not Wilson now, hasn't been for years apparently, and they don't live in Sheffield any more, no, they're down near Bakewell, husband has some kind of business in Chesterfield, Janet thinks.'

There is a substantial silence.

'One thing,' says Lynn. 'Let's keep this to ourselves, for now. Let's not tell the girls, or anyone, till we've had time to think it through. All right?'

Silence.

'What are you thinking?' says Lynn.

'I'm thinking,' he says, 'that it's just one thing after another. I can't keep up. I'm seventy-one, Lynnie, I can't keep up with all this. I shouldn't have to.'

'You don't have to,' she says. 'We can say, it's none of our business. We can leave them to work it out.'

'What,' he says, 'retire from the family, like retiring from a job?' He waits for her to respond, then does it himself. 'No, no, that's not going to happen. Is it?'

A mile away Tasha is seated on a kitchen chair, her father silent across the table, her mother leaning, arms folded, against the washing machine.

'And where,' says Gemma, 'did you get this information from?' Her voice is quiet but it is trembling with the effort of keeping her temper.

'Not just me,' says Tasha. 'Melissa were in it too.'

'That's not what I asked. I know what you've done. I've seen it. I've told you already what I think of a person who broadcasts family business – private business – all over the internet. Who thinks they know better than their parents. Who meddles in things they don't understand. What I'm asking you now is this – where did you get this information from? Who told you?'

'Melissa –'

'I've said,' says Gemma, 'I don't want to know about what Melissa said or did. She doesn't know anything.'

'She does, she does,' insists Tasha. 'Mum, she heard you. She was outside the door and you and Niecey were talking and she heard you. And we already thought something was going on cos everyone were that funny –'

'What do you mean?'

'Like, you and Niecey were having all these talks, and Mel's mum and dad were having all these arguments and we knew something must be up and we thought, well if we can find these twins it will all be sorted out. I was trying to help.'

'So tell me,' says Gemma, 'step by step, what you did to – help. As you call it.'

Tasha does not speak for a long time. 'I looked at your laptop.'

'And?'

'Mel was going to look at her Mum's phone too but she couldn't get it.'

'So – texts, emails. Grown-up communications. *Private* messages. And you two have been spying on them.'

'No –'

'Yes. And then spreading it all round the city, and all your friends will be spreading it, further and further, and who knows – Tash, didn't you think for one *second* about the trouble you might cause?'

'Like what?'

'Like if there are good reasons for those kids to be kept away from their mother. Like if they don't even know

190

anything about her. Like if they are with their Dad and he's married again and they have brothers and sisters and they're quite happy and you blunder in – whether anyone likes it or not – and turn everything upside down.'

'That's not what you said to Niecey though, is it? Mel heard you talking about looking on Facebook, and Social Services. How is it any different, what we've done? You just want to keep us out of it. You think we're children.'

'You are,' says Gemma.

Mark speaks for the first time. 'Have you had any replies? You know, on Facebook?'

'Yes, replies,' says Tash, 'but nothing positive – just people saying they'll pass it on, that's all.'

'That's another thing,' says Gemma. 'What settings did you use?'

'Don't know,' says Tash. 'Can't remember. Whatever it was set on.' She is screwing up her eyes the way she does when she is angry.

'These replies,' says Gemma. 'Any from people you don't know?'

'Don't think so.'

'I'll check,' says Gemma wearily. It seems that her anger has deflated. 'Thank goodness Melissa's out of the country. Though I suppose she'll have her phone with her, she'll still be in contact with all these friends. So-called. I have to call Sarah and let her know.'

'Don't!' says Tash. 'Don't tell Auntie Sarah. Please. She's being horrible to Mel, honestly, Mel's really miserable at home, there's nothing but rows, she says.'

'Well, she shouldn't have gone shoplifting should she. Does she expect her parents to behave like nothing happened? When she has social workers coming round and they have to go to court with her?'

'Not social workers Mum. They're called Youth Justice.'

'Same thing.'

'And it's not just getting at Mel you know. Auntie Sarah and Uncle Jon are having big fights –'

'Fights?'

'You know, arguments, shouting and that. Mel is scared her Dad is going to leave home.'

'That's not going to happen,' says Mark.

'How do you know?'

'Not your business,' says Gemma. 'Just like your Aunt Niecey, this is none of your business. And the first thing you can do now, my girl, is hand over your phone. Now, to me. And the laptop stays in this room, do you understand, where I can see what you're doing.'

'You're treating me like a child,' says Tasha.

'That's right,' says her mother. Tasha looks at her dad in the hope that he will be on her side but he had turned away already. She hands her phone to her mother and stalks out of the room. They hear her sobs of fury as she goes up to her room.

'Am I right?' says Gemma. 'She's got to be punished, hasn't she. Mark?'

Mark is facing the window but he turns and puts his arm round her shoulder. 'She'll get over it,' he says. 'No one ever said it was easy, having teenagers.'

'I'll be glad when they're back at school,' says Gemma. 'And we've got a week in bloody Filey to get through first.'

Lila and Oliver have grown up in an unusual position. They are not the only kids who live *not* with their own parents; they know others. There is Kieron, Oliver's best friend, whose mother is periodically hospitalised – Kieron doesn't tell anyone what for – and when she is he and his little brother go to stay with an aunt, sometimes for the whole of a term, sometimes only for a week or two. There is Belinda who lives in term time with her grandparents so as to be in the catchment area for her preferred school. There is Gwennie, who lives with her grown up half-sister, because their mother died and their father says he can cope with the brothers but not with a teenage girl. Lila sometimes walks home with Gwennie, though she is in the year below, and they discuss possible reasons why a father cannot look after his children. But Lila and Oliver, so far as they know, have never met anyone else who cannot remember their mother, who know so little about her, who have no family, apparently, beyond a father who lives thousands of miles away and doesn't even skype, a grandmother, and a step-grandfather. And each other.

They cannot clearly remember living in any other place than where they live now. This house is where they learnt to eat sitting at a table, these armchairs are where they sat with Granny Jac while she read them stories, this garden is where they rode their balance bikes and pushed their toy wheelbarrows, this road is the one they walked along into the town, into nursery, into school. These views are the ones they know will be there when they open their curtains each morning.

'How old were we?' said Oliver. 'When we came to live with you?' He was seven when he asked this.

'You were three,' said Granny Jac. 'Just two weeks off being three.'

'Did we have a party?' said Lila.

'Of course.' It was one of the lies that Jacqui seemed to be stuck with.

'Was our mother there?' This was a question Lila had not thought to ask before.

'No she wasn't.'

'Why not?'

'I've told you haven't I –' Jacqui's voice strained not to sound impatient '– she wasn't able to look after you, so your Daddy brought you to live with me.'

'Was he at our party?'

'Certainly,' said Jacqui. It was almost true – Adrian, under some duress, had stayed for a matter of weeks with his children, so if there *had* been a party he would no doubt have been there.

'Is there photos?'

'No, I don't think so.'

'Why not?' This was Ollie joining in.

'Well – I couldn't really say. Maybe we were too busy having fun. Now, I have to go and get the washing out of the dryer.'

Lila ran after her into the utility room. 'Can our mother come to our party when we're eight?'

Of course, as they have grown older their questions have become more searching. Jacqui has tried to be helpful, but not at the price of being honest. Their mother wasn't able to look after them. No, she's not exactly sure why not. Of course she loved them, but sometimes it happens that it's not possible to et cetera et cetera. Is she dead? Well, nobody knows for sure – Jacqui would have liked to tell them Denny was dead but she did not dare. Where did she go? Did she go to hospital? Did she go to America? Did we call her Mummy? Why is our dad in America? Is our mother there too? What was her favourite colour? Did she smack us? Did she shout? Did she love us *really*? Does she remember us? What school did she go to? Is she English? Do we have cousins? Why don't we have cousins? Which one of us is the oldest? Why don't you know? When will she come back?

Jacqui knows that they have always talked between them about their mother. She has heard them – Lila creeping into Ollie's room at night when they should both have been asleep and their whispering, serious young voices, trying to puzzle it all out.

'If she was dead she would have a gravestone.'

'Where though? Where would it be?'

'Why aren't there photos of her?'

'There aren't any of us even, until we came to live here.'

'Maybe she kept them.'

'When Dad comes we'll ask him.'

But when he came, which was seldom, and briefly, he appeared not to hear them if they asked questions about their mother. He pretended his phone had made a noise, or he went into the kitchen saying he was going to help with dinner.

The confused ideas that the children were left with amounted to this: that their mother's name was Denise, or Denny; that she lived – if she still lived – in London; that she had some sort of disability that prevented her from looking after children – for many years Lila imagined a woman with no arms and the image never went entirely away.

They have tried to describe to each other their earliest memories. They believe they remember, because Jacqui has told them, sitting in high chairs in the cafe. Ollie says he remembers being lifted up to look out of a window at a fire engine. Or maybe it was a JCB. Whoever lifted him then stood him on a kitchen worktop so that he could see out. He says he can remember – whoever it was – holding on to his T-shirt. 'Who was it though?' says Lila. Of course, she thought, her mother had arms – they would surely have been told if she hadn't.

Lila says she remembers falling out of bed and someone – their mother? – coming in and picking her off the floor and taking her into her own bed. 'Was Dad there?' asks Ollie. Lila would like to say yes but as she believes they are working seriously and scientifically she suppresses the urge and says she doesn't know. 'Shouldn't we have been in a cot though?'

They have been told they were born in Norwich – why do they picture their mother – and themselves – in London? Why do they picture themselves as babies living in a house with a garden when Granny had told them many times they lived in a small flat. Why did Lila, when she was eight, draw a picture of their mother with brown skin like theirs, darker even, more like their father's?

'Who is this Dad?' she said, and when he couldn't guess and she told him it was Denise, 'Who?' he said. 'Oh –' and then he laughed and called Granny to look.

Lila was cross and embarrassed, and then upset, and it was not until Dad had gone that Granny explained that their mother was white, and drew a whole family tree with coloured pencils to show how their skin colour – the colour of almond shells, Lila's slightly darker than Ollie's – had come about.

'When we grow up,' said Ollie, 'we'll go and find her.'
'How though?'

'There are ways,' said Ollie. 'This boy Daniel at school, his dad has found out that some old great grandfather fought in the Civil War. And he's *dead*. So if you can find a dead person – well, even if she is dead we can find her. I bet there are books. And you know, you can look things up on the internet. When we're allowed, that's what we'll do.'

Jacqui kept them away from online as long as she could, but when they went to the comprehensive they had to have tablets of their own. Anyway, she thought, they can't stay ignorant for ever.

It is late and moths are flying round the dark garden. Lynn and Dave are still sitting there; they are tired and ready for bed but they sit there still.

'I could have had a load of ironing done by now,' says Lynn.

'What if –?'

'Dave, I don't want any more of your what-ifs. We've what-iffed every which way and there's no good way. What if we pretend that Janet never phoned? We don't know anything. It's none of our business.'

'You keep coming back to that. You want to hide from it. But how would you look Niecey in the face –?'

'How can she look us in the face? Like she has been doing all these years? Why should we do anything for her?'

'Like I said, and I've kept on saying, and I keep on saying, you can't keep secrets in a family.'

'*She* did.'

'And in the end it's all come out and look at the upset it's caused. Far better if she'd told Jamie right at the start.'

'So you keep saying. And Dave, I not disagreeing with you. If she'd said at the start then by now it would be ordinary. Maybe Janet would have told us years ago if it had been out in the open.' She brings her hands up to her face. 'Oh I can't bear to think of it. Why didn't she *say*? What was she so afraid of?'

'No good thinking about it Lynnie, it's past. Come on, let's go to bed and sleep on it.'

Lynn stands up wearily and allows herself to be led indoors, leaving the clearing up until the morning.

'I have had this weird message. Have you had it too?'

'On Facebook? This one?' says Lila. 'Yeah, I've had it three times now.'

'Do you know anyone called Tash?'

'Not in our year. There's one in Year Eleven –'

'So why,' says Ollie, 'why isn't it our mother who is posting this? Who is Tash? We don't have a cousin called Tash.'

'I know.'

'We don't have any cousins. Unless our mother had another baby. If she's not dead. Maybe Tash is our –'

'She'd be our sister. Half-sister.'

'I don't get it.'

'Me neither. What should we do?'

'Delete,' says Ollie. 'No, don't do that. We'll be getting some more. If it's got to kids in our school it will get to all of them. Keep them all. But tell them it's not us. Just go, Oh wow, how weird, but it's not us.'

'Then what?'

'Well look, it isn't us is it? Cousins are your parents' sister's children, right? Or brother's. We know we haven't got any cousins cos our parents haven't got sisters or brothers, right? So Tash isn't our cousin. But –'

'How do we know though – she might have a brother or sister.'

'Granny said she didn't.'

'How does *she* know? It's probably just what Adrian said, and *he* might not know either.'

'So you mean we might have a cousin.'

'She might be somebody?'

'Like?'

'Like a relative. Someone in our family. There's second cousins aren't there.'

'What we'll do, we'll find someone at school and trace it back till we've got who Tash is and then –'

'What?'

'We'll take it from there.'

'Don't tell Granny Jac.'

'Li, don't tell anyone at all. If they don't know, don't tell em. If they've heard, we don't know anything, right?'

'What you scared of Ol?'

'I don't know. Scams, that sort of thing. Someone trying to get hold of us.'

'Suppose it's her, you know, our mother?'

'We'll find out eventually won't we. We've waited this long, we can wait till the kids at school have forgotten. We don't want everyone coming up and asking us stuff do we. Right?'

Dave pops round to Gemma's house, hoping to catch her before they set off for their holiday. He finds Mark loading the car, Jake helping and Gemma tidying the kitchen and sorting out food to take with them.

'Where's Tash?'

'She's not up yet. Actually Dad, let me make you a coffee, there's something I want to tell you while it's quiet.'

He sits at the table and watches her fondly as she spoons the coffee into two cups and pours on the water.

'What's up then?'

'Tash,' she says. 'You don't do Facebook, I know you don't, but just about everyone else in the world does and our Tash has been – well, been a little busybody and she's put this thing on about Niecey's kids.'

Dave nods carefully.

'You're not looking surprised, Dad. Do you know about this?'

'Janet,' he says. 'Your Aunt Janet. She picked up that message, or whatever you call it. She phoned your mother and told her.'

'Not surprising,' says Gemma. 'I don't suppose she put any filters on it, except for me and her Dad and probably Sarah.'

'Was Mel in on this then?'

'Some of it without a doubt. But it's Tash who's actually done the deed. And she's not sorry, she's quite proud of it really. She's helping, she says.'

'Will Jamie have got it? Niecey?'

'Well, I haven't heard anything. Jamie doesn't look at his very much and I happen to know that Niecey only keeps a page with her old name on it. Not much traffic on there, and I don't think she's even friends with anyone.'

'It's all Dutch to me,' says Dave. 'So you've had words with young Tash?'

'Oh certainly. She's grounded for the rest of this week and I've taken her phone off her, it's up there on the shelf.' Gemma lifts her hand to the shelf where she keeps her kitchen scales and measuring jugs. 'It's not there. Little madam must have sneaked down and got it.'

She moves towards the stairs.

'Just a minute,' says Dave, 'there's something else I need to say.'

But he is too late, because Gemma is already shouting up the stairs. 'Tasha! Get yourself down here, and bring that phone with you. Now!'

It's Jake who appears. 'Did you call me – oh, hello Grandad.'

'I called your sister,' says Gemma.

'Can I make some toast?'

'You had breakfast.'

'Cereal bar?'

'You can have an apple.'

He sits beside Dave and eats his apple. 'Nannan gone to work?'

'That's right. And I've just come round to wish you a happy holiday. Here's a bit of spending money for you, don't tell your mum.'

Gemma has gone upstairs to retrieve the phone and have an argument. There is no opportunity now for any more talk about what is on all the grown up minds. Dave leaves another tenner on the table for Tash, and calls up the stairs to say goodbye.

*

Every evening he and Lynn have the same conversation.

'How will we go on if we don't tell her?'

'What if we tell her and it all goes wrong?'

'How? How could it go wrong?'

'This Jacqui whatever-her-name-is, she could say she can't see them. They might be wards of court or something. She might know things we don't know, she might have reasons.'

'They might not even be with her any more, whatever Janet says. They might have gone back to their Dad.'

'If we don't tell Niecey and she finds out later that we knew all along – what's she going to think of us?'

'Suppose we tell Jamie?'

'But what has she told him already? I don't want to be the one to cause problems between them, do you?'

'Jamie told me,' says Dave, 'that Niecey had told him everything.'

'He might think she has, but she might not have. How would he know what she hasn't told him?'

'So to start with we'd have to ask him – do you know she was married before? Do you know she had twin children?' He does not mention the time in prison, she notices.

'He's seen the birth certificates – it seems a long time ago, doesn't it to you?'

'So we'd go to Jamie behind her back. We'd put the responsibility on him. What if he said, no, he's keeping quiet about it, if he said he didn't want anyone to tell her.'

'Well, so what?'

'We'd still know, wouldn't we? We'd be in the same pickle as we are now. We'd have it hanging over us every time we saw her, we'd be wondering too, will Tash tell her she knows all about it. Will Melissa say something? How long will it be before the boys find out? What if they say something to Leo?'

'But what if we tell her and it all goes wrong? What if those kids don't want anything to do with her?'

'I know. But until we tell her, nobody would have the choice would they.'

They are sitting in the back garden again. A cool breeze blows through the phlox and brings the scent to them. The sparrows in the hedge have gone silent now that it is nearly dark.

After a long silence, 'How about this,' says Lynn. "We – you and me, just us – we find this Jacqui woman and we make an appointment, a proper formal appointment to see her and we tell her who we are, and that we know the mother of the children and we know that she's not a criminal and that she's been longing for years that she could find the children and see them again – she has, hasn't she?'

'Oh she certainly has.'

'And we discuss with her what to do. She's their guardian after all, she should have a say in this, they are minors, they're children like Tash and Melly, they can't be expected to make sensible decisions. What do you think?'

He smiles at her triumphantly, as if it has been his idea. 'I think you're right, love. I think that is far and away the best thing we can do. I'll do the finding out – we'll see what Janet can tell us, where his business is, home address, that sort of thing, then you can phone her and speak to her – best coming from a woman do you think? – and then, as soon as you've got over being retired, we'll arrange to go and see her. The kids will all be back at school by then. It's a plan.'

She sighs wearily. 'Good. Can we stop thinking about it now?'

'I should say so. Shall we have a beer?'

The dusk falls over them as they sip the cold beers.

Jacqui is finding the children rather tiresome as the holidays draw to an end. There is obviously some secret between them, and some difference of opinion. Ollie is twitchy and Lila is excitable in a more positive way; then it will change and Ollie will be calm and Lila will be objectionable about decisions which a few weeks ago would have rolled over her. Bruce hasn't noticed any of this, engrossed as he is in the design of the new saleroom being built on his forecourt.

'Shall we go for a walk?' says Jacqui. It is almost eleven on a still, stifling morning. 'We could go along the river, may be a bit cooler there. We could walk to Ashford and have lunch in the pub.'

Lila shrugs as if it's all the same to her; Ollie says he was thinking of going round to see his friend.

'Kieron's away though,' says Lila.

'Oh yeah, I forgot.'

'You did not,' says Lila. 'You're not going to forget that are you? As if.'

'Stop it,' says Jacqui. 'It's not worth having an argument about. Do you want a walk with me or not. You don't have to. I've got plenty to do in the garden – in fact, you could both help me if you're doing nothing else.'

'I'm going to see people,' says Lila. '*My* friends haven't gone away and left me.'

'Don't be childish,' says Ollie. He turns and they hear his bedroom door close quietly.

Ten minutes later, when she can't wait any longer, Lila goes to Ollie's room.

'You're supposed to knock,' he says.

She stands in the room, looking first out of the window at the house across the road and beyond, at the water meadows; then looking at his bookshelf and at his computer, where there is nothing to be seen except the screensaver of an American footballer.

'What are you doing?'

'I thought you were going out with your friends.'

'Not really,' she says. She pulls a post-it note off a pad, writes on it and tries to stick it on his forehead.

'Leave off.'

'It's just a game,' she says. 'You have to guess what it says.'

'I know that,' he says. 'Think I'm stupid. It probably says 'dickhead' doesn't it.'

She screws it up and throws it in the bin.

'What we should do,' she says, 'is write a private note to that Tash, just asking who she is.'

'But then she'll have us as a contact and she'll know who we are. Even if we're not the people she wants us to be she'll be able to go on contacting us.'

'So what do we do?'

'We could use someone else's account.'

'Like Jacqui's?'

'Bruce's better still.'

'And say what?'

'Write it like it's from him, like – It is possible that I may have some information for you, but initially I would need your full name and address and assurances that –'

'But then he would get a reply and he'd know –'

'Yeah.'

'Should we ask Granny Jac if she knows anyone called Tash?'

'Stick to the line we're on Li. I've never known you so all over the place.'

'Cos you're perfectly calm and in control of course.'

'More than you are.'

'I'm going for a walk with Granny Jac,' she says suddenly.

'Shall I come?'

'Go on then.'

'What is the matter with them?' says Jacqui to Bruce later. 'They've always got on so well, they've always looked out for each other, now they're in each other's faces all the time. Not in a violent way, I don't mean that, just niggling and sniping.'

'Probably their age,' says Bruce. He is searching his phone for a cricket score.

'I'm tired,' says Jacqui. 'It feels like these holidays are never-ending.'

'Another year,' he says, 'with no break. Next year they'll be fifteen – they can go stay with someone, I don't care who.' He has found the cricket score and it is not to his liking.

'There's only the Nuttalls,' says Jacqui, and shudders as she customarily does when she thinks of them.

'We can do better than that,' says Bruce.

Jacqui laughs. 'Certainly couldn't do any worse.'

Some years ago, driven by guilt, and a need for support, and annoyance at their silence, and – quite honestly – curiosity, Jacqui had dropped the children at school, got back into her car and driven to the Nuttall's village. She found the house.

They were not at home; the cleaner told her they were at work. 'But you're lucky,' she said. 'Mrs Nuttall said she'd be home at lunchtime – don't ask me why – if you'd like to come back a bit later. I'd ask you in but I'm not allowed. Come back, say – half past twelve?'

Jacqui walked away and wandered round the village, smiling scornfully at the idea of having your cleaner refer to you as Mrs. Of being "not allowed" to invite someone in. How feudal it was.

The village was nothing special. Quiet. A couple of shops, church, pub, primary school. A small playground, football goalposts, and swings where two mothers were entertaining a toddler each. A row of council houses where no doubt "Mrs Nuttall's" cleaner lived. Some tidy allotments.

When, passing the house again, she saw a car on the drive she did not wait for twelve-thirty but went and rang the bell again. The cleaner opened the door. 'Who shall I say it is?' she said.

'My name is Jacqui Thwaite,' said Jacqui firmly.

'And what is it regarding?' Even the cleaning woman seemed embarrassed at having to say this.

'It's private,' said Jacqui, just as firmly. She was surprised then that the woman stood back and held the door open for her to go in.

'Yes?' Denise's mother was a small woman, very thin, wearing a navy blue suit – skirt not trousers – no make-up, heavy glasses. She was in her stocking feet; Jacqui could see her sensible shoes on the hall floor. For her size she was surprisingly imposing.

'My name is Jacqui Thwaite,' said Jacqui again.

The woman said nothing.

'I think you are Mrs Nuttall.'

Still nothing.

'I would like to talk to you about your daughter Denise.'

Mrs Nuttall did not allow her face to change. 'Are you from the court? The police? Social Services?'

'None of them,' said Jacqui. 'Would it be better if we talked somewhere private?'

'No,' she said after considering. 'I think this will be adequate.'

Jacqui, she told Bruce afterwards, was ready to run by this point but she had come all this way and clearly only was going to get one shot at this. Already though, she had written off the idea that she would ever leave the twins with this woman. 'I'm Adrian's mother,' she said. 'Adrian was married to your daughter.'

'Yes.'

'I have care of the children.'

'Yes.'

'They live with me. With me and my husband.'

The woman – Mrs Nuttall, Denny's mother – was a small statue, more rigid than iron. Then she said, 'I am going now.'

She picked up a briefcase and a small pile of slippery plastic folders. She pushed her feet roughly into her shoes; Jacqui could see that the backs were tucked in, probably painfully. She lifted her keys from the hall table and called loudly, 'Sylvie.'

The cleaner appeared.

'Open the door Sylvie,' she said.

'Would you mind,' Jacqui addressed Sylvie more than her employer. 'Could I use your loo?'

'In there,' said Sylvie, pointing down the hall.

When Jacqui came out the front door was closed and she could hear the car crunching the gravel. Sylvie was waiting in the hall.

I can push my luck here, thought Jacqui. She said, 'I'm sorry to bother you but could I have drink of water. I've got a long drive home.'

Sylvie looked over her shoulder as if Mrs Nuttall might be coming back into the house, and said, 'I can make you a cup of tea if you like.'

'So,' said Jacqui, standing by the cooker as Sylvie filled the kettle. 'Have you been in this job for a long time?'

'Not that long. Nobody stays that long. But I've lived round here long enough. I know Denise all right. I know what happened to her.'

'You mean –?'

'Going to prison for drugs, yes. I dare say she'll have been out by now. They never do their whole sentence do they.'

'But she's never been back home? Back here?'

'She wouldn't. She couldn't wait to get away in the first place, and who can blame her.'

'So her parents were always –?'

'Hard. Her mother was anyway. She had no chance, Denise. No backbone. Couldn't stand up for herself. Never allowed to be a child, supposed to be perfect from Day One. Well, we know how that turned out don't we?'

'What about Mr Nuttall?'

'Her Dad? Well he's nicer to talk to but he's under the thumb of his old lady.'

'You mean –?'

'Her. She has to be the boss. Everything has to suit her, no one else gets a look in. Shouldn't have been allowed to have a baby, her.'

Jacqui sipped her tea. 'He's a head teacher, right?'

'At the grammar school. She's at the college. Makes em all jump to it, them poor kids. Denise, she was a poor thing, soft as lights, big fat girl, plain as a bread roll –'

'Fat!' said Jacqui. 'She wasn't fat when I saw her.'

'Fat like her Dad,' said Sylvie. 'Though, mind you, by the time she went off down south she'd lost a good bit of it. How she did it I don't know.'

'Her mother's not fat,' said Jacqui. This was turning into a cosy gossip.

'Doesn't eat,' said Sylvie. 'Drinks though.'

'Ah,' said Jacqui. 'So, her dad, Mr Nuttall, do you think he might be interested in his grandchildren?'

'Oh, them children. Fancy having children and carrying on like that, selling drugs and everything. Where she got those ideas I don't know.'

'Well, neither do I,' said Jacqui, though to herself she acknowledged that Adrian might know more about that lifestyle than he had ever let on. 'But she doesn't see the children now. I don't know what has happened to her, if, as you say, she's out of prison by now. I just wondered – I thought it might be nice for the children if they knew their other grandparents.'

'Probably not,' said Sylvie, and they both laughed. 'I tell you what though. You're right, old man Nuttall, he might want to know. Just so he can leave them all his money when he pops off, eh. If you want to leave me your address I don't say I *will* give it him, but if the occasion arises, if you know what I mean –'

'That's a good idea,' said Jacqui. 'Thank you Sylvie, for the tea, and all your help.'

'I don't suppose you feel better for seeing *her*.'

'She's not what you'd call welcoming. Nor talkative. But at least I know now.'

'You won't be coming back, I bet.'

'Probably not. But thank you.'

They exchanged addresses and phone numbers, just in case. Jacqui offered her email address but Sylvie said it was useless to her; if there was anything she needed to say, she would phone.

Jacqui never heard from Sylvie again, but the following Christmas a parcel arrived, posted in Macclesfield, containing two books and two jigsaw puzzles – the books too old for the twins and the jigsaws too young – and a slip of paper bearing a name, R D Nuttall, a mobile number and an email address that clearly belonged to a school.

Sarah and Jon and the children return from Ibiza where they have had two weeks of precarious peace interspersed with awkward low-voiced arguments in the hotel room. The weather has been analogous – hot stillness broken by fierce thunderstorms. Melissa has played a lot of table tennis with the kids' club workers; Dom has perfected his backstroke. Each of them has been sullen when out with both their parents, brittle and bright when with only one.

Back home, there is work, and childcare, and the remaining school holiday weeks to cope with, and the tense waiting for a letter requesting Melissa to go to court. There is Dom to get equipped for starting at the new school; he is becoming anxious and tearful about it and needs reassurance that he won't be picked on because of Melissa's behaviour; reassurance which Sarah is unable to give.

Gemma and Mark and the children are home from Filey. It wasn't the best of holidays. Jake borrowed heavily against his future pocket money to fund sessions in the arcade; Tash, deprived of her phone, took to reading books, pugnaciously, beating each one into the ground like an enemy and immediately starting on another. The days were hot and windy and Mark was painfully sunburned. Gemma patiently rubbed Aftersun on his shoulders and made him stay in the shade from Wednesday onwards.

Back in the shop, the children left in the house, or with Dave, Gemma feels fretful.

'It's six weeks,' she says to Mark. 'Give or take, it's six weeks since I laid eyes on Sarah.'

'Go and see her then,' says Mark.

'Why should I be the one? She started it. And I looked after her kids for her and I never got a thank you. Not even a postcard from Ibiza.'

'Text her,' says Mark.

'What would I say?'

'Call her then. Go out for a coffee. Ask if she can keep Jake overnight for some reason. Just make contact and it'll all work out.'

Gemma, appears not to hear him. 'We've fell out before. But never for this long.'

'You're worried about her,' he says. 'I bet you're worrying about her and Jon. You don't want to take notice of Melissa. You know she's a drama queen. She's only making it all up to give herself an excuse to be upset. Has Tash seen her?'

'I told her to stay away from her,' says Gemma miserably. 'We've missed her birthday and everything. Jake was in the park with Dom yesterday but you know what boys are like. They won't have enquired about each other's families.'

'They might.'

'Trust me,' she says. 'They won't. What I'm going to do, I'm going to ask Dad if we can have a little do when Mum finishes work on Friday. Then we can all be there and there won't be any arguments. All right with you? Maybe you could make one of your cakes.'

'Sounds like a plan,' says Mark, though his eyebrows are raised in a way that if Gemma had been looking, would have communicated doubt.

Leo has found some friends on the beach. His parents sit together, watching as a slightly older boy and his even older sister organise the digging of a canal from the sea to their sand construction.

'See,' says Niecey. 'He's fine. He can get along with anyone. He can make friends just like that.'

'He would have liked a brother or sister though,' says Jamie.

She shakes her head silently, and no more is said for the time being.

The beach scene is one that could have come off a travel poster. There are people, but enough space between them; there is calling and laughing but none of it too raucous; the sea is cold but not so cold that it remains empty; there are clouds in the sky but the sun shines between them enough that children are well rubbed with sunscreen.

'Newquay,' says Jamie. 'That's my favourite seaside. I always wanted to surf but I wasn't old enough, or else the sea was too rough, or too calm, or I'd spent all my money and couldn't hire a surf board.'

'You never got to do it then?'

'I got to canoe. I liked that but it was a bit tame after watching the surfers.'

'How old were you?'

'Young I think. Younger than Leo. My sisters didn't want to do it, that were the trouble. They always got their own way so I had to do what they wanted.'

'So brothers and sisters aren't always an advantage.'

'You told me you wished you weren't an only child. You told me you hated being on your own.'

'I did,' she says. 'But that was more about what my parents were like. We're not going to be like that, are we, all strict and critical of everything he does. If anything we'll mess him up some other way, being too soft maybe.'

'Did your parents ever bring you here? It's not that far from where you lived is it?'

'Not here, no. Too down-market. Too tacky. We were supposed to be above things like candy floss and bingo.'

'Where did you go then? In the holidays. You've never told me about where you went.'

'Historical places,' she says. She shades her eyes to watch that Leo is still in sight and doesn't look at Jamie. 'Castles, ruins, things like that. Rome, Athens. My mother was a historian – you know that – and she wanted me to like history. My Dad's degree was geology so we used to walk up hills and see rocks and stuff.'

'He should come to Derbyshire. Plenty of rocks there.'

She shudders. 'He can go where he likes as long as I don't have to see him.'

'That bad?'

She brushes away something – a sand fly probably – from her eye, and looks briefly at Jamie. 'I know, I've never talked to you about them but now you know everything, there's no harm. Unless you've had enough miserable stories from me. I don't want to go on about it.'

*We are talking more than we ever have – at least I am. But he never mentions the twins. Afraid of upsetting me? Afraid of being angry with me? Maybe I have to be the one to say something, it's only fair.*

He reaches out and gently squeezes her arm. 'All this is stuff we could have talked about years ago. You know what my family's like, they like to know everything about everybody – you've been like the mystery woman. The woman with secrets.'

'The woman who's told lies,' she says. 'Your mum and me – I don't know how we're ever going to get back to getting on together.'

'You will,' he says. 'You watch, once she's retired she'll be that chilled, she'll be a different woman.'

'We'll see' says Niecey. Then, 'I didn't mind so much going for the walks with my Dad. I was quite interested in him telling me about granite and volcanoes and schist and things like that. You know when you see piles of rocks on a beach and they look like they've been upended somehow – he would know what had happened, and how long ago, and he knew where to look for fossils and he had a hammer that he used to break open rocks and there would be a fossil inside.'

'Did he keep them?'

'Oh yes. He had loads of rocks and fossils in the garage, all labelled, on shelves. My mother thought they were pointless. She only liked the sort of history that had written records. She used to make me translate old things in churches, you know, Latin, and I found it so –'

'Boring?'

'Stressful. Like an exam when we'd just gone out for the day and I really wanted to talk to someone my own age, or at least go round the shops and look at stuff.'

'That's what my sisters and my Mum would like to do on holiday. Sit on the beach for a bit, put their toes in the sea, sit a bit more, then, Ooh I could do with a cup of tea, or Can we get an ice cream, or Can we go and look in the gift shop?'

'I should have come on holiday with you. What did your dad like doing?'

'He used to swim in the sea – I think he's stopped that now. He taught us all to swim in the sea. And if there was something to go to, like a castle, he'd have a walk round it but he wouldn't make it a big deal. Anything there was to do – crazy golf, or a bouncy castle, or a sandcastle competition – he'd have a go, or he'd let us have a go. Just not surfing – he thought I'd be disappointed I think.'

Leo comes running up to them, takes some gulps out of the bottle of water and runs back to his new friends. They fall silent as they watch him go.

'You've been very good about it all,' she says, tentatively. 'You know, all the stuff I kept from you. You never gave me a hard time about it.'

He props himself up again and puts a hand on her bare shoulder. 'Nee, why would I give you a hard time? You didn't mean all those things to happen to you.'

'They were my own fault, a lot of them. It's like I was living with my eyes closed, of course I was going to bump into things. But I should have opened my eyes. I should have grown up.'

'People do the best they can,' he says. 'That's what my Dad says anyhow.'

'Nice man, your Dad.'

'They all say that. Mum's nice too –'

'Of course she is.'

'– but people don't always see it. She can be a bit snippy. The sisters too.'

'Gemma's been lovely lately,' says Niecey. 'I've never got on so well with her before. Sarah – well, I don't know what's going to happen there. She seems to have fallen out with all of us.'

'Look,' says Jamie. He props himself up on an elbow and looks down at her. 'I should have said this before. Like when you first told me, the other week, I should have said it. I don't care what you did before I met you. You're my wife, you're great, I'm happy, I love you – all that. If your other kids turned up on the doorstep, no problem. They can live with us if they want. I just want you to be happy, then Leo's happy and I'm happy. OK? And Sarah – she'll come round, don't worry.'

'OK,' she says, and he lies down again on the sand.

He makes it sound easy, she thinks. He thinks you can be happy just by doing it. He amazes her by the faith he has in her, in life, in the goodness of people. She has had to live up to this for six years now, you'd think it would get easier.

'I suppose,' she says, quietly, 'I wouldn't know the children if I saw them now. I wouldn't know how to speak to them. They wouldn't know me at all. I wouldn't be their mother, not after all this time. I should – move on.'

She looks at Jamie but he seems not to have heard; his chest rises and falls as if he is sleeping. As they often do, words of Blake come to her. *My heart is at rest within my breast And every thing else is still.*

At the Hedges, they are missing Niecey. Even Hilda has asked where she is, though she can't remember her name. Margot has asked every five minutes it seems. Lynn forces herself to smile and assures them she will be back next week. 'But I'll be leaving,' she tells them. 'You'll be missing me soon.'

Ron, being of sound mind, is missing his favourite cleaner but is able to understand how long – or short – a week is. He asks especially to speak to Katie.

'When I go,' says Ron, 'I want her to have my books.'

'We're not allowed,' says Katie.

'I know that,' he says, 'but what will happen to them otherwise?'

'Maybe we can keep them here for other people to read.'

'Not that likely is it, that other people will want to. They'll end up in the bin won't they. I'm not daft, am I, I know what's what.'

'I know Ron, I know you know the situation.'

'I want you to write it down,' he says, 'and I'll sign it. I want you to show it to your management committee, not to *her*, mind, so that when I go I can go knowing they'll be taken care of, and read, and appreciated. Will you do that for me?'

'Of course I will,' says Katie. 'But don't say a word to Niecey will you, or that could scupper the whole thing.'

'Mum's the word,' he says.

*

At the end of Lynn's last day at work Dave is waiting outside for her in the car.

She appears late, encumbered with flowers and presents – as he knew she would be – with the signs of tears on her face. Katie accompanies her to the gate. Dave gets out of the car.

'You must be Katie. I've heard a lot about you.'

'And you must be Dave. I've heard a lot about you too.' She turns to Lynn and hugs her. 'I know I've said it before, but you feel free to come and see us any time you miss us. We'll always have a chair for you. Goodbye. We'll miss you.'

'Surprise at home,' says Dave as he puts the car in gear.

'Not the family,' she says – not surprised, not pleased especially, just resigned.

'Not all of them. Jamie and Niecey aren't back from holiday yet, as you know. Just the girls and the kids. Little tea party. Good job it's not raining, we can all sit in the garden.'

Gemma is in the kitchen, arranging cakes on plates; piles of sandwiches are already outside, covered with cling film. The kettle has boiled.

'How are you Mum? Let me take those. Go and sit down with Tash, tell her to put her book down and talk to you. I'll bring you a cup of tea.'

There is noise in the tiny hall as Sarah arrives with Melissa and Dom. She hugs her mother first and turns to her sister, cautiously.

'Hi Gemma.'

'Sarah.' Gemma does not look at her; she keeps her eyes on the chocolate cake she is cutting into ten not quite equal pieces.

'All right?'

Gemma finishes what she is doing and puts the knife down, carefully, and turns to Sarah. 'Fine thank you. You?'

Sarah looks away, down towards her feet and says nothing.

'Come here,' says Gemma suddenly and grabs at her, no matter that her fingers have chocolate icing on them. 'I've missed you, give us a hug.'

But it's an awkward hug, not entirely entered into by either of them. It seems more to pose questions than provide reassurance. Anyway, it's done.

'Can I help?' says Sarah.

'All done,' says Gemma, 'if you can take the tray.' And they go out into the garden together.

'This is nice,' Lynn is saying. 'I didn't know anything like this was going to happen.'

'Mark will be here in a bit,' says Gemma.

'What about Jon?' says Dave. 'Will he make it do you think?'

'Probably not,' says Sarah, but Dom says, 'He said he would try his best. I think he'll come, but maybe late. He said to save a piece of cake for him so I think he'll come.'

Melissa and her mother exchange a glance that shares how gullible Dom must be.

They talk about how sad everyone must have been to see Lynn leave – these are things everyone has said before – they look and admire her presents and read the cards and

Tash takes them indoors and arranges them on the mantelpiece. They ask her how it feels. They ask Dave how he will feel having their mother around all the time.

'No more sneaky visits to the pub at lunch time,' says Gemma.

'Once,' says Dave. 'Not more than once since I retired, and you won't let me forget it.'

'Once,' they mock. 'We've seen you, we know what you get up to.' And he smiles broadly, happy at being teased by his daughters, by both of them together.

They eat the sandwiches, the boys taking more than their share down to the end of the garden where they sit on the wall and look out over the valley and discuss how far into the country they could ride their bikes if only they were allowed. Tash and Melissa are as wary of each other as their mothers are.

'What are you reading?' says Melissa.

Without speaking Tash holds up the book to show the cover. Melissa has nothing to say. After a bit, 'Was Ibiza good?' asks Tash.

'Buzzin,' says Melissa.

'Did you go to a night club?'

'Of course she didn't' says Sarah. 'She's not old enough, as you well know.'

'They had discos at the hotel though. It was like a night club, except there was old people there, and kids. Mum got drunk.'

'Take no notice of her,' says Sarah. 'She doesn't know what being drunk is.'

'Ha,' says Melissa, and Dave breaks in to suggest more tea, more Coke, what about that chocolate cake?

'What do you think?' he says to Lynn in the kitchen. 'If I got the girls – the young ones I mean – to help with the dishes, do you think they'd start to come round a bit? You know, speak to each other? Properly.'

Lynn shrugs, wearily. 'No harm in trying.'

The cake is passed around. Dom carefully puts aside the piece reserved for his dad. Gemma picks the especially small piece she cut for herself. The cake is eaten, the drinks are drunk. They are quiet as if they are working out what to say.

'Now then young ladies.' Dave pushes himself out of his folding chair. 'Who is going to help their old Grandad?'

Tash looks up from her book and Melissa from her phone, then back down again.

'First off,' says Dave, 'I want you both to go down the garden and bring back any plates, glasses and stuff that your disgusting little brothers have left lying around.'

The girls do not move, though they look at each other. Tash gets to her feet, slowly.

'You too Missy Melly,' says Dave.

'Come on,' says Tash and they go together, and soon return walking closer together, though they stop talking as they approach.

'Now then,' says Dave. 'Your old Grandad needs a bit of help with the dishes. Can you bring them all into the kitchen for me.'

There really aren't so many dishes – no pans to wash up, only mugs and a few sandwich plates.

'We'll do it Grandad,' says Melissa. 'You go and sit down.'

'What with all those old women!' he says, pretend horrified, and pulls Melissa to him for a quick hug, and puts the other arm round Tash so that the two girls are face to face, laughing, before he goes back into the garden and leaves them alone together.

The boys are mostly out of sight behind the bushes. They have made up some game of throwing things at the fence and the three women, sitting in silence, hear their exclamations and groans. Dave sits back in his too-small garden chair.

'You're very quiet out here,' he says. 'I haven't heard about your holidays yet. How was Ibiza then, Sar?'

'It was OK,' she says. 'You know, Mel is too old now to play on the beach, she was at a bit of a loose end. Dom enjoyed the pool.'

'Nice weather?'

'Some thunderstorms, but you know, they pass over quite quickly.' She sounds tired, as if speaking is an effort.

'Been working hard since you got back?'

'Feels like it. You know, you pay all that money for a holiday and you wonder why you bothered. You come back and everything's the same. Same old, same old.'

'Well, not for you Lynnie love, eh? Holiday every day from now on. That's right isn't it?'

'That's all you know, David Wilde,' she says. 'For a start there's going to be some spring cleaning done. There's curtains in this house that haven't been washed in years. There's stuff gathering dust in the loft that should have been thrown out decades ago, there's cupboards want turning out and the kitchen wants painting and that vinyl on the floor has to go before someone breaks their neck.'

'Right then,' says Dave. 'That's the weekend sorted. What shall we do on Monday?'

'Less than a week and they'll be back at school,' says Gemma. 'I bet Jake's grown out of his school trousers.'

'Dom too,' says Sarah. It is the first time she has spoken directly to her sister. 'And Mel's blazer is too tight for her now. I think it might fit Tash if you need it. It's nearly new but Mel's not as skinny as she was. She's going to have big boobs, the way she's going.'

'Thanks. What shift are you on next week?'

'Three nights, starting Monday.'

'Send Dom round to ours, then you can get some sleep. Mel too, if she wants to.'

They can hear the two girls in the kitchen, talking and laughing. There's a shutting of cupboard doors and they come back into the garden and throw themselves down on the grass, still laughing.

'Last week of holiday then,' says Dave. 'Any plans?'

They shrug in unison.

'I think there may have been some homework set for the holiday,' says Sarah. 'I've not seen any sign of it being done.'

'Tash has done hers,' says Gemma.

'Yes,' says Tash scornfully. 'On holiday in *boring* Filey, because there's nothing else to do in boring *Filey*.'

'I hope,' says Lynn, 'that Jamie is having a good time in Wales. The weather is always a bit uncertain there I believe.'

'Wouldn't it be funny –' says Tash, and stops.

'If– ' says Melissa.

'If what –?'

'If Niecey had a surprise, like –'

'Like maybe –'

'Like maybe –' Melissa is laughing so much that her words are hard to hear. '– maybe she would hear something about Oliver and Lila.'

'That would be a nice surprise,' says Tash.

Only Sarah does not know what they are talking about. 'What are you on about?'

'Tash knows.'

'I know,' says Gemma firmly. 'And if you're wondering why Tash doesn't have a phone any more, that's why. I would have told you Sar, but you were away on holiday when I found out, and then we were away, and then I thought I might as well let it lie.'

'What?'

'Tell you later,' she says. 'When little people with big ears and big mouths aren't around.'

'Well, I can't say I'm surprised,' says Janet.

They have had to tell her everything.

'What do you mean, not surprised,' says Dave. 'Do you think it's normal, going to prison and losing your children?'

'It happens,' says Janet, accepting a small sherry as there is no gin or tonic in the house. 'What I mean is – I always thought there was something about that Niecey. Not saying anything against her, but you wouldn't trust her would you.'

'"*That Niecey*",' says Lynn, 'just happens to be our daughter-in-law and I think you ought to watch what you're saying.'

'She's our Jamie's wife, see,' says Dave, conciliatory. 'Whatever she did before, she's one of the family now.'

'And I see,' said Janet, 'that your Melissa has been getting up to mischief too.'

'Which is all it is,' says Lynn. 'It's mischief, all kids do it. She won't do it again, I do know that.'

Janet, with the help of some Fulwood ladies, has provided an address and phone number for Jacqui Thwaite, as well as information – old now and quite unreliable – about her son Adrian Wilson and his promising life that turned out to be less illustrious than people thought it might turn out to be.

'So it seemed to knock him off course,' reports Janet. 'The trial and giving evidence and all that sort of thing. So he missed some sort of deadline, and he didn't get his PhD – although some people tell me he did, later, in America – so it's an American PhD so he has to work over there. He's had more children, so they say, but he never brings them when he comes to the UK – that's what I've heard, but you can't always believe what people tell you, can you.'

'Where?' says Dave. 'Where in America?'

'Now you're asking. I think it's somewhere beginning with P.'

'Philadelphia?' says Dave. 'Portland, Pittsburg. Phoenix?'

'I don't know now. You've confused me – they all sound the same. Anyway, he lives in an apartment, with his family or on his own I couldn't say. Some people told me one thing and someone else would tell me something different. Anyway, his mother would know. She was always a woman who was on top of things. Fancy your

Niecey being her daughter-in-law. Isn't it strange how things come about, her ending up in Sheffield, what a coincidence.'

'Not really,' says Dave. 'She came here to look for the children because she knew Adrian's mother lived here – or she thought she did. There's a reason for everything if you can find it.'

'Maybe that's why Jacqui moved away,' says Janet thoughtfully. 'Maybe she didn't want her to find them.'

Lynn has been leaving the conversation to them. She gets up now and goes to put the kettle on. 'Coffee is it? We've only instant.'

Janet makes a face. 'I'll just have a glass of water, if you don't mind. So, you've retired at last then Lynn. What's brought that on?'

'I'm sixty-four,' says Lynn. 'I think I'm entitled.'

Next day, when Dave has gone out, Lynn picks up the house phone, puts it down again and picks up her mobile. Dials.

It is a young person's voice that answers.

'Can I speak to Mrs Thwaite please.'

'Oh,' he says. 'She's not here.'

'OK,' says Lynn. 'Thank you.'

'Um – shall I give her a message?'

'No thank you, no message.' Lynn almost drops her phone in her hurry to switch it off. That must have been Oliver, that nicely spoken young man. Niecey's son, Jamie's stepson. Step-grandson to her and Dave. What would Niecey do if she knew? The weight of it all is too much and Lynn sits down in her armchair with her eyes closed for quite five minutes before pulling herself together and embarking on cleaning the kitchen windows.

It takes two more goes before it is actually Jacqui who picks up the phone.

'I'm sorry to bother you.' Lynn has debated with Dave whether she should say this. *Is* she sorry? Is she bothering her? Does it sound too apologetic, should she be more assertive? But in the end, though she decided not to say it, it just came out. 'My name is Lynn Wilde – you don't know me.'

There is a pause where she hopes the other woman will say something, but she doesn't, she waits.

'I'm ringing about Niecey –'

'I don't know any –'

'– Denise. Denise who was married to your son.'

There is an even longer wait this time.

'Is that right?' says Lynn desperately. 'Have I got the right person? Are you –?'

'Look,' she says, this woman on the other end of the phone line, 'I can't do this here. Now. I've got to go out.' Which Lynn took as being a lie and did not answer.

'Leave me your number,' says Jacqui. 'I will ring you when it's a better time. I will ring you, if I don't, well, you know how to get hold of me. It's just – now is not a good time. I need to –'

'You'll have my number,' says Lynn. 'When do you think you will call me?'

'Soon,' she says. 'In a day or two.'

'Tomorrow,' says Lynn. 'Make it tomorrow, it will be better to get it over with.'

'Tomorrow,' she says. 'That should be do-able.'

When Lynn tells Dave about this they can think of lots of other ways the conversation could have gone, should have gone, but there you are, that's how it was, that's how it is, let's see what will happen tomorrow.

Unexpectedly, Lynn has a good night's sleep and keeps herself busy in the house, sorting out cupboards and hanging up her clean curtains. Dave has been hanging around at a loose end now the children are back at school. She sends him to buy groceries, knowing that he will call in at Gemma's shop and come back feeling better.

'Take your time,' she says. 'No rush.'

'Wouldn't you like me to be here when she rings?'

'I'm quite capable,' she says. 'I have taken phone calls before you know. I won't keep anything from you, you know I won't, but it will be easier if I don't have to take account of you being in the room. Go on, have a walk, it will do you good.'

'Is this going to be how it is from now on?' says Dave, 'I'm an encumbrance in my own home. You're going to do it all, even though I've been doing it for years and you've never complained, not once.'

'Don't talk rubbish,' she says. 'See you later.'

Jacqui has had a disturbed night worrying about what might be going on. Denise – well, she was bound to be somewhere; someone, some day was almost bound to try to find the children. It was more surprising that it had taken this long for something to happen. She has not mentioned yesterday's phone call to Bruce, and now waits for him to go out before she sits with her mobile in her hand waiting for her courage to gather.

She hadn't asked the woman's name, nor where she lived. In her imagination over the years she has pictured Denise – Denny – in prison, long after she knew she must have been released. And then, when it was really no longer feasible that she was still locked up, when the twins were about ten or eleven and beginning to ask awkward questions, she pictured Denny in London, with some other man, with some other children, living a life on the margins of crime, being still an unsuitable person to look after her children. But the woman on the phone had not had a London accent. Jacqui was almost sure, replaying the brief conversation in her head, that it was a Sheffield accent.

She wishes now that Bruce was in the house; she wishes she had spoken to him about it. But he had always left anything to do with the children to her. They had been married only a year or so when it all happened; picking up the pieces of that little episode had nearly cost them their marriage, before it had properly been settled into. Eleven years now since it happened, and Bruce and she had come to an understanding about the best way for them to get on. He had nothing to do with the children – with decisions, or discipline or responsibilities – he provided money for the family and held himself back from interfering, so conscientiously that it was by now hardly possible for her to consult him. It was like being a Victorian family, she thought.

Of course she has not mentioned the phone call to Oliver and Lila. It would be cruel. She knows – though these days they try hard to hide it – that they are curious, more than curious, obsessed at times – about their mother. Naturally. She believes, without thinking herself a paragon, that she has done a better job of bringing them up than Adrian would have done, with or without Denny. There is only one thing she can feel ashamed of doing in all the years she has had them – and that was more of a mistake, she tells herself, than a deliberate wrong. It was one time when Lila, ten years old, was going through a sad patch at school – a bit of bullying, a bit of name-calling which she had probably started herself, being rather on the bumptious side.

'Martha's told everyone my mother's dead. Everyone's saying it.'

'That's right,' said Ollie. 'They were all saying it.'

'So what did you say?' said Jacqui.

'I just told them to leave me alone and I went in and told a teacher.'

'Well, that was good,' said Jacqui.

'But they'll do it again tomorrow. I'm not going to school ever again.'

'I think,' said Ollie very seriously, 'that it would be better if we knew for sure where our mother is. Like Adrian.' – They had stopped calling him Daddy by now – 'We know where *he* is and no one says anything to us about it or calls us names.'

'But –' said Jacqui.

'So she *is* dead,' shouted Lila and began to cry loudly, punching the arm of the chair.

'I didn't say that.'

'You said But. You said But.'

'Do you actually *know*?' said Oliver. Jacqui could see that he was trying very hard to use the thinking skills that everyone said he had.

'I don't *know* – that's what I was going to say,' she said. Inside her head a voice told her, Go for it, there'll never be a better time, she's upset already, you won't make it any worse. 'But what I think –' she paused, thought again, and again, and plunged in '– I think it's likely that she *has* died. I think she would have got in touch if she was able to, by now.'

It's better, she thought, better to give up the idea of their mother. Get used to it, stop niggling away at it. Both children were crying now and she pulled them beside her on the settee and put an arm round each one.

'But you're not certain,' said Ollie. He wiped his nose on his sleeve and she did not tell him to use a tissue. 'You're not one hundred per cent certain. You could be wrong.'

'Ninety-nine,' she said. 'I'm certain ninety-nine per cent.' Thinking, Oh God, why did I say that, I've just made it worse than it was already.

She knows why the children stopped asking about their mother, and she knows they haven't put the idea of her out

226

of their minds. She knows too that if their mother has got this close – that phone call – there can be no turning back, no escape in the long run.

She sighs resignedly and picks up her phone.

When her phone rings Lynn is standing on a step-stool, spraying the cooker hood with cleaning stuff. She gets down carefully and lifts her phone from the table. Sits down before she answers.

'Hello.' She knows who it will be.

'Hello.'

'My name is Lynn Wilde,' she says, formally. 'I wanted to talk to you about the children. Lila and Oliver Wilson.'

'Are you a social worker?'

'No. Not at all.'

'What do you want?'

'It's a long story,' says Lynn, though in fact, when she tells it, it isn't really so long.

Jacqui grasps the situation straight away. 'So she doesn't know? That you've found me. Us.'

'Not yet.'

'You would know if she had?'

Lynn thinks. 'Probably. Not straight away maybe, but we would get to know soon enough.'

'You know,' says Jacqui, 'what I'd like to do, is to meet you, just you. First of all. What do you think about that?'

'That's what we thought. Could I bring my husband?'

'If you like. I'll try to bring mine, if he has the time. In the meantime, you won't say anything to your family will you. And I won't say anything to the children.'

'It should be soon,' says Lynn.

'Tomorrow?'

They arrange to meet at Chatsworth, in the café at the garden centre. 'I'll wear a blue top,' says Jacqui. 'I'm quite tall, grey hair. I'll wear white trousers.'

'I'm not very tall,' says Lynn. 'I'll wear a blue top too. Grey hair too. Half past ten.'

She switches off her phone, shaking slightly, and finds that Dave is standing in the doorway.

'Have you been listening?'

'Not really,' he says. 'I only heard the last bit. Are we going to meet her? What's your impression of her?'

'She seems all right,' says Lynn. 'Reasonable. Not stuck up really. She didn't ask me very much – I mean no personal questions, nothing like what's Niecey like? Has she stayed out of trouble? Is she a good mum? Nothing at all really. You'd think she'd want to know.'

\*

Lynn is much more nervous the next day. She and Dave are at the garden centre at ten past ten, having left plenty of time to get there no matter what the traffic situation. They walk round looking at the plants, the planters, the accessories, the furniture, Lynn eyeing up all the other customers, all of whom seem to match Jacqui's description of herself, and by the time they get to the seed stands it is still not half past.

'Should we get our cup of tea before they come? Would that be rude?'

'We'll wait for them,' he says. 'I'll buy the first round.'

'Are we doing the right thing?'

'Too late now,' he says.

'It's not. We could turn round and go right now and they would realise we'd just changed our minds.'

'Then what?' says Dave.

She sighs. 'I know. We can't back out now. I know.'

Jacqui and Bruce, it turns out, also arrived early and have been sitting in the car park, watching the arrivals and wondering which are the ones they are meeting. Bruce, willing as always when asked, has taken the morning off work, though he is busy on his phone as they wait.

'Lynn?'

'Jacqui?'

Dave and Bruce are introduced – they look surprisingly like each other, could be brothers, though Bruce is considerably younger. He takes the chance to go with Dave to buy refreshments and they come back as if they have some sort of understanding.

Meanwhile Lynn and Jacqui attempt some sort of conversation which will not commit them to either liking or disliking each other.

When they are all four seated, stirring their drinks thoughtfully, Dave commences.

'Well,' he says, cheerfully, 'who'd have thought this would ever happen? Eh?'

Jacqui and Lynn are not cheered.

'What I think –'

'The thing is –'

'Hold up,' says Dave. 'Let's do proper introductions.' He looks round as if he owns the table. 'I'm Dave Wilde, this is my wife Lynn. Our son Jamie is married to Niecey – that is Denise – and they have a little boy called Leo.'

'Oh,' cries Jacqui, 'she's had another baby.'

'Not a baby any more,' says Lynn. 'He'll be six in December.'

'What we believe,' says Dave, 'is that Niecey – that's what we call her – had a pair of twins and that you are their grandparents.'

'I am,' says Jacqui. 'Bruce isn't.'

'I can imagine,' says Dave, 'that you aren't wanting to give too much away just yet. I can understand why you might want to meet us –'

'I don't want anything to happen too quickly,' says Jacqui. 'It will come as a shock to them if they –'

'They must know they've got a mother somewhere.'

'Of course. At least – they think – at least I think they think – that she died.'

Lynn makes a small gasping sound.

'Who told them that?'

'It's more like,' said Jacqui, 'that they've got that idea and we don't know, it might be true, and in a funny way –'

'It doesn't sound funny to me,' says Lynn. 'I can understand you might have to tell children a bit of a story – but pretending she's *dead*. That's taking it too far.' She puts her mug down with a hand that is trembling. 'That's what I think anyway.'

'No one's heard from her,' says Bruce. 'Not Adrian, not her parents –'

Lynn and Dave exchange a look to communicate that Niecey's parents may not be as dead as they have always assumed.

'Her parents?' says Dave. 'Do they think she's dead? Does Adrian?'

Jacqui holds up a hand. 'Do you know, I think we're going up a blind alley here. I think we should start from where we are. Tell me again, with all the details, everything you know about the children, and their mother.'

Lynn and Dave are silent, looking at each other.

'For a start, then,' says Jacqui, 'is Jamie your only child or do you have others? Do you have other grandchildren? Start from there.'

'Jamie's our only son,' says Lynn, on easier ground now. 'We've two daughters, they're older, they've both got kids too, a boy and a girl each. It's our Tash – our Gemma's girl – who's put it on Facebook. She's in some right trouble about it too I can tell you.'

'What? It's on Facebook?'

'That's what I was trying to tell you on the phone,' says Lynn. 'But I don't use it myself and I don't know the names for how it's done. It's all a mystery to me. Anyhow, that's how my sister saw it and she put two and two together and it was her who said she knew how to get in touch with you, on account of her living in Fulwood and knowing people who know you.'

'And you couldn't just leave things as they were,' says Jacqui, a shade bitterly.

'Ask yourself,' says Dave reasonably. 'Would that have been possible? From the time my son found the birth certificates – and she'd hidden them, she didn't tell him till he found them – from that time on it was bound to come out. See, he asked us what to do about it and his sisters were there, and then, though *he* just put it out of his mind, his sisters took it further and they went investigating and found out all sorts. So then our Melissa's been listening at doors and such and her and Tash have decided to help find the twins. It was like a mystery to them, they got carried away. But sooner or later it was bound to come out.'

'Had Denise not been looking for them?' says Bruce.

'They were on her mind all the time,' says Dave. 'You could tell – knowing what I know now I can see that if you were with her anywhere, in town, or walking in a park, whatever, she were looking round her all the time, searching like, looking for – well I know now she were looking for them.'

'I always wondered,' says Lynn, ' I mean when we didn't know about the twins – I wondered if she was scared of meeting someone. Someone from her past I mean. Because she's always been very buttoned up about that. And now we know why.'

'I were never altogether convinced,' says Dave, 'that her parents really were dead. I wondered if she were scared of them finding her. She was always funny about them.'

Jacqui shudders a little. 'What do you mean, funny?'

'Very off-hand. She doesn't like you to ask about them, not in any way at all. She's told us all sorts of lies about where she was brought up and what her parents did, and I know she's told our Jamie they were dead. So what they did to her to make her that scared I don't know.'

'They're not dead,' says Jacqui. 'Far from it, though they are a bit odd. We don't see them, they send – well, he does – sends presents at Christmas, that's all.'

'They must have seen the children.'

'Only once – and only the grandfather. Not her. She stayed in the car, wouldn't get out. We went all the way to Chester Zoo, didn't we Bruce, and she never looked at them. He was better, but they were scared of him I think. They've never asked to see them again.'

'Who hasn't, the children or the grandparents.'

'Neither,' says Jacqui. 'Thank goodness.'

'Here,' says Dave, suddenly, 'I brought some photos to show you. He pulls out of his canvas bag most of the photos that stand on the shelves at home, having left behind only his and Lynn's own wedding photo. They clatter on to the table among the mugs and milk jugs and he picks them up at random.

'So that's our Sarah getting her degree, she's the clever one. That's our Gemma and Mark's wedding, she didn't want a big do but she looked lovely didn't she Lynn? Look, this one is Leo, it's his first school photo, so he'll be half brother to your twins.'

Jacqui looks at the picture of Leo, his dark blond hair, his ebullient grin – she looks for a long time it seems, then puts it down.

'This is Jamie and Niecey with our Leo when he were a tiny baby. It were New Year weren't it Lynn. We went round to wish them a happy new year and they were just sat together on t'sofa with him and I took this picture and it came out so well I put it in a frame and we have it on t'shelf.'

Jacqui looks at this one too for a long time. Jamie, seeming mildly embarrassed at being photographed but smiling holding the baby, Niecey looking down at the baby, impeccable make up hiding the dark rings under her eyes, the baby, eyes open, gazing back at her.

'That's a lovely picture,' she says to Dave. 'I should have brought something to show you but I didn't think of it.' Her voice does not sound regretful.

'There'll be some on your phone,' says Bruce, and she casts at him what Lynn would call a Look.

'Not any more,' she says. 'I transferred them to the computer.'

'Could you send us some?' says Dave. 'Even just one.'

'Not yet at least,' says Jacqui. 'Not until we've decided how we're going to proceed.'

'That sounds like a legal word,' says Dave. 'I hope this isn't going to go that way.'

'Nobody wants that,' says Bruce. 'But we do need to decide on our next step. Or steps.'

The café is becoming noisy now – a large party of large women have pushed tables together and are calling and laughing loudly to each other.

'We could go outside,' suggests Dave. 'Have a bit of a stroll by the river. Quieter than in here.'

At first they walk in their marital pairs but then, after crossing the road and going through a gate into the meadow, they have somehow adjusted and Lynn is walking next to Bruce, and Dave with Jacqui.

'The thing is,' says Bruce, 'they're not my children, obviously. You know that. But I've lived with them for years now – Jac and I had only just got married when it all blew up. First we knew was Adrian on the phone saying he needed us to go and get them – we thought it was just for the weekend, but since then they've never been away from us, not for a single night.'

'Do they see their father? He's in America isn't he?'

'They don't see much of him. I think he's come over here nearly every year, but only for a week or so. They don't really know him.'

'Haven't they been over there to see him? Why not?'

'It's all a bit difficult, apparently. He only has a small apartment and Jac says he doesn't seem to know what to do with kids. And of course they haven't got passports.'

'He hasn't married again then?'

'He's had a number of girlfriends. One of them has a child which is his but we've never seen her. Jac's a bit cut up about that, I know. And she'd like to be closer to Adrian, but he's not really that sort of person.'

'Selfish?'

'I suppose you could say that. Impression I get is – withdrawn. Keeps himself to himself, you know, not one for socialising.'

'He works though?'

'Got a good job. Something in marketing, which you would think – well I think of it like selling, you need a bit of personality. But he is more behind the scenes I think. What does your son do?'

'Jamie. He has a plumbing business – it was his uncle's, that's Dave's brother. Jamie went to work for him – he's a plasterer and tiler, and then when Steve retired he had no one to take over the business so he sold it on to our Jamie. He's not doing badly, always plenty of work.'

'Good business to be in,' says Bruce. 'I suppose he has a van.'

'Two.'

'That's my line,' says Bruce. 'Vans, pick-ups, tradesmen's vehicles. I won't deal in cars, people don't know enough about what they want. Tradesmen are different – you tell Jamie, next time he wants a new van – new or used – tell him to come to me.'

'I will,' says Lynn. 'Not that he's likely to listen to me.'
'Tell me about Denise,' says Jacqui to Dave. 'I've seen that picture of her and I must say I would not have recognised her. I didn't know her well – only met her three or four times – but she used to be quite different.'

'We like her,' says Dave. 'I would say she's not that easy to get to know – not shy, I don't think, but not exactly chatty. My daughters thought she were a bit stuck up when we first knew her, but then she doesn't have the Sheffield accent of course, so she sounds more posh – stand-offish, that's what they were thinking. But no, she's got no airs and graces, just gets on with her job, good mum to Leo.'

'She goes to work?'

'Lynn got her the job. See Lynn's retired now, last week actually, but she worked at this old folks' home and she got Niecey a job there, cleaning. They think very well of her, so I'm told.'

Jacqui does not look impressed. 'Is that what she wanted to do, cleaning?'

'I know what you're thinking. Waste of all them exams she got to go to university, but she says to me, Dave I haven't got qualifications, I haven't got a CV, I'm just glad of a job where I can get to school in time to pick Leo up and I can feel like I'm doing my bit to help. She says they don't need the money – our Jamie's doing all right – and she's putting her wages away to save for if Leo gets to go to university. You hear so much nowadays about students being in that much debt. She's got her head screwed on, our Niecey.'

'She's changed a lot then,' says Jacqui.

'I can see,' says Dave, 'that you wouldn't have a very good opinion of her. I dare say I wouldn't have either if I'd known her then, and Lynn and my daughters – well, they were downright shocked and disgusted when we found out about the drugs and the neglect of them kids. But I can only speak as I find, and what she's like now – well, there's nothing like that these days I can assure you.'

'What do you think we should do?' says Jacqui. She sounds exhausted. 'I know we've got to do something. I'm even sure that Ollie and Lila have to meet their birth mother – they would want to I know. But how are we going to go about it? I mean, does Denise – Niecey – know anything at all about this?'

'What she knows – what I know she knows – is that we all know about these two children. She doesn't know – even Gemma and Sarah don't know – that we've traced you. None of them know we're meeting you. It's possible that some news has got back to Tash on that Facebook thing – but Tash isn't allowed her phone at the moment, and Gemma's got the laptop in the kitchen, and it goes everywhere with her all the time so that Tash can't get hold of it.'

'She sounds a firm woman, your Gemma.'

'Oh she is. A nicer person you couldn't hope to meet, but she takes a firm line with her kids. Mark – that's her husband, he's a lot softer with them. Very nice chap though.'

'I'm sure. But what do you think should be our next step?'

They have reached a bridge across the river and all four lean on the wall and look down at the Derwent flowing past.

Jacqui is now next to Lynn. 'What do you think we should do next?'

'I wish I knew what would be the right thing to do. Do you know what I mean? It feels like we're walking along in the dark and we don't know if there's traps or holes in the ground, or what not. You know?'

'I know what you mean. I'm thinking, if I just go home and say to the kids, we've found your mother, she's just down the road in Sheffield, they'll want to see her, of course they will, but it will be a shock. I would want it to go well, if you know what I mean, but I have to say this to you – I'm not prepared to let them go and live with her – however nice and good and everything she is nowadays – I'm not prepared to let them go until they're eighteen and old enough to make decisions.'

'I knew it would be like this,' says Lynn. 'I don't mean that you're saying anything wrong – I'm sure I would feel the same as you. It's just, I suppose when we found you it felt like the end of a long search – I mean Niecey's long search because we've only been involved for a few weeks. I probably wasn't thinking any further than our Tash was thinking. But it's not simple is it? We're not going to please everybody.'

'We can't let it lie,' says Bruce, turning round. 'The cat's out of the bag now, as they say. What would the kids do, Jac, if they found that we knew all this and we kept it a secret?'

'Then there's the Nuttalls,' says Jacqui. 'Do they have a right to be consulted? If they found out – which they might – will they be coming over here to see their daughter? It doesn't sound to me as if Niecey would welcome them.' She leans her head on her arms on the stone parapet. 'There's too much to take in. There's too much to take into consideration.'

'I have a suggestion,' says Dave. 'We're tired now, we're all tired. It's been a heavy morning. We'll go home – I know, I know – we need to make some decisions, but let's go home and have a bit of a rest and get in touch tomorrow. Maybe you give us an email address and we'll give you ours and we can send suggestions to each other and see which we think is the best one. Cos I don't know about you three, but I'm done for today. How does that sound?'

'I'd hoped,' says Lynn, 'to have something sorted this morning, but you're probably right. But we can't leave it too long because if we do events will overtake us, just wait and see if they don't.'

In the car park they come over all formal and shake hands, and drive away in their respective cars.

'What I'd like to do,' says Lynn, 'is see what Gemma thinks of all this. Sarah's got too much on, but Gemma –'

'Sarah will think she's being left out.'

'She won't know. She's got Mel's court appearance to worry about, and Gem says there's been some arguments at home between her and Jon – I don't want to dump anything else on her.'

'All right. Let's see if Gem can drop in this evening.'

'Not so soon. We should let it settle first. In our heads I mean. Let's take it slowly – there's no rush after all.'

'If you want,' says Dave.

Lynn suddenly sits up. 'Do you know what he said? That Bruce? It's only just struck me – he said *of course they haven't got passports.* Why? Why wouldn't they? Why *of course*?'

Dave slows down to approach the roundabout. 'Figure of speech probably.' He slows down for the pedestrian lights. 'No, I know what it will be – she told me, Jacqui did, that she changed the twins' names. They're Thwaite, the same as her, unofficially. She said it was easier that way.'

'Sounds a bit – I don't know, like she wanted to hide them.' Lynn considers. 'I suppose it was reasonable, in the circumstances.'

He drives them the country way home, avoiding the city traffic.

'Do you know,' says Lynn, 'the way I see it, why would those children even *want* to belong to our family. They've got money haven't they. Got everything they want. Why should they even bother to make contact with their mother?'

'Wouldn't you? I mean, when your mum first left you – wouldn't you have wanted to see her?'

'At first I would have. But I was ten, remember, I was old enough to know what was going on, I was old enough to miss her. But these kids, they won't remember will they, they won't miss her, like I didn't miss my mum, after the first few months.'

'If you say so,' says Dave, and changes gear to go down the steep hill.

'Those people,' says Jacqui, fastening her seatbelt, 'are not going to take the children away from me. I'm not going to allow it.'

'It won't happen,' says Bruce, waiting for the lights to change on the bridge. 'After all, it's Adrian who gets to make the decision isn't it.'

'Oh god,' she says. 'Adrian. I hadn't even started to think about Adrian. This whole thing is like one of those funguses that spread and spread till there's no end to it.'

'Don't get dramatic,' says Bruce, quite kindly. 'It feels like a mess now but it will get sorted out. This time next year it will all be in the past.' He pats her hand. 'We'll cope. We always have.'

'There is absolutely no way,' says Sarah, 'that I am going to get out of bed two hours after I've got into it after a thirteen hour shift. You know what you're asking me to do, you know what it will do to me. You're in town already, all you have to do is walk up to the court house, your bloody store will survive without you for an hour or so.'

'You have no idea how difficult it can be to get away. Surely they would give you some time off, for a thing like this.'

'Surely they would give *you*–'

'It's different. I never know what might happen if I'm out of the store.'

'You're being ridiculous. How come you could go on holiday? Did the store close? Did it burn down? You're not indispensable.'

'Neither are you.'

'Yes I *am*. And my sleep is indispensable too, if I'm to be able to do my job properly when I get back on duty.'

'For Christ sake. Can't your Dad go with her?'

'It says "parent" on the letter. The woman who did the assessment said "parent." Not "grandparent." I was here for the assessment, if you recall. You weren't. I had to get up an hour early, you didn't even ask about it when you came home. It's time you did your bit Jon, I do everything round here, if you're not working you're out in the evenings, Dom never sees you, you don't know what's going on with the kids, no wonder Mel gets into trouble –'

'That's my fault as well is it?'

Melissa, sitting on the stairs with Dom, hears his breathing change and puts her arm round him, knowing he'd like to cry. She'd like to cry herself. She'd like it all to go away. She'd like to rewind time, back to when she was a good girl, in Year 8, before she fell out with her old best friend, and Tash didn't want her with her crowd, and she was forced – she had no choice – to start hanging around with Bethany and Gaby and them. She knows they are not her friends, she knows they used her to carry out the items that they took off the shelves, she knows they will beat her up if she tells anyone their names.

School has not been too bad. Being in Year 10 means that she is in different sets, mostly, sometimes with Tash – who is friendly again, ish – but almost always not with Bethany, who is in lower sets, and sometimes with Dani, who is also trying to settle down, as the teachers put it.

And Dom is there too, in Year 7, so there are times when she can say to other girls, when they ask is she going round the back of the gym for a fag at lunchtime, Oh I just have to go and check my little brother is OK, I'll see you later. She is angry still, at the shop which reported her to the police, at her father who seems to believe that stealing from Accessorize is the same as stealing from him, personally, at Debenhams. Angry at the police, and the Youth Justice people who seem to have nothing better to do than to interfere in the life of someone who certainly knows right from wrong and are wasting their time if they think that she needs their help to change anything. She can do it herself. And it's not her fault anyway because look how her parents are arguing again. Surely it can't be long till one of them leaves.

Her phone tells her she has a text – it also tells her parents she is close enough by to hear their argument. Their mother comes out of the kitchen, shouting at them to go upstairs. Dom bursts into tears. Dad comes out, pushes past them up the stairs, slams the door of his office.

*

Lynn's phone tells her she has a text.

'Who's that from?'

'Sarah,' she says. 'She's coming round.'

'What for?'

'Doesn't say. I was hoping for a quiet evening.'

'Me too.'

It is not long before Sarah arrives. Her nose is pink and her face is pale.'

'What's up?' says Dave. 'Not Melissa again is it?'

'Worse,' says Sarah. She sits on the sofa and says nothing for a while, until Lynn has brought her a cup of coffee and put it beside her, without speaking, as if there has been a bereavement.

'It's Jon,' she says. 'Me and Jon. Feels like it's all over.'

'Now then,' says Dave. 'Everyone feels like that at some point. You've had a lot on. It's a strain, you know it is. But all over – that's a bit dramatic isn't it.'

'It's what he said,' she says. 'He went out last night, he didn't come back till late, he's not answering calls – at least not from me. He's come home from work today, he's stormed off upstairs –'

240

'What did he say?' says Lynn. 'About yesterday? Were you having a row?'

'Of course we were. It's all we ever do.' She begins to cry again. 'He's been a pig – all this summer he's been selfish and bad-tempered. The kids are upset, Dom's in tears for any little thing, Melissa – well you know what she's been up to. We've got a date for her to go to court and Jon just won't take the time off to go with her. Like it's my job, only my job to do anything for the kids. Like he thinks I only work part-time –'

'Well you do, sort of,' says Dave, unwisely.

'I do thirty-nine hours a week,' she shouts. 'If that's not full-time tell me what is. And I never get away on time – if I added it all up it would be nearer forty-nine. Don't you tell me –' She stops, to blow her nose and get her breath.

'We know love,' says Lynn. 'We know how hard you work. We know it's not easy. But it's been like that for years – what's changed?'

'He has. He's changed.'

*

Niecey is at the end of her shift when Katie calls her into the office.

'I have some news,' she says. 'Two bits of news actually. One, not to keep you in suspense any longer – your DBS check came back. I've shown it and discussed it with the management committee, and we are all quite happy for you to continue working here. Two, I would like to start you on training to be a carer. You would make a good carer and we can always use good carers.'

Niecey's eyes are shining and she blinks to hold the tears back. 'Thank you. Thank you so much.'

'I don't think you've taken in what I said,' says Katie. 'Training to be a carer – is that something you'd like to do?'

She thinks. Then, 'No. Thank you but no. I'll stick to cleaning. It's more me. But I'll be a caring cleaner. I'll always work for you Katie, one way or another.'

'Silly,' says Katie. 'Go on now, I know you have to pick up the boy from school. See you tomorrow.'

Melissa and her father have to sit on a hard bench outside the courtroom for an indefinite length of time before they are called to go in. Jon is fidgety and uncommunicative, and hoping that no one he knows will see and recognise him. Melissa is in her school uniform, fiddling with the buttons on her new blazer, rubbing her eyes like she did when she was a baby and getting ready to cry.

'How much longer?' she says.

'How do I know?' he says. 'It depends on the case in front of us.'

She kicks her feet against the bench.

'Stop that,' he says. She stops. 'You're not five years old,' he says.

'I've stopped haven't I.'

'When are you going to stop being rude?' He looks at his watch. 'When are we going to get in there?'

When they do get in there it is over and done with quickly. The Youth Court has bigger fish to fry than Jojo bows, clearly, and dismisses her with barely a look. Even then though, they can't go straight home but have to see someone else before it's all over.

'My name's Orla,' she says. 'I just need to take a few details so that I can do a visit and make a report –'

'Another one?'

'– and then we can get the order started. I need to talk with Melissa and find out what her needs are.'

'She doesn't have "needs,"' says Jon. 'Now, I need to get back to work.'

'I'll be as quick as I can,' she says.

'You're not going back to work,' says Melissa when they are outside again, looking at the late afternoon sunshine in a daze. 'Why do you always lie?'

'Sometimes,' he says, 'you've got to. It wasn't a lie, it was an excuse, nothing wrong with that.'

'So how come,' says Melissa, 'it's an excuse when you do it and it's a lie if I do it. Or Dom.'

'Enough,' says Jon. 'Get in the car.'

'Are you and Mum splitting up?' Melissa says this before she is properly in the car, half-hoping perhaps that he won't hear her. She has buckled her seat belt and he has turned on the engine before he answers.

'What gives you that idea?'

'Der,' she says.

'At the moment,' he says carefully, 'there are no plans to split up.' He heads out along the Penistone Road and she waits. 'Actually,' he says, 'I'm sorry Mel. We've all been a bit grouchy lately.'

'Dom's really scared,' she says.

'And you?'

'A bit,' she says.

When they arrive home, Sarah is up and dressed and waiting for them.

'Thought you'd still be in bed,' says Jon.

'Couldn't sleep,' she says. 'What happened?'

Melissa shrugs, and heads towards the stairs.

'Where are you going?' says Sarah. 'Tell me about it. One of you tell me about it.'

'If it's that important,' says Jon, 'you might as well have gone yourself.'

'Six months,' says Melissa from the top of the stairs. 'Six months referral order.'

'Come back down here,' calls Sarah.

'Going to my room,' says Melissa. 'Leave you to argue in peace.' But instead of raised voices she hears the front door close and from her window sees her father's car pulling away.

'Wow,' says Lila.

'I know,' says Ollie.

Jacqui has left them to themselves in the room. She said she was going to put the oven on, and she has; and she has taken the opportunity to take a swig at the cooking sherry.

'Is that amazing or what?'

'Yeah,' says Ollie.

'I want to meet her, don't you?'

'Suppose she's awful,' says Ollie. 'How do we know she's not – Granny Jac hasn't met her, we don't know anything. She might be horrible.'

'And she's got a husband – he might not like us.'

'And a boy.'

'But he's our brother,' cried Lila. 'How cool is that? A little brother. Called Leo, which is a really cool name.'

'Li, you're getting sidetracked again. You always do it. The issue is whether we want to know her at all.'

'I'd like to have a hidden camera in her house,' says Lila, 'so we could see what she was like. And then I'd like to ask her lots of questions –'

'Like what?'

'Like, why did she leave us, and why didn't she come back and get us, and does she even want to know us –'

'Granny Jac says she really does.'

'But she's not spoken to her, only to these other people. They might not know what she thinks. So I want to ask her, straight out, why did she let all this happen. And see what she says.'

'I don't want to go and live with her,' says Ollie.

'Why not?'

'We'd have to go to a different school for a start. We'd be miles from our mates.'

'We'd miss Granny Jac and Bruce.'

'Yeah, we would.'

Jacqui, standing in the hall listening, finds her tears starting again and retreats to the kitchen, to put the casserole in the oven and, this time, pour herself a proper drink, in a glass.

'How was Sarah?' says Dave.

'Struggling. I told her she should take some time off but she won't. Looks shocking.'

'Is Jon still there?'

'Says he's not leaving. Now she's saying she wishes he would.'

'Is there someone else then? Or not.'

'Who knows,' says Lynn. 'Make us a cup of tea will you. I'm about dead on my feet.'

'I don't know if you're ready for this,' says Dave, bringing in two mugs. 'I've had a call from Jacqui.'

Lynn sits up. 'And?'

'She wanted us to know that she's had a talk with the twins about Niecey, just a first mention, like. To say that she's made contact, through us. That's all so far. She's going to let them know that they can meet her if they want. Then, when they've had chance to think about it, she'll let us know.'

'Oh my,' says Lynn. 'I feel like I'm in one of them soap operas. Did she say when she'll get in touch next?'

'All depends, she said. I were thinking, Lynnie – it made me think – suppose the kids say No, they don't want to meet their mother –'

'Then it won't happen.'

'But we'll still know, won't we. We'll be holding all the cards, if we want to play them.'

'She knows that. She's no fool. She'll have been thinking of nothing else. It's just as well for her that we're reasonable people.'

'Can you imagine it though – Niecey's kids getting out of a car and walking up to front door? Niecey's face. Explaining it to Leo.'

'She won't be taking them to the house, believe me. She won't want the kids to know where she lives, not until she sees how it pans out. Anyway, I don't want to think about that right now. I'd rather think about Sarah. One good thing, she's made it up with Gem, so it seems. They're meeting up tomorrow.'

'Oh,' says Dave, remembering something. 'I've been a bit out of line, I've gone and told Gemma about meeting them – you know, Jacqui and Bruce. She'll keep it to herself though, she won't pass it on.'

'Only to Mark. And probably Sarah. That's all.'

'Sorry. It just slipped out.'

'Actually,' says Lynn, 'I mentioned it to Sarah too. I thought it might take her mind off her troubles but she didn't seem to even listen.'

\*

'Whatever you do,' says Gemma, 'don't tell Tash.'

'Course not,' says Mark. 'But just run it past me again. It's a lot to take in.'

'I don't see why,' says Gemma. 'It feels like we've talked about nothing else all summer. Dad and Mum have been to see this woman, and this woman is the grandmother of Niecey's kids.'

'Not Niecey's mother?'

'Not Niecey's mother. God, Mark, keep up. The mother of the father of the kids.'

'So your Mum and Dad have seen the kids?'

'No, but they've seen her, they've talked to her, they've both gone away to think about it.'

'To think about what to do next?'

'And how to do it. Think about it – it's a complete life-changer. Not only for Niecey and Jamie – what about Leo? What about the twins? Us? Everyone?'

'So what does Niecey say?'

'Nothing yet because she don't know yet.'

'Doesn't seem fair does it? You'd think she'd have a right to be the first person to know. I mean before you and me –'

'And Sarah.'

'I'm surprised your Dad has let it happen. He's always fair with people. Always tries to do right.'

'I know. But it's complicated. There's the twins' father, he's in America, they say they have to consult him. There's the kids – what if they say they don't want to meet her? Will someone make them do it?'

'Tash has got a lot to answer for –'

'But if it all works out, she'll be –'

'Too big for her boots.'

'Yeah, probably. But she was only trying to help.'

'Interfere.'

'Same thing.'

Neither Lila nor Oliver can sleep. Lila comes softly into his room and they sit in the dark together. Jacqui, lying awake too, beside a sleeping Bruce, has heard the door open and close, hears them whispering, like leaves rustling, but cannot make out the words.

'If she's horrible we don't have to see her again.'

'Can she go to court though, and get us?'

'We could run away.'

'What do you think Granny Jac wants us to do?'

'She must want us to see her or she wouldn't have told us.'

'But she doesn't want us to live with her.'

'And we would meet Tash. Probably. If we wanted to.'

'What would you say to her?'

Long pause for thought.

'Depends doesn't it. If it all worked out fine and everyone was happy –'

'But if not. If we end up with this horrible family and we have to run away –'

'I think Granny should go and check it out for us. First, before we have to go.'

'But I wish she could have one of those secret cameras. I want to see her *so* much.'

'I know.'

Jamie parks his car outside his parents' house. He and Niecey get out into the evening air – pale grey cloud over all. She grips suddenly on to his hand as they walk up the path.

'Honest,' he says. 'I don't know what it's about. I told you.'

'*I* know,' she says.

'Don't worry,' he says. 'It won't be anything.'

There is a tray of mugs on the coffee table, a plate of biscuits. Dave and Lynn are sitting in their accustomed chairs; Gemma is sitting on the settee. She is looking worried too, but smiles at her brother and Niecey, as if to say, I'm on your side. Niecey does her best to smile back.

Dave puts down the mug of tea which he has just picked up and sits up straighter as if he is going to make a speech. Which he sort of is.

'What it is,' he says, 'is, we've got something to tell you, and it's not easy, you'll see, there's no easy way to break this. So, what it is, I've asked Gem to come over because she can do it better than me, and what it is, see, it's sort of following on from what we were talking about back in the summer, if you remember, and so –'

'It's all right Dad,' says Gemma. 'What it is, you two, it's exciting news really, but we have to take it a step at a time. What it is, we know where Lila and Oliver are.'

Lynn takes a tissue from up her sleeve and blows her nose. Niecey looks stunned. So does Jamie.

'So where?' says Jamie eventually.

'We haven't got their address exactly,' says Dave. 'They live with their granny, somewhere in Derbyshire. We've met her.'

'You've met her?' says Niecey. 'What, Jacqui?'

'She's all right,' says Lynn. 'Sensible, you know? We've got along quite well.'

'But the –'

'We've not met the twins,' says Dave. 'That's what Gem means to say – a step at a time.'

'Are they all right?' says Niecey.

'All right?' says Lynn. 'Of course they're all right, they've been well looked after, you can tell she's the sort of woman who would do a good job.'

'But are they –?' Niecey does not know what to ask, she feels faint, her words stumble, she can only think of babies, she can see babies crawling across the floor, she can see them sleeping, she can see them sitting in those high chairs in the café in Norwich, crumbling cake in their fingers.

'So the thing is,' says Gemma, 'where we're up to, the next step – their granny would like to meet you.'

'Me?'

'It's reasonable,' says Dave. 'I mean, we know you've turned it all around, we've got used to the idea now, we can see how it might happen – but think of her, Jacqui, she's got this picture of you – what? – eleven years ago? She wants to –'

'But –'

'It's reasonable,' says Lynn. 'She's a reasonable woman. I've met her, and I've talked to her on the phone I don't know how many times, and I know she wants nothing but the best for the children. You've got to see her point of view.'

'But they're alive –'

'Of course they are. Why shouldn't they be?'

'And they're in England. Where do they live?'

'We can't tell you that,' says Dave. 'Not yet. Actually, to be honest, we don't know, exactly. She wants –'

'She wants it all her way,' says Niecey.

'And why shouldn't she,' says Lynn. 'She's the one who's been putting the work in all these years. Through no fault of her own.'

'Mum,' says Gemma.

'So,' says Jamie. 'What are the steps? How's it going to work out?'

Gemma waves her hand at her dad to tell him to let her say it. 'OK. Jacqui meets Niecey and you.'

'Me?'

'Of course you. If the kids are going to have contact with Niecey she wants to know that you're an all right person too, of course she does. She's responsible for them.'

Niecey says, '*I* should be responsible for them.'

'Nee,' says Jamie softly, 'we have to start from here, not from however many years ago.'

'Then,' says Gemma, 'if she doesn't have a problem with you – and she won't, I'm sure she won't – then if the kids are up for it, you meet them. With Jacqui there. In somewhere that's not your house and not theirs.'

'Why?'

Gemma looks at her and she shrugs, resigned.

'So,' says Gemma, 'gradually, a bit at a time, they can meet Leo, and Jamie, and maybe, if it's all working well, they can meet the rest of us, and –'

'How long would all this take? When can they come and –'

'They're not going to live with you,' says Lynn. 'She's made that very clear. They'll stay with her.'

'Where's Adrian?' says Jamie. 'Where's their Dad?'

'U.S,' says Dave. 'Not a lot of contact.'

'So do they know? That I'm here? Do they know?' She means, but can't say, Do they know I love them, and I always have loved them, and I always have missed them, and this, this is almost worse than losing them because they are there – wherever there is – and all these people are standing between me and them, and I have a right, and they have a right, and it's like knives in my brain, all this talking and it's not fair.

'They know about Leo,' says Dave. 'Jacqui says they're thrilled at the idea of a brother.'

'When then?' says Niecey. Her voice is dull, as if she has lost an argument. 'When does she want to meet me?'

'Us,' says Jamie. He takes her hand.

Gemma, sitting the other side of her, puts her arm round her shoulder and hugs her roughly. 'I'll come round tomorrow,' she says. 'After Leo's in bed. We can talk about it. You'll have had some time to get used to it.'

'Thank you,' says Niecey.

'Well,' says Dave. 'How did it go?' He carries the tray of mugs into the kitchen.

Lynn is waving from the window as Jamie's car drives away. She shrugs, though Dave is not there to see.

'Well?' he says again, coming back in.

'I never saw my mother again,' she says. 'I could have but I wouldn't. I believe she would have wanted to see me –'

'Of course she did.'

'I could have,' says Lynn again. 'It scared me too much, just thinking about it – I'm thinking how those twins must be feeling. They'll be scared. Confused.'

'Only natural,' says Dave. 'But at least, you know, they've got each other. Some support.'

'I hope it's better than the support I got from my sister,' says Lynn.

'It's different,' he says, after a small silence. 'I know, it's a bit the same, but it's a different set of circumstances, and besides, it's not our problem is it. We'll set up this first meeting and then it can carry on without us. Come Christmas it will all be sorted.'

She looks at him, looks away, out of the window at the houses opposite, the setting sun breaking through the cloud to shine on their upstairs windows.

'You,' she says. 'Always looking on the bright side.'

'And what's wrong with that? Niecey will get to know her kids, they'll get to know her. Our Sarah will sort out her marriage and be happy again. Melissa will behave herself. All the kids will grow up and go off to college or something like it. We'll be here, together. Everything will be all right.'

'Ooh look,' says Lynn, 'a flying pig.' But she says it softly, too quiet for Dave.

'What was that?'

'Nothing,' she says. 'You're right, I know you are.'

'I am *so* not looking forward to this,' says Ollie.

'Like, which bit?' says Lila.

They are sitting on a bus, upstairs at the front, and the branches of the trees in their late summer fullness are bashing at the windows as they go through the lanes.

'All of it,' says Ollie.

'Like what though?'

'One, we're on a *bus*. If you'd passed your test we could have borrowed Jac's car.'

'At least *I* got as far as the test. *You* failed your theory. And you're supposed to be the geeky one.'

'And then we've got to go shopping.'

'Ok, but if you'd come with me when I asked you to we could have done it in Bakewell –'

'I was busy.'

'Sure. So now you have to do it in Sheffield.'

'You could do it without me.'

'I could,' says Lila, 'but I won't. One little birthday present is all it is.'

'*Then* we've got to go to this stupid tea party.'

'And? What's wrong with that? She came to our birthday didn't she.'

'They'll all be there. The grandparents being all nice-y nice-y and those two annoying kids who think they're so smart. Showing off.'

'What Jake, showing off? I admit Dom does sometimes – but so do you sometimes. I want to go. I like seeing Tash, she's sound. Melissa not so much, but hey, she's family isn't she.'

'Not really. And she's not someone I want to go out with, in Sheffield, on a Friday night. We don't know the places, you don't know where she'll want to go, it'll be busy –'

'It won't, more likely it'll be dead with all the students gone home –'

'So, even worse. And then we've got to stay at Neicey's –'

'I like doing that. And she just loves it.'

'It's all right for you. I have to share with Leo.'

'And? He's your brother.'

'He's annoying. He only wants to talk about football.'

'Not to me he doesn't –'

'Well, he has a very gender-stereotypical view of the world.'

'He's only ten. You can't expect him to be woke yet.'

'I don't expect him to be boring. I've heard all I ever want to hear about his crap Sheffield Wednesday.'

'Look we could get off here. There's some smaller shops. We don't want to end up getting something from John Lewis.'

'What are we going to get for her anyway?'

'Oh,' says Lila airily, 'something blingy. She likes all that. She's got loads. Her dad keeps giving it to her. Guilt.'

'Then maybe she should have something a bit more classy?'

Lila turns towards him as they go down the stairs. 'Ol? You don't fancy her do you?'

'Of course I don't. She's practically like a cousin isn't she.'

'No. Not at all. It was you that said they're not family. You *do* don't you.'

*

Dave is in the garden looking at the bindweed that has come through from next door. He has nothing against his neighbours, but they are not gardeners, not by a long way. This is their bindweed twisting its way up his roses and – yes – up his lilac bush too, shoving its big white trumpets where they're not wanted and wreaking havoc in amongst the roots of his precious plants.

There is a cry and a crash from the kitchen and he goes to see.

'What's the matter love?'

Lynn is sitting at the table, looking at a cake tin on the floor. He goes to pick it up.

'Don't touch it,' she cries. 'You'll burn yourself.'

'What's going on?'

'Look at it,' she says, bitterly. She has the oven glove still on her hand and picks up the tin to show him. 'Call that a Victoria sponge? It's more like a biscuit.'

'Did you drop it love? Hey, these things happen, it's not the end of the world is it.'

'I threw it,' she says. 'I was that disgusted with meself I threw it. Look at it.'

'I expect I shall eat it,' says Dave, 'whatever it looks like. No need to get upset.'

'Look,' she says, pointing at the worktop.

'What am I looking at?'

She stands and picks up a bowl, shoves it under his nose. 'Eggs,' she says, tragically. 'I've got them out, I've beaten them, I just haven't put them in the mix.'

'Never mind,' he says. 'You'll not forget next time.' He bends down and rubs at the floor. 'Melted the vinyl,' he says. 'But only a little bit. We'll never notice it. No harm done.'

\*

Tash and Jake, their parents being at work, are raiding the fridge, in which there is a considerable amount of provision.

'Mm, coleslaw,' says Tash. 'Look there's Danish pastries there too. Do you think they'd miss a couple?'

'She said we're only allowed a tin of soup or beans on toast,' says Jake. 'All this is for later. And she said don't eat too much cos there'll be loads later on.'

'She only said that to you, fatso,' says Tash. '*I'm* not on a diet.'

'I'm having soup,' he says. 'Tomato or chicken?'

'Don't fancy soup,' she says. 'I'll just have this little custard slice. Don't tell will you.'

'How you gonna stop me?'

'It's more a case,' she says, 'of how I'm gonna punish you if you do.'

'I'm so scared,' he calls after her as she goes back upstairs.

She hears someone at the door and goes to the top of the stairs to listen but it's only Dom.

'Man,' says Dom. 'I had to get away. It's fucking mental round our house. You'd think it was fucking Buckingham Palace garden party the way my mother is cleaning everything. I tell you, I've been carrying chairs and moving tables since the sun came up. Honest, you'd think fucking Princess Thing was coming. Got your bike? Come for a ride?'

'OK,' says Jake. 'Just got to put my plate in the dishwasher.'

Dom opens the fridge. 'What you got in here then? Wow. Look at that. I'm a have some of that.'

'You can't,' says Jake. 'Not till later.'

'She won't know,' says Dom. 'She'll think it were you anyway.'

'Hands off,' shouts Tash from the top of the stairs. 'I can hear you Dom. Lay off that stuff or I'll tell your mum.'

He comes into the hall and grins up at her, a pastry in his hand. 'I've touched it now,' he says. 'So I've got to eat it haven't I.'

'Out,' she says. 'Both of you. Go out and leave me in peace. I've got work to do.'

'Yeah right,' says Dom, but he goes, and Jake follows.

Tash goes back to her room and looks at her reading list again. She has even bought two of the most important looking books but somehow, every time she picks one up and tries to get into it, she finds herself drifting into a daydream of Uni. She will be an undergraduate. She sees herself on University Challenge – 'And Liverpool's captain.' 'Hi, I'm Natasha and I'm studying journalism.' Though she doesn't think she has ever noticed a journalism student on University Challenge; they all seem to be scientists, answering questions about the periodic table and the distance between Mars and Mercury.

She sees herself handing in assignments that impress her tutors (is it tutors that they have?) as much as, maybe more than, her English and History essays did at sixth form college. She sees herself running the University newspaper – 'You've really turned it round, it's amazing how much you've achieved.' She sees herself on the TV news – because surely all those old people will have given up by then – interviewing ministers and celebrities. 'Natasha Parkin, outside the Houses of Parliament; and now back to you in the studio.'

'Don't go getting big ideas,' her mother had said to her. 'You'll be lucky if you end up on the Sheffield Star. If it's even still in existence.'

But Tash has flown high for years now; she's not about to come down to earth.

\*

Lila shops with enthusiasm. 'What's the matter with you?' she says. 'You could join in a bit more.'

Ollie shrugs. 'I guess this is just me turning into a grown up man,' he says. 'I've decided to be a stereotype.'

Lila finally decides on a small handbag. 'It's pink,' says Ollie, with scorn.

'That,' she says, 'is exactly the thing – in exactly that tone of voice – that Leo would say. *That's* how grown up you are. It's actually perfect.'

'It's too small to put anything in.'

'As long as your phone will go in what more do you need? Not everyone wants to carry round an entire toolkit on a night out.' She gives him a small push that nearly knocks him into the road and says, 'It's all right. I love you really.'

He shrugs again, then smiles.

They are quiet on the bus and when they get off Ollie says, thoughtfully, 'You're sort of right. About Mel. I like her when I'm with her. I like looking at her – I suppose that means I do fancy her. But afterwards, when I think about her, I don't remember anything nice about her.'

'Do you think she likes you?'

'How would I know? What do you think?'

'I've never noticed it,' says Lila. 'Shall I ask Tash what she thinks?'

'No. *Don't.* I'd never speak to you again.'

'Ok then, little brother, deal with it on your own.'

*

Sarah shouts up the stairs for Dom but there is no reply. Sighing she goes up – Dom is not there but she finds Melissa in her bedroom – Sarah's, not her own – trying on clothes in front of the big mirror.

'Seen Dom?'

'I think I heard him go out.'

Sarah sits on her bed – her single bed – and sighs again.

'This one?' says Melissa. 'Or that one?'

'That one,' says Sarah.

'Hm. No, I think – maybe – no, I think this one.'

'I could do with some help,' says Sarah. 'You know your Nannan and Grandad will be here early and I don't want them to have to pitch in and help. Dom was supposed to tidy the garden and put the chairs out, and the table, and now he's disappeared.'

'Mum, I'm dressed. I can't go out *gardening*.'

'Just pop your jeans back on.'

'I haven't done my make up yet.'

'Come on Mel. This is your do after all. It won't take us long if we're both doing it.' Sarah sighs again. 'Please.'

And Melissa, whose better nature is really not hard to reach, joins her mother in their small back garden – so much smaller than the one they had in their previous house – and while her mother picks up various footballs and pots and bits of bike, she sets herself to reorganising the furniture, counting how many chairs they'll need.

'We haven't got enough,' she calls down the garden where Sarah is struggling with the shed door.

'As long as Nannan and Grandad can sit down,' says Sarah. 'You kids can sit on the grass.'

'I'm not,' says Mel. 'The boys can sit on the grass. Not Ollie though.'

'I'll call Grandad – see if he's got a couple he can bring over.'

Mel is not listening – she has a message on her phone. She should pass on the information to her mother but decides to forget that part of it.

*

'That was our Sarah,' says Dave. 'Needs more chairs.'

He goes out to the shed to fetch them. When he comes back Lynn is still sitting where she was, at the table, the cake tin and its failed cake still in front of her.

'Lynnie,' he says. 'Now then lass, I thought you'd be getting ready by now.'

She shakes herself a little, 'I were miles away. What time have we to be there?'

'Any time, she said, but if we've to take chairs with us we'd better be early, so folks can sit on them. I'm ready, just got to wash me hands. Come on love, go and get changed into your party clothes.'

'As if anyone will care what I'm wearing,' says Lynn, but she gets to her feet and goes upstairs.'

Dave stands for some minutes gazing expressionless at the chair she's been sitting in.

*

Leo has been to his holiday football club all morning and returned red in the face and sweaty all over.

'Shower,' says Niecey, 'and don't take all day.'

'But I just want to tell you something.'

'Go on then.'

He tells her about his goals, his tackles, his sentences tumble out, he slides across the kitchen in his socks to demonstrate.

'That's enough,' says Niecey. 'Save it for Ollie and your dad.'

'Can I have something to eat?'

'There'll be food there, you know that. Auntie Gemma and Uncle Mark are doing all the catering. There'll be plenty.'

'I'm famished.'

She laughs at his new word and points at the fruit bowl. 'Shower first, then you can have a banana to keep you going.'

She goes back to her preparations, tidying the paperwork that spreads over the dining table. She and Jamie usually set aside Friday evenings to get up to date with the invoices and quotes and receipts and orders, but tonight will be different. Lila and Ollie will come back with them from Melissa's family party, and spend the evening with them until she and Tash come to collect them for a night out in town. Then the twins will come back to sleep and will be there till they go home some time on Saturday.

Niecey smiles to herself as she checks the rooms where they will sleep. When Leo comes out of the shower he finds her piling his belongings into his wardrobe and his clothes into the washing basket.

'Anything you're going to need tonight or tomorrow morning,' she says, 'take into my room. You're on the floor tonight, in with me and your dad.'

'I want to sleep with Ollie. I've got things to tell him.'

'I know love. But he'll be coming back really late and I don't want him to wake you up. You can tell him all your news this afternoon.'

'It's not fair.' But he looks cheerful enough, towelling his hair and pulling on his favourite T-shirt before he's properly dry, so that it sticks to his skin.

'And you can stay up late and see them before they go out.'

'Where will they go?'

'Down town.'

'Yes I know, but which club? I want to know.'

'I don't know. They don't know themselves I expect. They'll see where their friends are.'

'Did you go to clubs mum?'

'Only once or twice,' she says. 'When I was a student, before I had children. Since then, no, never.'

'Why do I like Ollie Mum? I really like him. Like, he's my favourite cousin.'

'But Leo, remember he's not your cousin, he's your brother.'

'I know, but he feels like a cousin. Cos we don't see him all the time. So why do I like him so much?'

'Is this a quiz?' she says. 'Do you know the answer?'

'Sort of. Cos he's grown up. It's cool having a grown up brother. And he's going to be a scientist which is like, really cool.'

'You know he's going to live in Manchester don't you? I explained that didn't I?'

'Yeah yeah, I know. But Lila's not going.'

'Not yet. Probably next year. She's going to art school first for a year, so she'll stay at home with her Granny.'

'Like Tash is going away but Mel is staying at home.'

'It's not like school,' says Niecey. 'It's not like everyone does the same thing. Once you've left school you get to choose.'

'I could choose football.'

'Well, you have to be good at it too.'

'I am though.'

'I know.'

She ruffles his hair, and he has to take his comb and arrange it carefully back into place.

*Good grief*, she thinks, *feels like I've only had him five minutes and he'll be a teenager any minute now.*

\*

The family begins to assemble at Sarah's house, Dave and Lynn first, as she predicted.

'Mum was going to make you a Victoria sponge but it came to grief,' says Dave.

'You didn't need to Mum. Gemma's bringing enough to feed us for a week.'

I know,' says Lynn. 'But I wanted to contribute something. It just – well, you know, they don't always turn out as you want do they.'

'Mum,' says Sarah, smiling for maybe the first time all day. 'I've never made a Victoria sponge in my life, and I don't intend to start. I've had you feeding me cake, and then Gemma feeding me cake and it's a wonder we're not all twenty stone.'

On cue, Gemma and Mark arrive, bearing trays of food, Jake too, carrying the cake, Dom, carrying nothing, and Tash, encumbered only by Melissa's present in its posh shop bag.

'*There* you are,' says Sarah to her son. 'Fat lot of help you've been today. Go and get changed.'

'I'm all right,' he says.

'He's all right,' says Dave, and Dom smirks and wanders back into the kitchen.

'And don't touch the food,' calls Sarah after him. 'I've a good mind,' she says softly to Gemma, 'to send him to live with Jon. He takes not a blind bit of notice of me.'

'Don't let Dad hear you,' says Gemma. 'Tell me later.'

Lila and Ollie arrive with Niecey and Jamie and Leo. ('You know that's what she'd like us to do,' Lila had said to Ollie.)

They are well into food and conversation – the same conversations as they always have – when the front door bell rings.

'Probably Janet,' says Lynn. 'She said she might call in if she wasn't busy.'

Dave makes his dismissive snort, the one reserved especially for Janet.

But Sarah's voice is raised in the hall and they can hear another voice too.

'It's Dad,' cries Melissa and she and Dom run through to see him.

'Hello darling,' he says. 'Happy birthday.'

Sarah makes a similar sort of noise to the one Dave just made, and stalks back into the garden.

'I don't want him here,' she says. 'He has no right to come. I didn't ask him.'

'P'raps Melissa did,' says Gemma. 'You can understand it sis. He'll want to see her on her birthday, and she'll want to see him.'

'You should see the size of the bag he's carrying. He must have raided the stock room. I bet there's stuff there for Dom too. He spoils them, he never consults, he brings them stuff every time he sees them and it makes them think I'm mean. Right, he's had long enough, he's given her presents, he can go.'

'I'll go and tell him,' said Mark. 'He'll take it better coming from me. We don't want any bother do we. And Mel needs to come back and be a proper hostess.'

And being Mark, he manages to say a civilised farewell to his one-time brother-in-law and brings Melissa back in, eyes shining with excitement at her packages, and with tears as well.

'At least it's a nice day,' says Lynn, for what may be the third time.

'Our birthday was awful,' says Lila. 'Rained all day, we never went out at all.'

'Did you have a party?' Lynn has forgotten being told about it by Tash.

'We had a tea party in the afternoon, like this but indoors. Niecey came and Jamie and Leo, and Tash and Melissa. And then in the evening we had a big party at home for our friends from school and Tash and Melissa stayed for that and came back home next day and it was lovely because our friends are all going away to different places so it was sad too and we took loads of photos and we've got a huge Whatsapp group –'

'A what?'

'Oh it's a phone thing. Look, I'll show you.'

'Don't bother,' says Dave. 'We've got phones you know, but not these smart phones that you've all got. It's as much as we can do to make a phone call, but we don't need more than that. And phone calls aren't always good news, at our age.'

'I don't think,' says Lynn, '– it's all very clever I know but it seems to make life a lot more complicated. And getting an email – or a text is it – it isn't the same as getting a letter. Oh! I've remembered. Did we give Melissa her card?'

'She's got it,' says Dave, 'along with about a hundred others. And all those presents. It'll take her rest of the day to open them.'

Jake and Dom, having eaten, say they are going down to the rec for a kickabout. Mark says he'll go with them. Jamie, seeing that Leo has monopolised Ollie for the whole afternoon, wonders whether he'd like to go too.

'You'll see Ollie tomorrow,' he promises. 'He'll be there in the morning.'

'You come too,' says Leo to his brother.

'I don't play football,' says Ollie.

'I'm no good at it either,' says Jake. 'That's why I go in goal. But you can go in goal if you like.'

'It's all right,' says Ollie. 'I'll stay with my sister.'

Jacqui and Bruce have taken their Friday evening bottle of wine into their garden. Bees buzz softly and crawl over the globe thistle flowers; butterflies land on the buddleia; the afternoon sun slants across the lawn.

'Will you miss Ollie?' says Bruce.

'Of course,' she says briskly. 'But I bet he comes home for weekends. He's not much of a one for mixing easily is he. And we won't see much of Lila I don't suppose.'

'We could have some weekends away,' says Bruce. 'You know, city breaks, mini-holidays. Make up for lost time.'

'That would be nice,' she says, absently.

'You don't sound as if you want to.'

'Oh I do, of course I do. We've always wanted to haven't we. I thought, when they first started seeing Niecey, that we could organise some time away but it never seemed to work out –'

'One or other of them always had something on, couldn't possibly spend a night away–'

'– Niecey would have had them for a week, we know she would. I think – you know I've said this before haven't I – I think they had some sort of separation anxiety, from being babies.'

Bruce pours more wine.

'Remember the first time?' she says.

'What about it?'

'Oh the whole thing. We went to meet Niecey didn't we, just us, and she was so distressed I thought I could never, *ever* trust her with the children. I thought she'd wreck them, their confidence, their feeling of security. And we gave her photos of them didn't we, but old ones so that she wouldn't recognise them if she saw them, and she just broke down looking at them.'

'Hm,' says Bruce.

'You couldn't cope,' says Jacqui. 'You said you'd go and sit in the car and I had to hold on to you.'

'Can't be doing with all that crying,' he says.

'I know. And even I thought she was going a bit overboard. But she'd been waiting for so long. And then she pulled herself together and she gave us tea and cake didn't she, and Jamie came back and we met Leo and she was so proud of him and I began to see that she was not as flaky as I thought.'

'She's kept to her side of the arrangement at least,' says Bruce.

'What choice did she have? We held all the cards. She didn't know how much the children wanted to see her.'

'She didn't know how much we needed a break from them.'

'Don't be so cynical about us. We never put ourselves first.'

'You didn't. I would have.'

'And the first time she met the children, do you remember? Ollie was sick he was so nervous and Lila was high as a kite and we met in that park –'

'Millhouses Park. I remember the leaves coming down around us, it was so windy.'

'We thought – I thought – that somewhere public would stop it being so emotional and in fact –'

'It was like bloody Wuthering Heights. Never seen so much crying. Remember that poor little kid, Leo, hanging on to his mum telling her to stop crying?'

'And poor old Jamie, wondering what he'd got himself into.'

'He's a decent chap though.'

'He's been very supportive, from what I know of it. It can't have been easy for him. The kids like him and as far as I know he's never objected to them going there whenever they want. Not a great brain, but as you say, a decent chap.'

'Like me,' says Bruce.

'Of course like you. This whole time, all these years, I couldn't have got through it without you.'

'You always say that Jac, but you would have. You're a strong woman.'

'He's been wonderful,' Jacqui has told her friends. 'He's supported me, and paid for them and never moaned, but they're *not his*, do you see.'

And those same friends who were concerned that allowing the twins to meet their birth mother, who told her scarily tragic stories of the numerous ways it could all go wrong – she has been able to tell them that, yes, it was difficult, there were tears (Ollie) and tantrums (Lila) but their other family was a *nice* family, *good* reasonable people. 'Not our sort maybe, but very close family, very respectable. Taken all round, it's been a good thing, for everyone.'

The grandparents start to clear away the dirty dishes. 'You have a sit down,' says Dave to Sarah. 'Have a quiet chat with Gemma. We'll get this tidied up.' There is, after all, no room in the tiny kitchen for more than two people.

Melissa leads Tash and Lila up to her room. Halfway up the stairs she looks down at Ollie standing in the hall. 'You can come too,' she says. 'We're not gonna be taking our clothes off.'

Ollie blushes. 'Not yet anyway,' says Melissa.

It's a cupboard of a room; all the rooms in this house are small; even the attic where Dom sleeps has a cramped feel to it, containing as it does the water tank and a redundant chimney breast as well as all of Dom's possessions.

The three girls sit on the bed; Ollie sits on the floor, folding up his long legs and remaining quiet.

'Congratulations,' says Tash to Mel. 'You're the same age as me – for the next three weeks that is.'

'I don't care,' says Melissa. 'In fact I think eighteen is just a perfect age. I shall feel sorry for you when you're nineteen and all wrinkled and your teeth fall out.'

'Come on then,' says Lila. 'Anyone got any news? Tell us about your job Mel. Do they actually pay you now?'

'It's good,' says Mel. She has a BTec in Hospitality Management, came out the best in her cohort and has been snapped up, as Dave puts it, by the Crown Plaza Hotel.

'Do you get famous people?'

'Only footballers,' she says. 'But there's a swimming competition next week; we've got two of the teams booked in with us.' The way she says 'with us' makes it sound as if she owns it.

'What about you Li,' says Tash. 'Are you sorry you're not going away?'

'A bit. Only a bit. See, it's the Art degrees. I want to have ceramics as my major subject but I've never done any –'

'How do you know you want to do it then?'

'That's exactly what I say,' says Ollie to Mel.

'I just know. Like Ollie's never done Materials Science but he thinks that's what he wants. Anyway, I have to do a foundation course, that's all. And I'm going to get a job too, in a shop or something, and save some money.'

'I wish I'd done that,' says Tash. 'I'm gonna have to be *so* poor.'

'I'm not,' says Mel.

'So this is it,' says Lila, looking round. 'It's us, grown up.'

*

On Saturday morning Leo is in such a state of impatience for Ollie to get up that Jamie gets out the bikes and forces him to go out for an hour's ride. When they come back Lila is in the kitchen with Niecey, telling her about their evening.

'I didn't lock the back door when I got in,' she is saying. 'Sorry, but I didn't know if Ollie was home or not. We lost him. And Melissa, she disappeared too.'

*Home*, repeats Niecey in her head. *I know it's just a figure of speech but she said Home.*

'He's back now anyway,' she says. 'Maybe he took Melissa back to hers. But you had a good time.'

'Of course. Sheffield's better than Chesterfield for going out. Some of the places were closed up for like, refurbishment, but that didn't matter. We found Mel's mates and they were good. We had a laugh.'

'Was Ollie all right?'

'Oh I know what you mean,' says Lila. 'He doesn't really like going out, and drinking, and the banter and that. He can't really handle it. Jac says our dad was similar.'

'I suppose he was,' says Niecey. There is a small pause while they both process again the idea that Adrian was once connected with Niecey. 'I think I was socially awkward as well,' adds Niecey. 'But I'm glad you're an outgoing type. It makes life easier I think.'

'Ollie's OK though,' says Lila. 'I mean, he does have friends. He's just serious that's all.'

'I wish he could laugh a bit more,' says Niecey. 'But I'm sure he'll be fine. You all will.'

She gets up to put the kettle on and when she sits down again there are tears in her eyes. 'I'm very proud of you, you know. Both of you. I've never said that to you before because it felt like I might be – I don't know – putting pressure on you to come and visit. But, you know, you've both been so lovely since – you know – and I do appreciate it. I've seen you every week since then – nearly – and I love to see you and so do Jamie and Leo. You know that don't you. I'll miss Ollie when he goes to Manchester.'

'It's not far,' says Lila. 'I bet he'll be back every weekend.'

'He won't have time to come and see us,' says Niecey. 'Neither will you. I get that. Things have to change now you're grown up.'

'Grown up,' says Lila. 'Isn't it amazing.'

*

Lila and Ollie take the bus back to Bakewell late in the afternoon.

'Not many more weekends,' says Ollie. 'Five more times to go and see her before I go away. Will you still go?'

'We were talking about that,' says Lila. 'She was, like, giving me permission not to go so often.'

'So will you?'

'I miss her if I don't go,' says Lila. 'It's like she's not our mother, though I know she is, it's like she's a big sister or something.'

'Better than Adrian as a parent at any rate.'

'Ol, you do like her really don't you.'

He screws up his face. 'I do, of course I do, but I think you're closer to her. Sometimes I didn't want to like her, or Jamie either, but I did. I feel all right when I'm there. I didn't at first but I do now.'

'You never said.'

'We were sort of obliged weren't we. Because she'd been so sad. But she used to cry every time we saw her and I couldn't handle it.'

'You did handle it though, Ol. And she doesn't cry these days does she.'

'No, hardly at all. And I wouldn't be freaked out by it now. I've grown out of that.'

'You must send her photos and stuff while you're away. Little messages. At least one a week.'

'Yeah. I can do that. Selfies of me in the physics lab. No, it's all right, I wasn't saying no. I'll do it.'

'It's funny isn't it,' says Lila. 'In all our life, in all our memory, there's been no one we call Mum. We've never said it, never.'

'I never thought of it like that,' says Ollie. 'I suppose we might have done when we were two. Can two year olds talk?'

'Course they can. But we don't remember doing it do we. As far as we remember, we've never called anyone Mum.'

*

'Did you have a good day,' Niecey says to Leo. She asks him this nearly every bedtime. 'Did you have a nice time with Ollie?'

'I made him laugh,' says Leo.

'How did you do that?'

'I told him a joke.'

'Will you tell it to me?'

Leo stuffs the corner of the duvet into his mouth. 'I can't. It's too rude.'

'Who's been telling you rude jokes? Was it Dom?'

'I can't tell you that,' he says. 'But Dom says – no, Jake says – if you're not old enough to understand them, well, you just don't get it do you, and if you get it then you must be old enough.'

'So you got it did you? And Ollie got it.'

'Of course *he's* going to get it – he's grown up.' Leo punches his pillow into shape and lies down. 'You don't even know when someone's grown up. You're funny, you are Mum. No, leave my hair alone.'

But she ruffles it anyway.

## ABOUT THE AUTHOR

Susan Day has been making up stories since before she could do joined up writing, but it took a while before she became brave enough to let other people read them. *Who Your Friends Are* was her first book, and she hasn't stopped writing since.

Susan was brought up in Enfield and lived in Colchester, Leicester and Paisley before settling in Sheffield. She has a husband, three children and a garden.

*Also by Susan Day*

## WHO YOUR FRIENDS ARE

Plain Pat and Lovely Rita – childhood best friends who shared lives and confidences through the 1950s and 60s.

As the two friends follow different paths through the 70s, they grow apart, but Pat stays loyal to her friendship with Rita and her sisters.

Now, years later, Pat finds herself with time on her hands, and begins to look back on her relationship with Rita – at the same time as she has a crisis in her own life and problems in her grown up family.

*A wonderful book about rites of passage – from the 1950s to the present day. Sometimes raw; often poignant; with deft dialogue and a feel for the realities of teenage friendship and subsequent family life and its unexpected twists and turns.*
Robin Kent, author of *Agony Aunt Advises*

*A deceptively simple story that makes you think about relationships, self-deceit and how we fail to spot the obvious.*
Barbara Bannister, author of *The Tissue Veil*

THE ROADS THEY TRAVELLED

Four girls set out one wartime morning, on a day that will bind them together for years to come. Work and marriage, children and divorce, change and death.

Many years later they are still in touch, and still trying to resolve the tragedy that has been a constant in their lives. What did happen to Marcie?

Read carefully and you may recognise some of the characters from *Who Your Friends Are*.

*Ordinary is made extraordinary by the intricacies shared in this beautifully woven tale of lives shaped by the forces of history… The reader is drawn into a skilfully painted picture of lives, changed forever by war.*

Bryony Doran, author of *The China Bird*

*Offers fresh new perspectives on lives lived — its pages are filled with moments and stories that are a pleasure to take into the imagination.*

Docs and Daughters Book Group, Bristol

## HOLLIN CLOUGH

CONCEALMENT: (*Verbs*) To conceal, hide, put out of sight, screen, cloak, veil, shroud, muffle, mask, disguise, camouflage.

There are families that would fall apart if the truth came out.

Jen admires her father and Frank believes that his daughters are happy, but no one in any family knows the whole story.

This family has fractured before, and been patched up by secrets and evasions.

Now things are about to change.

*The more I read, the more I enjoyed it. A real page-turner – well-written and believable.*

Laura Kerr, Botanical Book Group, Sheffield

*A book that makes you think. Susan Day expertly tackles the relationships within families and their dynamics; her characters are very convincingly drawn and deftly written. Thoughtful and entertaining.*

Steven Kay, author of *The Evergreen in Red and White*

BACK

Joan Jones leads a quiet and orderly life until she receives a postcard from an old boyfriend.

Viv feels on top of things until she becomes intrigued by the new member of her choir.

Bill is hoping for someone to love.
Road trips, crises and confusion ensue.

*An enjoyable romp through some ordinary yet extraordinary lives. Full of all too believable characters whose inept communications result in missed meetings, long car journeys, petty rows and tricky situations. A look at human life which reflects both its amusing and poignant aspects. Well worth a read.*
    Tilly Northedge, Cobnor Book Group, Sussex

*The dialogue and interplay between her characters vividly reveals them, drawing out and colouring their contrasting natures, histories and motives with little need of further description.*
    Brian Sellars, author of *The Whispering Bell*

WATERSHED

During the coronavirus pandemic lockdown Pam Dearly is more grumpy and resentful than ever, having not got over her sister's death. Confined to her house as the world changes, she reflects on disasters –two Sheffield floods and her family's loss in the North Sea inundation of 1953 – and she wonders if there is any way forward for her.

*A beautifully written, compelling read which had me hooked until the final line.*
Lucie Brownlee, author of 'Life After You'

*Like its characters, this book has an unassuming style, which masks great depth, emotion and insight. It's an interesting read for all those who, until the pandemic, thought they 'had the right to safety and plenty and freedom'.*
Janet Rees, Agglestone Rock Book Group

*Other Leaping Boy titles*

THE CHILD WHO FELL FROM THE SKY
Stephan Chadwick

Untold secrets of a post-war childhood.

A true story of a child born in war-torn London soon after the Second World War whose early memories are of the care and security given to him by his grandmother and a guardian angel who watches over him. At six he finds out a devastating secret that changes his life. He withdraws into his own world, searching for understanding and meaning. Isolated from his family and children of his own age he turns to his angel for love and guidance but even she cannot save him from what is to come.

*'Sometimes a book can just sneak up on you and contradict your expectations and this is such a book. There is nothing flashy about it, but nor is it didactic, and it has a raw, poetic quality that to my mind puts much more scholarly writers to shame.'*

Amazon review

*'This is an extraordinary, raw, and powerful book.'*
James Willis, **author of** *Friends in Low Places*

*Books by Lucinda Neall*

## A LIFE GUIDE FOR TEENAGERS

There are many things teenagers need to know to navigate their way through adolescence: from information about drugs, sex and alcohol; through how to deal with stress and peer pressure; to how to negotiate with parents and avoid being nagged! This easy-to-read book covers all this and more with quirky illustrations, lots of colour and buckets full of wise advice.

*Absolutely brilliant. Straight-forward, non-judgmental and accessible advice... which I wish I had growing up as well.*
Hans Svennevig, Croydon College
Head of Citizenship and Progression


## ABOUT OUR BOYS
### A Practical Guide to Bringing out the Best in Boys

This book looks at what motivates and de-motivates boys and how to help them navigate the journey to manhood. Written at the request of parents and youth workers who had read Lucinda Neall's book for teachers, it is packed with practical examples from everyday life.

*'A really accessible, practical and useful handbook.'*
Sue Palmer, author of *Toxic Childhood*

*'This book gives us all a hope of turning boisterous boys into confident young men.'*
Superintendent Mick Doyle
Thames Valley Police

HOW TO TALK TO TEENAGERS

If you have teenagers in your life – at home, at work, or in your neighbourhood – this book may stop you tearing your hair out! It will give you insights into how teenagers tick, and strategies to get their co-operation.

- ➢ Explains how teenagers see the world
- ➢ Packed with examples from day-to-day life
- ➢ Focuses on what to say to get them on board
- ➢ Includes 'maintaining boundaries' and 'avoiding conflict'
- ➢ Gives tips on how to stop the nagging and shouting
- ➢ Encourages adults to see the positive in teenagers
- ➢ Concise chapter summaries for easy reference

*'Lucinda has captured the art of dealing with teenagers in a fantastic, easy to use guide.'*

John Keyes, Social Inclusion Manager
Arsenal Football Club

*'A superb guide – the key issues and techniques of interacting with young people are covered in a practical, easy to understand way. A great introduction to working with young people. I'd recommend it to anyone.'*

Mark Todd, Chief Executive
Ocean Youth Trust South

*Books for children*

### The TOM AND JAKE Series
### Helen MccGwire

Six charmingly written and illustrated little books about Tom and Jake, two small boys who live with their family and animals in an old farm-house in Devon. The stories are based on the experiences of the author's five children during the 1960s, whilst living in the countryside.

*Tom and Jake*
*More About Tom and Jake*
*Tom and Jake & The Bantams*
*Tom in the Woods*
*Tom and Jake & Emily*
*Tom and Jake & The Storm*

*'Enchanting ... it takes us back to the 1960s and the adventures of the two young heroes, living in the countryside with the world to discover. Ideal for grandparents and young listeners, and a springboard for reminiscences, too. The story and prose are realistic and precise, the illustrations nostalgic and have detail for young eyes to explore and absorb. Thoroughly recommended.'*

Richard Newbold, Amazon
Top 1000 Reviewer

THE VERY SKINNY WHIPPETY DOG
Kate Tomlinson
Illustrated by Sue Luxton

A beautiful picture book about a skinny whippet who finds joy playing hide and seek in the woods and fields of Devon, and contentment in the comfort of a loving home.

The delightful illustrations make this a perfect book for dog lovers, or to read to small children.

Other work by artist Sue Luxton can be viewed at www.sueluxton.com

*Any of our books can be purchased online at:*

www.leapingboy.com